S/A LOOP

Death and the Dogwalker

On an early morning walk with his dog, Jason Lynx, antiques dealer and interior decorator, come... acquaintance shot dead ... soon finds out that a terr... his investigation arouse... betrayal and retribution.

Death and the Dogwalker is a gripping, darkly compelling novel and Jason Lynx a sophisticated sleuth who is as charming as he is irrepressibly curious.

Death for Old Time's Sake

Jason Lynx is administering his recently-dead foster-father's bequests to various charities, when his duties are interrupted by a corpse left on the doorstep of a family planning clinic being blockaded by anti-abortionists.

The corpse is soon identified as Simonetta Fixe: many people knew her, but who knows what she did long ago that brought murder to the clinic's doorstep, killing her – and perhaps trying to kill Jason as well – for old time's sake?

'Lynx is an American version of Lovejoy, but blessed with higher principles…a thoroughly sympathetic character…I hope we'll see more of him.'

JAY LLIFF, Sunday Express

By the same author

A LITTLE NEIGHBOURHOOD MURDER

A. J. ORDE

Death and the Dogwalker

Death for Old Time's Sake

Diamond Books
An Imprint of HarperCollins*Publishers*
77–85 Fulham Palace Road
Hammersmith, London W6 8JB

This Diamond Crime Two-In-One edition published 1994

A.J. Orde has lived in or near Denver for decades, and knows many
parts of it intimately. Despite this, the author frequently chooses to use
fictional locations to avoid giving offence through unflatttering
references to specific address, neighbours, or places of work.

Death and the Dogwalker

CHAPTER 1

Grace Willis, my friend and favourite policewoman, had to go to San Francisco to get her brother Ron out of trouble. No particular trouble specified; the subject mentioned with an attitude of stiff-upper-lip which prevented my pressing for details. She asked me to please take care of her cat until she got back. I had never seen her cat, though I like to think that my fondness for Grace would have made me say yes even if I *had* seen him. I owe Grace a great deal more than a mere cat-sit.

She had, however, neglected to say that the cat was a mature Maine Coon bullcat named Critter who weighed in at roughly twenty-eight, twenty-nine pounds.

'You don't mind if he sleeps on your bed?' she asked doubtfully, cradling the red tabby monster in both arms while he regarded me balefully.

'Where does he sleep at your house?' I asked dubiously. I had spent a few memorable nights in Grace's bed, and this monster had not shared our couch, which, in any case, would not have had room for him. I recalled that on one or two of our more athletic evenings it hadn't even had room for us.

'With me,' she admitted, blushing a little. 'Except when I have company.' Grace was not, she was at some pains to tell me, in love with me. She forgot that, once in a while. Not quite often enough for my taste, but thank God for any loss of memory.

The cat yawned widely, displaying teeth capable of dispatching fairly large herbivores. Then he blinked at me, lazily, deciding I was no threat. His eyes were amber.

'Why is it I've never seen him before?' I asked, still clinging to the idea it might all be a joke.

'Jason, when I first met you Critter was at the vet's for almost a week because he had a hurt leg, and then I had to keep him quiet until the leg healed, so he was in the little back room I haven't finished yet . . .' Grace was converting her grandmother's Victorian house into four apartments, and the unfinished ground-floor unit was occupied by herself. 'And then, later,' she went on, 'I took him up to my cousin Charlene to breed her two female Coons—that's my cousin in Cheyenne who raises these gorgeous-shaded apricots—and then after that you went on a trip for a while, and . . .'

'What does he eat?'

'I brought a sack of kibble. And I usually give him some of whatever I'm having. Chicken. Or fish. Or whatever.'

Since dining with Grace was an exercise in trying to get some for myself before she ate it all, I was surprised that she and Critter shared. 'I suppose he uses a what-you-call-it.'

'Litter box. It's in the car. And a sack of litter to go in it. I thought you could put it in the hall by the back stairs. And he'll get along with Bela fine, he likes dogs . . .'

Likes them for breakfast, I thought.

'I wouldn't take him outside for a while, Jason, until he knows you, because he might run off, trying to go home, and there won't be anybody there.'

Critter had his own ideas about staying in the house. He regarded staying inside as cruel and unusual punishment, and he let me know it clearly and continuously. He sat on the windowsill and cried, heartrending little cries, like a grief-stricken toddler. If he kept it up, someone was going to turn me in on suspicion of child abuse. After two days of this I gave up and bought him a harness and leash.

Which explains, more or less, what Bela, the hundred-pound Kuvasz dog, Critter, the thirty-pound cat, and Jason Lynx, the hundred-eighty-pound dealer in old furniture and related stuff, were doing entering Cheeseman Park shortly after dawn. We were having our morning constitutional. It had taken Critter about three minutes to figure out the leash, after which his attitude conveyed that Maine Coon cats had invented leashes as a kind of ornamental linkage indicating the relative status of the two creatures involved—

the one in front being in charge. Critter paraded, tail lashing. Bela slouched, nose to ground, smelling what was new, his heavy tail making a steady drumbeat against my leg. I strode along, taking deep breaths, trying to convince myself I needed these jaunts because the doctor said exercise the leg, no matter how much it hurt. Which, since I'd had it shot out from under me by a bad guy a few months ago, it did.

Just inside the park there's a grove of big old spruces. The ground beneath them is usually dry and needle-covered and in midsummer and fall it's littered with the chunky white-fruiting bodies of *Agaricus nivicens*, which are great with hamburger or scrambled eggs if Bela and I get there before the mushroom kickers and the squirrels do. Squirrels you can't blame, but mushroom kickers ought to be hung up by their heels. At this season, *nivicens* were not in evidence, their space being occupied by Frederick Foret. He was lying under the spruce farthest from the path, one knee up, one arm draped dramatically over his eyes. This world-weary, emotionally exhausted posture was a frequent accompaniment to what Fred called the 'essential surrender of meditation, the passive aftermath of positive motion.' Fred was always eager to talk about essential surrender or any other emotion he happened to be feeling. 'I have just experienced an insight,' he might say, summoning me over with an imperious wave. I need to tell someone . . .'

I can't recall his ever saying, 'How have you been, Jason?' or showing any interest in anyone other than as a potential audience.

The path went directly by him. There was no way to avoid him, but I decided not to see him. If I zoomed by, eyes front, he might meditate right through my passing. If he was still there when we left, I could call a hurried greeting and plead the pressure of business prevented my staying to hear his latest saga of the human spirit.

The latest, as of a few days before, had been ominous hints that Fred might be thinking of getting involved, once again, with World Peace. His youthful interest in the

Rosicrucians—about which I had heard much—had been followed by a long-time involvement with est, which had given way to Carlos Castañeda and, more recently, a brief flirtation with Shirley MacLaine's more-things-in-heaven-and-earth cosmobabble. I had refused at least twenty times to attend meetings or get involved in any way, but this had not discouraged Fred, who, since his recent retirement, was totally indefatigable in his own mystic interests. The latest thing seemed to be to 'walk for peace' while carrying 'the light of peace' (i.e., burning candles) from place to place, or, in Fred's case, to fly about, mostly in Europe and England, getting other people—mostly small children—to carry candles into people's offices and shops, generally making a nuisance and fire hazard of themselves while doing nothing identifiable to reduce international tension. Fred had accompanied the children into some fairly high places, and the name dropping (the Minister of Education, the Secretary of State, the Prime Minister, blah-blah) could go on for several hours.

Critter, Bela, and I speeded up to a gentle lope and went quietly past, though Bela jerked nervously at the leash, making an abortive lunge in Fred's direction. Fred did not move his arm, though I caught the white gleam of half-opened eyes as I went by. So. Biding his time. Or maybe he hadn't recognized me with the cat.

We made the usual circle, about thirty minutes' worth of brisk walking and occasional jogging, slowed this morning by people stopping me to ask about Critter. Most of them were regulars, people I saw every morning when I walked the dog. The grey-haired couple in the purple outfits. The two guys with the soccer ball. The very stout white-haired woman in sweats, dark glasses, and flowered kerchief. The redhead with the serious runner's body. No one could believe the size of the cat, and all I could tell them was that I didn't believe it either.

We made the turn at the flower plots—recently bedded out and still sparsely grown enough so that Critter could find plenty of toilet room between the petunias—and then started back the way we'd come. Fred was still right where he'd been when we came in. This time Bela did not go on past. He stopped, pulled hard on the leash, and howled.

Fred didn't move. Bela stared at the recumbent form and howled once again, a long, lugubrious sound. When he stopped, he gave me a significant look from his dark, mournful eyes. The scars on the back of my neck prickled. If I'd had any hair there, it would have stood up.

'Sit,' I said to Bela, realizing all at once, and not for the first time, that he had better sense than I did. Bela sat. 'Stay.' Bela would stay until hell froze over or until I called him, whichever came first. I still had one animal left over. 'Hold it,' I said, putting Critter's leash in Bela's mouth. He held it while I skulked into the grove of trees. Fred hadn't moved. His eyes were still half open under the concealing arm. I thought at first he might have fallen asleep or have had some kind of seizure, then I saw he wasn't breathing. I said something obscene or blasphemous, half under my breath. Bela whined. I said again, 'Stay. Hold it,' as I reached down and moved Fred's arm. His eyes glared up at me, unseeing. My first feeling was one of guilt that I hadn't spoken to him earlier. Then I realized it wouldn't have mattered. I wasn't the only one who'd gone on past without noticing that Fred wasn't his usual, very important self. He'd been dead long enough to get pretty cold.

I stood up to see a Laurel and Hardy duo jogging towards me along the path, guys I'd seen out there most recent mornings. I hailed them, told them what had happened, and asked them to call the police. The skinny one zoomed off down the path towards Thirteenth Avenue; the other one, a stout, fiftyish man already red in the face, stayed with me.

'My neighbour,' he said between puffs. 'Thinks he's doing a marathon every morning. Makes me feel like a couch potato.'

I turned back to Fred as the potato stared down at the body with no visible emotion.

'Think it was a heart attack or something?'

I shook my head. 'I don't know. I don't think we should touch him. He's been dead a while.'

He nodded. 'He was here when we came into the park. We just speeded up a little so he wouldn't catch us.'

'You know him?'

'Well, not really, but I know who he is, you know what I mean? The guy's here most mornings, almost always sprawled out under a tree, or on a bench if the ground's wet. Talk your arm off if you let him, makes no sense so far as I can tell, and he's hard to get away from. Lately it's been this walk-for-peace business. My God, there must be a lot of people in the world with nothing to do, you ever think of that? I guess maybe he runs, but I've never seen him running.'

I'd never seen Fred running either. 'His name is Foret,' I said. 'Fred Foret. He lives over there in that high rise next to the Twelve Hundred building.'

'No kidding? He's a neighbour, then. I moved in there four months ago.' He mopped at his face, eyes fixed on Critter. 'I been meaning to ask since I saw you yesterday, is that a regular cat?'

We talked about the cat. I sat down on the ground; Critter climbed on to my lap and washed his face. Bela leaned over one shoulder, his lop ears, black nose, and dark eyes making a sad mime's face against his white fur. We were sitting like that, my companion talking about pets he remembered from when he was a kid and scratching Critter's stomach, when the police arrived, two cops in a white car with the blue logo on the door.

It turned out the fat man's name was Clive Corvallis, of the Corvallis Funeral Home, which explained his lack of emotion on viewing the body. He gave his business and home address to the officers and told them he'd seen Fred lying there earlier. His friend, Ben Maurier, arrived, panting, and told them the same thing. I repeated the information for the third time and added that I knew who he was.

'He got a wife, family?' the officer asked.

'Divorced,' I said, trying to recollect what Fred had told me. I had, literally, not listened to him most of the time. He was so full of how he felt about things and what he thought about things, so unaware of there being another human being present who might also have thoughts and feelings, that I had usually just turned him off. 'Divorced,' I repeated, feeling foolish not to know more. 'But I think his ex-wife and kids live here in town.'

'How well did you know him?'

'We met at a party at his sister's; her name is Marge Beebe. That was over a year ago. Then I saw him here, one morning a little later, and since then we've chatted about this and that when I've been walking the dog.' I decided I didn't have to say I'd avoided him whenever possible.

Marge's husband, Silas, is my broker. I have taken them out to dinner a few times. Also, the Beebes throw occasional mob-scene barbecues at their farm, and I usually drop by briefly to show my face, drink one beer, and sneak off before the burned meats are served. At last summer's, Marge had introduced me to her baby brother Fred; he'd stuck to me like strapping tape, talking about est. Since he was completely impervious to social signals like 'I've got to run', or 'I'm meeting a plane', I'd sneaked away while he was in the bathroom, thinking the rudeness wouldn't matter because I'd never see him again. The rudeness didn't matter because he didn't recognize it for what it was, and I saw him altogether too often. Fred was incapable of believing he was boring. I gave the officers Marge Beebe's name and told them she was listed under S. R. Beebe in the phone book.

'What made you go over to take a look at him?' the officer asked.

I pointed to Bela. 'He howled,' I said.

The officer nodded as though this was the usual thing. Then he asked me, 'Say, is that a regular cat?'

When we got back to 1465 Hyde Street, which is both home and shop, I took the leashes off the animals while admiring the tulips, daffodils, and grape hyacinths among the ever-greens out front. Mark MacMillan, my assistant, had planted the bulbs the previous fall, and I had to admit they brightened the rather dowagerly façade. I took my usual good-luck swipe at the brass plate by the front door that reads: 'Jason Lynx Interiors'. Some people immediately think, 'Ah, interior decorator,' which isn't quite it. Every paint and fabric shop has someone on staff they call a decorator. I can do that, of course, but I don't, except as part of a total design for a room or rooms, furniture and all. Mostly I'm into antique furniture, period rooms, and occasionally some good reproductions. Before my name went on the entry, the business was Jacob Buchnam's, my foster father's, and when he had his stroke, he asked me to come back from the East Coast and take it over. He got a nice cheque from it every month, and I got a business it had taken him fifty years to build.

Once inside, the three of us went under the latest in a series of crystal chandeliers, $8,000; over the current Persian rug, $24,000; past the pair of Edwardian rosewood chairs, $3,400; and the English oak dresser, $5,200 (but I'd take four-eight), that I'd bought from a suddenly impecunious Londoner who'd found himself stranded in Colorado with all his furniture (which is another story). And up the curving stairs to the private part of the house. Bela galumphed along at my heels and Critter bounded ahead like a huge, furry basketball. We stopped in the kitchen, them for breakfast, me for coffee to drink before, during, and after my shower. By the time I was dressed, Critter was on my bed deeply involved in his morning wash and Bela had gone down the back stairs to the dog door and the back yard. During the fifteen or twenty minutes that had passed since we'd arrived, I'd been trying to decide whether I should go see Marge Beebe.

If the police mentioned my name as the one who dis-covered Fred's body, she'd be justifiably hurt that I hadn't told her personally. Maybe the police had already informed her, maybe not. I'd told them she was next of kin, but who knew how prompt they'd be. Though Fred had not been a particular friend of mine, he had been Marge's brother, and any debt I owed, I owed to her.

Marge didn't work, so the chances were, this early in the morning, she'd be home. The calendar said nothing on Wednesday A.M. until ten-thirty, so I left a note for Mark and for Eugenia Lowe, the showroom person, saying I had a personal errand to run but would be back by ten-thirty. They both had keys to the shop and would let themselves in.

The Beebes live outside of Littleton, a sprawling suburb that once had been a rather nice small town. The town, or what remains of it, perches like a pimple on a vast suburban carbuncle, and is notable for having had one of the ugliest Main Streets in the urban US. Some con artist sold the city fathers an endless line of concrete umbrellas, which, until recently, stood along the kerbs like so many upended stumps, offering neither shade nor grace and ruining the façades of the few good buildings in town. The once elegant town library had been remodelled into a restaurant that has changed hands so often no one remembers what it's called. The once authentically Victorian courthouse has suffered from chronic accretionosis. A little south of Main Street is the prison-grey bulk of Arapahoe Junior College, an accidental-looking concrete pile possibly stacked by the same guy who put up the street umbrellas.

I don't have to drive past the courthouse to get to the Beebes', but I always do, just to get my animosity flowing. Betweentimes I can't believe it's as bad as I know it is. The Historic Preservation people call it 'remuddling', and there's a lot of it around.

Marge and Silas live west of town on what remains of an old farm property off Bowles Avenue. When I drove in, Marge waved at me gaily from the stables out in the front pasture, so I knew no one had called her yet. She left the horse she'd been grooming and met me near the front door with her usual friendly hug. Marge offered coffee. I accepted. We sat at the kitchen table. I took her hand and said I had some bad news for her. She thought I was kidding, and that didn't make it any easier When she finally heard what I was saying, she just sat there, her face very still, not crying, not anything. Marge has a plump, jolly face. When she stopped smiling, it looked old and yellowish, like an almost healed bruise.

'Marge?' I said. 'Marge.'

'I was thinking it happened too late for Shannon,' she said in a shrill, empty voice. Then she burst into tears. I put my arms around her and let her cry and wondered what in hell she meant about too late for Shannon. I seemed to recall Fred mentioning a daughter Shannon: Shannon and Keith, the names popped into my mind, daughter and son.

'Do you want me to let her know?' I asked gently when she quieted a little. 'His daughter?'

She turned her stricken face on me and said, 'God, no. No, Jason. I'll call Lycia, and she'll tell Shannon.'

'That's his ex-wife?'

She nodded. 'Oh, God, Shannon will feel so guilty.'

I must have looked confused, because Marge said, 'Only the other day Shannon said she wished he was dead.' She went back to crying.

On occasion, I had wished Fred Foret would drop dead, and the desire had not occasioned excesses of guilt. Still, it did seem an extreme emotion for Fred to have evoked in a daughter. I wondered what he'd done to deserve it, confident that the Fred I'd known was fully capable of doing whatever it took.

'Marge, would you like to go to your sister-in-law's? I'll drive you. Maybe it would be better if you told her in person.' I wanted to give her something to do, and I didn't want her to be alone. A thought occurred to me. 'Unless you don't get along . . .'

'Me and Lycia? Oh, no. I like Lycia. We were never really close, but we like each other. I think you're right. I should go over there. If you'll take me . . .'

I took her. We went back into town and ended up at a building not far from my own place, a tall, impersonal apartment house with a phony French name (the Louvre, for God's sake) and bad-fake Louis XIV lobby furniture. Marge asked me to come in with her, so I followed along while she pushed the button and spoke her name into the mike and got buzzed in through the security door. A stout, red-faced man with two toy poodles got out of the elevator, and one of the poodles started to lift his leg, using me for a tree. I jumped back, and the man peered at me apologetically through thick-lensed glasses as the assembly of dogs and man rushed untidily for the door. Poor pups. Probably hadn't been outside since yesterday, and the dumb sod that owned them expected them to hold it forever.

Lycia Foret, a smooth-faced woman with a charming smile and short grey hair, came to the door in a housecoat, obviously bewildered by this early visit. It was half past nine but I felt it should be about noon. Marge didn't even wait for the door to open. She launched herself through the crack, already bursting with tears and explanations, while I stood behind her staring at Ms Foret with a very strange feeling of . . . what? Recognition? No. Certainly not recognition, but a weird, inexplicable sensation nonetheless. I couldn't stop staring at her. Luckily neither of them noticed as they noisily sorted it out. Then Lycia turned to me and asked, 'How did he die?'

I was so intent upon trying to figure out what it was about her that troubled me, it took me a minute to apprehend the question.

'There was no cause of death I could see, Ms Foret. The police didn't invite me to stick around and wait for the medical examiner. Since I happened to know Marge, I thought it would be appropriate to tell her . . .' Ms Foret turned back to Marge, and I resumed my analysis. Her hair was gray. That didn't describe it. It was the colour of falling water. And her eyes were water-coloured, too, the darkness that lies in deep, slowly moving rivers, almost green, almost brown, and utterly still. Quite honestly, until that moment I hadn't been particularly curious about what killed Fred Foret. I think I had rather assumed a heart attack. He was at the age when that happens, not to oneself but to other people. Meeting Lycia, I was suddenly interested. Seeing her, I wanted to know everything about her, even if that meant getting posthumously involved with Fred.

She shook her head at me sorrowfully. 'Come into the kitchen,' she said. 'The children and Ross and I were just having breakfast.'

Marge followed her closely, dabbing at her eyes with a soggy tissue. I went after Marge, wondering how I'd ended up here. I hadn't intended the good deed to become a half-day expedition, though it was turning out to be interesting. As we walked through the apartment, I gave it the professional eye. This was a place where people lived, a place alive with colour and life and healthy-looking real plants. We went through the dining-room, through a swinging door into a sun-drenched kitchen where two shelties looked lazily up from their baskets under the window and three people sat at a round table over the remnants of a sizable breakfast. The daughter: pale blonde with dark brows and lashes, a sweet, slightly pensive expression, and none of her mother's tranquillity. The son: same colouring; lean, hungry face; husky body; pouting, demanding lower lip. Both of them in baby-blue sweats and white headbands. She looked about twenty, twenty-two. He was a little older. There was another guy at the table, fiftyish, bearded.

'Keith,' Lycia said to her son. 'Shannon honey. I'm afraid your Aunt Marge and this gentleman have brought some bad news.' Though there were no tears, there was tension in her voice and she choked, unable to go on.

Shannon threw me a fearful glance, light hair falling across her open, childlike face. There was no guile in it. She stared up at her aunt, at me, lips already trembling. She didn't know what the news was, but she was ready to cry. Her brother furrowed his brow in my direction. Marge was busy wiping her eyes and making swallowing noises. Lycia Foret wasn't saying anything. The room teetered with expectation. One of the dogs whined, and I didn't blame him. I don't tolerate tension well either.

So I pushed us off dead centre. 'I was running in the park this morning,' I told them. 'And I found your father's body. He'd evidently come to the park sometime earlier . . .'

'Dead?' asked the bearded breakfaster in a deep, matter-of-fact voice. 'Are you saying he's dead?' He moved his short, compact body out of the chair and I stepped back, almost behind the kitchen door, to give him room. 'Fred?'

I nodded. 'Body' usually meant dead, to me. Shannon started sobbing. Her brother just looked at me, as though I'd said it was raining outside. 'Son of a bitch,' he whispered. A dog got out of her basket and came over to him, putting her head on his knee. 'Son of a bitch,' he said again, stroking the dog gently.

I couldn't tell if he meant the words as an imprecation or an expletive.

'How?' he asked.

'Yes,' the older man agreed. 'How?'

'Mr Lynx doesn't know,' Lycia told them, laying a hand on my arm as though to forgive me for not knowing. My skin actually quivered where she touched me. 'The police will know. Ross, will you call and find out what you can.'

The bearded man moved from the table to the wall phone at the other end of the kitchen. He mumbled into it while I answered what questions I could. Where Fred had been lying. The jogging suit he'd been wearing. I fluffed over my first view of him, saying I'd seen him there but figured he was meditating.

'Meditating,' his son snorted. 'Oh, sure, meditating.'

'Keith,' his mother said warningly. 'Keith!'

'Well, Mother! You know Dad. He was about as far from being able to meditate as you can get. He couldn't forget his audience long enough!'

'Oh, Keith, don't,' the girl cried. Her Aunt Marge went over and sat by her, hugging her. 'He shouldn't say things like that . . .'

Lycia shook her head warningly at her son.

'I hate that park,' the girl cried. 'Melody was in that same park!'

'He was shot,' Ross said as he hung up the phone.

'Murdered?' Keith breathed. 'Murdered?'

'Melody was shot, too,' Shannon cried hysterically. 'And I hated her. And I hated Daddy. They'll think I killed them both. After what I said . . .'

'Shannon. Don't be silly!' Marge shook her, then hugged her again. 'You didn't mean what you said. We all know that.'

I started to excuse myself, but Lycia was speaking to Shannon in a low, intent voice, so I extricated myself from where I was standing, beside the kitchen door, untangling the dog leashes that had wrapped themselves around my arm and straightening the several framed award certificates I had unsettled. As I went quietly to the front door, I heard Lycia saying, 'Shannon, no one will think you had anything to do with it. We've been together, all four of us, since yesterday afternoon. There's no way you could have had anything to do with it at all.'

I thought how convenient it was that the whole family could alibi one another. Considering that victims' husbands or wives, even ex-wives, are usually immediately suspected, it was nice to know that Lycia could not be. The thought surprised me. I didn't even know her. Why would I care? I wondered who Ross was. Then I told myself it was none of my business who he was, and anyhow, Lycia was considerably older than I, so forget it. I looked at my watch and realized the day had begun, ready or not, and I had a customer coming in at ten-thirty.

I had parked the car in my garage before I noticed that Marge had left her purse in it. I took the bag upstairs with me and asked Mark to call her at Lycia Foret's place and tell her I'd bring it to her that evening. When I came back from getting a cup of coffee, Mark said Marge needed her purse, so her nephew Keith was driving her over to pick it up. Fine, well and good.

My ten-thirty customers showed up and we spent almost an hour choosing among four carpet samples for their new family room. Normally I don't do jobs which are totally unrelated to the antique business, but he was the son of a client and I had promised his mother I would 'help'. He was decisive enough, but his wife liked to play cutesy games with him. 'On the other hand, Bobsy, this is a lot like the one your sister has. Do you think she'd mind?' Or: 'Which one of the others, after we take out the one I don't like, do you really like best?' Since I'd seen the room in question and had picked the samples myself, I knew any of them would do. In this case, 'do' meant that the carpet would not detract from the general effect they had managed to achieve on their own. In other words, it wouldn't do any harm. They finally compromised upon my least favourite, and Mark winked at me over their shoulders. He had bet me lunch at Cliff Young's that they'd choose the one I liked least. They and I parted with mutual groans of relief.

'I hear there's been a murder,' Mark said in the unenthusiastic voice he'd been using lately. His love life was not going well. 'Are we involved up to our ears?'

'We? *We* don't get involved in this one at all.'

'Oh, come on, Jason. You like murders.'

'I don't like murders. I like solving puzzles, but that's a different matter. Fred Foret's death may not be much of a puzzle. He probably got mugged and shot by some drugged-up kid.'

'Not mugged,' said Mark.

'What do you mean, not mugged?'

'Not robbed, anyhow. He had a wallet in his pocket with over five hundred dollars in it.'

'Who told you that?'

'Some funeral director guy named Corvallis. He called here while you were gone. Said he thought you'd be interested. Evidently he stuck around while the medical examiner took a look. They went through his pockets. The corpse's pockets, that is.'

'Maybe somebody shot him, then got scared off before they could go through his pockets.'

Mark shrugged at me. 'Corvallis said he'd been dead for at least two or three hours.'

That gave me pause. I'd passed him at about six o'clock. I'd come back by at six-thirty. The police had arrived ten minutes later, and the medical examiner shortly after that. Say almost seven. So Fred had been shot at four or five in the morning.

'What the hell would he have been doing in the park at that hour?' I wondered. 'Very few people up at that time.'

'So few a murderer could hide and come back if somebody did come by,' he offered.

I visualized the scene. There was dense shrubbery only a few feet from where Fred had been, lilac bushes, fully leafed out, excellent cover, the fading blooms hanging thickly. I'd smelled them at the time without noticing the bushes. Them and something else. Fred had lain in the open, of course . . .

'He was lying on his back with one arm over his eyes,' I said.

'He was shot in the back, according to Corvallis.'

In the back? Mark and I stared at each other. If Fred Foret had been shot in the back, he had not fallen gently supine with one knee up and one arm over his eyes in his usual dramatic posture. He had been, one might say, arranged.

Marge and her nephew Keith came by about one. Something had been nagging at me, and when she came upstairs alone (leaving Keith to roam around the main showroom, running his fingers either disdainfully or covetously over the eighteenth- and nineteenth-centuries) I decided to ask her about it.

'Shannon said something about someone else having been in the park,' I said. 'Melody someone. What did she mean?'

'Melody Steinwale.' Marge nodded. 'She was killed in the park, but that was some time ago. Shannon was just being hysterical this morning. People get killed in parks all the time. I guess that's true in any big city.'

Somehow I do not think of Denver as a big city. It is still the cow town I grew up in, with all a cow town's virtues and faults. Nonetheless, the population makes it 'big' enough to stack up a respectable homicide score, that much was true. 'Who was Melody Steinwale?' I asked.

'A sort of neighbour of Lycia's. Harriet Steinwale lives upstairs from Lycia. In the penthouse. When she's in town. She has a place in Mexico, and she spends a lot of time there.'

'Harriet Steinwale?'

'Barge Steinwale's widow. You know, Jason. Steinwale Steel? Lycia and Harriet are friends. Harriet's son is Greg Steinwale, and Melody was married to him. Greg and Melody lived in the penthouse, too.'

'Gregory Steinwale.' The name rang a bell. 'I should know that name.'

'He's an artist. He was written up in *Time* magazine.'

I remembered an article, though I hadn't seen the one in *Time*. 'In *Art & Antiques* last month,' I said. 'He signs himself Grale. Said to be quite the up-and-coming painter just now.'

'A rather strange one,' she said. 'At least, I've always thought so.'

I was remembering what else the article had said. Something about an emotional or psychological collapse? When his wife was killed, perhaps? I was sure I remembered something soap-opera-ish. Well, the back issues of *A & A* were downstairs in the basement. I'd look it up later.

Marge was shaking her head. 'Fred was my brother, Jason, but he was such a . . . I don't know. It wasn't that he was stupid. He was very intelligent. He had a high IQ. He was a physicist, a professor up at CU until he retired a few months ago.'

I nodded, indicating I'd known that.

'Before that, he worked with the Department of Defense, some kind of science adviser.' She sighed. 'He made a good living. It's just that with people . . .'

'He never shut up.' The words came out without thought, and I flushed.

She didn't take offence. 'Oh, Jason, that's so true. When he was a little boy, he used to drive me crazy. He never shut up. And he got these strange ideas about his relationships with other people. Like what he did to poor Shannon . . .'

'What was that?' I asked, curious.

She squeezed her mouth into a prim little line, opening it just enough to say, 'I shouldn't have said that. I'm not going to talk about him, Jason. I'm just not. When somebody dies like this, the least said, the soonest mended. Silas says I talk too much, and this is one time I'm not going to.'

I didn't press the matter, but despite myself, I was becoming intrigued. I asked her who Ross was. His full name was Dr Ross Whitfield, Dr Lycia Foret's significant other. I wished, with a pang, that Grace Willis were back from San Francisco. It was sometimes convenient to have a police detective as the closest thing I had to a significant other. If she were home she could get me a look at the police report.

A funny thing happened when I got back to the office. There was an envelope in the mail with a local postmark and no return address. Any mail addressed to me personally, I open, and I did so. Inside was a plain piece of paper with words and letters pasted on it, words and letters cut out of slick magazine paper.

'If you want to know who you are, get ten thousand together and put an ad in the personals that says, "JL wants to know all."'

The quote marks were huge, probably from a big ad of some kind. The initials were of two different type styles. The paste-up job was neat, as though done with a ruler. I sat there staring at it for maybe ten minutes.

I was abandoned at a Home when I was three, and my parentage is a complete mystery. Not knowing who I am used to bother me a lot. From the day I'd come under Jacob's tutelage, however, he had insisted that a person's identity is not dependent upon knowing his family name or history. Firmly and repeatedly, he'd told me that Jason Lynx would be who I made myself be. Now, being true to Jacob's tenets, I told myself my identity was my business, and no filthy anonymous letter writer was going to con me out of ten thousand.

I had to repeat it to myself several times. Finally, I put the letter in the bottom drawer with the three almost like it that had come in the mail over the past six months. Somebody was trying to get my attention. I wondered how long I could refuse to notice. I wished Grace was here so I could talk to her about it.

Next-best thing to a look at the police reports on Fred was a look at the newspaper accounts of the Steinwale killing. Not that I had any reason to think they were connected, but Shannon had mentioned Melody Steinwale in the same breath. If you're going to start prying something up, any old corner will do to insert the wrecking bar, or so I often tell myself. I asked Mark to go down to the offices of both daily papers, buy back issues if they were available, or get photostats. It gave Mark something different to do, too. He'd been depressed for the past several weeks since his longtime roommate had left him to move back to California. They'd fought about something, God knows what, and Mark was feeling betrayed and lonely. He didn't get along with his father well enough to make going home a suitable alternative, and with the current health problems among what is called 'the gay community', a rebound affair wasn't sensible either. Getting him interested in one of my puzzles might be therapeutic.

Myron Burstein called from New York City around five o'clock. I asked him what he was doing working so late.

'Late,' he snarled. 'It's barely dinnertime.' Myron hated being late for meals. Or maybe it was his wife, Leah, who hated his being late for meals. Since he did commission buying for people in the western US, he got caught by the difference in time zones and stayed in the office until seven or eight, but after twenty-five years of being married to him, Leah still put dinner on the table at seven. I'd been a guest in Myron's home often enough to be aware of this particular source of marital dissension.

'So? What can I do for you, Myron?'

'So, you sent me this list of furniture from the treasure trove you uncovered.'

'Myron, you've had that list for two months.'

'The list I've had; buyers I haven't. Now I maybe have buyers.'

Something in me whooped with joy. When the owner of the house next door had died intestate with no relatives anyone could discover, the city had auctioned the house and, separately, the houseful of American antique furniture. They'd put it up as one lot, and I'd come up with the winning bid. The bank and I, that is. The bank with some protest, some glowering, some portentous remarks by senior officials. Then Mark and Eugenia had put together a gorgeous, very expensive brochure, and we'd sent copies everywhere. Since the bank had made it clear it was only in for the very short term, I had to lay off about half the contents of that house immediately at what amounted to little more than dealer prices, and time was getting very, very short. Myron's mention of buyers got my full, enthusiastic attention, and Myron and I talked deals for over an hour. If he could do what he thought he could do, my immediate financial troubles would be over. Then I could take my time with the remaining pieces and end up turning a profit. Jacob Buchnam, my foster father, would approve of that. Since I was making monthly payments to him, buying the business, his income depended on mine. When I'd told him I was borrowing money to swing the deal, he'd been a little worried about it. Jacob had become rather feeble over the past year, and worrying wouldn't help him any. I resolved to go over soon and give him the good news—cross my fingers—about the New York sale.

While I sat there, massaging my aching leg and thinking positive thoughts, Bela nosed me questioningly. I heard Mark shutting the front door as he went out. It was five o'clock. Eugenia had locked the showroom and gone home half an hour ago. Critter came to the door and made a questioning half growl, somewhere deep in his throat. So, all right, why not another walk. The leg often hurt less at night if I walked it twice during the day. I stood up, ready to go get the leashes, and stopped, astonished. Both of them lay on the floor behind Critter. I'd hung them on a hook in the kitchen when we'd come in that morning.

I looked at Bela, who seemed unaware of anything strange, and then back at Critter, who now had the leashes in his mouth and was dragging them closer, as though he thought I hadn't seen them. Somehow, he'd gotten them off the back of the door.

'Critter?' I asked.

He made the growl noise again, leashes dangling from either side of his jaws. A cat to reckon with!

We went downstairs together and out the back door to the parking lot. It had occurred to me that Nellie Arpels, the old lady who lived upstairs across the alley, might like to see Critter. She is a cat fancier who spends most of her waking hours peering out of her upstairs window at anything happening up and down the alley. I waved in her direction, holding up Critter for her delectation. We went down the alley to the cross street, across, half a block over to Hyde, and then down Hyde the two blocks to the park. This time of the evening the traffic was heavy. Both Fourteenth and Thirteenth are one-way streets, though, so we found holes in the traffic and made it into the park.

Something had been itching at me all day. Something I'd seen that morning? Something I'd smelled maybe? When we got to the spruce grove, I stopped, staring. There were no crime-scene tapes, no chalked outlines. The body was long gone and so was any effort to find clues. The dried needles under the spruces had been raked. Little windrows of them stretched here and there across the grove. There was a single dark spot where Fred's body had lain.

Bela sat down and stared with me. Critter prowled to and fro at the end of the leash, three steps one way, turn, tail lash, three steps the other. I put his leash in Bela's mouth as I had that morning. 'Hold it,' I said. There was something in that grove. I could feel it, like an itch in my head. I stood under the tree, musing, and Bela nosed my leg. I hadn't told him to stay. I patted him; he barked softly, releasing Critter, who went up the tree like a panther, leash dragging.

'Critter, dammit,' I said, trying to see where he'd climbed to. I walked around the tree, to the side away from the path. There was a large bush there, screening the path from view. Something white against the trunk of the tree caught my eye, something below the level of my chin. A tuft of something. I pried it out from behind the bit of bark where it had lodged, a dozen or so bits of hair or something that looked like hair, white as Bela's fur. I ran a hand up the trunk and felt a shred of something else. Something black. Was this what I'd subconsciously noted earlier? I had no idea. I might have seen the tuft of white. The more I thought about it, though, the more I thought I'd smelled something. Still, nothing came to mind.

'Critter!' I demanded as I folded the white tuft and the black shred into a clean tissue and stowed it away in a pocket. 'You come down here.'

He came down out of the tree, trailing the leash Bela had dropped. I got hold of the leash and then waited while Critter groomed his jaw whiskers, looking pleased with himself. In addition to size, Maine Coons have these enormous muttonchop whiskers. He finished his whiskers with a final exhibitionistic lick, then we went on with our walk.

When we got home, I hung the leashes up in the kitchen, paying particular attention as I did it. They were on the back of the kitchen door, on a hook a good five feet above the floor. Critter could not possibly have brought them down. I must have forgotten to hang them up that morning.

Then I took a look at the tuft of stuff under a magnifying glass. It looked like hair to me. No follicles, but no twisting as thread was twisted either. That didn't rule out some monofilament like nylon. The black stuff was woven. It looked familiar but I couldn't figure out why. I don't have a microscope, so I couldn't look for fine structure. What I really should have done was turn the tuft over to the police, but they'd had their chance. Hell, maybe what I had was a policeman's hair. Maybe some detective had leaned up against the tree while he was supposed to be raking the ground. There was nothing to tell me how long it had been there. I put it away in a sealed, labelled and dated envelope.

When I went into the living-room, I found a pile of newspapers neatly stacked on my coffee table with a note from Mark. He'd gone down and picked them up after work and come back to drop them off. Poor guy. He really had nothing to do with himself, and I resolved to invite him to dinner soon. Not tonight, however. I was hungry, and the day had been longer than needful.

We, dog-cat-person, suppered. We retired early. I opened the window and turned on the ceiling fan to let the cold night air into the room. At ten o'clock Grace woke me from a doze, calling from San Francisco to say Ron was in jail and would I mind very much keeping Critter for another few days.

'Grace,' I said, 'do you want to talk about it?'

'Not really, Jason. No. Not now.'

I could visualize her pale face under that tow hair, her eyes looking gray, the way they did when she was sad. When she was joyous, she sparkled. When she was down, she looked like Poor Pitiful Pearl. In the Home, when I was a kid, someone had given one of the girls a Poor Pitiful Pearl doll, and I'd never forgotten that pale, sad, freckled face. 'Can I help you?' I asked, longing for her to be closer, where I could hold her.

'Maybe. If you can, I'll call you, all right? I'm not being closemouthed, really, it's just he's so damned dumb! And you hate to tell people your own brother is just stupid, don't you? After being a cop as long as I have, I should be able to be sort of detached about this. I keep telling myself that, but it isn't working. I always took care of Ron when he was little, and I keep thinking I should have taken better care of him lately.'

'He's a grown man,' I told her.

'I know,' she said sadly. 'I know. He is, but he isn't. Somehow when he looks at me, all I see is a little boy with a skinned knee.'

I made sympathetic noises. To get her mind off it, I told her there'd been a murder, that it was someone I knew, and asked if there was anyone at the station she'd recommend I talk to.

'Don't!' she said. 'Not until I get back!'

'Well then, Grace, you'd better hurry back,' I said. 'They may ask me more questions any day now.'

Long silence. Then: 'You're not really involved, are you?'

'I found the body,' I said. 'Maybe I found a clue in the park.'

'Damn.' Another long silence. Then: 'Don't do anything until I get home, Jason. I'll call you again soon, honest. Is my cat all right?'

Critter looked lazily up from my feet, where he had been chewing my big toe through three layers of blanket and bedspread, and purred.

'He's fine,' I said. 'Don't you worry about him.'

She said goodbye and we hung up. I missed her. After all those years without anyone, really, I'd gotten out of the habit of missing anyone except for Agatha, my wife. My wife, who had disappeared, whom I'd searched for and never found. I'd missed her for years, at first in a kind of hopeless agony, then doggedly. Last year I'd found out what had happened to her, found out she was really dead. Now that I knew that, I could miss Grace instead, even though she wasn't in love with me. She said.

CHAPTER 2

It was raining when we got up the next morning. Our usual run in the park was cancelled by mutual consent. Bela had his breakfast and crawled back into his dog bed. Critter accompanied me into the office—Mark and I have offices next to my living quarters on the second floor—and curled up in a velour-covered wing chair he'd adopted. I made a mental note to trade the wing chair for one of another colour. Critter's red tabby fur was garish against the wine upholstery. I had a green chair downstairs he'd look great in. To each of us our own small concerns.

I drank coffee while reading the accounts of the Steinwale murder.

According to the papers, Melody Steinwale had been the thirty-one-year-old wife of 'artist Greg Steinwale, better known as Grale, which is how he signs his paintings'. As in the Holy, maybe, I told myself, having known a few artists who took themselves very seriously indeed. Melody had managed a small gallery in North Cherry Creek, one of the few interesting parts of town so far as strolling and shopping go. Denver, like most cities, has been malled to death, but Cherry Creek is a nice combination of residential and commercial and arty. The gallery was called Just the Right Touch, which I'd thought a trifle precious each time I'd passed the place—recently taking note of some interesting ceramics in the window: big architectural pieces with unexpected lines and bright glazes. I wondered who ran it now.

In accordance with what Marge had said, the paper reported that Melody and husband had lived at the Louvre in the penthouse apartment of husband's mama, Harriet Steinwale. Melody usually walked or ran in the park in good weather. On this particular October Thursday morning, Melody had left for the park early. At ten in the morning, her body was found on a bench, slumped over a magazine. She had been shot once, at close range, by a small-calibre firearm. Park regulars had passed her without noticing she had been shot. So said the *Post*.

There was an interesting discrepancy between what the *Post* said and what the *News* had to say. According to the latter, Melody's husband had been out of town on a 'business trip'. On this rather important point the *Post* was mute. I wondered why.

The story was on the front page of both papers on Friday morning, with pictures. Melody looked closer to twenty than thirty, a breathtakingly lovely face with medium light hair piled carelessly above it. I wondered what colour it had been. Light brown maybe. Dark ash blonde. The eyes were wide and deeply fringed, the nose straight, the lips delicately curved. Pretty, pretty girl. Miss Gorgeous, right down to her collarbones. Gregory, on the other hand, was bony, lumpy-faced, with an odd nose. Of the two, he was more interesting-looking, though he showed every one of his close to forty years.

The Saturday papers carried a joint statement from Greg and from Harriet Steinwale's spokesperson: '. . . confident that the police will do everything possible to bring the perpetrator of this outrage to justice.' No rape, said the paper. No robbery. Melody was wearing her wedding ring, a complete circle of diamonds. No indication that the husband was suspected, even though husbands usually are . . .

'Jason!'

I looked up to find Mark staring at me. 'You looked deep into that,' he said. 'I spoke three times before you heard me.'

I grunted at him. 'Did you read this?'

'Umhm. Yes. Not much to go on, is there?'

There wasn't, yet. A few niggles, but nothing to talk about except for one curious thing. 'I think both murders are remarkably similar,' I said.

Mark dropped his jaw at me. 'Oh, come on, now. They were both shot, sure, but according to the Corvallis guy, Fred had quite a hole in his back. The Steinwale woman was shot with a lady's gun!'

I shook my head at him, telling him I knew that. 'What interests me is that both of them were shot but people went by without noticing they were dead. I went right past Fred yesterday. Hurried, as a matter of fact. People went right past Melody. People who knew her.'

'Maybe people were avoiding her. Maybe she was a talker, too.'

I stared at him with my mouth open. Of such small comments are puzzles further complicated.

*

I do love a good puzzle. Even as a kid I enjoyed them. Riddles. Conundrums. Word games. Better yet, a real mystery to figure out. The first one I remember was when I was about eleven. Three of us boys from the Home, Jerry Riggles, Prense Brown, and I, used to sneak over to City Park and go fishing. I say sneak because there were certain things we'd been told not to do by one or another of the staff at the Home. Mrs Opinsky, one of the cooks, had told us not to go to the park because of the 'preverts' waiting in the men's bathroom over near the band platform. Better that boys didn't go to the park, she told us, but if we did, we should pee outside, in the bushes.

This was a mystery. What was a 'prevert', and why did Mrs Opinsky warn us against them?

I looked up 'prevert' in the dictionary, sounding it out, just the way she'd said it. I couldn't find the whole word, but I found both 'pre' and 'vert'. 'Vert' was green cover, like bushes, where deer could hide. 'Pre' was before or outside of. Therefore, it seemed to me, these creatures, whatever they were, hid outside in the bushes, and it was bushes we had to watch out for, not toilets. When Mrs Opinsky told us to go into the bushes, she must actually be setting us up for some monster!

I told Jerry and Prense, and we figured maybe the monster was a relative of hers. Maybe her father or some old guy that ate kids. We stayed out of the bushes, and when we had to go, we used the toilet. Except for one old guy showing off his dick, there was nothing strange there at all. We laughed at him and he put it away. Poor Mrs Opinsky. If she's still alive, she's probably still wondering why these three brats took such a dislike to her.

I sometimes remind myself of the preverts when I think I've got an answer. Hidden in the bushes of easy certainty, I tell myself, there's probably some prevert waiting!

So, on this fall morning months after the death of Melody Steinwale and one day after the death of Fred Foret, I did not cry 'Eureka!' I merely noted, in passing, that Fred's body had been purposefully arranged, and that the newspaper account did not give me sufficient information to know whether Melody's body had been similarly trifled with or had simply slumped where it was shot. The park benches slope sharply back. A body could stay in place without falling over. I confess that I wondered if anyone in authority would take the trouble to check and how, with Grace out of town, I was going to find out.

When Mark finished with the mail, we composed a letter to Harriet Steinwale acknowledging her interest in American antiques (everyone with money *must* be interested in American antiques), referring to our recent 'acquisition of exemplary pieces', and enclosing one of the slick brochures.

'You think she'll call?' Mark asked.

I shrugged. I had no idea whether she'd call or not, but at least the signature on the letter would help establish my bona fides if we ran into one another. Which might happen, one way or another, if I started poking around. Meantime, there was Just the Right Touch awaiting. When and if I had time to get around to it.

'You've got to see the Hoopers today,' Mark instructed me.

His words were echoed from the door by Eugenia, just arrived. 'Yes, Jason, you simply must.'

'John and Lucinda Hooper have been talking about buying antiques for over a year now,' I growled. 'Meantime, they've bought a ranch over at Glenwood Springs, they've been into and out of the classic-car business, they've invested heavily in an AM radio station, and they have still to buy their first piece of antique furniture!'

How did I know all this? Because the Hoopers had told me. People talk to me. Ever since I was a kid, people have talked to me. I come across as the boy next door, I guess. The unthreatening nice guy they can confide in. Other men tell me that when they're alone, say late at night, and they get into an elevator with a lone woman in it, the woman looks frightened. If I get into an elevator late at night and there's a woman in it, she tells me what she had for dinner and about the fight she just had with her boyfriend. I'm not sure that's flattering, and don't ask me what it is, but I've got it, and I know more about some people than I've ever cared to know, believe me.

'It's a waste of time,' I said firmly.

'You could charm them,' said Eugenia.

'Flirt with her,' suggested Mark.

'She looks like a Scotch Highland cow,' I told him. 'All that hair!' I knew about Highlander cows because Jacob's niece Charlotte raises them on a spread down near Elizabeth, Colorado—which she calls Lizzieville.

'Mrs Hooper has a thing for you,' Eugenia suggested with a well-bred little moue.

'Whatever the thing may be,' I remarked with a moue of my own, 'she may keep it. Look, Eugenia. I know the type, I really do. They don't buy things because they want them. They buy things to prove they can. We've been going at it all wrong. Tell them the pieces they're looking at are too expensive. Tell them I recently got some new auction catalogues, and after looking at the reserve prices on similar pieces, I've raised the ante. Tell them that highboy they've been wearing the varnish off with their stroking and sniffing has gone up twenty per cent. It's now ninety thousand, and it will probably be a hundred by Christmas.'

She started to tell me something for my own good, but I scowled at her and she went away. She'd do it, just to prove I was wrong. Which, heaven help me, I might well be.

'All right, Mark,' I said. 'What else?'

'Willamae Belling wants you to come over today, anytime, she says, and look at that wallpaper in the entryway. Mrs Belling says it isn't the same colour she picked out. She says it's purple.'

'Of course it's purple. We agreed on purple.'

'She says it's too purple.'

I sighed and made a note. 'Anything more?'

'On your way to the Bellings', you should stop at that place on South Broadway and look at the Mexican reproductions for George Gorham's office. They came in yesterday.'

I grunted. George Gorham, who had bought a very nice and very expensive dining-roomful of furniture from me for his residence, was a collector of Southwestern art. He had asked me to provide a 'Southwest' décor for his office and to do it inexpensively. Which meant reproductions of colonial pieces, made in Mexico, usually of wormy pine. They were crude as a drunkard's humour but they did look old. Unfortunately, in some of the pieces, the woodworms were still working. I can remember vividly the first time I moved a genuine eighteenth-century diagonally braced Taos chest in the showroom and found those telltale little piles of sawdust. Actually, the things aren't worms. They're tiny black bugs, no bigger than a pinhead. One solution: put the furniture in an unheated garage in midwinter for a day or two. Or borrow somebody's walk-in freezer. The bugs are perseverant, but they don't adapt well to zero degrees.

With my day neatly laid out for me by other people, I had another cup of coffee and got started on it. If I did Gorham and Belling in the morning, I could stop by the gallery in Cherry Creek at lunchtime.

The colonial furniture looked all right for what George Gorham wanted. There were no piles of sawdust under the legs of the pieces. Of course, the drawers were made authentically—that is, crudely, which meant one couldn't draw them out without their falling on one's feet. No guides, no stops. I made a phone call from the shop to Art Baker, a cabinetmaker who does a lot of work for us, and arranged for him to pick the pieces up: a long table with three drawers, a *trastero* (armoire), and two lamp tables with drawers. Art could salvage the fronts of the drawers while completely rebuilding the backs and sides. He could also insert drawer guides in the frames. None of his work would show, but it would make the pieces functional. Since they were only reproductions, authenticity wasn't an issue, and the added cost still fell within Gorham's budget.

I left South Broadway and headed east on Alameda. Willamae Belling lived in the Denver Country Club, a very pleasant and expensive area of old, large homes and old, large trees. In Denver every tree has been planted by someone—something I have to remind my eastern acquaintances of when they wonder 'why you cut down all your forest'. There was no natural forest before our city was built, only shortgrass prairie with a few cottonwoods huddled along the creekbeds. Every bush and tree over eighty years old was lovingly planted by some verdure-hungry settler who most likely kept it alive with the weekly bath water.

I'd brought along the Belling file. It had in it, in lightproof envelopes, a sample of each paint colour and each wallpaper we had selected. When I walked in, poor Willamae greeted me almost in tears. I saw why. The entry was purple as Cartland prose. Magenta, really. I spotted the culprit almost immediately, an old pair of rose curtains across the window on the stair landing. The light coming through was bloody. I told Willamae to sit down for a minute, then went up and took down the curtains—being thankful that I'm reasonably tall—then went back down and collected her.

'Willamae,' I said, pouring on the smarm, 'we should have taken those old curtains down before we did anything at all. Look at it now. *All* the difference!'

She admitted it did look better. I got out the sample, and we compared. It was purple, rather towards the blue. It looked nice. She invited me to have coffee, and I said yes. We sat in the living-room and talked. Poor thing. She was lonely. I meet a lot of lonely old ladies. They call me because they bought something years ago from Jacob and they know I took over his business. They call me because they got one of my brochures offering to appraise their furniture. They call me to consult about refinishing some piece of old furniture for the children or for a grandchild. They call me because they don't know who else to call. In Willamae's case, an upstairs bathroom had flooded and brought the plaster down in the hall. She had a fixed income which inflation had not treated kindly, and her insurance did not cover broken pipes. So she had offered to let me buy her great-great-great-grandmother's silver candlesticks provided I would see to repairing and redecorating the entry hall, which I was glad to do because the candlesticks were beauties! At least in this case, the work was necessary. Often I get calls from old ladies who want to change furniture around just to have something happening. My bread and butter, but I'd give it up if someone could just figure out how to keep old ladies from being so all by themselves. Maybe I only feel for them because I have no old ladies of my own, no grandmas or elderly aunts. And perhaps because I feel for them, I seem to collect them like honey does ants. Old ladies and sad gay guys like Mark and girls who aren't in love with me, like Grace.

Willamae and I decided together that hanging a white sheet over the landing window would do until the new window treatment arrived. 'Window treatment.' That's decoratese for a pair of filmy, unlined curtains to let the light through plus a pair of heavier, lined drapes to shut the night out. And a fancy pouf at the top for elegance' sake. None of which would solve her real problem with the hall, which was that there was too little traffic in it.

I hung the sheet, then had three cups of coffee and a muffin and saw for the third or fourth time the pictures of her grown-up grandchildren and one great-grandchild who live a thousand miles away. She was lucky if she saw them once a year. I told myself if I had a family, I wouldn't move a thousand miles away from it, but maybe I was only kidding myself. I saw the pictures of her dear departed Flopsy and Mopsy, too, miniature poodles of discouraging mien.

'I keep thinking of getting another dog,' she said. 'And then I think how selfish that would be, to keep some young puppy from having a home with a whole family just to keep an old lady company . . .' I nodded and said I understood.

From the Country Club it's only a few blocks east to Cherry Creek. They're building a new shopping centre there, so the streets are all torn up and will be for the next several years. Street parking is always difficult. I parked in the garage next to the Tattered Cover Bookstore, one of the largest in the country and certainly the largest in our town, and walked north a block and a half to the Right Touch.

There are galleries, and there are galleries. There are those that try to appeal to everyone with bits and pieces of this and that, some representational, some kitsch, some way-out. There are other galleries that appeal to a certain taste. The Right Touch was of the latter type. The certain taste in this case would be for the fantastic, the outré, the slightly bizarre. The huge ceramic pieces were still in the window, organic-looking planters, like dinosaur innards, gizzardy swellings and intestinal coils. Behind them was a display of skeletal animals made out of wood and steel rods and wire. The wood had been burned and then scraped with a wire brush to give a feel of age and lively decrepitude. Each creature was very much itself, no fantasy except for the semi-skeletal forms. There were feral dogs with their teeth showing, deer bugling, fish swimming, hawks flying, a nightmare menagerie, life-sized. Not weatherproof, unfortunately, or I could have used two or three pieces for an outdoor job I had.

Upstairs there were small totem-pole-like sculptures, heavily decorated with feathers and rough fabric and beads. One of them I coveted immediately. It reminded me of something from my childhood, though I couldn't think what. Someone, perhaps. That straight, upward-peering outline, that feathery lightness at the shoulders. I have these flashes of recognition sometimes, outlines of something I think I recognize. Once these bothered me a lot, but I've gotten used to it. I tell myself.

'Can I help you?' a voice asked. I turned to find a pair of bright green eyes under a cap of sleek red hair, a light-footed person of obvious vitality, sparkling at me like a whole cageful of bright birds.

I got out my card. 'I've been noticing the pieces in the window,' I said. 'Since I had a few minutes to spare, I thought I'd drop in and see what you have. I don't do a lot of modern work, but sometimes one needs something a bit out-of-period.' Which was basically hogwash. One can put things of any periods together if one wishes to do so and arranges them properly. There's no law against it. I think Green Eyes knew the hogwash for what it was, though she looked properly awed by my pronouncement. I gave her an apologetic grin, one redhead to another.

We walked through the gallery. She told me about the artists. I told her what I liked, and there were a number of things I really did like. Her name was Nina Hough, pronounced Huff, and she was a graduate in fine arts from a prestigious eastern university. That made me think of my wife, Agatha, and I set the memory aside, ruthlessly. I can't afford to think of Agatha, of what we had or what we might have had. Whole days can get lost that way.

After Nina and I had established rapport, I got around to the real reason for my visit.

'I think I know the family that owns the gallery,' I said. 'Steinwale, isn't it?'

She got a funny look on her face. 'Harriet Steinwale,' she agreed.

'Oh,' I said, blank-faced. 'I thought the daughter-in-law, the one who was killed, owned it.'

'Harriet has always owned the gallery,' she said firmly. 'Her daughter-in-law used to run it.' She snipped off the final word as though to prevent other words from following. There had been a peculiar emphasis on the word 'run'.

I let it pass for a few moments while we talked about a painting I liked. 'You were here when Melody was alive?' I asked, returning to my subject.

'I was here,' she said. The peculiar emphasis told me that most of the time she had been the only one.

Pique will out. I nodded wisely. 'Melody thought it would be fun to play art gallery, did she? Well, that doesn't surprise me.'

'You knew her?' A half-suspicious glance.

'Of her.' I shrugged. 'A friend of mine knew her rather well.'

'Male friend, no doubt,' she snapped, then became contrite. 'I'm sorry. It's just that I'm still trying to undo . . .'

I told her that I understood, suggested that since I was about to have lunch, why didn't she join me and we'd talk about art. She looked doubtful.

'Come on,' I begged. 'You have to have lunch, too. And I hate to eat alone.'

'If you can wait until twelve-thirty,' she said. 'I have a gal who comes in every day for a few hours. She watches the gallery while I'm out and addresses show announcements, things like that.'

I wandered while I waited. The gallery also exhibited one-of-a-kind jewellry, woven wall pieces, several series of paper sculptures, plus a series of exciting ruglike-felt 'soft paintings' done in coloured wools by an Israeli artist I'd never heard of. When the gallery sitter arrived, Nina and I walked over to Soren's. The sun was out, temporarily, so we asked for a table on the patio. I had artichoke lasagna. Nina had what turned out to be a very authoritative chicken curry, and kept reaching for her wineglass, tears in her eyes.

'They don't fool around,' I told her.

Weeping but happy, she agreed, and I ordered her another glass of wine. So far she'd had three. She was beginning to be voluble about a lot of things.

'So tell me about Melody Steinwale,' I said when the plates had been taken away and another glass of wine for her and a cup of coffee for me had been delivered.

'I wouldn't want Harriet to think I'd been talking about the family,' she said. 'Harriet's a perfectly nice woman, but she can be a holy terror if you do something disloyal to the family.' She sipped, turning the long-stemmed glass.

'The family being?'

'Her, I guess. And Greg. And maybe a new wife, the way things are going.' She sipped again.

'What's she like? The new person? Any similarity between her and Melody?'

She snorted, caught herself, then snorted again. 'No, Jason. No similarity at all. In the first place, Trish already has one child—she's a widow—and wants more. Melody didn't.'

'You know that for a fact? Melody said so?'

'No. She said just the opposite. She and Greg were desperate to have children, to hear her tell it. She spent half her time going to gynaecologists and infertility specialists. They'd put her on pills.'

'And?'

'And she'd dump the pills down the john at the Touch. I saw her. She made some lame excuse about it being an old prescription, but it wasn't.'

'Well, that's only an isolated incident. Maybe she wasn't feeling well or the pills made her sick.'

'The only time she was sick was when the doctor suggested she might best get pregnant. Then she was sick. She had fifty and a half excuses for never making love at the right time.'

'You know that for a fact, too?'

'Lord, you couldn't miss it! Greg and she had arguments almost every month. He'd come into the gallery, the compleat angler, bearing little baits of flowers or perfume or cashmere sweaters, ready to catch her for lunch and then take her to bed, and she'd scream at him that she hadn't felt like it last night and still didn't feel like it. I mean, I wasn't eavesdropping; you could hear it down the block!'

Wine had loosened both her tongue and the sill cock on her metaphor tank. I enjoyed the thought of Steinwale as fisherman until I applied the same comparison to myself. What I was doing was also fishing.

'Why didn't she just take the pill?'

'Because then she'd have had to admit she was being dishonest with Greg, that she really didn't want children. So long as she could come up with excuses, she could tell herself it wasn't her fault. You know the kind, Jason. She was good at lying to herself.'

'What did she do with the other half of her life?'

'She took art classes, at DU. So she could—and I'm quoting—"share Greg's mental processes, be more attuned to his needs, as well as expressing her own talent." Christ! At least poor Greg doesn't have that to put up with any more.'

'She wasn't talented?'

'Jason, she did these really painful little paintings. Cramped. Full of fussy detail. No line, no composition, terrible colour that always ended up muddy. The instructor was very much on the make—I know him, he always is—so he fed her a bunch of crap about her talent. She used to quote him until I turned blue! The talent he had in mind wasn't on canvas.'

'So the new person is not like Melody,' I said. 'Which is odd, you know. Most of us men tend to go for types.'

She considered this. 'Well, Trish Watson *is* kind of like Melody, in appearance. Same chestnut hair. Same blue eyes. Same build, even. She's lovely-looking. I admit I was surprised when Harriet brought her in to the gallery . . .'

'Harriet brought her in?'

'About two months after Melody died. Harriet brought her in, asked if I could use her since I couldn't run the place alone. That was the first I'd known I was going to run it at all. Trish had no art background, particularly. Just what one gets as part of a liberal arts degree. I took one look at her and thought, "Uh-oh, here's another one."'

'But you were wrong.'

'I was wrong. Trish is just solid, you know? One of those women who had a nice family life, no real hang-ups, pleasant disposition. If I ever really got into trouble, I'd go to Trish for help, she's that kind. And she's got this adorable little girl who looks just like her.'

'You know Greg well?'

'Not really. He never looked at any woman but Melody, and he never looks at any woman but Trish now. Greg— well, you'd have to understand about Greg. He never went looking for a woman, you know? He never had time, or let himself have time. And yet, he's a perfectly normal male, so he needs a woman, so he stares around vaguely bellowing mating calls, and then settles on the first reasonably attractive thing that bugles back. That's what he did with Melody, and that's what he did with Trish. After about two weeks with me, Trish left the gallery to manage the studio for him.

He gets a lot of visitors, you know, and he's one of those single-minded men who can't cope. He really *needs* a wife, but except for that, people just aren't important to him. His mind is always doing something else. He's perfectly polite, but he's elsewhere.'

'He had some kind of mental breakdown, didn't he? When Melody was killed?'

She shook her head. 'Before. Months before. It was bad. I thought Harriet would lose her mind, too.'

'I wonder what caused that.'

She flushed, shaking her head. 'It could have been money worries, I suppose.'

'I thought Harriet was very well-off.'

'Harriet is, but both she and Greg feel very strongly about his being self-supporting. He wants to live on what he makes, not what his mother has, even though he'll probably inherit it someday. Harriet talks a good bit about building character. Then, too, Harriet could have gotten tired of supporting Melody in the style Melody preferred. Melody wanted a home of their own, and not just a plain house, you know? Greg's becoming a very popular artist just now. He will make very good money, but he's got debts and it will take time. Melody wanted a million-dollar house right now, and nothing else would do. I honestly don't know what caused the breakdown. I do know he spent a while in a private hospital. He was there when Melody was killed.'

'The papers said . . .'

'Oh, I know what the papers said. The Steinwale lawyer issued a statement, and then Harriet came zooming back from Acapulco or Yucatán or wherever and issued one of her own. The paper went along with the "business trip" because the editor is Harriet's cousin or nephew twice removed or something. I guess it's okay. There was no intent to interfere with the investigation. I mean, Greg was definitely locked up in the hospital when it happened. It wasn't a case of anyone suspecting him of anything. It was just protecting the family reputation. Harriet is very big on family.' She yawned. 'Jason, I've had too much wine. I'm talking too much. Harriet's going to fire me, sure as summer.'

'I'm sure she won't. You're far too knowledgeable to be fired. My guess would be that the gallery makes a profit.'

'Now it does,' she agreed, letting me assume what I did, that in Melody's day it had not.

'Tell me something,' I asked her, suddenly remembering Mark's comment. 'Did Melody talk about herself a lot?'

Nina gave me a wink, and a slightly tipsy giggle. 'There were two things Melody could do, Jason, better than anyone I've ever known. One of them was talk about herself and how she felt and what she thought and what she was going to buy.'

'And the other one?'

She grinned. 'She could spend money. God, could she spend money.'

I walked with her back to the gallery, then took myself back to the parking garage. Clouds had blown in suddenly, and there were tiny spatters of icy rain on the windshield as I drove back to 1465 Hyde Street. I hadn't learned much of help during lunch, except for the answer to the first question that had come up in the puzzle. Yes, Melody, too, had been a talker. And so was Nina Hough.

Eugenia greeted me with the news that the police were upstairs waiting for me and that the Hoopers wanted the highboy if I'd let them have it at the previous price.

I breathed in deeply. 'Tell them no. But I will come down ten thousand, simply because they've been looking at it. However, that price is only good until tomorrow. Tell him we're going to retag things over the weekend to reflect new values.'

'Mr Hooper wants to know how much of a deposit to hold it for them.'

'I won't hold it for them because I have a possible buyer coming up from Santa Fe on Sunday,' I fantasized out loud. 'A very wealthy man to whom I have sent pictures of various pieces because he is redoing his three-million-dollar house in an exclusive suburb. Tell the Hoopers I'm very sorry.'

Growing up in a Home, particularly playing cards with the janitor, teaches one how to bluff with a completely poker face.

Eugenia gave me a look: her 'I hope you know what you're doing' look. She has quite a repertoire of looks. There's the 'You have just made a complete ass of yourself' look, and the 'You should have had a mother to teach you manners' look. None of them has ever been quite insubordinate enough to make me do anything about it, though each has a definitely laserlike quality. You can turn your back on Eugenia and still feel the Look, like a small bonfire between your shoulder blades.

I found the police in my office, two plainclothes types, glancing through back issues of *Art & Antiques* and looking bored. Mark stuck his head in the door and asked if they'd like coffee, and they both said no in a tone that said yes, so I told Mark to bring a tray in case they changed their minds.

We went over the same ground I had gone over with the uniformed men. I had seen Fred on the ground when I went into the park.

'You didn't say anything to him?' the fatter cop asked me.

'I hoped he wouldn't see me,' I confessed. 'He was the world's worst bore.'

They cast one another significant looks, as though I had just confirmed a private theory.

'Well, he was,' I said. 'Ask anybody.'

'We did,' said the fatter cop. 'They all say the same thing.' Mark came in with the coffee, and the fatter cop poured himself a cupful and sugared it liberally.

Then we covered where the dog, cat, and I had run, who we had seen—I didn't know many names, but I could describe the regulars—and what we had said. Critter wandered into my office about then, lending verisimilitude to what I was telling them about the cat remarks.

'How long have you had him?' the leaner cop asked.

I thought of saying he belonged to Grace Willis, but caught myself. These were her colleagues, and I didn't want to involve her in explanations she might not care to make. I said I hadn't had Critter long.

'So then you came back the same way you went in,' the fatter cop prompted.

I agreed. That exit from the park was closest to the shop. 'So you saw him again.'

'I saw Fred again, but this time Bela howled. As soon as I saw he was dead, I stepped away from the body and hailed two passersby to fetch the police. I stayed by the body with Mr Corvallis until they came. Period.'

'Okay,' said the leaner cop. 'Now, how well did you know this guy?'

'Not well. His brother-in-law is my broker, his wife is an acquaintance. I met Fred at their house.'

'You have any business or personal dealings with him at all?'

'None whatsoever. He used to talk my ear off in the park, if I gave him a chance. That was my total relationship with the man.'

They went over the same ground again, from a slightly different angle, but they weren't pressing. They didn't really think I had anything to do with it.

I decided to try for some information I wanted. 'Have there been any other murders like this?' I asked. 'In the park?'

The fatter cop responded at once. 'There was a woman shot in the park last year. There was an elderly man shot this winter, sort of in the park, on one of the paths leading to his apartment house. That one was a robbery.'

'Any similarities?' I persisted. 'Between Fred's murder and either of the others?'

Aside from the fact they hadn't caught the perpetrators, either they didn't think there were similarities or they didn't intend to tell me. They were interested in why I asked.

I shrugged. 'I go to that park almost every day. I wondered if somebody was wandering around in the park shooting people, that's all. Did you work on the earlier cases?'

They had not. They accepted that I had a legitimate

concern. I said a few words more about possible similarities, which should have been enough to make them look at the former case files. Saying anything more than that might get me right into the middle of it, where I decidedly did not want to be!

'What did you find out?' Mark asked me as soon as the police had gone. I gave him an abbreviated version of what Nina had told me while he hmmed and wowed, and said maybe Mark was right after all about Fred and Melody both having been talkers. 'Are you trying to solve it?' he asked. 'What can I do?'

I'd been thinking up some nice, time-consuming job to get Mark involved. 'The people in the park tend to be regulars,' I told him. 'I've noticed it. Some of them are there every morning. Some two or three times a week. Some of them have been running or walking there for months or even years, certainly since Melody Steinwale's time. What I'd like you to do is take the picture of Melody from the newspaper and do a little jogging yourself. Ask the regulars if they ever saw her or talked to her or saw her with anyone.'

'You're concentrating an awful lot on her, aren't you?' he wondered. 'Wouldn't Fred's murder be easier. Since it's more recent?'

I considered it. 'What makes them both appetizing is the family alibis. The woman from the art gallery says that Melody's husband was in a mental hospital and her mother-in-law was in Mexico when Melody was killed. That removes the two nearest family members from suspicion in her case. Also, it seems Fred's ex-wife and her family alibi one another for the time Fred was killed. If all husbands and former wives were verifiably elsewhere at the time of the murders, and if, as I'm still assuming, the two killings are connected, we're looking for something outside the usual domestic-violence arena, something unusual. In my limited experience, with unusual things it doesn't make any difference where one starts, at the beginning or the end, or in the middle so far as that goes.' That sounded very pontifical, though I wasn't sure it meant anything.

'I wish Grace was here,' he said. 'That way we'd know what the police are doing.'

I agreed with him and told him about her having called me the previous night. We both said it was tough to have family in trouble, but when he began to look depressed at that idea, I quickly changed the subject back to Melody Steinwale.

'When I talk about Melody, what am I looking for?' he asked.

'Any reason anybody might have to kill her. I know her husband had a reason, though he might not have known it, but for the time being we're assuming he didn't do it. So we're looking for anyone else who knew her. You take the park, and I'll take the art school.'

Before the art school, however, I had the Hoopers. John Hooper called to say he'd be in within the hour, bearing a cashier's cheque for eighty thou. He didn't want the highboy to get away from him.

I grinned at Eugenia and she gave me a haughty glare. Score one for Jason, I told myself. Now that the dam was broken, maybe we could sell the Hoopers a few more excellent investments—something that would hold its value better than a shoe-string western-slope radio station at any rate.

I got tied up on the phone for the rest of the afternoon. The weather continued lousy, becoming worse along towards evening. I was trying to decide whether to thaw something for supper or go out, when the phone rang. Marge Beebe, asking if I'd come have a meal with her. Silas, she said, was out of town, which was good because she wanted to talk to me privately.

I drove the highway route, taking Bela and Critter along. Marge was an animal person, and I thought she'd like to see them. She told me to bring them on into the brick-floored family room, where they met her two dogs and all settled down among the saddles and tack and dusty boots to concentrate on the meaty beef neckbones I'd brought with me. Marge was broiling lamb chops for us, and we talked about Maine Coon cats for a while. She has quite a library of animal books—dogs, all kinds of livestock, cats. She pulled out one book that said something about Maine Coons, then another book that contradicted the first one. One authority said the cats matured at one year. The other book said at least two, maybe three. The first authority, a West Coast woman, said they weren't any larger than normal cats, ten to twelve pounds. I stared at Critter and wondered what kind of animal she'd been looking at.

Marge sat us down at her kitchen table. 'Jason, I know you sometimes get involved with solving things. Betty Garrison told me you did for her.'

I'd done a little thing for Betty Garrison, who had been married to a man who had an identical twin, though I was very surprised that Betty would have mentioned that embarrassing occurrence to anyone at all.

'Betty didn't tell me *what* you did,' Marge went on. I silently sighed with relief. 'But you know, Jason, the police aren't going to get anywhere with this. They as much as told me so just today. They don't have anything to go on. They say murder is usually someone the killer knows, or it's during the course of a robbery or other crime. Well, he wasn't robbed. I've told the police the names of anyone I knew that he knew. Lycia and the kids and Lycia's friend Ross—they were all together from four o'clock on Tuesday until we showed up there Wednesday morning. No way any of them could have been involved . . .'

'All four of them slept together?' I asked.

'Well, no.'

'Then they weren't together.'

'Wait. Listen. Lycia got burgled two weeks ago. Somebody got in and she doesn't even know if they took anything, except she does know they went through her things. I'd dropped by to return her hot pot I'd borrowed, and I was right there when she came out of her bedroom, really angry. She didn't say much, but I could tell how upset she was.

Well, wouldn't anybody be? It isn't the first time it's happened either. It happened last year, and that time she bought herself a little twenty-two, even though I don't think she's ever fired it, even for practice. I doubt it's ever been out of her dresser drawer. Ross has a gun, I know that, but he was in the military for a while and learned how to use his. Well, anyway, so this time she ordered a new lock put in, and day before yesterday, Tuesday, was the earliest the lock man could get there. He put the lock in and gave her one key, only one. This kind of lock you can only unlock with the key—no buttons or combinations or anything like that. She locked up that night, after supper, with the only key. She intended to have keys made for the family, of course, but at that time, Tuesday evening, she still had only the one. About eight o'clock Wednesday morning, she took the key out of her jewel box and unlocked the door to get the morning paper, and Ross was with her when she did it. The apartment only has the one entrance. There's no way anyone left that apartment during the night.'

'Where was this jewel box?'

'In her bedside table in the room she was sleeping in, her and . . . well, her and Ross. I guess in this day and age nobody has to apologize for sleeping with somebody they aren't married to. It still comes a little strange to me. Particularly since she was my brother's wife.'

'Does she plan on getting married?' I don't know why this seemed important to me, but it did.

'Lycia says no. She says once is enough. She isn't going to go through that again.' Marge busied herself with her knife and fork, a little pink in the face at the implied criticism of Fred.

'Could either Lycia or Ross have wakened and got up without the other knowing?'

'Ross is a trauma surgeon. Lycia says he sleeps like a cat from having to get up in the middle of the night all the time. And since Lycia's a doctor, she's a light sleeper, too. I don't think either of them could have gotten up and left the apartment without the other knowing. Besides, Ross says he didn't know where the key was. He wasn't in the room when she put it away.'

'It sounds to me like there's been a lot of discussion of this.' Everything she had told me sounded carefully phrased and rehearsed.

'Well, of course it's been talked over,' she said in an exasperated tone. 'It was the police, Jason. They asked all the same questions you're asking, and they asked them over and over. Lycia told them, and then Ross told them, and then Keith. Poor Shannon was crying so hard she couldn't even talk. I was there and heard it all two or three times. They even wanted to know where *I* was early yesterday morning. It happened to be one of those mornings when Silas and I had an early ride and breakfast together, so that's all right.'

'What do you want me to do, Marge?'

'I want you to look around a little, Jason, please. He was my brother. I feel . . . oh, like I ought to do something.'

I didn't tell her I had already involved myself in her puzzle. 'I'll look around a little.'

'I can pay you, whatever you think . . .'

'No!' I said. 'Absolutely not. Buy some good antiques, if you want to, but don't pay me for this. So far as this little hobby of mine goes, I'm an amateur and determined to keep my amateur status.' I smiled at her, not letting her know how close to rejection her words had pushed me. Someone had tried to hire me once, to conceal information. As it happened, I'd thought concealment was the best idea, but I would not be hired to do it. That came too close to what Jacob called selling one's soul. I liked solving puzzles, but I would not commit myself to 'doing' things about them. Once you take money, you have to impose some sort of ethic or professional standard on what you're doing, and I didn't want to do that.

'Have you got anything to tell me, Marge?' I asked. 'Anything about Fred I ought to know?'

'I'm not going to talk about family,' she said. 'They're out of it. Nobody in the family is involved. I'll tell you anything else you want to know, even though I don't know much. Fred went to school half a dozen different places here and there, fooling around, using up all the money our daddy left him. He came back here for a visit in '58. He'd have been about twenty-two then. Silas knew I worried about my baby brother—well, being ten years older, I'd half raised him—so he told Fred he'd get him a teaching assistantship up at the university if he'd settle down and get his doctorate. Silas could arrange that because his family was very big in the alumni association. Well, Fred took him up on it and stayed. He didn't even go back to collect his things, not that he had much. He got his doctorate, and he got this job and that job in the department and stayed there for ten years. He married Lycia, she was Lycia Meyer, in '60, and the kids were born in '62 and '66, and then in '68 he got a job in Washington with the DOD.'

'How did he get that?'

'I don't know, Jason. Politics of one kind or another, I guess. Fred wasn't making much at the university. I used to worry about his family getting along. Though we've never talked about it, I think Silas may have pulled some strings, a political favour, you know. I figured if he'd wanted me to know, he'd have told me. He thinks I talk too much, and I guess I do, so sometimes he doesn't tell me things and I don't ask. Anyhow, Fred went to DC in '68, and the family went with him, but about four or five years later, I think it was in '73, Lycia left him and came back here. Some relative of hers had died and left her enough to live on for a while, so she went back to school, to medical school. She'd gone on taking courses all the time she and Fred had been married, so she was well prepared for it.'

'She left him in Washington?'

'Left him, yes. She didn't divorce him then, Jason, but I think we all knew it was just a matter of time. Whenever we spoke of him, she got this tight-lipped look. Something happened back then. She never said one word to me against him, give her credit for that. The only hint she ever gave me was she said once that Fred had some problems he should work on. Oh, and once she said he'd let power go to his head. He was something or other on some committee at the DOD, and I guess he did have a little power of some kind. Well, maybe it had gone to his head.'

'When did he come back to town?'

'In '78. While he was in Washington, he'd done some favours for people at the university here—seen to it they got some grant money, that kind of thing. He told me he was going to "call in the IOUs", and evidently it worked, because he got a job at the university. The funny thing was, he expected Lycia to move in with him as soon as he got back, and he was really surprised when she didn't. She fought with him about that—if you can call it a fight when one person yells and the other one just sits there and looks superior, which is what Fred always did—and then she filed for divorce. Fred talked some about getting custody of the children, but they'd been living separately from him for years, and Silas told him not to make a fool of himself. Fred always listened to Silas. By that time, Lycia was a doctor, making plenty of money to support herself and Keith and Shannon.'

'And you're sure they had nothing to do with Fred's death.' We had come full circle. I knew a few more unsurprising facts about Fred, but no more about who might have killed him.

'Nothing. Couldn't have. Now, I know Fred made some enemies at the university. He used to talk about that. I know when he was with the DOD, there were people who didn't like him because he reviewed grant proposals . . .'

'Grant proposals?'

'For money, Jason. Scientists who wanted grants of money to do certain kinds of research. Fred was on this committee, and he turned a lot of them down. He said a lot of them were just half-assed.'

'Did you tell the police that?'

'Yes. Of course.'

'Did he do anything at the university besides teach? Any committees there?'

'The postgraduate committee, that's all.'

'That's the committee that reviews applications for scholarships or fellowships or teaching assistantships for graduate students, some of whom are also half-assed?' I was beginning to see a pattern.

She flushed. 'Well, Jason, some of them probably are.'

'Still, if graduate students were told so, they might be very angry. Murderous, perhaps?'

She looked away, uncomfortably.

'Did you tell the police that?'

'I didn't think of it.'

I didn't press the matter. 'If the family's out of it, do you have some other names for me, Marge? People I can talk to?'

'He worked most closely with a Professor Simmons. There were other people, too, but I only remember Professor Simmons. He came out here with Fred a few times, to go riding.'

I made a note. She hadn't given Simmons's name to the police because she hadn't thought of him as possibly implicated or involved. We finished our coffee. I gathered up dog and cat and went out to the car. The sleety squall had blown over. Though the city glow paled the northern sky, the country night above me was velvet black, stars everywhere, so many it made me gasp. There's a lot of talk about cities being crowded, polluted, unhealthy, but all in all, I think cities are man's proper milieu. How could we get on with our everyday business if we were confronted, night after night, with stars like these? How could we maintain our necessary sense of self-importance? We probably need that haze of sodium vapour playing on exhaust fumes to conceal what's too magnificent to be lived with. Like frogs need their muck, down in the bottom of the pond, to hide the existence of the uncomfortable stars.

On Friday morning I had an appointment with a plastic surgeon. I've had a mutilated ear and burn scars on the back of the head since I was an infant. I had the injuries when I was abandoned at the Home, and I don't remember how I got them. The records at the Home say they were not fully healed then, so it must have happened when I was three. Kids don't remember much from that early. At any rate, the scars don't bother me too much. I wear my hair a little long to cover them. Agatha used to say they made me mysterious. I'd rather have a nice saber cut, quite frankly. Something a little more traditional and less accidental-looking.

One of my customers happens to be a plastic surgeon, however, and he had mentioned to me that he could do hair implants where the scars are, not one hundred per cent guaranteed, but worth a shot. He'd said he could take hair from the back and sides and implant it along the neckline. The first session was Friday morning.

An hour after entering his office, I walked out. The back of my head was still numb, but he said it would hurt later. Like ant bites, he said. He'd given me some painkillers. I felt depressed and sad. Thinking about my origins does that to me sometimes, but it's a familiar woe that I don't let get to me much. The doctor had said he could fix the top of my ear, too, and I was considering that. When I got back in the car, I just sat for a while. I had no appointments. Mark could take care of anything that came up. Hooper's cheque would make the next bank payment with a little over, so I didn't feel compelled to go drum up cash business. I decided to drive up to Boulder and talk with Professor Simmons.

The University of Colorado at Boulder is a flawed extravagance of Italian provincial architecture. The flaws are new additions. The dollar is not what it used to be. All that tile and exterior detailing takes a lot of dollars, and concrete is cheaper, alas. Ralph Simmons was officed in a science building which looked like a packing crate and was only marginally better inside. His office was pleasant enough, if one ignored the dusty piles of papers.

'Fred's sister called to tell me you'd be in touch,' he said in a prissy voice. He had a face like an unblanched almond, lined and brown, with a pointy chin above which tiny features struggled with one another for supremacy. Seemingly the mechanism that moved his face could only work one feature at a time. If his mouth was open, his eyes were shut. 'I can't tell you how distressed I was to hear of Fred's death,' he said, like a blind man. His eyes flickered open, closing again when his mouth cracked to say, 'Our society must find ways to protect itself against this casual crime. Muggers! Thieves!' Eyes and mouth shut, his nostrils flared. He sniffed at me through his closed eyelids, like a blind bloodhound.

'He wasn't mugged,' I said. 'He wasn't robbed. He was probably killed by someone who knew him.'

Eyes opened again. This time they sagged half closed while he hissed, 'Surely that's impossible!'

I nodded, conveying certainty. 'Which is why I'm here, Professor Simmons. Marge Beebe tells me that you knew Fred as well as anyone.'

'We weren't really close,' he said with sudden caution. 'Not . . . bosom friends.' The old-fashioned phrase came out like a cockroach, peeking from a hole, waving its antennae in alarm, as though he were afraid of being accused of friendship. If they hadn't been friends, I wondered what they had been.

'Nonetheless,' I continued.

'What do you want to know?'

'I'd like to know who had reason to dislike him. Who had reason to think Fred needed killing.'

'That woman,' he snorted. 'Sally somebody.'

'Woman?'

'His neighbour. Where he lived, in his apartment house. She tried to kill him, but he took the gun away from her. Heaven save me from hysterical women!'

'His neighbour, you say?'

'She's not there any more. Streeter, that was the name! She moved. Too ashamed to face him.'

'Can you think of anyone else?' I asked, making a note of the name Sally Streeter.

'There is someone who might have wanted to kill Fred,

though it would have been totally without justification,' he snapped at me, eyes closed. 'Totally without justification. Fred was quite right to deny financial aid to that young ruffian.' There was a little foam of spittle at the corner of his mouth. From this, I assumed (rightly, as it turned out) that Simmons was also on the committee and had also been exposed to the ruffian, whoever he was.

I asked him for details and was told of a certain Martin O'Toole, who had only last week been denied the teaching assistantship he needed to continue his work at the university.

'He shows no scholarship!' Simmons pronounced. 'Calls himself a physicist. He might as well be doing alchemy!'

I wondered out loud why Fred was still on the committee when he had retired from the faculty.

'He would have stayed on for the rest of his term,' Simmons said with an impatient gesture. 'He would have received a small stipend. Retirement is not, after all, an incapacitating condition . . .'

I thanked the professor and slipped away. Since this was the physics building, finding a graduate student who was at war with a couple of physics professors shouldn't be difficult.

I asked here and there. A plump blonde in the office told me, wistfully, that Marty O'Toole was at war with everyone, and further that he hung out at a local tavern. There I found him, ensconced at a rear table, working on a monumental drunk all by himself. In front of him were several empty glasses plus the ones he was working on. From the colour of his eyes, I estimated today's bout to be at the tail end of a lengthy series.

I sat down across from him and asked if I could buy him a drink. He glared at me.

'For what reason? To corrupt my soul? To assist my descent into Hades? Or to offer the pleasanter comforts of Lethe?' He was so lean as to be almost skeletal, huge-eyed, like a lemur, his mouth compressed into what looked like a permanent sneer. 'Are you astonished that I, a mere scien-

tist, should be aware of such references? I had a mother
who read-to-me . . .' Every few words, his shoulders would
jerk, as though something had bitten him.

'Actually,' I said, 'I wanted to talk about Fred Foret.'

He pointed a finger at me, cocked as though he was ready
to fire it. 'Dead,' he intoned. 'Freddy For-it is dead. There
is justice. It is slow and incomplete, but there is justice. The
mills, as it were, of the gods.'

'I take it you didn't like him.'

'I hated him. I should've shot him myself! Him, and
Simmons, and Graybull. The know-nothing triumvirate!'
He circled his half-empty beer glass with several completely
empty shot glasses, an alcoholic's solar system. An almost
empty bowl of peanuts was Jupiter.

'Tell me about him,' I suggested. 'I really want to know
about Fred.'

He sat back, arms above his head, reaching for something
I couldn't see and he couldn't find. Finally he came back
to earth. 'Why?' he asked.

'His sister wants to know why he got killed. I'm trying to
find out for her.'

He drank, thinking about this. While he thought about
it, I went over to the bar and picked up a couple of beers.
If I could keep him on beer, maybe he could tell me
something.

His glass was empty by the time I got back. I set a full
one in front of him.

'I'm going to tell you,' he said. 'I'm going to make clear
what no one understands. I'm going to diagram for you the
parameters of the man's stupidity. I'm going to show you
what an idiot he was.'

'Fine,' I said, sipping.

'You know anything about physics?'

'Nothing,' I admitted.

He thought about that. 'This may be more difficult than
I had thought,' he said. He drank a few swallows, drumming
his fingers and blinking rapidly. 'I shall speak in the general
rather than the specific.'

'Fine,' I encouraged him. Anything would do. If I didn't understand it, I could always get someone sober to explain it to me.

'There is a certain method which has been taught in departments of physics for the past thirty or so years. It is a method of making calculations regarding the structure of substances. Are you with me thus far?'

I told him I was.

'This process is assumed, eventually, to have a practical consequence. It is supposed to be predictive. Engineers and metallurgists very much desire some kind of predictive method which will tell them that if they mix element A and element B, the resultant material will behave in such and such a way.' He spoke with the precision of someone who has used the same words before—often before. 'There would be no reason to engage in these calculations if they had no practical consequence.'

I understood him. I was surprised that I understood him, but I did. O'Toole's alcohol content didn't seem to be affecting his tutorial powers.

'For thirty years, maybe forty, physicists have been getting grants from metallurgists to develop a method of prediction. For thirty or forty years the physicists have been promising that any day now they would perfect this process and start predicting things.' He nodded at me: great, ponderous nods. 'Forty years.'

My mind made the intuitive leap. 'You've found a new way to do it,' I said. It was the only thing that made sense.

His eyebrows went to join his hairline and he smiled, like a sunrise. 'Not I.' He shook his head at me with the pleased smile still wandering around on his face, trying to find a place to settle. 'Not I alone. Several people. Here and there. The man I studied under at MIT. Some people at Oxford. We have found a way to do what these idiots have been promising . . .'

'Fred Foret?' I suggested, pronouncing it For-ay. 'Him?'

'Freddy For-it was one of them. Simmons was one of

them. Graybull was one of them. They've been doing the same things over and over for decades. They've been giving all the financial aid to their students, whom they've taught to do the same things over and over. So I come along and say, hey, fellas, here's a way to get somewhere with this, and you know what they do?'

I had a pretty good idea. 'What?' I asked.

'They say I'm arrogant. They say I'm wet behind the ears. They say I'm no scientist. They say I make mistakes, which I sometimes do, like they never made a mistake. God! What kind of a scientist does the same calculations over and over again for forty years without figuring out he's not getting any place!' He finished his beer, looked startled, as though he'd swallowed something alive, then collapsed face forward into the bowl of peanut shells.

The bartender came over, not hurrying. 'Marty passed out, huh?'

'Looks like it,' I said. I stood up and put my hands in my pockets, waiting for it. I could see it coming.

Sure enough. 'You wanta take him home?' the bartender asked.

I didn't, particularly. 'Where does he live?'

He named a street I knew. I told him I'd get my car. When I drove up in front, he hauled Marty across the sidewalk like a sack of grain and dumped him in the back seat of the Mercedes, commenting, 'Nice car. I'd get him home right away. Sometimes he whoops after he's been drinking.'

I drove as quickly as was consonant with good sense. There were two guys lounging on the front porch amid a litter of empty beer cans when I got O'Toole there. With a minimum of comment, and that jocular, they helped me get him into his place and on to the bed, not much helped by what seemed to be their own customary state of inebriety. When I pulled the pillow over to put Martin's head on it, a gun slid on to the floor.

'What's that doing there?' said one of them, picking it up in a manner that posed imminent danger to himself and me. I took it away from him gently, pointing it in a less dangerous direction. A .38 revolver, fully loaded. Both the gun and the cartridges were filthy. I doubted it had been fired in twenty years, which didn't mean it couldn't do a lot of accidental damage.

'He was going to shoot somebody,' the other guy said. 'Some professor or other. Don't you remember the other night?'

'Oh, right,' he replied, without interest. 'Old Freddy Forit. Well, considering what Freddy did to O'Toole, he's got it coming.'

Evidently the two of them had not yet heard about Fred's death, or were not sober enough to have taken it in. I didn't enlighten them. I put the revolver away in a drawer under some dirty socks and left without telling them that Freddy no longer had it coming.

On the way back home, the back of my head started feeling as though it had been attacked by a nest of fire ants. I stopped at a service station to get a can of citrus-flavoured fizz to chase the painkiller with. After about fifteen minutes, the pain let up enough so that I could get back in the car, wondering whether it was worth it or not to look merely normal. The face looking back at me in the car mirror was the same stranger I always see in the mirror, and he refused to say.

CHAPTER 3

Jason Lynx Interiors opens at noon on Mondays. We close at noon on Saturdays, except by appointment. On Saturdays, Eugenia often doesn't come in at all; sometimes Mark's appearance is merely a gesture. This morning he arrived in jogging clothes to report no luck so far on the park circuit. 'I'll give it another try tomorrow,' he said.

'People run a little later on Sundays,' I told him. 'Or maybe it's just that I do. I do tend to see the same people on Sundays as on other days, though, so I guess I'm not the only one.'

'Are you going to tell the police about O'Toole?' he wanted to know after I'd filled him in on yesterday.

I said no, I wasn't. At least not yet. They could find him the same way I had, and besides, I didn't think he'd done it.

'Why is that?'

'I think he was too drunk to have hidden the fact if he had done it. I think he wanted to do it, sure. Got out his gun from wherever he usually keeps it, loaded it, talked drunkenly to his housemates about shooting the bastard, then fell asleep on top of the gun. When he woke up, he felt like hell and went out to get some more of what ailed him.'

'Could have been,' Mark agreed. 'Is he an alcoholic?'

'He may be merely a genius who drinks,' I opined. 'If he gets some help pretty soon, and the establishment doesn't beat him down. On the other hand . . .'

'What, on the other hand?'

'On the other hand, he could be a very clever killer counterfeiting drunkenness. He's still on the list, Mark.'

Mark gave me a lopsided grin and left. It was the most cheerful expression I had seen on his face for some time. I fervently hoped he would soon meet someone . . . someone what? Someone nice. Someone non-promiscuous. Someone. Well.

I had a quiet morning, doing paperwork, mostly figuring bills for people. Sometimes I add a little for aggravation. Sometimes I add a lot for aggravation, then have to go back and refigure it when I cool down. The entry bell rang a couple of times during the morning. Package delivery. A peerpointer. I call them peerpointers because that's what they do. Peer, and point. They seldom buy anything. I locked up at noon, got some stuff out of the refrigerator for Jacob, took a little box of chocolates out of the 'go visiting' drawer, and started the afternoon by dropping in on Nellie Arpels.

Her daughter, Janice Fetterling, was looking very spruce

and at least five years younger than fifty-five. I complimented her on her outfit, and she told me she was going
shopping with a friend as soon as Jeannie arrived to sit with
Nellie. I told her I'd stay until Jeannie arrived, and she took
off with a smile and an expression of anticipation. There
had been quite a change in Janice since Jeannie had started
coming three times a week to cat-sit for Nellie, which was
actually equivalent to Nellie-sitting for Janice. Jeannie's
salary was a small gift that I gave Nellie. I hadn't planned
it as a present for them both, but it's nice it worked out that
way.

I took the box of chocolates on upstairs. After I'd told
Nellie all about Melody Steinwale, at least the part that I
knew, she licked the sticky chocolate truffle off her fingers,
rocked herself briskly back and forth in her wheelchair, and
said, 'She reminds me of Hope Dodson. I went to school
with Hope, back in the twenties. Her daddy had run off
with another woman when Hope was eight. Hope spent all
her time looking for her daddy. I don't mean her real daddy,
I mean anybody who'd be her daddy. She had no use for
boys. She wanted men. She made up to a doctor for a while,
but when his wife ran her off, she got involved with a lawyer
about twenty years older than she was.'

'I don't see the similarity, Nellie.'

'Well, they got married. And she never got pregnant. And
her husband was so nice about it, saying it was probably
his fault they couldn't. But I knew it was because that
doctor had given her some kind of cap—not a diaphragm,
something else—to keep from it. That doctor's nurse was
my sister-in-law, that's how I knew. We figured out why
Hope was that way. Because she was the little girl, don't
you see? If she had a baby, she'd have to grow up, and she
didn't ever want to.'

I had a few fleeting thoughts about a female Peter Pan.
'The woman at the gallery says Melody could really spend
money,' I said.

'More of the same,' said Nellie, push-pulling at her chair,
back and forth. 'Money takes care of you, too. Money and

the right kind of shepherd dogs and horses and men, we always used to say. They'll take care of you. Best is a nice older man with money. Sugar daddy is what we used to call somebody like that when I was a girl. I'll bet this artist was her sugar daddy.'

Gregory Steinwale was eight or nine years older than Melody, not nearly old enough to be her father. Still, he seemed a lot older, while she'd had a nubile quality. I gave Nellie high marks for perspicacity, as usual. Grale and Melody could have looked almost like father and daughter, and who knows what roles they had played to one another. I had known couples where one of them played the parent most of the time. Still . . . 'He didn't have money, Nellie! His mother did.'

'Well, you can bet his wife used him to get money out of his mama, then. Bet you anything she spent it faster than he could paint it and his mama kept having to help.' She rocked and peeked in the chocolate box, teasing herself, finally giving in and taking another one. 'You know, Jason, it's like that old saying. It's a wise child knows his own father. All these little girls looking for their daddies, picking the wrong ones or maybe not knowing them when they show up.' She nodded, pleased with herself. Her cat, Perky, came out of the closet and jumped up in Nellie's lap. Perky had been a gift from me, one that suited both cat and old lady.

'I've seen that big cat you've got,' Nellie said, scratching under Perky's chin. 'Where did you get that monster thing?'

She knew Grace, so we talked Grace and cats until Jeannie Rudolph showed up. Before I left, I promised to bring Critter over so Nellie could get a closer look.

The next stop was at Jacob's place. Francis Fairweather, Jacob's male nurse, opened the door to my knock.

'How is he, Francis?'

'Doing better this week,' he told me. Jacob had a stroke a few years back, and he had good and bad days, often perking up with the weather. I handed over my gifts. Jacob likes double cream, soft semi-ripened cheeses, and he's a tiger for caviar, so I'd brought some of each.

I told Jacob the story of my newest puzzle. He subscribed to *Art & Antiques*, and we dug out the article on Grale for him to review.

'I read this when it came out,' he said. 'I thought at the time we had another Hockney.'

The styles were similar. Not derivative, merely similar. A lot of very bright colour. A similar use of diagrammatic landscapes, though Grale's were less spontaneous, more controlled, and he eschewed the bright magenta Hockney used a lot of.

'He's good,' Jacob said. 'He's making a name for himself.'

'Now that he's out of the mental hospital,' I agreed. 'He wouldn't have made much of a name for himself in there.'

Jacob sighed. 'I've always thought that genius and madness were close kin. I always told myself to be thankful I had neither of them.'

He laughed. I laughed. Francis brought in some toast and butter and chopped egg. We had caviar on toast. We had cheese. Jacob really was looking a lot better.

'So what do you do next?' he wanted to know.

I shook my head at him, not sure. 'I need to know more about them. Why they were as they were. I thought I'd go down to Grale's studio. It's open to the public. His new girlfriend manages it for him.'

'That sounds like a good idea,' he said with a satisfied little sigh, his eyes sagging closed. Over his shoulder, Francis grinned at me. Jacob had eaten himself into a nap.

Back at my place, I came in the door just in time to catch the phone: Grace, with her voice full of suppressed emotion. I couldn't tell whether she was trying not to cry or trying not to scream.

'Jason, I've called the personnel office down at the department, and I'm taking all my accumulated leave.'

I gulped. 'Lord, Gracie, is it that bad?'

'It's that bad. My stupid, stupid brother got himself mixed up with some real rotten people. He's in for drug trafficking, Jason! He's only an accessory, they know that. But they think he can tell them something, and he can't. At least, I don't think he can. If he could, he would have told me. Unless he's dumber than ever before. Oh, God, Jason,' she yelled, 'I am not being at all professional, and this is such a *mess*.'

I could see her, her eyes squinched shut, tears at the lashes, shouting at me. 'Grace, do you want me to come out there.'

'Would you? Would you really, Jason? That's so nice. That's really nice. No. I don't want you to. There's nothing you can do, and I'd only feel guilty taking you away from business when there's nothing. I'm just going to stay here until I get Ron sorted out.'

'Do you need any money?'

'The rent on Ron's apartment here is paid through the end of the month and it's one of those places that get the last month as a deposit, so next month is paid, too. I'm living there. He had a roommate, but the guy moved out when all this came down. If I need some, I'll call, okay? Will you go by my place just to check? If I'm still here the first of the month, will you or Mark collect from the tenants for me? Will you keep Critter?'

I told her I'd do anything she needed doing. I said I'd keep Critter. I asked her if she was sure this was the right thing to do.

'Jason,' she cried, 'it's family. When it's one of your own, you have to do everything you can. You know that. You can't just stand around and let people ruin your family.'

I had no family any more except for Jacob, but I agreed with her. When I hung up, I felt alone and sorry for her and sorrier for me. Not that we were an indivisible twosome. We weren't. Grace had let me know in a very gentle way that she didn't think I was ready for that kind of relationship. She hinted that she thought I needed more time to get used to the idea that Agatha was dead, and that was possibly part of her real reason. Though Agatha had disappeared eight years ago, I had only found out last January that she had been murdered by people she and I knew, people who were playing a part, people who sympathized when she disappeared, who acted like ordinary people until the day came when someone killed them both. My son, who had been injured when Agatha disappeared, died soon after we found out about his mother.

Grace was partially right about all that. It had been sad, and I probably had needed some time to adjust to the realities. I'd mourned a lot over both of them, however, and it was time to get on with life. I believe Grace's real reason was that she was afraid I'd compare her with Agatha at some point. Agatha had been beautiful. Grace didn't think she was. Agatha had been a college graduate. Grace hadn't gone to college. Agatha had been an artist. Grace was a cop. Grace saw herself at the short end of any comparison, even though I didn't. I was letting things ride. Either she'd straighten it out for herself or I'd have to figure out some way to let her know there were no comparisons. Not any.

Be that as it might, I didn't want to spend Saturday night worrying over it, or Sunday either. I couldn't very well call Mark for company while he was grieving over his absent lover. Almost everyone I knew was part of a couple. Finally, I called Nina Hough. Nina was, as might be supposed, busy that evening. Discoing, she said, with an artist from out of town. She was free on Sunday, however, and we made a date for lunch and to catch the new exhibit at the Art Museum. Busman's holiday. That still left Saturday night.

The Ogden Theatre was having a Kurasawa festival. I went to that, alone. Four hours later, overdosed on pageantry and Round the Corner hamburgers with avocados and barbecue sauce, I made it to bed. Critter curled up in the middle of my back and purred. I thought it was nice of Grace, and the very least she could have done, to have arranged for the substitute.

I was just leaving to pick Nina up at noon on Sunday when Mark came zipping up the stairs, face pink and healthy-looking, eyes shining. I hadn't seen him smiling like that in weeks!

'You found out something,' I said unnecessarily. He

was only waiting to catch his breath before he told me.

'Found a guy,' he said. 'About forty-five, forty-eight. Good-looking guy. Has a whole floor in that high-rise condo just past Thirteenth? The new one? The one with the lanais?'

I told him I knew which one.

'His name is Ambler. Neal Ambler. He's something in oil. And he knew Melody. From the way I read him, he knew her pretty well.'

'What makes you think so?'

Mark considered this. 'The way he talked about her. Very knowingly. He said things like "her bitch of a mother-in-law". And "Her husband never understood the kid, of course."'

'Whoop-de-do,' I said.

'Yeah, that's the way I felt.'

'Did he express wonder at your interest?'

'Well, Jason, what I did was, I gave him the impression you were looking into her death for the family. I told him you'd be in touch with him. I didn't . . . well, I didn't say what business you were in.'

I thought about that. I *was* looking into Fred's death for *his* family. Melody was part of the same puzzle, or so I believed, so one could say I was looking into Melody's murder for *a* family. A small change from that to *the* family. Make it the definite article. 'Right,' I said. 'When I meet Mr Ambler, I'm not necessarily an antiques dealer or decorator and I'm looking into it for the family.'

'I wandered around and asked people for a couple of hours. Several people remember her, used to see her, even spoke to her, but he's the only one I've found so far who actually knew her. He says he used to talk to her during their morning dog walks. He has a Kerry Blue. Big thing. It growled at me when I tried to pet it.'

'I've heard Kerries are one-man dogs,' I replied absently, focusing on something else he'd said. 'Melody had a dog?'

'Ambler mentioned her collie. Why?'

'The papers didn't say anything about a dog. Was she walking the dog the morning she got killed?'

He shrugged. We stared at each other for a moment, then he went home and I went to pick up Nina, which soon made me forget all about the question of Melody's dog.

Nina and I fought about art, not with any rancour but continually, starting with lunch and without surcease during the museum visit. Her taste and mine were not so much diametrically opposed as they were antithetical. She liked the kind of thing she showed at the gallery. Fine. I could take some of it, even like some of it. However, I could also like twelfth-century church art and craft pottery and half a dozen other things Nina cast aside as part of an outmoded canon. With her it was the cutting edge or nothing. Despite the fact that we knew within an hour that we would never be able to share any aspect of our lives except purely social ones, we had fun. I was almost getting used to having fun again.

Our day together was both enjoyable and late: enjoyable enough that we finished up the afternoon at a pizza place, and late enough that when I got home the animals complained about neglect. There's always dog kibble and cat kibble available, so they weren't starving. As is customary, the dog eats the cat kibble and vice versa. They get good stuff in the evening, however, and that's what they were waiting for: people food. Since I'd been with Nina, not Grace, there had been leftover pizza, and I'd brought it home.

Along about nine-thirty the doorbell rang.

Marty O'Toole was on my doorstep, leaning against the door, very pale-faced, his eyes, as Mrs Opinsky used to say, 'like two holes burned in a blanket'. He was carrying a crumpled paper sack.

'You're the guy I talked to in Boulder the day before yesterday? The one who took me home?' His eyes were so red, I wondered that he could see me at all.

I said I was the man. I hadn't told him my name at any point. I asked him how he found me.

'Jerome Needleman,' he said. 'Jerome K. Needleman. He

has one of those what-you-call-it memories. He remembered your licence number.'

Jerome must have been one of the men who helped me carry him upstairs. 'You went down to the vehicle licence bureau and paid your two dollars?' I suggested. 'They told you who I was?'

He nodded and gulped. 'Listen, could I come in?'

I led him up the stairs, past the offices to the living-room, and suggested we both have some coffee. He nodded with a miserably sick expression on his face, and I told him where the bathroom was before I went to make coffee. I heard the toilet flush, then water running. When I got back from the kitchen, he looked a little better. The front of his hair was wet.

'I am so hung over you wouldn't believe it,' he said.

I told him I would believe it.

He drank coffee. I drank coffee. After a while, he said, 'From what I remember, you were asking about Freddy For-it. Old Jerome K says you saw the gun.'

'Yes, I saw that you had a gun.'

'I didn't kill him, honest.'

I told him I'd have called the police if I'd thought he had. Not that I was sure he hadn't, just that I didn't think he had.

'I wanted to,' he admitted. 'If I hadn't been so drunk, I would have. That bastard. He was such a freaking bastard. You have no idea!'

'Why him, more than the others? Simmons is on the committee, isn't he?'

'Simmons is just ignorant. How he ever got a doctorate, only his keeper knows. But Freddy For-it, damn him, he knows he's destroying people.'

'Why him?' I pressed. 'Why Fred?'

'Because of what the bastard did,' he said. 'First, the committee shot me down. He was only one of them, maybe the most important one, but only one. But then afterward, he called me. He wanted to meet with me. Said he thought he could improve my "standing in the academic community". I hate guys that talk about the "academic community" as though it was something real! But I said all right, why not. Maybe the guy has had second thoughts about the reaming he'd given me.'

'When was this?'

'I don't know. Last week. Ten days maybe. What's today? Never mind, it doesn't matter. So, since Freddy For-it is retired from the university, he borrows old Simmons's office and I went there. He sits there with this prissy expression on his face, being kind. He says he believes I am fundamentally an intelligent young man. He thinks he can help me. He thinks I've just been badly taught at MIT. He talks about my professor there, what a nut he is, what a weird reputation he has, how he can't blame me for "having a crush on someone who seems messianic". All of which is true. The guy is a nut case, I do admire him, he is messianic, but he's also right! He's eccentric and he's a genius . . .' He gulped at his coffee, burning his tongue, waving his hand to cool himself before spewing out words again, as though they were bullets.

'Here's Freddy at this puking state university, got on the faculty by bribery, which everyone knows, not even on the faculty any more, ignorant as a tuna, about as much of a physicist as I am a paperhanger, and he talks in this patronizing way about a guy who's a genius. So anyhow, Freddy For-it goes on about anyone who knows anything in the field knows that the only way to do things is the way they've been doing them for forty years. And he quotes me this guy, and that guy, none of whom have made any progress since the sixties. They're still doing their damned calculations to more and more decimal places, and they still can't tell you what the numbers mean or if they mean anything.

'So, okay, I ask him how he can help me. Well, he says, I should take some of Simmons's courses. He can give me a reading list. I mean, look, Jason—can I call you Jason?— here this guy is, he doesn't know anything about what I do, he hasn't bothered to read up on my field, and he sits there with this fatherly, superior smile and tells me I should go back to being an undergraduate!

'So I tried to tell him. I told him what they're doing at MIT. I told him what they're doing at Oxford. I told him we can predict outcomes. I had a bunch of stuff with me, and I dug out a bibliography for him. I had some reprints, a couple where I'm even one of the authors, you know? And he smiles, and he smiles, and finally, when my batteries run down, he says, "But, Marty, this can't be more than superficially interesting because it's based on error."'

'What error? I ask him.

'It has to be error, he says, because it wasn't done the right way. Which, as you may have guessed by now, is the way he and his friends do it!'

'He hadn't read any of your material?' I asked.

'Not a word. It was like arguing with some guy who comes to your door and wants to talk about the Bible. No matter what you say, he has some answer from the Bible, and you have to be wrong because what you're saying isn't in his damned book!'

'So then?' I asked.

'So then I told him I'd just have to go to some other university where people cared a little less about how they'd always done things and a little more about reality. And he says . . . he says a bunch of stuff. About men like him with over twenty years' investment in their careers. About giving up kith and kin in order to serve science. About young tomcats rampaging around ruining other people's lives. About he knows exactly how I feel, senses my keen disappointment, how he's an expert in est and could have told me how to deal with my feelings if I'd been halfway respectful . . .'

'And . . .' Somehow I just knew there was more. What he'd told me so far, no matter how awful, was not enough.

'And, he said, since I'd come across as intransigent and disrespectful—get that, like I was some kid in military school—he says wherever I go, he'll know somebody there and he'll write to them and tell them they shouldn't give me any support, and just in case they do, he'll also write to his old buddies at the DOD and tell the DOD to blacklist whatever school I'm at. God, do you know how much research money comes from the DOD? Can you imagine what kind of weight they swing?'

I sipped coffee, thinking. 'In other words, he promised you a vendetta?'

'Exactly. That's a hell of a good word. He promised me a vendetta. He did it with this expression of kindly concern on his face, and behind it he was so angry he was shaking. I saw his hands, and they were white around the knuckles. I thought the guy was going to hit me, but he didn't. Instead, he talked about the mystical purposes of life and came damned close to saying it was for my own good. That's probably the only cliché he didn't use!'

'Do you think he could have done what he threatened to do?'

'Oh, he'd have tried. What I don't know is whether anybody would have listened to him. I don't know how many old cronies he's got at the DOD. Considering the puking state of science in the US right now, he's probably got some and they're probably running things.'

'And you'd like to have killed him.'

'Oh, man, would I.' He sighed, tears in his eyes. 'But I didn't.'

I thought about it for a while. 'You know, Marty,' I said at last, 'you're right about one thing. Our university has a reputation, as I understand it, for being a good place to go if you ski, party, play football, or drink a lot of beer. It is not known as a bastion of independent thought, high scholarship, or research achievement. Why did you come here?'

'I grew up here,' he said. 'I love it here. I was naïve, I guess.'

I shook my head at him. 'If I were you, I'd go back to MIT.'

'Don't I know it,' he said, head in his hands. 'Or a couple of other places I can think of.'

I refilled his coffee cup and asked him if he'd like a sandwich. He would. I made him one. He ate it, and we chatted, about other things. I told him I wouldn't say anything to the police, not yet, especially if he didn't plan to leave town soon.

'Are you kidding? I've got this term to finish and it's paid for! I can't afford to run out on a whole semester's credits. The credits will be good for something, somewhere . . .'

'Where'd you get the gun?' I asked him.

'My dad's,' he confessed. 'After he and Mom died, I put it in a box with some of my stuff. I dug it out after that meeting I told you about. It was already loaded.'

So. A fellow orphan. That, in and of itself, was enough to make me feel kindly towards him. 'Either put it somewhere safe or learn how to use it,' I said sententiously, thinking that drunks and loaded handguns were a very bad combination. 'Your friend Needleman almost shot me in the lower torso.'

'I brought the gun to you,' he said, fishing around on the couch for the paper bag he had carried in. He was sitting on it. 'Needleman said you knew how to handle it. I figured you'd keep it for me.' He looked sheepish. 'I don't manage frustration real well, and maybe I shouldn't have it around.'

After Martin O'Toole left me, I put his gun away in the iron safe in the basement. Jacob had the safe installed to keep working capital in, but then Jacob liked the feeling of money in the house. I don't, so I've never used the big box for anything except my own handguns. They've been there for years, and Marty's revolver would be safe enough in their company. I considered firing it into an old mattress, then digging the bullet out and sending it anonymously to the police, but it would be easier to wait until Grace got back. She could credit an 'informant,' and nobody would push her too hard to know who. Besides, she'd told me not to do anything yet.

As I was dozing off, I tried to remember if I'd ever been as young as Marty O'Toole. Young enough to go get drunk as a response to crisis. Not that only young people do that, just that it's always seemed to me to be a thing kids do. Maybe I'd never really been a kid.

The next day would be Monday. I wasn't in favour of it.

Mrs Richard Duchesne, whom I did not know, called me at seven-thirty on Monday morning, on my private line, which is unlisted, almost in tears, telling me she had to have her guest suite done over within the next ten days. Finished, completed, within the next ten days.

I demurred. I said I preferred not to do interior decoration except period rooms or as ancillary to the sale of antiques. She cried. Her daughter was getting married. The groom's parents were coming to visit next week and the guest rooms were wrong, all wrong, and she didn't know what was the matter with them. And Mrs Duchesne's brother had told her to call me. Mrs Duchesne's brother was Mr Utterly Powerful, the vice president and loan officer of the very same bank from which I had borrowed a great deal of money at very high interest for a very short time.

I told her I would be over as soon as possible after breakfast. When I arrived, she took me upstairs, talking incessantly. The suite had been done not long ago. She'd been very happy with it. Now she just knew it was all wrong. Something was wrong. She thought something was wrong, maybe she was mistaken, and it wasn't wrong but it looked . . .

The suite consisted of a small sitting-room with fireplace, a sizable bedroom with walk-in closet, and an adjoining bath. I stood there looking at it, trying not to howl.

'You had it decorated a year ago,' I said.

She said she had.

I told her who'd done it. 'Either him or so-and-so,' I said. She admitted to one of them and wanted to know how I knew.

When she asked, I was standing in the door to the bedroom. From where I stood I could not see one square inch of unencumbered surface except on the floor, and space was at a premium there. There were two bedside tables with floor-length geometric-print cloths on them in various shades of brown, almost brown, and quite brown. Each table supported a tiny lamp with an opaque black shade. In addition, between them they held a pair of marble bookends, three leather-bound books by Dinesen, an ostrich egg in a gilt stand, a turned ebony vase with ostrich plumes in it, two carved ebony animals—lion and giraffe—an ivory(?)-framed tinted etching of someone with his foot on a lion—presumably dead—and a collection of little boxes covered in different kinds of faux animal skins: a zebra box, an alligator box, a tiger box. I went over and turned one of the lamps on. A forty-watt bulb cast a dim, conical glow downward.

The queen-sized bed was a heavy four-poster. Draped oh so casually and artistically over the top of the posts, à la mosquito netting, were a dozen yards of filmy white fabric. The chairs on either side of the bed were an undistinguished rattan upholstered in yet another brown. In the corners of the room were wicker baskets, campaign chests, folding canvas chairs, and more than sufficient other stuff to give the impression the safari hadn't quite unpacked yet. Any space not occupied by this impedimenta was filled by potted palm trees, presumably fake since the rooms faced north and there was insufficient light for real ones. The wall around the Georgian fireplace had been covered with plastic wallpaper in a bamboo texture. More carvings and a few spears on the wall drove the point home. Welcome to the Dark Continent. I sighed.

She heard me. 'It *is* wrong, isn't it? What's wrong?' She faltered.

I tried to speak gently. 'Mrs Duchesne, let us suppose that your future in-laws retire for the night. Let us suppose that Mrs What's-her-name . . .'

'Mifflin.'

'Let us suppose that Mrs Mifflin likes to read in bed before she goes to sleep.'

My client nodded doubtfully, as though she could scarcely

imagine anyone wanting to read at any time, much less at bedtime.

'She has a book. Let us suppose also that she needs to blow her nose. She has a package of tissues. Let us suppose she needs to take an aspirin. She has a bottle of water and a glass. Where does she put any of these things and how in heaven's name does she see to use any of them?'

She stared at the tiny laden tables and their contents, her face turning an ugly red. 'He said little lamps were cozy. He said lots of things carried out the theme and made the room look lived in.'

'If you lived in this room, you would have a hundred watts on each side of the bed and you'd have put all that junk on the tables somewhere else by now. You would also have thrown out those tables and replaced them with others with larger surfaces and at least one drawer to hold a box of tissues and a book. You'd have a luggage rack in the corner instead of all that useless junk, because your guests will have suitcases.' I gave her my 'I am very much annoyed but I understand you were misled' look, the one I'd learned from Eugenia.

I sat on the bed. At least it was all right, comfortably firm. When I stood up, the draped material caught me around the forehead and ears, shedding dust all over my dark jacket.

I snarled, 'Also, the first time you got out of bed in the dark, stood up, and wrapped your face in six yards of dusty fabric, you'd get rid of that.' The dust was inevitable. No cleaning person of my acquaintance would do anything more than shake a duster at it, or at best a vacuum attachment. It probably wouldn't be taken down, washed, and artfully rearranged any oftener than maybe once a year.

Aside from the African 'decor', the whole room was depressingly brown and brown and brown. The carpet was that tan color that looks dirty even when it's brand-new. Aside from everything else the place needed, the touristy African junk should be carted out and buried. I had tallied up the separate jobs in my head. We needed a painter, a

wallpaper hanger—unless we got Maggie, who could do
both—a carpet layer, a slipcover and drapery seamstress,
someone to take the ordinary but well-made rattan chairs
down to the spray-paint place, a mover to get rid of the old
stuff, plus two or three people at my end to get everything
picked out and delivered to the right people in time to get
it done in ten days. It could be done. It wasn't a large enough
job to make the prospect attractive, but it could be done. I
considered briefly whether it might not be possible and
preferable to get a loan at some other bank.

I shook off the urge to howl, explained what had to be
done, told her the minimum it would cost, and got a budget
figure out of her. She wanted everything green. I told her
green was out. There was no green, and hadn't been for
four years and wouldn't be for four more years. We are
between greens. We are at the end of mauve, violet, grey,
and thank God for that. My best guess is that we are in
for a period of saturated, so-called tropical colours: coral,
mustard, and hot pink. She said coral and cream and maybe
violet, and we went with that. We agreed on re-covering the
love seats and painting the rattan and re-covering the bed.
What would replace the tables would depend on what I
could find immediately available. 'We are not,' I told her
pontifically, 'New York.'

She suddenly wanted to argue. She'd seen some tables at
a friend's. She really liked them.

'What's the number one priority?' I asked her.

'Getting it done on time,' she admitted.

'Then we go with what we can get, not with something
we'd need to order months in advance,' I said sternly,
hoping to heaven she wouldn't make difficulties.

I measured windows, walls, and furniture and told her
Mark and I would be out that afternoon with samples, not
to leave home under any circumstances. She bridled in a
put-upon fashion, and I decided to add fifteen per cent over
my usual charges for annoyance. I never would have gone
into this business except for Jacob, and sometimes I wonder
whether it's any way to earn a living. Whenever I visualize

myself as something else, however, I have trouble taking it seriously. Jason Lynx, the Used-Car Salesman. Jason Lynx, the Insurance Man. Actually, at one time it had been planned as Jason Lynx, the Art Historian, or Jason Lynx, the Museum Director, but all such roles faded when Jacob had his first stroke and needed me to come home. As close to home as I'd ever had, at any rate.

By three o'clock Mark and I had samples and Polaroid pictures of the tables that were available, including a pair of slightly restored, very nice Portsmouth, New Hampshire, birch end tables, c. 1800, I happened to have at the shop. By four we were back with Mrs Duchesne, who, forbidden to leave the house, had had frequent recourse to the premixed margaritas.

Margaritas made her happy. She had another one to mark our arrival, offering Mark and me the pitcher. We smiled and refused. She continued cheerful. Indecisive, but cheerful. It took until six to get the necessary decisions out of her and her name on the dotted line. I got a door key as well and told her to forget everything. It would all be taken care of. We went back to the shop. There was still work to do before we collapsed.

Mark was busy with his notebook. 'Fabric order tomorrow if you can get Myron to expedite. The one she picked is stocked from New York, and we can fly it in.'

'The seamstress needs five days,' I said. 'Not counting weekends.' We talked about timing and getting everything scheduled. I crossed my fingers, hoping we could get people in time.

'Go over the scheme with Eugenia and ask her to find a couple of really nice little things,' I said, yawning. '*Only* a couple. Maybe we can use that porcelain clock with the flowers on it . . .'

'What's her first name?' Mark asked. 'Mrs Duchesne's.'

'Gladys,' I told him. 'Don't forget to arrange for someone to take all that stuff out.'

'Pity she didn't do it right the first time.'

'She didn't think in terms of anyone staying there,' I said.

'Just of people looking at it. You know, she says to her visitors, "Would you like to see the house? This is the guest suite." And everyone oohs and aahs. She's never actually had anyone stay in it. Well, we'll have it comfortable by the time the Mifflins arrive. The groom's parents are to be suitably impressed.'

'This is not our kind of job! Why are we doing this?' he asked with aristocratic distaste. Mark was also in the business because of an interest in fine furniture as art, an interest he could have fully explored with his own resources. He had chosen to work at it instead, and I gave him a good deal of credit for that.

I explained about money and bankers and loans, and Mark made an appropriate face. Annoyance and apprehension, nicely mixed. No awe. Not Mark. His family has too much money for that.

'Shower curtain,' he sighed. 'There's no shower enclosure in that bathroom.'

'We'll find one,' I promised. 'Or have one made. Or something. Towels, too, but they're the least of our problem.'

He said good night. I said good night. Bela whined from the door where he'd been sitting. When I got to the kitchen, Critter was sitting there looking disgustedly at his empty dish. We all went out for Kentucky Fried Chicken—thighs for me, breasts (which I deboned) for my friends. Score for the day: a living earned, if you can call it that, food on the table, but not one damned thing done on the puzzle.

Once Mark and Eugenia had been pointed in the right direction, I left the Duchesne job up to them. It was mostly a case of seeing that things got where they were needed. I called Myron and asked him personally to pick up the fabric and put it on the plane. He said he would. He wouldn't, but one of his assistants (read: brothers-in-law) would, which was good enough. Then I cleared the Tuesday afternoon decks and told everyone I was going to be out.

Mark gave me a questioning look.

'Grale's studio,' I said.

He went discontentedly back to his cajoling conversation with the upholsterer.

Grale's studio was on the top floor of an old warehouse down on Lawrence Street, part of a row of remodelled turn-of-the-century buildings given a new lease on life by private entrepreneurs who found they could buy cheaply, renovate inexpensively, rent at fairly low rates, and still make a frugal buck. Of course, seeing them do it led later and greedier owners to assume they could charge an arm and a leg for the buildings and someone would still buy them. Wrong assumption. Renovation in the area has pretty well stopped as a result. There are lots of For Sale signs and not much traffic.

I walked up two flights. The door was open. Inside was a room with a couch and chair. It had a tiny kitchen along one side wall next to a door leading into a bathroom and another one leading into a tiny bedroom. A glass wall separated this living area from the studio below: lofty space with a skylight and a row of tall north windows. Pictures hung on the walls in both areas. Gregory Steinwale was down in the studio with his back to me, working on a picture of two women, a wicker chaise, and a potted palm. The chaise and the palm and one of the women were in front of him. Trish was his model. I recognized her from Nina's description. She saw me, said something to Grale, then got up and came up the stairs and through the glass door, a slight, graceful figure with a mind-melting smile. 'May I help you?'

I told her I knew Nina. I told her Nina had told me to introduce myself to Trish and had also told me what a truly fine artist Gregory Steinwale was. I gave her my card.

She warmed up immediately, glad to meet me because I knew Nina, wasn't Nina a wonderful person, so full of life, so knowledgeable! She offered me coffee or a soft drink (I accepted coffee), got out a sheaf of exhibition information on Grale's works, directed my attention to the walls and to a fat notebook on the table, and then sat down across from me, happily waiting to see what I'd do next.

What I did was look down into the studio. Greg hadn't turned, even when she left. His eyes had remained fixed on the canvas. No, not his eyes. His whole body. Hands, feet, legs, arms, head, even torso seemed somehow bent and focused on the painting. When his hand moved, it moved as though directed by his whole self, like an attachment moved by a huge robot. He was working on the face of one of the women, almost an abstract shape against the background. 'He doesn't do portraits, does he?' I asked, noting the lack of detail.

'He can,' she said. 'Actually, he can do fine portraits. But what he's interested in right now is the sculptural qualities of human figures.'

'A nose is a nose is a nose,' I offered.

She giggled. It was a nice giggle. 'I think that's sort of it. People as compositions, not people as individuals.'

'I'm glad to see he's working so well,' I said. 'Nina told me he'd had a rough time, been hospitalized for a while. We have too few good artists to be able to spare any.'

She nodded, soberly, not offering any comment.

'Did you know him then?' I probed in my kindliest voice.

'No,' she said. 'I met him after that.'

I let the silence alone.

'We're getting married. I suppose Nina mentioned that?'

'She did say something like that.' I gave her my best boyish grin, the one that makes Willamae and Nellie open up. 'Nina said he'd had a hard time with his wife. His first wife.'

'I guess she . . . his first wife. Melody.' She stopped, giving me a slightly suspicious glance. 'Did you know her, Mr Lynx?'

'No,' I said, surprised, letting it show. 'And please call me Jason. We're both Nina's friends, so we're friends of each other, right?'

She flushed. 'That would be nice, and I didn't mean to be . . . It's just that I hear about Melody knowing so many . . .'

'Men,' I said in a sympathetic tone. 'Nina told me about that.'

The comment overcame her reticence and she leapt to Greg's defence. 'But it wasn't that she slept around. Even Greg says that. She didn't sleep around that much. It was just that she kept . . . collecting them. Older men, mostly.'

I nodded thoughtfully. 'Why do you suppose she did that?' I asked.

'Looking for her father, I guess,' Trish said. 'According to Greg, that's what she was doing. He's explained to me very carefully that he was never jealous because he understood what she was doing. Evidently her father deserted her when Melody was an infant and Melody kept trying to find him, or a substitute.' She bit her lip. 'Why am I telling you this? This isn't why you came.'

I smiled noncommittally, taking my mental hat off to Nellie Arpels. Bull's-eye! 'In a way it *is* why I came,' I said, sitting back and sipping. 'I won't repeat what you say to me. I'm not a gossip, but I am sincerely interested in puzzles and mysteries, and Melody is—or was—both. Nina told me about her. She died mysteriously, and I'm trying to figure out why.'

'You don't think Greg . . .'

'No,' I assured her. 'I don't think Greg. I don't think her death had anything to do with Greg. It's just a mystery. Call it an intellectual exercise. Did Melody think her real father was here in Denver?'

With the caveat that I wasn't going to involve Greg, she seemed to regard my interest as acceptable, if not totally legitimate. 'From what Nina said, Melody's mother died when she was born. She lived with her aunt, and the aunt said Melody's father came from Englewood, Colorado.'

'What was Melody's maiden name?'

Trish thought for a while. 'I'm not sure either Nina or Greg ever . . . No. I remember. Harriet said it. She was talking about Melody once, and she said, "Greg should never have married Melody Maudlin." But then, Harriet believes Melody drove Greg into that hospital.'

'What do you think?'

She flushed again. 'I think she probably did. Well, she

drove him to the point of a breakdown.' She stood up, stared through the window intently, sat back down. 'You see how he works, so intent, so very concentrated? He needs quiet to do that. According to Harriet, she was always at him. About everything. Harriet used to buy him clothes, and Melody didn't like them, so she fussed at him all the time about what he wore. They lived with Harriet, and Melody didn't like that. She was always complaining about the way Harriet had decorated the place, or about something Harriet said.'

'Mothers-in-law,' I said sympathetically. Not that I'd ever had one. Agatha's mother had died long before we were married.

'No,' she said. 'It wasn't that. Harriet's an old bat, she says so herself, but she's a nice old bat. She's opinionated, and she has a right to be. She's over sixty years old. She has a right to have her own property the way she wants it. She even bought the gallery so Melody would have something to do, but Nina says all Melody did was pout or have a tantrum whenever Harriet tried to teach her anything about business, or threaten to fire Nina when Nina did.' She turned back to me, her face pink, her mouth angry. 'That's not fair. Nina's a good person, and she breaks her neck working in that place. When I was there, I saw how hard she works. I guess Melody couldn't deal with just being a grown-up workaday person. Everything had to be personal with her. Instead of getting to work and doing the job, she kept getting her feelings hurt.'

'Doesn't sound like a good bet to manage a business.'

She shook her head. 'I'm extrapolating. I could be wrong. I get so . . . so mad sometimes when I hear things about her because I know what she did to Greg, even though he always makes excuses for her. He doesn't talk that much about her, so I'm putting things together that he's said and that his mother has said and things that Nina tells me. The way I understand it, Harriet finally gave up trying to teach her anything, backed off, and just left the gallery alone. It's a pity, too, because Harriet would have been good for

Melody if she could have just accepted there being someone else in Greg's life. She was good for me. If it hadn't been for Harriet, I wouldn't have met Greg.

'She hired you to work at the gallery?'

She refilled my coffee cup. 'That was really funny. I hadn't worked since I graduated from college. I got married. I had a baby. My husband and I, jointly, decided I'd stay home until our child . . . or children . . . were in school. Then the accident happened, and suddenly I was a widow with a baby girl. Burt, my husband, was very responsible about insurance and there were benefits from his job, so I had enough to get by on for quite a few years if I went to work and if I was careful, but I did need to get a job. So, as soon as I felt I could, when Frosty was a little older, I started looking. Right away I saw this ad.'

'Harriet ran an ad?'

'Right. It said she wanted a working mother between the ages of twenty-five and thirty with a college education who knew something about business. And it said to enclose a photo. How about that?' She got up and stood at the glass wall, looking down at the man hunched before the canvas.

'Did you know something about business?'

'My family had a paint business, back in Chicago. I worked there as a kid, and during summer vacations. I knew about inventory and invoices, and how you keep books. Things like that. So I sent in my picture and my résumé, and she called me up. Took me to lunch.' She spoke to the glass, not to me. Our reflections swam dimly in it, like ghosts.

'And hired you.'

'And hired me. Took me over to the gallery that afternoon and told Nina I was her new help.'

'Nina said she was surprised.'

'Nina was mad, to tell you the truth. It was two days before she simmered down enough to get to know me. We got along fine, though, once she found out I really meant to work.'

'And then . . .'

'And then Harriet visited me at home. That was kind of a shock, but she and Frosty hit it off—Frosty's three years old. Martha Frost. Frost was my mother's maiden name. Then Harriet invited me to dinner, and I met Greg, and a week or so later, here I was helping him instead of working at the gallery. And a month or so later, he asked me to marry him. Sort of diffidently, between brushstrokes.' She turned from the window.

I was staring at her. She caught the look, returned it, then looked away, reading my mind.

'Do you get the feeling . . . ?' I started to ask.

'That I was handpicked? Oh, yes, I sure do. I'd have had to be blind not to see what she was doing. The first time I saw a picture of Melody, I knew exactly what Harriet was doing. She was being a meddling mother. You'd have to know Greg to understand, but I don't blame her for it one bit.' She turned back to the studio, peering at the concentrated stance, the wild hair of her fiancé. Her feelings were plain in her face.

'You love him, hmm?'

After a moment she said, almost in a whisper, 'Oh, yeah. Yeah, I really do.'

'Does he ever go out? To a movie? To dinner?'

'Sometimes.'

'If you'd like, you and Nina could get your heads together and see if you're free this weekend,' I suggested. 'Let's all go to dinner on me. I'd very much like to meet him.'

I left, wishing I knew exactly what tap I'd turned to let all that gush out. As I've said, people often talk to me, people I've just met. Women. Men. Even children. Here in the West, people talk more anyhow. About themselves, their jobs, what they think or believe. When I've been back East I've noticed that people aren't as open or friendly. They're more suspicious, more held in, and yet, even there people talk to me. Sometimes I think people need to talk, and any halfway attentive, sympathetic face will loosen the floodgates. But maybe, and I keep coming back to this thought, it's because of the lack of families. The conversation Trish had just had with me was one she might have had with a sister or her mother if they'd been near enough to talk to. Chances are, her sister or mother is a thousand miles or more away. Which reminded me of Willamae Belling. Which reminded me of Nellie Arpels.

Which reminded me that since I had no mother of my own to fret over, or cuss at, I could possibly do a little something for those ladies. I got out my pocket notebook and made a suggestion to myself.

Since the afternoon was yet young, I decided to see if I could locate the woman Simmons had mentioned, Fred's neighbour, Streeter.

The ground-floor apartment was the manager's. I rang several times before she came to the door. She had just washed her hair. The whole place smelled of shampoo and steam with a faint stench of something I recognized, after a while, as home perm, though I could not imagine where I had smelled it before. Agatha had had naturally curly hair. The manager had bare white arms and a great expanse of pillowy chest above a scoop-necked blouse. She had plump cheeks. She had worms of hair dangling on her forehead, like wet springs. She looked like an old-style Campbell's Soup kid, head wrapped in a towel. I told her I was looking for anyone who had known Fred Foret, like Ms Streeter. Did she by any chance know Ms Streeter?

'Sure I know Sally Streeter,' she said. 'She lived here for over five years. She'd still live here if it wasn't for that prick Foret.'

'You didn't like him,' I said with great perceptivity.

'You're Sherlock Holmes!' she crowed.

I blushed.

'No, I didn't like him,' she said. 'I liked Sally. We were friends, her and me. She was ordinary people, just like me, except her husband left her fairly well-off when he died, but she was lonesome, and we used to go to bingo together, and we'd bake stuff for sales at the church. Fred Foret lived across the hall from her, and she used to go over to his place sometimes with a plate of cookies or something. Hell, there's nothing wrong with that.'

'I didn't say there was.'

'You said you were looking for anybody that knew him. Somebody must've told you she didn't like him.'

I took the bull by his figurative horns. 'Somebody told me she tried to kill him.'

The manager turned her attention to her head, towelling furiously. 'Oh, hell, she didn't really mean to kill him. She was mad, though. Hell, I'd've been mad.'

'Why was she mad?'

She blushed. 'Because he . . . he misled her, that's why. And then, afterward, when she tries to tell him how nice it is to be close to somebody, he tells her not to think she's close to him, because she's not up to his standard.'

So Fred had been into seduction. Somehow I could imagine Fred saying that to a woman. It was the kind of thing he said. 'Being frank,' he called it. 'He said that?' I asked, trying to look doubtful.

She tried to convince me. 'He said that and some other stuff. About her not being his intellectual equal, plus some junk about his just trying to be nice to women of "her age". So she grabbed her little gun and waved it at him and told him to get out and stay out. Hell, it probably wasn't even loaded.'

'She told you this.'

'She told me why she had to move out; she was so embarrassed, she didn't want to run into him again. He grabbed the gun and took it away from her and called her a silly bitch. She moved out the end of the month and over to the other side of town, halfway to Lookout Mountain. That was six, eight months ago, now.'

'She told you all about the incident?'

'She had to tell somebody. She cried and her face got all puffy and she said she wished she'd killed him, because then when they arrested her, the trial would've at least given her something to do.'

'Well, somebody shot him,' I said.

'I know somebody did, and good riddance,' she said. 'But

you don't think Sally? Oh, my Lord, no. She wouldn't ever have looked that man in the face again.'

'Do you have her address?'

She started to tell me, then shut her mouth, firmly, shaking her head. She told me her lips were sealed and to please leave so she could get her curlers in. I didn't press her. If Sally Streeter hadn't changed her name, I could find her one way or another.

Since I was in the neighbourhood, I walked a block down the street to the building Neal Ambler lived in and rang his bell from the lobby. No answer. I jotted a message and dropped it into his box. It had been a day for disclosures. Maybe there was another one who wanted to talk.

There was, but it wasn't Neal Ambler.

Mark was just closing up as I got home and he asked if I'd mind talking to him for a while. What does one say? No, I didn't mind, I said. But yes, I did mind. I didn't want to share his troubles, but I owed him that much.

We went back upstairs to the living-room. I pulled the curtains against the evening grey, telling myself, as I had many times, that I wanted a real home, one that didn't look north, into offices. Not that Agatha hadn't made it look like a real home. The curtains were deep wine. The rug was a Pakistan remake of a Persian pattern, burnt orange and deep blue and wine and cream. Jacob's choice, originally, but Agatha had left it there after we moved in.

I poured us both a drink, and Mark said, 'I got a letter from Rudy.'

'What did Rudy have to say?'

'He said he's going to get married.'

'I didn't know Rudy was bisexual,' I blurted, in complete surprise.

'He's not,' Mark said. 'I don't know who he thinks he's kidding. He says he wants a family.' He got up and stalked across the room, one hand working at the back of his neck. Mark is extremely good-looking, and emotion had coloured his face. I thought, not for the first time, that he really should be an actor.

I didn't know what to say, so I didn't say anything.

'I told him he should find some lesbian who wants children,' he said. 'She could have them by AI, he could be a daddy, and neither of them would be disappointed in one another. He says no. He wants a straight woman. He says most lesbians are too angry.' He turned back towards me, tears in his eyes. 'Jason, what am I going to do?'

How the blazing hell did I know?

Apply common sense, someone said in my head. Some female voice. Agatha maybe. Maybe Grace. Maybe Nellie Arpels. Common sense.

I thought it out as I went. 'Mark, I think you'll have to accept that Rudy's desire for a family is natural, that it has nothing to do with you or his feelings for you, and that you can't solve his problems.'

'They're my problems, too.'

'Not really,' I said. 'The way you feel is your problem, but Rudy's desire for a family isn't. There's no way you can be involved in that. You can't provide him with children. I suppose it's a little like before there was AI, a woman who wanted babies might leave a man who was sterile. If babies were more important than the man, she would. If the man was more important, she wouldn't.'

'I thought I was important,' he said brokenly.

'Rudy was raised in an Italian Catholic family,' I said. 'What is he, about forty?'

'Thirty-nine.'

My age. I sat and drank. 'This isn't the first time he's left. Six months ago you went through this with him.'

'He just went home for a visit is all. He was only gone a few weeks.'

'He just went home and realized what home meant,' I said. 'He measured home against his sexual inclinations and decided which was most important to him. Five years ago, he felt differently. Five years ago, he wasn't pushing forty.' I knew how that felt. 'I've been thinking a lot about this lately,' I said. 'Families, I mean. People aren't meant to live alone. People aren't meant to grow old alone. The nuclear family is all well and good, but it means a lot of people are left over.'

'I can't even manage a nuclear,' he said, trying to laugh.

'I don't know what gays do about families,' I said. 'I don't know how you plan to grow old. I've always wanted to do it with wife and children and grandchildren. If I had a mother, I'd want her around, and maybe an aunt or a cousin or two. Except for Jacob, I've been alone most of my life, but it wasn't my own choice. To me, family is a very powerful concept. I wouldn't let anyone deprive me of that.'

'What if one of your kids turned out to be gay? What if there weren't any grandchildren?'

'Maybe that's what Rudy came up against,' I suggested.

'I was thinking of my father,' he said. Mark's father hadn't really accepted Mark since he'd found out his son was disinclined to marry and produce an heir.

'Rudy has a father, too, remember. An Italian Catholic father, probably sixty-five or so, and Rudy's the only son. Think about that and you'll know what he's been up against.'

'Damn,' he said. 'Jason, I wanted sympathy, not logic.'

'I'm sympathetic. Have another drink.'

Since he was so alone, I suggested we have dinner together. We fed the animals, then went down to Cliff Young's and pigged out on pasta and two bottles of wine. He told me all about Rudy, in exhaustive detail; I told him what Trish had said about Melody Steinwale and about needing to find Sally Streeter.

When I got home, there was a message from Neal Ambler, Melody's park friend, on the answering machine.

CHAPTER 4

Neal Ambler suggested breakfast. I rose at the crack of dawn to meet him at Le Peep. He was a broad, friendly-looking man with steely eyes. If you listened to his mouth, you liked him at once. If you looked at his eyes, you were careful. I knew those eyes from somewhere, so I played it close to my chest.

'I don't understand what your authority is in all this,' he said.

'None at all,' I confessed cheerfully, taking a large chunk of omelette to give me something to keep my mouth occupied. I'd discovered a long time ago that it's hard to read a man while he's chewing. 'I'm looking into the case for family members who want to augment the police investigation. I'm a complete amateur. I have no status.'

'That's what I mean,' he said with a little smile belied by an ice-cold glance. 'She had no family who would want to look into it. I was probably as close to her as anyone.'

'You?' I cocked my head at him, making a question. 'She was a friend of yours?'

He thought about this. 'Yeah. I was her friend. About the only one she had.'

'Her husband was deeply grieved at her death,' I said.

'Her husband was a nut case who couldn't take care of her,' he replied. 'Grief from somebody like that is about as useful as tits on a bull.'

'We might suspect her husband of killing her, of course, except for the fact he was hospitalized at the time.'

'Yeah, and his mother was out of the country. That doesn't mean they couldn't have hired someone. Or she could have, the mother, by herself.'

'Why would Harriet Steinwale have done that?'

'The Steinwale woman hated Melody.'

'Why?'

'Because Melody was young. Because she was beautiful. Because Melody was talented in her painting, and the old woman wasn't willing to have her son share the spotlight.'

'You gathered this from things Melody said?'

'Gathered, hell. She right out told me. She said, "My mother-in-law hates me because I'm young and pretty and her son loves me and I can paint as well as he can." That's about as clear as you can be.'

I remembered Nina's assessment of Melody's talent. 'I thought she only took art lessons so she and her husband would talk the same language.'

'Maybe that's the way it started. Her teacher told her right off she had a very great talent.'

'You saw her work.'

'I bought some of her things. I'll take you back to the apartment and show you. Very—uh—mystical.' For a moment his eyes were clear and unsuspicious, like a child's. Most people he watched like a dog with a bone, but he had evidently felt differently about Melody. He waved for more coffee, which gave me a minute or two to chew and think.

'Had you known her long?' I asked.

He leaned back, coffee cup cradled in both hands.

'Ten years, more or less. I met her before she ever married that guy. I met her when she started living with Rich.'

'Rich?'

'He's an oil buddy of mine. Rich in name and rich in fact, he says. I guess he's right about that. There's guys that make it and lose it, and there's guys that make it and make it. He's one of those. Anyhow, Melody came out here in about, oh, '76? That'd be about right. Nineteen, twenty years old maybe. No money. Not trained to do diddly, you know? She had enough money to last her about two weeks if she'd been smart, and it would have lasted her about three days because she picked the most expensive hotel in town to stay in. Rich picked her up in the bar. She told him she'd come out here to look for her daddy. Rich felt sorry for her, took her home with him, gave her a room, a little salary, told her she could keep books for him. Shit, Rich's got six accountants on full time and needs a little girl bookkeeper like he needs an extra ball. Anyhow, she settled in, and pretty soon he had her playing hostess for him. That's when I met her. Her and me used to talk, about her looking for her daddy and so forth.

'Well, a couple of years went by and I guess she got a

little bored. Rich was good to her, but he's been around. He didn't hang around her much, you know what I mean? He expected her to be there when he wanted her and kind of disappear when he didn't. I told Rich that wasn't fair to her—hell, she was just a kid—but he just laughed. You'd have to know him. She asked Rich to pay for her to take some courses, maybe get her college degree. So Rich said sure, honey, go to school if that'll keep you quiet. She started taking these art courses. That's where she met the crazy artist.'

'Greg Steinwale.'

'Him, yeah. Well, she started sneaking off to spend time with this Steinwale, and after a few months she told Rich she was going to leave him and marry the artist. I told her she was making a mistake, and so did Rich. Hell, anybody could see what she needed was somebody to take care of her, somebody that didn't take her too serious, and anybody short of a hundred per cent blind could see the artist couldn't do it! Talk about babes in the woods!'

'So she married Greg.'

'That was about '81. She married Greg. He was living in some studio place he had, and Melody wouldn't move in there, so they had to move in with his mama.'

'I understood that Mrs Steinwale offered to buy them a place of their own.'

'Well, sure, his mama offered to get them a place, but hell, Melody'd been living pretty good with Rich. Rich has one hell of a nice place. Melody wanted something at least that nice, and the artist couldn't provide it and Mama wouldn't pay for it. Mellie was used to nice things. Clothes. A fur coat. Everything cream and clover. Rich used to kid her about how much she'd spend on clothes. Anyhow, so the two of them moved in with the artist's mama, right near the park here, and my place is close by, so we used to talk when we'd run into each other, me with Blue Boy and her with that fat collie dog she had.'

'You're telling me she wasn't happy.' The waitress put a full pot of coffee on the table, and I reached for it.

'First couple of years weren't bad, but no, she wasn't happy. I know for a fact she was always pretty happy with Rich. I don't know what gets into women! Rich would've taken care of her as long as she lived, one way or another, or somebody else with plenty would have, and here she had to leave him for this guy. She didn't really want to eat beans in some dirty studio. Melody got herself in over her head.'

'Maybe she just wanted to be married.'

'Why? She didn't want kids. Rich must have asked her a dozen times if she wanted a family, and she said no every time. Rich was married twice, and he won't do it again, but he's not one to keep a woman tied to him if she wants kids either. He likes his comfort, but he isn't really a user, you know what I mean? He's got a conscience.'

I thought about Rich's conscience for a minute, chewing slowly. 'Most women want children,' I offered.

'Well, Melody wasn't most women. She didn't want to stretch herself out of shape, for one thing. She used to laugh and tell me she wanted to be beautiful when she found her father, so he'd be ashamed of having walked off and left her.'

'Tell me about that,' I suggested, sipping at the hot cup. 'Had she had any luck finding her father?'

'She knew his name. Rick Maudlin. She knew he was supposed to live out in Englewood. Rich hired some guy to search the city records for her. Nobody of that name had ever lived there, according to the city directories and the phone books. No Maudlins at all.'

'Is that all she knew about him? That isn't much.'

'Her mother died when she was born, in Baltimore. Her mother's aunt brought her up. All the aunt knew was that her niece had been married to a man named Rick Maudlin from Englewood, Colorado.'

'I suppose the search extended past Englewood. Out to Littleton and around to the other suburbs?'

'Rich spent a few thousand looking. I don't think the Maudlin guy ever lived here. I think he lied about it.'

'So who do you think killed Melody?'

'Who the hell knows? Rich didn't do it. He'd picked up with somebody else by then, and besides, he was in Texas when it happened. He was really knocked off his perch when I told him about it. Maybe that old guy she used to talk to in the park shot her for her wristwatch. She didn't have it on when they found her.'

'What old guy?'

'Some guy she used to talk to. Some friend of the family. I used to see them sitting on a bench, over by the walk.'

Ambler couldn't remember what the man looked like. Thin, he thought. Fifty-five or sixty.

Ambler insisted both on paying the tab and on taking me back to his apartment, where he showed me Melody's works of art hanging on the very expensive grass-cloth walls of his very expensively decorated apartment. I smiled and commented and escaped, wondering what his friends thought of the paintings. When it came to estimating Melody's talent, Nina had hit it on the nose. No line. No colour. No composition. No technique. Muddy little daubs of no charm, and yet Ambler's face, when he looked at them, was open and enchanted, like a child looking at a circus. He himself had no æsthetic sense, so much was obvious from the few personal touches he had added to the place. I wondered what he saw in the paintings. I wondered if, perhaps, he hadn't been in love with Melody himself.

There was a message from Trish when I got back to the office. She'd left the studio number, so I called it, waiting while it rang and rang. I could visualize her having to stop her pose and come up into the living area to answer it.

'Grale's,' she said at last, breathlessly.

'Jason Lynx, Trish,' I said, realizing I didn't remember her last name.

'Hi there,' she said. 'You asked about this weekend? Friday night there's a family party and you're invited to join. Harriet and Greg and me, and Lycia and Ross, and Shannon and Keith with their dates. You bring Nina.'

'I wouldn't want to intrude,' I demurred.

'It's not an intrusion. You wanted to meet Greg, and Harriet already had this thing planned—it's Greg's birthday that weekend, but we're not taking much notice, since he's forty—and Harriet is very fond of Nina. So.'

I accepted, provisionally, then called Nina. Yes, she'd heard about it. Yes, she'd love to have me as an escort. So. I would meet the whole cast of characters.

I suddenly recalled that I'd already met some of them when I'd been in Lycia's apartment with Marge. Well, my presence would have to be terribly coincidental, that's all. Unless they, like me, did not believe in coincidence.

I had noted the name Rich, Neal Ambler's friend 'in oil'. I had some friends 'in oil', and it took only about half an hour to identify him as Richard Beacon of Beacon Exploration and Leasing. Mike Lessing, one of my informants, even remembered Richard's former live-in wife-surrogate.

'We used to go over there every now and then for dinner,' he told me. 'Melody was a bit more than a mistress but a good bit less than a wife. Sort of a cross between bedmate and daughter, I'd say.' Which fit right in with everything Ambler had to say. 'Beacon kept a cook, a houseman, and some other help, so she had it pretty easy. Several of us were rather surprised when she left him, though Vicki, that's my wife, said Melody left because Rich didn't pay much attention to her. My wife said Melody was cute but boring, I guess that's why.'

'Boring how, Mike?'

'Vicki said she was the only person she'd ever met who could talk for a whole hour about choosing the dress she was wearing. Vicki said Melody could talk about picking out shoes the way some women talk about picking colleges for their kids. She was real full of herself, even though she'd never done anything or been anywhere. She didn't even read anything. At least, that's what Vicki said.'

I thanked Mike and hung up. Puzzle, puzzle, and so far I was getting absolutely nowhere. Wednesday was Mark's day to fix lunch, so I filled him in as we ate. Chicken enchiladas with sour cream, guacamole salad, and flan. Mark makes great flan, only he calls it *crème brûlée*.

'Why did she leave Beacon?' Mark wanted to know.

Why had she? Love? Boredom? Disinclination to be Rich's bedmate any longer? Desire to be with someone who would pay more attention to her? Or from whom she could demand more attention, which was perhaps more likely. She had probably had very little luck whipsawing Rich, or teasing him, or getting him to do anything he wasn't already willing to do. Greg, on the other hand, could have been an open season, without defences. She might have thought Greg could tap the Steinwale money at will. She might not have realized he wanted to make it on his own, and her consistent attempts to access Mama Steinwale's money through him might have pushed Grale over the brink. Mark and I talked about possibilities. Mark did not discount love as a reason for her leaving her snug nest; I did not discount boredom or pique. No way to know, for sure, unless she had told someone. Ambler had his opinion; I had mine. She might have told Greg, but I couldn't very well ask him. Maybe I could ask Rich if it became necessary. If he knew. I made a mental note.

And there was the other man she talked to. The fiftyish guy on the bench. The family friend. I'd have to find out who that could be.

'I have another job for you,' I told Mark. 'The people you talked to on Sunday, the ones who recognized Melody?'

He nodded.

'According to Ambler, Melody used to talk to someone else in the park. A fiftyish man, probably thin.' I paused, trying to remember what else he'd said. 'He said the bench by the walk. That would probably be the walk nearest to his apartment building . . .'

'The bench he was talking about would probably be one of those just off Twelfth.'

'What we need is to identify the man she talked to on the bench. See if anyone saw her talking to him, and see if you can get a description.'

'Are you getting anywhere with Freddy?' Mark asked.

I laughed, shaking my head at him. 'I've got a woman who may have tried to kill him, a student who talked about killing him, and several people who probably thought he ought to be killed. Which is to say, nothing so far.'

And I got nothing else for several days. The rest of Wednesday went on by in a clutter of little jobs. Eugenia Lowe had a problem with a client charging misrepresentation. The first I knew of it was when a large angry man invaded my office yelling and using words I didn't find particularly coherent. After I asked him for the third time to explain what his problem was, he calmed down enough to thrust an invoice at me and shout, 'You rotten liar, you told my wife this was an antique chair, and it says on the bottom it was made by this company in Michigan . . .' and more words to that effect. Even when I pointed to the invoice where the words 'Colonial reproduction' appeared in large letters, he still wanted to yell about it. I told him I'd be glad to take the piece back for exactly what his wife paid for it, and he got suddenly quiet.

'She told me it was an antique,' he grumbled.

'It's a reproduction,' I told him. 'Normally I don't handle reproductions, but this one came with a roomful of furniture I bought from an estate. A real chair of that period would cost at least three or four thousand dollars, and it would look very little different from the one you have.' I didn't mention that to those who care about such things, that little difference is supremely important. The chair she'd bought was well made and worth every cent she'd paid for it. 'As I recall, your wife thought she was buying you something nice for your birthday. So she fibbed a little and said it was antique. You don't like it, I'll take it back.'

He grumbled again, then left, saying he'd bring the chair back that afternoon.

'Honestly!' Eugenia was steaming. 'That bastard!'

'Don't sweat it,' I told her. 'You get one like that every now and then. I can see the scenario. He asks her what she paid. She tells him. He rages. To justify the price, which needs no justification if you know good furniture, she says it was an antique. He sees the invoice, maybe he yells at her about it, so she screams misrepresentation, and everything degenerates from there. Put their names in your no-no file and forget it.' Jacob had always kept a no-no file. People he would not, under any circumstances, do business with again. Funny how some people will threaten to sue you one day, then come back a week later thinking you'll be glad to see them.

That night Grace called, collect.

'How are you?' I asked her, suddenly missing her more than I'd thought I possibly could. 'How are you, Grace!' It wasn't a question. It was a demand. I needed to know.

'I'm lousy,' she said in a depressed voice. 'I'm terrible. I'm so down, Jason. I've finally found Ron a lawyer, but the man wants the mortgage on the homestead as a retainer. God, I hate to do that. I've put everything into that house.'

'Grace, do not, I repeat, do not give him anything but a cash retainer which I will send you in the morning.' I caught myself yelling at her. It was usually the other way around. Usually she yelled at me.

'Jason, I can't let you do that.'

'Grace, you can owe it to me, interest-free. Put it down to passing on a kindness, okay? Jacob was good to me, I'll be good to you, you be good to Ron. Maybe someday Ron'll be good to someone . . .'

'He doesn't have sense enough to be good to himself even. Can you spare five thousand, Jason?'

I gulped deeply and lied. 'I can spare it, Grace. Is that what the guy wants as a retainer?'

She fussed about paying me back. I told her if it got tough, I'd take her grandmother's Eastlake bed as security. It was the one piece of Grace's grandma's furniture I hadn't sold for her, the one piece still in her garage. Grace hadn't wanted to use any of her grandmother's furniture—too many memories, she said.

'Grace, while Ron's in jail, while all this is being sorted out, you don't need to be there, do you?'

'If I come back, I could have trouble getting away again, Jason. They weren't real thrilled about giving me this leave.'

'Do they have to know you're back?' I asked. 'I mean, just a quick flight home. For a day or two. You could stay here, with me.

We talked about that. She said yes, she said no, she said maybe. We left it she'd think about it and let me know. She gave me the lawyer's name, and I told her I would call him in the morning and arrange payment. I told myself I'd also arrange a cap on legal fees. 'How long will you stay?' I asked her, wondering how long I could do without her.

'Until he gets arraigned or not. Or they let him go. Or something. So far they've just been playing games, trying to get information out of him. He doesn't know anything, that's his trouble. He's never known anything.' She laughed weakly, and I made comforting sounds. She asked about Critter. Critter was pressed tightly against my side in a furry ball, fast asleep, making little chirpy noises from time to time. I told her I missed her. She said likewise.

I hung up resolved to go to San Francisco and get her if she didn't get things straightened out soon. Or at least be there with her while she did. She was not sensible about Ron, any more than I had been sensible about Agatha. Cutting the cord between her and her baby brother was being very hard for her.

Thursday was a replay of Wednesday, minus the aggravation. I called the San Francisco lawyer and had a heart-to-heart talk about what Grace could afford. He told me he'd hold the expenses down and refund anything not used in the case at hand. I wired him the money.

Along about three, things loosened up and I decided to see what Melody's art instructor might tell me. Nina had mentioned his name, and I'd already found out that he had a Wednesday afternoon class which would end about the time I reached the University of Denver campus out on South University Boulevard.

His name was Conklin. Stan Conklin. He was feverish-looking, dark-haired, eyes glittery from contact lenses, about five foot ten, give or take an inch, with something predatory in his stance. I moved into the classroom when the students moved out, standing by while he said a few dictatorial things to a flirtatious female student whom he patted absently and familiarly on the bottom while he spoke. When she left, I asked him if he could spare a few minutes. He asked what about, and I told him. He gave me a looking-over.

'Are you related to her?' he asked.

I told him no, that my interest was really ancillary to another matter. He suggested a beer. I acquiesced. We went to the bar across the street.

'Melody was cute,' he said, after dipping his nose into the foam and wiping it off on his sleeve. 'She was cute as a button. I would have loved to do a nude study of her. Like a fairy, a sprite, one of those little ones.'

'I've never met one, personally.'

'Some famous illustrator used to do bodies like that for fairy tales,' he said.

'Rackham?' I suggested.

He waved his hands. He didn't know. 'So thin she looked breakable, but with proper little plumpness in all the right places.' He sighed. 'And no more talent than a cockroach.'

'I thought you encouraged her,' I said in an innocent tone. He blushed, grinning at the same time. 'I'm rotten to the core,' he said. 'Mother always told me so. I lie.'

The wry grin betrayed a rudimentary conscience. I decided he wasn't so much predatory as just opportunistic. 'She told people that her instructor told her she painted as well as her husband,' I said.

'She may well have.' He laughed. 'Who was her husband?'

'Gregory Steinwale. Grale.'

'Oh, my God!' He turned pale. 'You're kidding. Oh, God, why don't I learn to keep my libido zipped? She was married to Grale?' He leaned forward and knocked his head on the table a few times with a dull, thunking sound. 'Oh, shit.'

'Those who heard her quoting you may have wondered about your eyesight.'

'All she ever said to me was that her husband didn't want

to talk about his painting. She never said who he was. And she didn't register as Steinwale either. That would have rung a bell with me. She was Melody Maudlin.'

'That was her maiden name. She met her husband here,' I said. 'Some years ago.'

'I've only been here three years.'

'What can you tell me about her?'

'She talked like a magpie, mostly about herself or her next shopping expedition. She had no talent for painting, but talked about it anyhow. She had the neatest little body I've ever seen. She thought her mother-in-law had no taste and hated living there but had to because the old lady was crippled and needed her son.'

'The old lady is not noticeably crippled,' I said. 'The consensus seems to be that Melody lived there because it was more luxurious than any of her other choices.'

His eyebrows rose. 'Oh. Well. Whatever. I am guilty of telling her she had talent. I lied. She sometimes started out with colour and form, but by the time she was finished with it, everything was grey and itsy-bitsy. She had no confidence, no eye. I probably should have told her the truth for all the good lying did me. I never got anywhere with her. She said I was "too young and callow", laughing like crazy the whole time.'

'Did she have any friends? Close associates?'

'She talked to Bess Trumble sometimes. Poor Bess. Oh, and Shannon somebody.'

'Shannon Foret?' I think my mouth dropped open. Since Shannon had first mentioned Melody, I'd been looking for some connection between them, but this was the last one I would have expected.

'Shannon . . . Foret is right, isn't it? She audited a class. Last year, I think. The summer term, July, August, something like that. Melody seemed to know her pretty well, maybe better than Shannon liked.'

'How do you mean?'

He puzzled, remembering. 'I seem to recall Melody introduced Shannon as a relative. No. No, she said she knew

they were soul sisters because they looked so much
alike. Shannon said she wasn't Melody's sister and they
didn't look anything alike. They didn't, of course, except
that they were both pretty girls. Melody wasn't too serious
about it, kind of kidding, but Shannon was really
annoyed.'

I thought about that, but it took me nowhere. Melody
hadn't resembled Shannon at all, so far as I could remember
from the pictures or even the way Conklin described her.
'Did Melody ever mention her father?'

'Not that I remember.'

'What about Shannon? Did she have any talent?'

'She was taking an art history course, no talent required.
I don't remember much about her, to tell you the truth.
She'd graduated the year before. She was thinking about
graduate school. That happens a lot. Particularly with girls
like her.'

'What happens? And girls like what?'

'Fragile ones with reasonably good minds but no . . . no
gristle. They get through school assuming that they'll have
some kind of career later, but they aren't really equipped
to do anything, and they aren't suited to the brutalities of
the marketplace, so they think about graduate school. It's
a way of forestalling decision. A way to put off getting
involved with real life. Usually they end up getting married.
It's about the only thing they're even modestly equipped
for, and I'm not being sexist.' He leaned forward and gave
me a sincere look.

I knew he wasn't being sexist, at least not in this case,
though I wouldn't have given a dime for his not being sexist
in all other connections. His words had brought back my
own impressions of Shannon, very tremulous, very, as he
said, 'fragile'.

We had another beer and parted. I made a mental note
that Conklin might be interesting to know better. He was
about my age, presumably unmarried. Pity he was into
girls. Mark would have liked him.

*

Nina told me that Greg Steinwale's birthday dinner was being held out at the Wilshire, a restaurant I like more for the ambience than for the food, which is often quite good, though sometimes pedestrian. Nina didn't know whether gifts were to be proffered or not—Trish had said they were 'not taking much notice', but that could mean simply a much appreciated absence of cardboard birthday cake and singing waiters—so I pocketed a little something just in case, a sterling silver snuff box, dated about 1760, useful for stamps or pins or even pills. I wouldn't give it to him unless the atmosphere was right for it. Gifts from virtual strangers can be embarrassing. Hell, gifts from friends can be embarrassing.

The eleven of us were given an alcove and no menus. Harriet had evidently ordered the meal in advance. I was seated between Nina and Trish, with Ross across from me, Greg at the foot of the table, and Lycia between Ross and Greg. Harriet was at the head of the table with Keith's date, Stephanie, on one side of her and a dark, spectacularly handsome young man on the other, next to Shannon.

'Ancel Ancini,' Nina whispered to me. 'Shannon's escort.'

From the glowing look on Shannon's face, he was a good deal more than an escort. 'New boyfriend?' I asked.

'Old boyfriend,' she whispered. 'Something or other happened and they broke up, but they got back together just recently.'

'Isn't there an Ancini who's running for the Senate?' I asked.

'That's Ancel's father.'

I recalled pictures of the father. Stephan. He wasn't and had never been as good-looking as his son. The son was Prince Charming, Superman, and the guy in the white hat, all rolled into one. Eyes that glittered. Dark, velvety skin. Hair that looked as though it might reach out and grab you, it was so alive. The contrast between his dark good looks and Shannon's pale beauty was striking. As a couple they were breathtaking, an illustration for a romance. I know this sounds gushy, but Conklin had set me thinking about fairy-tale illustrations and they could easily have been Cinderella and the Prince.

I remarked, 'Good-looking couple.'

Nina agreed. An arm came across her shoulder delivering a hot lobster appetizer, and I turned to talk with my neighbours across the table. Or tried to. Lycia was charming, remarking on having met me before under difficult circumstances and being happy to see me under better ones. Ross, however, seemed to have a chip on his shoulder about something. He was almost abrupt. To escape his inexplicable belligerence, I found my conversational gambits directed more and more at Lycia Foret.

Her face was not as pretty as her daughter's. Still, of all the faces around the table, hers was the most attractive. It radiated with a kind of tranquil strength. Not quiet, for she was very animated. Still, her expression displayed an inner peace or satisfaction, a kind of ageless tranquillity. I found myself wondering how old she was, counting years, realizing that though she might be considerably more, she could be as little as five or six years older than I. Not too old, I told myself, then stopped the thought, wondering what in hell I was up to. Not too old for what?

For yourself, buddy, I told myself.

Don't be idiotic. She's spoken for, I replied. There was no doubt of that. The way she and Ross looked at one another was enough to make their relationship clear. Close, and loving, and apparently honest, though why she loved the touchy bastard was more than I could figure out.

So what *is* it about her?

I passed the salt and smiled and replied to Trish's comments and Nina's gibes and let my eyes slide gently over Lycia's face. Something about her. Something I almost recognized.

Appetizers were succeeded by Caesar salad, by cold curried chicken soup, by breast of duckling in apricot sauce with wild rice. There were several bottles of wine. No one was in a hurry. I had plenty of time to indulge myself in my little obsession. After the third glass of wine, Greg became almost voluble—that is, he actually used sentences of seven or eight words, some of them in series. Trish and Nina talked across me about the gallery. I talked across the table to Lycia. Unlike many doctors I had met, both she and Ross seemed to know and care about other things than medicine or hospitals or medical society politics. When Lycia spoke about her profession, which she did, passionately, in response to something Nina asked her, she mentioned the enormous responsibilities it entailed and was very clear about the value she placed on life. She spoke of a beloved older sister who had died needlessly, and of her desire to prevent others from dying in similar fashion. Everything about her impressed me, and I found myself wondering if this evening might be the start of a friendship between her . . . between the two of them and me. If it happened at all, it would have to be with the two of them. So much was obvious.

Raised voices from the other end of the table drew our attention. Harriet was holding forth to Stephanie about someone abusing a child. With her grey-white hair and virtually unlined face, she looked like a prophetess laying down the law. I raised an eyebrow, and Lycia explained.

'Harriet and I work for the Lighthouse,' she said. 'It's a home for battered women and their children. I got interested in it when I was in medical school. That's how I met Harriet. She was—still is—on the board.'

'She was talking about child abuse just now?'

Lycia's face was concentrated, a little angry, though not at Harriet. 'The women who come to the Lighthouse are battered, and frequently the children are abused, too. She's trying to talk Stephanie into volunteering. I think Steph's about ten years too young to care.'

'Harriet seems very dedicated.'

Nina snorted. 'If you want a three-hour lecture, get Harriet started on children and their rights and how they ought to be protected. She's a fanatic!' She said it fondly, which was a good thing, because Lycia picked up on it.

'I agree with Harriet, and I don't think that one can be

too fanatical,' she said, the little anger hot in her tone. 'There just can't be any limits where children are concerned. Children have all their lives ahead of them. If you ruin a child, you ruin a whole life. Harriet feels we should feel about every child the way we feel about our own, and most of us mothers have pretty unlimited feelings towards our own.'

Her voice had risen slightly, tight with feeling, and Keith cast a slightly ironic look down the table towards her. 'Soap-box, Mother,' he said.

Lycia looked down, embarrassed. Ross chuckled. Harriet looked up, caught several sets of eyes on her, and said, 'What?'

'We've been caught on our usual lecture platform, Harriet,' Lycia commented. 'Keith told me to get off the soap-box.'

'Oh, we really should stay off it tonight,' Harriet said. She was a big, tall woman, with a deep, almost mannish voice, and square, expressive hands that moved in accompaniment to it. Every statement was accompanied by gestures, pointing, prying, fist folding. 'Oh,' she said, lifting open hands on either side of her face, 'we really should,' laying them palm down on the table, disposing of the subject. Then one hand flew to her eye. 'Damn,' she said.

Concerned, Trish turned to her. 'Did you lose a contact, Harriet?'

'Just blinked the silly thing out,' Harriet said. 'Piffle.' She found it, put her napkin down, and pushed her chair back. 'If you'll excuse me, I'll retire to the ladies' room.' She rose to her full height, slightly over six feet; Lycia followed her. After a moment's pause, so did Shannon and Stephanie, Nina and Trish, in couples. The men were left at the table while a busboy trudged around it, readying it for dessert and coffee.

'Not many women your mother's age wear contacts,' I remarked to Greg.

'She has trouble keeping glasses on,' he replied. 'She says

contacts are a godsend. I hate glasses, too. I tried them, and I couldn't paint at all. I can't see in them. All I'm aware of is the frame.'

'You wear contacts?' I asked.

He nodded, widening his eyes at me to make them shine. Keith leaned across the table and said something to Ancel Ancini. The two of them rose, excused themselves, and went across the room to speak to someone at another table. Ross, Greg, and I were left alone.

'I gathered from what you said the other morning that you knew Lycia's former husband,' Ross said to me, apropos of nothing.

'Not well,' I said. 'I met him at his sister's. I used to run into him occasionally in the park.'

Ross frowned, staring at his hands, which were manipulating a dessert fork, turning it over and over. 'Now Marge tells Lycia you're looking into his death.' The tone was unmistakably annoyed.

Aha, I thought, so that's it. 'She asked me to,' I said in a noncommittal tone.

'We met Fred once,' said Greg, almost volubly. 'Melody and I, at that swimming party Lycia gave for Shannon's twenty-first birthday. Shannon said her father wasn't invited. He just showed up. And he had webbed feet.' He smiled into his wineglass, privately amused by some image only he could see.

'Webbed feet?' I didn't think I'd heard him correctly.

'Webbed toes,' Ross corrected, his voice still angry. 'Fred had webbed toes. He insisted on joining the swimming party, and I remember Keith was kidding him about his feet.'

'Is that rare?' I asked.

Ross pursed his lips. 'I suppose. It's not really a deformity, more of an anomaly. Any good surgeon could have removed them in five minutes.'

'Melody said it ran in families,' Greg said.

'It's true that Shannon had webs like it,' Ross said. 'Between her big toes and second toes. I removed Shannon's webs a few years ago. She wanted to wear thongs and couldn't.'

'Webbed feet and sticky fingers,' Greg said solemnly. He was nodding over his fourth or fifth glass of wine.

'Sticky fingers?' I asked, keeping my voice carefully neutral, hoping he wasn't talking about Shannon.

'I mean Fred Foret. Melody told me. After she met him at the birthday party, she used to run into him all the time in the park. She said he had sticky fingers.'

For a moment I didn't realize that he had just told me who Melody's park companion had been. Though Fred might not have said much to a woman he had just met at his daughter's birthday party, he wouldn't have hesitated to build on that acquaintance. So Fred must have been the man Ambler had seen Melody with. I noted this second connection between Fred and Melody. One that Conklin had mentioned between Melody and Fred's daughter. One that Greg had mentioned between Melody and Fred himself.

'That's what I mean about him,' Ross snorted, with a hard look at me. 'I think the police should be let alone to do their own thing without some . . . well, some amateur messing in. Fred wasn't worth the effort. Nothing about that guy would surprise me. I know damned well he stole Shannon's house keys out of her purse and had a copy made. Then he'd pick times he knew we were all going to be gone and sneak into Lycia's apartment.'

'Why?' I asked, genuinely curious. 'Why would he do that?' I had placed the anger now. It wasn't at me but at the former husband. I was only catching the reflection.

'After some private stuff of Lycia's came up missing, she realized what was going on. I should have realized before. Shannon told us one time she'd been over at Fred's, she'd lost her key. He called her a day or two later to tell her he'd found it. We didn't think anything of it at the time, but then when Lycia missed her stuff and Shannon told us the kind of things he'd been saying to her, it was obvious what he'd done. He was sneaking in and reading private letters, looking through Shannon's diary—she's kept a diary since she was about ten—then he'd be able to come over all omniscient with Shannon. You can imagine the kind of thing. "I know something's troubling you, dear. It's a man, isn't it? He's said something that's upset you. Let me see if I can figure out what it might be." Stuff like that.' Ross's nostrils flared with frustrated fury. 'Poor kid. He had her buffaloed. Like some kind of evil spirit. The Great All-Knowing Father. Know all, see all, tell all. He damn near broke up her relationship with Ancel, too.'

The Ancinis were another family 'in oil', and they'd managed to hold on to their money when the collapse wiped out the economy of several western states. 'How did Fred do that?' I asked.

Ross turned the fork over and over. I could tell he was thinking he had already said too much to me, but his anger and annoyance at Fred got the better of his reticence. 'Ancel invited Shannon home to meet his family. She was jittery as a cricket, scared, happy, half out of her head. She was sure he was going to propose. For the last six months it had been Ancel this and Ancel that. Lycia and I kept trying to calm her down . . .

'Then, along the middle of that week, Fred called Shannon and told her he needed her to come to his apartment that weekend, that he had something very important to talk to her about and it couldn't wait. You'd have to know Fred and his "talks" for this to make sense. You'd also have to know Fred to realize that the only reason he'd picked that weekend was that he knew she was going to the Ancinis'. A kind of test of his power over Shannon. He did that a lot. I'm pretty sure it's one of the reasons Lycia left him in the first place.' He closed his mouth into a tight, straight line for a second, as though he'd almost said something he shouldn't.

I did indeed know Fred and his talks. 'What did Shannon do?'

'She said she had an engagement, she told him with whom.' Ross shook his head. 'No guile in that girl at all, even though she should have known better. Fred already

knew, of course. You know what that damned Fred did?'
He waited, poised, lips compressed. He had to tell me. He
had to tell someone.

I tried to think of the most outrageous thing I could. 'He
called the Ancinis and said she couldn't come.'

'Worse!' Ross slammed his hand down on the table,
making the coffee cups rattle. 'He called Mrs Ancini and
invited himself along as chaperone. Poor Mrs Ancini didn't
know what to say. Here was this *father* on the line, and he
wouldn't shut up. Well, Shannon went out there Saturday
afternoon—they've got a huge, expensive showplace out in
Cherry Hills—and who was the first person she saw but her
daddy. Ancel brought her home early Sunday morning, his
face like a thundercloud. Shannon was in tears. She couldn't
talk to us for hours. Ancel's father had been insulted somehow. According to Shannon, everything was over.'

'Good Lord. What had Fred done?'

Ross shook his head, like a dog with a rat, as though he
would shake the words to death. 'Who knows what he did!
Shannon told us almost nothing except that Fred had invited
himself along on her weekend. Aside from that, she wouldn't
talk about it, not then and not since. It was all I could do
to keep Lycia from going straight out and . . .' He realized
what he was saying and bit off the words. 'Well, Lycia cried
on Harriet's shoulder instead. None of us knows what Fred
actually did, though we can imagine. Ancel hasn't said
anything to us. At any rate, the upshot of the whole thing
was that Shannon and Ancel broke up. They only got back
together after Fred was killed.'

I could see it all in living colour, full of anger and
embarrassment. 'Maybe Ancel killed him,' I said, without
thinking.

Ross's jaw dropped.

'No, no, Ross,' I said, embarrassed. 'I didn't mean it. My
mind works that way, trying to solve things. Looking for
motives. Looking for possibilities. That's why Marge asked
me to look into Fred's death. You said he wasn't worth the
effort, but she cares. She wants to know why he died.'

He scowled at me. 'Well, if anyone had a motive, I did. When Shannon told Lycia and me that Fred had showed up at the Ancinis', I was ready to kill him myself. I wouldn't have shot him, though. I'd have slit his throat. For sheer, unmitigated gall, Fred Foret took the silver buckle. Shannon didn't eat for a week. She didn't sleep either. All she did was cry. And to top everything off, Fred had the nerve to call her and tell her she was better off!'

'When did this happen? The Ancini thing.'

'Oh, I don't know. Six or eight weeks ago. Long enough for Ancel to think it over and make up with her. Thank God. You know the word "distraught"? I've never seen it anywhere except in old romances, but that was Shannon.' He sighed, his dammed-up anger talked out and gone. 'Sorry about seeming unpleasant. It's just . . . the bastard was always causing trouble. Now that he's dead, I'd hoped it would be over.'

Quietly grateful for whatever emotion had made him so talkative, I added Ross's name to my list of suspects. What he had told me should have strengthened Lycia's motive, too, though I could not imagine her killing anyone. As I pondered this, I saw her across the room, stooping to speak to someone on her way back to the table, her face calm and glowing. Ross shook his head at me, finger on lips. I wasn't to say anything to Lycia. I nodded agreement and took a firm grip on my suspicious self. Both Lycia and Ross had alibis. As did Shannon, who probably couldn't kill a mouse, and Keith, who looked as though he could kill something considerably larger if he cared to.

We stood up as the women returned. Keith and Ancel came back from their visit across the room. The waiters returned with an elegant dessert without even a hint of birthday cake or singing waiters. Several people presented small gifts. Since Greg seemed to be in a mellow mood, I gave him the snuff box. He asked the right questions about it and seemed pleased. He was a man improved by wine, made less self-conscious and less blunt. When I saw him like this, his face quite open and shining with interest, I

thought it quite possible that love had made Melody leave
her secure nest with the oilman.

I turned slightly and caught a glimpse of Harriet. She
was looking down the table, seeing no one but her son. The
way she looked at him, with a kind of brooding passion, left
me in no doubt about her feelings for him. Strange man.
Both Trish and Harriet loved him, and he basked in their
affection while remaining almost unaware of it.

After I dropped Nina off, I drove directly home, put the car
in the garage, and went in through the back door. Whenever
I get home, Bela comes to greet me, barking in muted
tones, semaphoring his heavy tail in a message of greeting,
sometimes almost knocking me over. I stood inside in the
darkness, half aware that something was wrong before I
realized what it was. No Bela.

I decided not to turn on the lights, and instead took the
large flashlight from the laundry-room drawer and flashed
it around the laundry and then the old kitchen we use as a
showroom for country furniture—pie cabinets, spice racks,
what Jacob calls kitchen clutter. The place looked as usual.
No mess. No sign anyone had been there.

The kitchen has two doors into the house, one opening
into the old dining-room, one opening into the back hall,
across from the back stairs. Back hall and front hall are
separated by another door, one we never use because Eugenia's desk sits almost directly in front of it. I had the
choice of the back stairs or the dining-room. Flipping a
mental coin, I picked the dining-room.

Shining tables, shining chairs, sideboards, serving tables.
Swagged drapes over sheer curtains with the streetlight
showing through. Nothing. Another mental coin, upstairs
or the other showrooms. Upstairs.

The stairs did not creak. They would not have dared.
Jacob had always said that nothing undermines confidence
in a piece of construction more than hearing it squeak.
Eugenia and I always pushed and tugged at things like
bedsteads and highboys to be sure there was no give. I went

up silently. Into the front guest room, nothing; the offices, nothing; my living-room and kitchen, nothing. Which left the bedroom. An ideal place for an ambush, really. A man comes in, probably with one arm half out of his suit coat, unsuspecting, a perfect target. Though who might be lying in wait and for what reason, my frantic brain didn't tell me.

My sensible self said go back downstairs and call the police. One of my other selves said Bela was missing, dammit, and I wanted to know what had happened to him.

I stood in the doorway, silent as a wraith, pointed the flash into the room, and flicked it on. It met the startled gaze of one very large white dog who raised his head from his bed and said *whuf* in a loud and irritated manner. There was a sound from the bed. I swung the flash and met another surprised pair of eyes. These were blue and sleepy, in a pale little face under a wealth of corn-silk hair.

'Grace!' I said.

'Oh, hi, Jason. I wondered if you'd ever get home,' she said sleepily. 'I was so tired, I decided I'd lie down for a minute.'

She had picked one of my T-shirts to do it in. It hit her at her knees, making her look like a little girl dressed up in some grown-up's clothes. She held out her arms like a little child, still half asleep, and I sat on the bed and gathered her up, while Bela subsided back into his huge basket, deciding everything was all right.

'How'd you get in?' I whispered.

'Through the dog door.' She giggled. 'I talked to Bela first, so he'd know who it was. He was on one side whuffing, and I was on the other side explaining. He let me in, though.'

'Oh, Grace,' I said, inadequately, holding her tightly.

'I'm so glad you got home,' she murmured.

'Why?' I asked, expecting some tender revelation, like separation had made the heart grow fonder.

'I'm awfully hungry,' she said.

So much for tender revelations. Grace did that to me all the time. In a mood of half-amused, half-annoyed affection, I changed into something more comfortable. Grace retained the T-shirt. We went into the kitchen and I made her a six-egg omelette and about half a pound of fried bacon, which she ate without pause. There were some English muffins in the freezer. She finished up with five muffin halves, liberally doused with ginger marmalade, and most of a quart of milk.

'You're sure that's enough,' I said sarcastically, noting the way the knit fabric clung to her breasts. Grace is small but shapely. At least that's the word I use to myself when I'm trying to control my breathing.

'I haven't been eating very well,' she confided. 'Mostly stuff at coffee shops. They never give you enough.'

I had never known Grace to have enough anywhere. Her appetite was a matter of constant amazement to me. Now, however, it seemed to be momentarily satisfied, for she sat back with a pleased little sigh and demanded to be told everything about the murder and the clue I'd found and everything.

'I don't want to think about Ron all weekend,' she said. 'I just want to be with you.'

'Fair enough,' I told her, mentally sorting out the Fred Foret case for her perusal while fighting the urge to drag her into the bedroom. After the meal she had just eaten, however, she was entitled to a little digestion time. Actually, the time stretched to two pots of coffee before everything was told with all the ramifications and bits and pieces.

'I worked on the Steinwale case,' she said, surprising me. 'I was one of the first people on the scene—that is, after they found out she was dead. She wasn't just slumped over. Her arm was sort of crooked into the arm of the bench.' She illustrated, bending her left arm and thrusting the elbow up and back. 'Those benches, the metal arms come down from the back, making a kind of triangle. Her elbow was shoved into the triangle, holding her up.'

'Did you think at the time the body had been arranged that way?'

She shook her head. 'I didn't think so at the time, no. There was no reason to think so. She could have been arranged, but she could have been sitting that way, too. If she had been sitting that way when she was shot, she might have just slumped forward without falling, the way we found her.'

'How about the magazine in her lap? Did you think that had been put there?'

She furrowed her brow, remembering. 'It wasn't a slick magazine,' she said at last. 'Or maybe it was, but it had a brown paper cover. Like a mailing cover. Like she'd grabbed it out of the mail and brought it along. I can't remember what the magazine was, so I couldn't have felt it was important. It'll be in the property room, down at the station. The case was never closed.'

We talked about that for a while, trying different scenarios, without getting anyplace. Finally, we ran out of things to say about the case.

'That's all very nice,' she said. 'Sounds like you've been busy. Now, what's bothering you?'

'I haven't a clue yet,' I said. 'Nothing fits together.'

'I don't mean about your puzzle,' she said. 'I mean about you.'

I had to think about that. What about me?

'Did you get another one of those letters offering to sell you information about yourself?' she asked. 'Last time you got one, you had those same lines in your forehead.'

Suddenly, surprisingly, for no reason at all, I had tears in my eyes.

'Shush, shush,' she was saying. 'Dammit, Jason. Who's doing this?'

'Some con man,' I said. 'Somebody who knows a little about me and thinks he can get money out of me.'

'You know, we could handle this. The police, I mean. We could set a trap for the person, find out who, without risking your money. I'm pretty sure it would be called extortion, you know.'

I did know. I'd thought of that. 'Grace, if we did that, suppose we did that. Suppose the person really does know something. Something I'd just as soon not know.'

'Like your daddy was a horse thief?'

'Like he was something worse than that. Or my mother was. Or the reason for my abandonment was . . .'

'None of that has anything to do with you!'

'That's what Jacob always says. I believe it. Intellectually. Privately, emotionally, I don't want to deal with the reality. I particularly don't want to deal with a reality which may end up in the papers, a "story", something for the curious to titillate themselves with. *Local Merchant's Lurid History Revealed*. I had enough ghastly headlines when Agatha disappeared. There were enough when they found her body. I don't want any more.'

She didn't protest. She nodded. She understood. 'Well then, you'll just have to wait until you know what you want to do. Eventually, he'll get tired of writing letters and try something else. Or he'll give up.'

And if he gave up, I'd never know.

Grace took me by the hand. We left the dishes where they were. Fifteen minutes later, I'd forgotten all about it and didn't care who I was or where I was or anything about the day-to-day world at all.

I called Eugenia and Mark early and told them not to bother to come in, to take Saturday morning off. Eugenia told me she'd planned to do just that, and Mark wanted to get together to talk about the puzzle. I told him Monday would be soon enough.

Grace and I talked about finding Sally Streeter. I'd already done the easy things, like looking in the phone book and calling Information. She didn't have a phone under that name, listed or unlisted. Since she'd moved only recently, she wouldn't be in any city directory. Public Service might have a listing, but that would require subterfuge. I went over the notes I'd jotted down just after my visit to the apartment house where she'd lived.

'Bingo,' I told Grace. 'And church bake sales. The manager of the place she used to live said Sally was into bingo and bake sales.'

She gave me a questioning look. 'Bingo?'

'Once an addict, always an addict,' I pontificated. 'You can help find her. Tomorrow maybe.'

Not Saturday, however. We spent the day in totally mindless and pleasurable doing-nothing. We soaked in my sybaritic tub. We drank wine. After a rushed trip to the deli, we ate enormously. At least, she did. We took a drive in the mountains, ending up at a favourite restaurant. In between, we went to bed together whenever we felt like it. Grace, being very solicitous of my feelings, did not tell me she didn't love me. Perhaps, I told myself, she had forgotten that. Sunday morning we parked outside the apartment house where Sally had once lived. We had a thermos of coffee in the front seat, Bela and Critter in the back. About ten-thirty, the Campbell-kid apartment manager came out of the place, bright brass hair frizzed like a pot scrubber, and walked down to the corner. Ten minutes later a station wagon pulled up and she got in. We followed the station wagon to the Church of the Living Gospel. Signs on the lawn of the Catholic church across the street advertised Wednesday night bingo.

The Campbell kid, an elderly couple, and a younger couple got out of the station wagon and went into the church. There was a remote chance that Sally might show up at the Church of the Living Gospel. If so, she'd probably come out with the Campbell kid. Dog, cat, Grace, and I went to a pancake house for a second breakfast (hamburger patties for animals, omelette for me, giant pancakes for Grace) and were back outside the church when it let out at noon. The Campbell kid came out with the same crowd she'd gone in with. No Streeter.

The four of us went to the park, got into a volleyball game, made friends, got home about four. Bela had scored the winning point by jumping at the ball and hitting it with his head. He still looked a little puzzled by the unaccustomed adulation. My leg hurt like hell. Which meant the exercise had probably been good for it.

The phone book listed the Church of the Living Gospel as a 'charismatic' congregation. I couldn't find a 'charismatic' church listed on the far west side of town. I turned my attention to the Catholic churches. There were half a dozen of those out towards Golden. I made a red mark beside each one that was located in a likely area. Tomorrow morning would be time enough to call.

'You going to drive me to the airport?' Grace asked from the living-room doorway. She was dressed, ready to travel. I hadn't even thought to ask her how long she was staying.

I swallowed my disappointment and asked, 'When does your plane leave?'

'About an hour,' she said. 'I can get a cab if you're busy.'

I wasn't that busy. I took her, and kissed her goodbye, and dropped her off. When I got back to the house, it seemed very, very empty.

When Mark came in on Monday, I gave him the phone book and pointed out the red check marks. 'Call these churches and ask if they have bingo. Ask if, by any chance, your friend Sally Streeter has been playing bingo there for the last six or eight months. If they don't know, find out when bingo is and make a note.'

I'd had another thought. While Mark was busy with the Catholic churches, I called the Church of the Living Gospel and asked the woman who answered if she knew of a charismatic church out towards Golden. She didn't know, but the minister, Mr McCall, might know. She told me I might catch him around noon, and I said I'd call back.

I didn't have to call back. Mark came into my office about ten-thirty, grinning up both sides of his face.

'Bingo?' I asked him.

'Bingo. She plays at Our Lady of Peace. Tuesday nights. A recent but very faithful player, according to the church secretary who runs the games with her mother-in-law.'

We spent some time considering the likely feelings of middle-aged women who have been 'taken advantage of', before agreeing on an approach for the following night. Back to business.

'How's the Duchesne job coming?' I asked Mark.

'Duchesne, Duchesne,' he murmured. 'Why does that sound familiar?'

'Mark!' I said warningly, suddenly having visions of Gladys coming after me with a meat axe, her daughter and the new inlaws close behind.

'It's fine,' he said. 'Paint's finished. Carpet's going in today. Curtains will be ready Wednesday. So far the only thing missing is a shower curtain and new towels for the bathroom. Someone said they'd take care of that.' His tone was unmistakably impudent.

'I don't remember anyone saying that.'

'I'm sure someone did.'

'Well, since I can't remember, you'd better take care of it.'

'Foul, Jason. Foul.'

I pretended not to hear him.

On Tuesday night we played bingo. At least Mark did, while I circulated asking questions until someone pointed Sally Streeter out to me. She was at the end of a long table playing eight or nine cards at once, the mark, so I hear, of a professional bingoer. Once I had her located, Mark and I settled into the game. We spent eleven-fifty and won a toaster-oven. Sally won a fifty-dollar pot. When she left, we approached her in the brightly lighted hall with fifty people around, hats in hands, so to speak, where she could not possibly feel threatened.

'Mrs Streeter,' I said. 'My name is Lynx, Jason Lynx. This is my associate, Mark MacMillan. May we please have a moment of your time?'

She looked around, doubtfully, taking assurance from the crowd. 'What do you want?' she asked ungraciously, her hands tightening on her purse, which she held up in front of her like a barrier to protect herself from us both. Sally was what Jacob would have called zaftig: light-haired, rosy-cheeked, definitely plump.

'Mr Fred Foret was a dreadful man,' Mark said. We'd

agreed in advance he would say something like that. 'Everyone knows he was a dreadful man. We're looking into something Mr Foret did, and someone told us you had known him slightly.'

She turned bright brick red and we both looked away, pretending to be interested in someone else. When we looked back, she had herself under control.

'We understand he used to talk to you,' I said. 'It's terribly important that we learn everything we can about him. If now isn't convenient . . . ?'

'It's just . . .' she fumbled with her purse, looking around again. 'This is very public.'

'There's a pancake house down the street,' Mark suggested. We'd located this and two other possible meeting places before we'd come to the church. 'It's open now. We could have coffee, or tea . . .'

'Tea,' she said. 'I'd like a cup of tea. I really would.'

'We'll meet you there,' I suggested. We'd decided it would be less threatening for us not to suggest driving her. She agreed. She went out. We followed, not too closely. She drove directly to the pancake house, as though she'd been there before. We met her inside. When we were seated and had ordered coffee and pie for us, tea and a muffin for her, we sat quietly, letting her look us over.

When I looked at her I thought of the faint smell of floor wax, lavender, hot ironing, and baked chicken. Though she was a few years older, she was Beaver Cleaver's mother, except around the eyes. They looked vulnerable, as though there was something in her house she couldn't get clean and she was afraid someone would notice.

'He wasn't a nice man,' she blurted. 'I thought he was. Last fall, he was very sweet to me for a while, and I thought he was a nice person, but he wasn't.'

'We know,' Mark replied, taking a bite of lemon pie. 'He was a louse.'

'He was a bastard,' she said, surprising us both. 'A real died-in-the-wool bastard. That's what my father used to say about someone like him. When I saw in the paper he was dead, I was glad!' She trembled an unsuccessful laugh. 'That's awful. That's just awful, but I was glad.'

'What can you tell us about him?' I asked.

'I don't know what you want to know,' she said, sipping her tea, tears at the corners of her eyes. 'I was very lonely, and I thought he was all right. Only it turned out he wasn't. And I waved my little gun at him and made a fool of myself.' She gulped, suddenly aware of what she'd said. 'I didn't shoot him! I couldn't shoot anything! But I didn't care when somebody else did.'

'Have the police questioned you?' Mark asked.

She shook her head, tears forming in her eyes, ready to spill over. I recalled the trail we had followed to get to her: from Marge to the guy in Boulder, to the apartment house manager, to bingo, to here. If Marge hadn't mentioned the man in Boulder to the police, likely they wouldn't have found out about Sally. Marge hadn't known about her.

Since she was very close to weeping, I tried to change the subject a little. 'Did he talk about himself?'

'All the time.' She tried the laugh again, at herself. 'Honestly, Fred never talked about anything else.'

'Well, just try to remember some of the things he said about himself and mention them. We'll try to figure out which ones are important.'

'Those things he got into,' she said. 'Est?'

'We already know about that.'

'The peace-marching thing with the children.'

'We know about that.'

She thought. 'He used to go into his ex-wife's apartment all the time.'

'Go into?'

'Sneak into. He took a key from his daughter's purse and had a copy made. He used to go over there when nobody was home and sneak in.'

Bingo. Ross's suspicions had been correct. Still, it seemed an odd habit to confess to an acquaintance. 'Did he tell you why he did that?'

'To find out what she was up to. Lycia. His wife. He told me she wasn't good for the children and he had to keep an eye on her for their sake.'

'They're scarcely children,' Mark said. 'In their twenties.'

She looked shocked. 'The way he talked, I thought they were young teenagers. He said they were still young and impressionable, particularly his daughter. He said his ex-wife gave his daughter too much freedom, that she ought to have more direction, more sense of purpose. That she'd be happier if she were kept away from undesirable people and didn't have so many decisions to make.'

'Undesirable people?'

'Some man she was seeing. He told me he was going to break it up. That the man's family was too much for Shannon. That Shannon wouldn't be able to cope with their level of sophistication.'

'Sophistication,' I repeated. So the breakup of Shannon and young Ancini had been planned. 'Anything else?'

'He said his ex-wife was trying to be a writer and she was no good at it, but maybe she'd pay him not to tell anybody. Then he laughed.'

I could make no sense out of that. 'A writer?'

'He said she was writing a book or something. Something like that.'

'When was that?'

'Oh, a long time ago. I really don't remember.'

'Did Fred ever mention Melody Steinwale?' I asked. 'The information we have suggests that he used to meet her in the park and talk to her there.'

'If that's the woman who married the artist, he used to talk about her a lot,' she admitted. 'That was before . . . well, when we were just friends, you might say. Acquaintances. I used to see them together, and I asked if she was a relative, and he said no, she was just a friend, that she needed someone to guide her.' She looked both angry and embarrassed. 'I think he wanted her to be more than that. I saw the way he looked at her. I heard his voice when he talked about her. He was trying to get into her bed.' Her face was red, and the words came out raggedly. 'But she was too . . . too smart for him.'

We gave her time to get herself together.

Mark said, 'Is that all you can think of?'

She nodded, then stopped. 'Except . . .'

'Except?'

'He said once he'd told the girl in the park she should get some back for herself.'

'What do you think he meant?'

'I'm not sure. He used to say things like that all the time. He said everybody needed to find ways to get theirs, more or less, and it was up to each person to make things come out even. He used to smile when he said that, kind of show his teeth. I told him it made him look like a wolf, but he just laughed. He said sometimes a little blackmail was a good thing, only he called it "calling in the IOUs", or something like that.'

Beyond that, she had nothing else to tell us. I asked for the bill and we walked Sally out to her car. She got in, started to shut the door, then stopped. 'It seems very odd to me now,' she said. 'Talking about blackmail and getting even and all that kind of thing. And him talking about that girl all the time. Looking back, I guess he was telling me over and over he wasn't a nice person. But when I was with Fred, he never made it sound like . . . anything unethical. He made it sound as though he was doing what was logical and right, what everybody did, or doing it for somebody else . . .'

'Or as though if you objected it was because you were stupid,' I suggested. I had noticed that tendency on Fred's part.

She nodded, tears at the corners of her eyes once more. 'Yes. As though anybody with brains would agree with him. He wasn't a nice man,' she said. 'He hit me once when I disagreed with him. I guess that's why I didn't argue with him. I don't know why I even went on seeing him.' She pulled slowly away from us, turning her head so we wouldn't see her cry.

We watched her drive off.

Loneliness, I thought again. The things it makes us do!

'She reminds me of my mother,' said Mark. 'Somehow you don't think of people that age getting sexually involved, getting sick and embarrassed over it.'

Mark's mother wasn't that much older than I am. Not that much older than Lycia Foret. I didn't comment.

CHAPTER 5

My phone rang Sunday morning about eight, just as the species-assorted three of us were about to have breakfast and then go out for a little exercise. It was Marge Beebe, sounding mysteriously aggrieved.

'I've found something among Frederick's things,' she said. 'Something you ought to see.'

'I was about to feed us and take the dog and cat to the park,' I complained. 'Can it wait till tomorrow, Marge?'

'You ought to see it, Jason. Really. I don't know . . . I can't imagine . . . I need you to come see it, really.' Her voice shrilled away in something approaching barely controlled panic.

I grumbled, but I got out the car. The animals didn't mind as much as I did, but then they didn't have to drive. Being Sunday, however, there was far less traffic than usual, so it only took half an hour or so.

Marge didn't even supply me with coffee before plunking down a nine-by-twelve brown envelope and a large square cardboard box in front of me. Then she went to the other side of the room and sat down, staring at me as though I was suddenly contagious.

'What is this?' I asked, indicating the box. It had been sealed all the way around with tape, but the tape had been cut.

'Open it,' she said. 'Just open it.'

I opened it. It was packed with money, new hundred-dollar bills in neat wrappers. I counted one bundle and multiplied in my head.

'There's over half a million dollars here,' I said in astonishment.

'I know,' she whispered. 'I know. It was in the bottom of a footlocker, from the storage room in the basement of Fred's apartment. I was going through his things, and there it was. With the other thing. Open it. Read it. I don't want to talk about it. I just don't know. You'll have to read it.'

So I read it. It was handwritten, several pages, and it seemed to be an outline for a mystery story, not a very original one. I'd seen the plot at least twice before, once in a movie and once on TV, involving A and B, each of whom has a person he wants to kill, but doesn't want to be caught. A offers to kill B's victim, and vice versa, at a time when, as the logical suspects, each will have an alibi. I couldn't see why this had occasioned Marge such distress.

'Whose handwriting is this?' I asked when I'd read part of the first page.

Marge tried to answer, but it took two tries before it came out. 'Lycia's,' she squeaked.

My mouth went suddenly dry. I tried to speak a couple of times, finally managing, 'Something Fred kept when she left Washington?'

'Read all of it,' she said in the same sombre squeak.

Half way down the second page was a date, as though she'd stopped writing a letter and then continued at a later date. The whole thing had that quality, like a memo or letter to someone else. The date was in June, two years ago. Therefore, this was not something Lycia had left behind in Washington when she left Fred. This was something she had written, at least in its current form, only fairly recently. 'How did Fred get it?' I asked, knowing damned well how he had. This was undoubtedly one of the 'personal things' Lycia had found missing before she changed the locks.

'Read it all,' said Marge.

So I read it all, not liking it particularly. Not liking it at all, as a matter of fact. The Lycia who fascinated and enthralled me simply would not have thought this way, though any real human being undoubtedly might have. The outline of the plot was fleshed out with a good many examples of why the victims needed killing. When I'd finished, I leaned back and gave Marge a sombre look of my own. 'The way this reads, there's an older woman with a destructive daughter-in-law, and a younger woman with a destructive ex-husband, and they agree to kill for each other, right? You figure this for Harriet Steinwale and Lycia?'

She nodded, silent, watching me as though I'd just crawled out of the earth carrying something dreadful. Her eyes were huge.

'Come on, Marge. You don't think that either of those women . . .'

'What am I supposed to think?' she shouted at me. 'It's all there, all planned out. How the older woman will be out of the country when her daughter-in-law dies. Harriet was out of the country! And all that money! Where did Fred get all that money?'

'I don't know where Fred got the money, Marge. Where Fred got all the money may have nothing at all to do with this other thing. And this other thing may have nothing to do with reality.'

'I don't care what it has to do with. Right there, in Lycia's handwriting, there's a plan to kill Fred.'

'Among other variances from fact, it says that the younger woman would be at an afternoon medical meeting when her ex-husband is killed,' I said. 'Fred wasn't killed in the afternoon, it was morning, and Lycia was home, with her family.'

'Lycia wasn't supposed to be the one who did it anyhow. And maybe they changed the plan.'

'Maybe they didn't do it at all.' I couldn't imagine the woman I had sat across the table from on Friday night killing anyone. She had cared too deeply about life and the meaning of it. She had cared too much about the saving of it to take it. She was . . . I would have sworn she was that most priceless commodity (*Proverbs*), a good woman. The Lycia I had met simply could not have killed another woman, however silly and destructive the victim was.

'I want you to find out,' Marge said, tears running down her face. 'I can't see Lycia or the family again, not any of them, not until I know.'

I went over to her and patted her on the shoulder. 'Come on, Marge. I don't think this is anything. At worst, a way of working out frustration on Lycia's part by a little day-dreaming. At best, an attempt to get a little variety, write something. Lots of people are closet writers, and lots of writers take out their own frustrations on their characters.'

'Lycia hated Fred. Ross hated him.'

'Marge, they disliked him. They had good reason. He was a real pain, particularly where your niece was concerned. Lots of us have people we dislike. We fantasize killing them or maybe we even joke about killing them. Hell, I've done it myself! That doesn't mean we actually do it.'

'Poor Shannon,' she sobbed. 'He was so . . . so overbearing with her. That's why Lycia left him, you know. She never said a word to me, but I think maybe he used to abuse her. Poor Shannon . . .' Her face flowed with tears.

'I will look into this,' I said. 'I promise you I will, Marge.'

'I want you to take the papers and that box,' she cried. 'I'm leaving. I told Silas this morning, before he left for work, I'm going to Arizona to see my daughter. I'm going to stay a while. This has all been . . . it's been too much.' The tears were flowing freely now, and I patted for a few minutes more before I asked her if by any chance there had been a gun among Fred's things in the storage locker. She said no. I'd been wondering where Sally's gun had ended up, ever since she'd said Fred had taken it away from her.

After a few more pats and a few more snuffles, I ran for it. I took the package and the manuscript with me. Even though I didn't believe it . . . Well. I wasn't sure. She called to me as I left. 'Silas will know where to reach me. You let me know if you find anything out, will you?'

I nodded, saying that I would. It wasn't a promise. I

didn't feel like making any promises, and once again I was glad I hadn't taken any money for whatever it was I was doing.

The money could go in the old safe in the basement, along with Marty O'Toole's handgun. I hadn't given Marge a receipt, but I would send her one as soon as I knew definitely how much cash was in the box. She'd have to decide what to do with it, eventually; there was nothing I could do about it but take it off her hands temporarily. There might be nothing I could do about the manuscript either. I considered whether I could approach Lycia about it, or Harriet Steinwale. Who else would know anything about it? It wasn't precisely the kind of thing one talked about to the family, or the kind of thing the family would talk about with outsiders.

When we got home, Bela and Critter were ravenous. Most unlike herself, Marge hadn't even offered them a drink of water. I fed them, then set about fixing my own breakfast with the manuscript on the kitchen table, where it could be perused again in the hope that some kind of sense would emerge.

I went over the handwritten pages again while I ate toasted bagels and jam, hoping it said something else. It persisted in saying the same thing I had read initially.

'Suppose,' it started out. 'Suppose two women were very good friends, and each of them had someone she wanted dead.' Then it went on to describe the daughter-in-law who was driving a son mad with her debts and her flirtations, and the ex-husband who was driving a daughter crazy with his violence, omniscience, and efforts at control, just as he had done when she was a child. Finally it talked about the two women each killing the other's bête noire, and the alibis each would have. One of the women was a doctor . . .

I chewed my bagel, not tasting it, trying to find holes in this unexpected and unacceptable revelation. Unfortunately, I didn't doubt that Fred had stolen this manuscript from his ex-wife's apartment. Marge said the writing was Lycia's, and I really didn't doubt that either. The only real question was whether the manuscript was an actual plan or only a bit of catharsis. If the thing was actually a *plan* and not merely a bit of wool gathering—if it *was* a plan, and if I set my prejudices concerning Lycia aside, then I had to accept that Lycia Foret might have killed Melody Steinwale as her part of a deadly bargain with Harriet. In which case, Harriet had killed Fred.

But if Lycia had killed Melody after Fred stole the manuscript, wouldn't Fred have assumed he was the next victim? There was all that business Sally Streeter had brought out. All that 'getting even' and suggestions of blackmail. The presence of the manuscript and the money together . . . well, it certainly suggested blackmail. I wondered if Lycia could have come up with half a million. One doctor might have trouble, but two surgeons might be able to raise that much. Suppose Fred had stolen this manuscript, then blackmailed both Lycia and Ross after Melody's death. 'Pay me, or I'll give this to the police.'

Would they have paid?

If the manuscript had been written only as a catharsis, Lycia would probably have told Fred to give it to the police and the hell with him. Which implied that if she had paid, she had also committed murder. And how had Fred tried to protect himself? If he had thought he was to be the next victim, wouldn't he have done something? Left the usual sealed letter with his attorneys? Or, more likely, wouldn't he have demanded blackmail from both Lycia and Harriet— Harriet had far more money than Lycia did—threatening them both with exposure?

As I sat there staring at the manuscript, I thought that in a way the fact that Fred had it might actually serve to exonerate Harriet. If she knew Fred had it, would she have dared kill him without recovering it first? Perhaps she had tried, but had been unable to find it. Even Marge had found it only long after the fact.

My eyes went glazed. I was totally preoccupied. Bela had become bored with his food and decided to steal an egg bagel from the back of the kitchen counter. Kuvasz dogs are tall and long and they can reach. He did it with a certain amount of decorum, actually, without knocking anything over, while I looked right through him, seeing him do it but thinking of Fred and Lycia and the whole ugly tangle. Once Bela had the bagel impaled on his front teeth, he tried to decide whether it was a rubber ball or something edible by dropping it and watching it bounce, then picking it up again and trying to chew it. The bagel fought back. Bela put a paw on it and pulled. Critter was crouched under the kitchen table, staring at this exhibition and growling. Suddenly aware of all this, I said to Critter, 'That's right, Critter. Tell him off. What's with this crazy dog?'

The words had an eerie resonance to them, that flash which is almost déjà vu, a remembrance of the thing itself, and I repeated the phrase to myself, testing for weird. 'What's with this . . . with this dog?'

Then the connection was there, the question I'd asked Mark once before but had not pursued. The morning that Melody was killed, she'd been walking her dog. What had happened to Melody's dog?

Dogs don't just disappear, not usually. Ambler said that Melody had had a fat collie. If she had a fat collie in tow when she was murdered in the park, one might expect the fat collie to set up one hell of a racket. Or maybe just run away, leash trailing. Either would have attracted attention, and since people might well have recognized the dog as belonging to Melody, they'd have noticed her 'sitting' on the bench, they'd have said something. 'Hey, miss, your dog's running away.' In fact, she hadn't been found for some time. Therefore, maybe there had been no fat collie in tow at the time. Or? Or someone took the dog. Someone the dog would go with?

I thought of the shelties I had seen in Lycia's place, all curled up in their baskets under the window, leashes hanging on the back of the door. If Lycia had murdered Melody, she could simply have taken the dog by its leash and led it away.

It was a tantalizing idea, one I didn't know what to do

with. It wasn't proof of anything. Or was it? Apologizing to both animals, I left them at home and went for a walk, not quite sure where I was headed until I ended up there, or right across the street at least, slouching in a doorway like a spy, staring at the Louvre apartments.

A man came out with two poodles; the same two I'd encountered before. They tugged him into the plantings and let fly while he pretended not to notice what they were doing. Through the plate glass of the lobby I could see Lycia Foret talking to someone while her shelties sat politely at her feet. She came out in a moment, the shelties tugging her down the sidewalk at a rapid walk. She passed the poodle owner with a nod and a pointed look at the defilement taking place among the plantings and zoomed off towards the park. Belatedly, the poodle owner steamed away in her wake. Not even considering what I was doing, I followed them. I didn't know what I wanted. I didn't know what I was after. The park was on the way home, in any case.

When we got there, Lycia was a long block ahead. The poodle owner found the first bench inside the greenery, gave a furtive look around, and slipped the leashes on both dogs. Evidently this was the usual thing. They zipped off into the shrubbery, snuffling and making treble conversation with one another while he sat back on the bench, wiping his very red forehead and settling his plump person into a slouch.

Lycia was too far ahead to catch up to. Nothing brilliant presented itself to mind, so I sat down on the bench and remarked, 'They'll wear you out, won't they?'

'I am not a dog lover,' he said sadly. 'They are not mine. I am merely stuck with them.'

'That's too bad,' I offered. 'Dogs take a lot of work if you do it right.'

'I don't want to do it at all,' he snapped. Then he sat up straight and scowled, as though at himself. 'Excuse me. I shouldn't talk this way. The dogs belong to my mother, and when she went into the hospital, she made me promise not to put them in a kennel because they're her babies. So I

promised. I'm sure they're perfectly nice animals and a lot
of company, but all they do is interrupt my train of thought
by whining to go out.'

'I see,' I said. 'You . . . ah, need to concentrate.'

He agreed with this, without giving any indication why
concentration was necessary. We sat in uncompanionable
silence, watching the dogs chase one another. Finally, he
said, 'I'm working on the ice-cube series.'

'Ah?' I said.

'I'm an inventor,' he offered by way of clarification.

'Ah!' I said again.

'The spider in the ice cube was mine. That sold very well.
When we were finished with it, it looked remarkably real.
Off centre, you know, so as not to look purposefully planted.
We tried all kinds. The long-legged ones work better . . .'

'Spider?'

'In an ice cube. For putting in drinks. Joke.'

'Ah.'

'That's what I invent. Joke products. I've tried to use
these animals for inspiration, but all the jokes to do with
dogs have already been taken . . .'

'I see,' I said. 'You mean like the plastic . . .'

'Yes. That's always been a good seller.'

'As a joke?'

'In the salad at parties, or on someone's bed. You know.'
I disclaimed any direct experience with faux dog excrement
in the salad or on the bed. 'My name's Jason Lynx,' I
offered. 'I have a shop over on Hyde Street.'

'Willie Stevenson,' he said, offering me a limp hand. 'The
spider sold so well that they want me to come up with some
other things to put in ice cubes. Not real cubes, of course.
Plastic ones. I've been thinking about fish . . .'

'Small fish,' I suggested sympathetically.

'Minnows,' he agreed. 'Little silvery ones. Somehow that
doesn't have the proper . . . oh, I don't know, impact.'

I couldn't think of any comment to make about that. He
pursed his lips and glowered. I presumed this was his
concentration expression and did not interrupt him. We sat,

he thinking of horrors to inflict upon the innocent, I thinking of my own horrors if it turned out Lycia was guilty.

After a time Lycia came back, jogging gently along behind the shelties. She saw me, waved and said hello, but didn't stop. Willie Stevenson rose to his feet and called the poodles. They came to his call, albeit reluctantly. Someone had trained them well.

'You really should walk them more often,' I said. 'You know, they can't hold it forever.'

'I know.' He gave me a guilty look. 'I usually take them out whenever I hear Mrs Foret go out. I live right across the hall, so whenever I hear her talking to the dogs, in the hall, you know, I take the poodles out. She's kind of my reminder.'

'Sometimes, maybe you don't hear her,' I suggested, remembering the morning I had first gone into the Louvre, the morning the poodle had almost peed on my leg.

'When the girl goes, I don't hear her,' he agreed. 'The Foret girl never talks to the dogs in the hall.' He regarded the two pups without either interest or malice. 'I'm really not a dog person. I'm not a cat person either. I'm just not interested in animals.'

Except spiders, I thought. And minnows. 'Well, we'll hope you won't have to look after them too much longer.'

He nodded solemnly without responding, and went in the direction Lycia had gone, leaving me to follow. I thought that in one sense it was a pity the poodles weren't his dogs. If they had been with him last fall, he might have been following Lycia on the October day when Melody had died.

Mark hinted for a progress report several times during the next few days, but I put him off. I had a seven-point-buck dilemma draped over the fender of my car, and no idea how to skin it or butcher it. On the one side, I had this passionate belief that Lycia couldn't kill anyone. But, just but, if she had, I wasn't at all sure I wanted to do anything about it. On the other hand, such evidence as we had indicated that she had at least thought about doing so and had probably been blackmailed because of it.

If Fred actually had blackmailed her. If that's where the money had come from. And where else?

I'd spent a lot of futile time trying to think where I might get more information. There were only a few sources who might tell me anything more. Sally Streeter maybe. If Fred had said a little more to her than she'd so far been willing to tell us. Greg Steinwale maybe. If Melody had said something to him, and he'd been paying enough attention to remember. Shannon Foret maybe. If Melody had confided in her, which didn't seem really likely, but there had been that strange, teasing relationship the art instructor had referred to. Though, how would one ask Shannon personal questions without sending her into hysterics?

Or I could get Marge's number from Silas, call her, and tell her I was bowing out.

Or I could lose the manuscript. I considered that for a while. William Sandiman, my old mentor at the Smithsonian, was often fond of saying, 'When in doubt, do nothing.' I took off my memory hat to Sandiman and resolved to do nothing at all for a while. I told myself maybe I'd get an idea in the middle of the night. Maybe it would all come to me in a blaze of celestial fire. Besides, I had a legitimate excuse for stalling for a day or two: I had another project in hand, one dealing with Nellie Arpels and Willamae Belling. I had written their names in my notebook, with a message to myself beneath: 'Since you have no aged mother of your own to cosset, take these lonely old ladies to lunch.'

'A worthy project,' I said aloud, trying to convince myself it was an adequate excuse to quit fumbling with the Steinwale-Foret puzzle.

'Were you talking to me?' asked Mark from his office.

'No.' I gave him what I confidently hoped was an angelic smile. 'I was telling myself to go out and do a good deed.'

'I didn't know you were a Boy Scout,' he mumbled. 'If you really want to do a good deed, find a shower curtain for Gladys. I can't find anything the right colour.'

'White,' I said. 'Buy a white one and take it over to that friend of yours who paints T-shirts.'

'Belly-boy?'

'If that's his name.'

'His name is Horatio Bell Hutchins III. And he only paints things that are either erotic or scurrilous.'

'Ask him to make an exception,' I suggested. 'As *his* good deed for the day.'

Mark's lips curled in a magnificent sneer. 'He claims to be a decorator of ephemera.'

'Tell him shower curtains are at least as ephemeral as T-shirts.' They were, too. When they get soap-scummy, four people out of five throw them away and buy new ones rather than try to clean them. At least so my acquaintance down at the Bath Shoppe had once alleged as he looked fondly over rainbow acres of shower curtains and stroked his cash register. 'Besides, they offer a wider scope. How much can you paint on a T-shirt?'

'Belly gets quite a lot on. One of the priests over at Blessed Sacrament wanted the Sistine Chapel ceiling on one.'

'All of it?'

'I think it was just the creation of Adam. Or Eve. One of them. No, it was Adam, because Belly painted him with an erection and the priest refused to pay him.'

'If he can do Michelangelo, he can do Gladys Duchesne's shower curtain. Have him do the same kinds of flowers as are on the wallpaper. Flowers are the sexual organs of plants, and he can be as erotic as he likes with them.'

I was trying hard, but even this silliness hadn't made me forget for one instant that I was suspecting Lycia Foret of murder. And Harriet, of course, though it seemed to be Lycia I chiefly regretted. All the nonsense did was delay the issue, making it less immediate. As would my good deed, which had assumed major-project dimensions.

Definition of *project*: Any job which requires more than one phone call to complete.

Definition of *major project*: Any job which requires more than one phone call and the cooperation of another person.

Taking Nellie to lunch wouldn't be easy. She had been out of her second-floor bedroom in the house across the alley only once in recent years. I figured one strong man could carry her down while I went ahead with the chair, if Janice Fetterling, Nellie's daughter, would agree. I could hire a hospital worker to do that. We'd go by Ambu-Cab, if Janice would go along to take care of any personal or sanitary matters that might come up. I had already checked with a few restaurants to find one that was what is euphemistically called 'handicap accessible'. This can mean that while they have a toilet large enough for a wheelchair, the tables are set so close together that no wheelchair can reach the toilets. Anyhow, I'd done the homework, and had decided on a new place on Seventeenth Avenue, which, though it looked exactly like the restaurant that had been there before, had the advantage of good reviews on the food and table spacing adequate to guarantee mobility for Nellie.

I'd also invited Willamae Belling, begging her to come as a favour to me. I'd told her I needed her along to make conversation with Nellie—as though Nellie had ever had any trouble conversing with anyone who happened by. Since the expedition was to be the following day, I had only today to buy each of the ladies a gift to make the occasion festive, one for Nellie for being herself, one for Willamae for being such a nice client, and something special for Janice for being helpful and coming along. I went out to do so, leaving Mark to struggle with the shower curtain.

Also, after the shopping trip I had another appointment with the plastic surgeon, and the least said about that, the better. That night I took my pain pills and slept on my stomach.

The fated day arrived. Janice and Nellie and I arrived at the restaurant to find Willamae already ensconced. I introduced the ladies. Nellie took one look at her and shrieked, 'Willa-*mae* Foster! Is that you?' And we were off to the races.

I don't know why Janice and I were along. We agreed that the weather had been nice. That Denver certainly was bigger than when we were children. That we wished it was more the way it used to be. That the restaurant was nicely decorated though a little noisy. That the food was very good. Meantime, Willamae Belling née Foster and Nellie Arpels née Wyler were reliving old times seventy years ago, around the time of World War I

It turned out that Willa-*mae* Foster (pronounced with the accent on the *mae* rather than the more gentil *Will-* amae I had assumed) had moved away when she married. When she returned, some years later, she had no idea her old school friend had stayed in town or what her name was. So, suddenly, here they were, and I smiled and nodded and said yes, ma'am, it really was amazing, and thanked whatever gods might be that they had been friends back then, not enemies.

'Remember Calvin Boome?' Willamae asked. 'Did you ever see his books? Remember Louise Storm?'

'Stormy,' mourned Nellie. 'She died real young. Only forty.'

'Drank herself to death,' said Willamae. 'She was so fun.'

'Remember Jackson Wetherbee and that Cosson girl?'

Both of them dissolved in giggles.

'Remember Cora Frame?' Nellie said. 'Wasn't that awful?' Willamae got a prissy expression and shook her head. 'Did you believe she didn't know?'

'Oh, I don't think she knew,' Nellie said. Then, catching my half smile of dazed incomprehension: 'Cora was a girl we knew. She was adopted, only she never knew it. People didn't used to tell their adopted children, you know, Jason. Anyhow, she fell in love and married this man, and he was adopted, too, and after they were married and she was expecting a baby, somebody told him he was adopted and it turned out they were full brother and sister. Willamae and me, we knew her. She was in school with us.'

'I just always thought something should have told her he was her brother,' Willamae asserted. 'She should have known.'

'They didn't look anything alike,' Nellie objected. 'They

didn't, Willamae. He was dark and she was light. She was a little bit of a thing and he was stocky. I don't know why you think she would have known. Animals don't know, and if anybody ought to, they should.'

'What happened to them?' Janice asked around a mouthful of quiche.

'It was annulled,' said Willamae with a grimace.

'And the baby?'

Nellie shook her head. 'Nobody ever knew what happened to the baby. Cora left. Just went right away. Maybe she had it and gave it up.' She chewed reflectively. 'It's a wise child knows its own father, Willamae. I was saying that to Jason just the other day.'

We had a good lunch. Afterward, Willamae came back to Nellie's with us and visited a while, and when she left she said she'd be over to visit again real soon.

Janice made a hmphy noise at me as I was leaving. 'If Mama starts having visitors, I'll have to clean house more,' she said.

'Do you care?' I asked her.

'Not if it'll make Mama happy,' she said with a kind of half smile. She was wearing some of the perfume I'd given her.

The next day was Friday. We plunged into work. I got a pile of invoices figured, talked to Myron, made a pest of myself over the Duchesne job, finally had Eugenia tell me to go back to my office and leave her alone.

Mark came in as I sat staring at the wall.

'What's the matter?'

I grumped something.

'Something's the matter, Jason. You don't usually go all over itchy like this unless something is.'

'I don't think Lycia Foret killed Melody Steinwale,' I said. 'I don't care how many outlines she wrote.' So then by way of explanation I had to show him the paper and tell him about the money.

'I wish Grace was here,' he said. 'She could go ask questions.'

I pondered this. Pondered whether I wanted Grace there, asking questions about Lycia Foret. I decided, on balance, I did.

I'd mentioned my strange attraction to Lycia. Now Mark asked, 'What is it with the woman, Jason? Is she beautiful or what?'

I couldn't answer that. I had no idea or what. She wasn't that beautiful. And she was older than I by some years. And she was spoken for. And I was inexplicably drawn to her. I threw up my hands.

'I think you'd better really dig into this,' Mark said with a serious look. 'If you really like her and think she's innocent, then you'd better get busy and prove it. Otherwise, Marge Beebe will come back and decide to turn all the stuff over to the police, and maybe it will be too late.'

'I have no idea where to go next,' I confessed.

'Well, usually when you don't have any idea where to go next, you sort of mull around through the mud until something jumps into the water and goes plop,' he said.

Which was a good enough description of the way I conduct myself.

So I made a list of all the mulling around I might do, and that took a good part of the day. At four o'clock, Mark came in, very pale, and said, 'Jason, we're in trouble.'

I looked up, wondering who was suing us for what this time. 'Belly-boy left town.'

'So?'

'He had the shower curtain. I told him I'd pick it up this afternoon, but when I got down there, he'd left town. Some relative of his died. The place is locked up.'

I found myself thinking that Belly-boy's relative might not be the only one who died. If Gladys Duchesne didn't get her guest rooms finished on time . . .

'What time are Gladys's in-laws arriving?'

'Seven. Tonight.'

'Where does your friend Belly live?'

He told me. Luckily, not one of the better parts of town. I

got out the lock picks and we went, with Mark muttering at my side. Words and phrases like 'You don't really mean to . . . You wouldn't really . . . What if we get caught . . . ?'

Jacob taught me to pick locks. One needs to in this business. People lock their desks or their dressers or whatever, and then they move away or die and somebody sells the furniture. It doesn't do an antique dealer's reputation any good to provide the vicarage with a seven-drawer high-boy full of unsuspected pornography or provide a little girl's desk fully equipped with lurid love letters. Therefore, one picks locks. I had found a few interesting things in my time, and a few I wish I hadn't.

Belly's place was an apartment in the near downtown north or largely ethnic side of town. Mark kept watch while I fiddled. I almost had it when the door across the hall opened and a brass trumpet of a voice demanded to know what we were doing.

Without a moment's hesitation, Mark said, 'Belly told me to feed his cat while he's at the funeral,' Mark drawled. 'But the key he gave me doesn't work. So I called the locksmith.'

'Oh,' said the voice. The door slammed, and I got the one I was working on open. The shower curtain was spread across Belly's worktable, a symphony of coral blossoms, each, if one cared to look closely, very reminiscent of certain aspects of human female anatomy.

'Oh, Lord,' said Mark.

'She'll never notice,' I told him.

'The in-laws will!'

'They'll be far too well bred to comment.'

I folded the curtain into its box and the two of us went scurrying away with it, like two white rabbits, muttering and looking at our watches. We let ourselves into the Duchesne house. I could hear voices in the back of the house, Gladys's high one and someone else. We slipped upstairs like thieves, and entered the redone guest suite. The wallpaper on the fireplace wall was an all-over coral and lavender floral on cream. The colours were picked up in the love seats and in the curtains. The carpet was cream, and so was the bed-cover. The rattan chairs had been sprayed lavender, with coral and white striped cushions. There were two large lamps with creamy shades next to the bed, and I tried them to be sure they worked and had large enough bulbs. We had used the tables from our shop. There were tissues in the drawers, along with a few readable books. We hung the shower curtain, straightened the towels, sneaked back down the stairs, and left the keys on the hall table. Gladys should be happy. Her brother the banker should be happy. He shouldn't call my loan before I was ready to repay it. I crossed my fingers and prayed.

The thought of the half million in the safe in the basement fled across my mind. I told the thought to begone, a little shocked that I'd been tempted. Jacob had taught me not to be a thief, and it was the first time I'd considered stealing in years.

Thinking of the loan, I made a mental note to call Myron and ask him how he was coming with our sale. Then Mark went off to his place and I went home in a sober mood to feed animals and refer to the list on my desk. Beginning tomorrow, if Myron gave me bad news, I was going to start scrounging for cash money. If Myron gave me good news, I was going to stir mud. I needed Grace to help me stir mud. And for other reasons. I called her.

'Jason,' said a weary little voice. 'What time is it?'

'About suppertime,' I told her. 'What are you doing asleep?'

'We got Ron out of jail. So he brought a bunch of his rowdy friends over here to celebrate and I didn't get to sleep all night.'

'You got him out? Great!'

'It was a plea bargain. We didn't even need the lawyer. He'll be in again inside a year, Jason. He doesn't have any sense. He talks this serious line about staying out of trouble, but he can't say no to anything.'

'Are you coming home?'

'Tomorrow,' she said. 'My plane gets there at six in the evening.'

A feeling of pure pleasure welled up from somewhere, and I stopped worrying about Lycia Foret.

I met her at the airport, took her home, helped her unpack. She looked worn out, and I suggested she catch a night's sleep and I'd see her the next day. She shook her head, looking sad and lonely, eyes squinched half shut.

'He hasn't learned anything, huh?' I asked. 'You really think he'll just get into trouble again?'

'I really do,' she said, crying. I gathered her up and we sat on the couch, her snuffling and me rocking her. 'What's worst is, I decided there was nothing I could do. I could keep running out there all the time, but it wouldn't do any good. He just hasn't any *sense*, Jason!'

I rocked and murmured nothing much.

She said the same thing three or four times, in different words, then there was quiet. I looked down to find her fast asleep. The only thing that would help brother Ron, so far as I could see, was if somebody hired him a keeper. He had that self-conscious naïveté Grace had often described as common among some youngsters, the kind that says, 'Oh, yes, I know there's tigers out there, but they won't bite *me*.' And they never believe the tigers will either, until they look down and find themselves disembowelled and the beast readying for the final blow. It always comes as a surprise. The girls who end up with a pimp, amazed that any such thing could have happened. The boys who end up in jail, sentenced to life, not knowing quite how.

I laid Grace on her bed, covered her with a blanket, and went out to get some food. I figured she'd wake up and be hungry, and there wasn't anything to eat in the house. While I was at it, I stopped by the shop and picked up Critter. He'd be company for Grace. When he got home, he explored every inch of the apartment, being sure all the pieces were there. His inspection included a few deep, diagnostic sniffs of the sleeping woman on the bed. Then he settled down on the couch and began to purr, as though some unhappy suspicion had been allayed. He had not been abandoned after all, merely sent on leave.

She woke up about ten to sit on the couch stroking Critter while I fed her supermarket burritos with cheese and green chiles and corn chips and guacamole and fruit salad and cookies and told her the latest about the case. Told her more, perhaps, than I'd intended. When I'd told her about it before, I hadn't dwelt upon Lycia.

'You say you think you recognize this Lycia woman?' she asked.

'Not exactly,' I said, unsure of what I'd said. 'It's a funny feeling . . .'

'Maybe you *do* recognize her,' Grace said firmly. 'The thing you've got to remember, Jason, is you were three years old when you were left at the Home. Kids that age can remember a lot, but not in words. They're really just starting to talk well then. So they remember faces and smells and sounds. This Lycia may look a lot like someone you remember, your mom or some other person who took care of you.'

I felt the back of my neck, feeling the spiky scabby little knots of hair growing there in the old scar tissue. 'I didn't think anyone had taken care of me.'

'Somebody did,' she averred. 'Even though you got hurt when you were real little, before you got hurt somebody took care of you.'

I wasn't persuaded, though it was possible. If Lycia resembled someone I had known, perhaps loved, as a child, it could explain my unwillingness to believe she had done anything bad, my desire to find any other explanation.

'Who are you going to talk to next?' Grace wanted to know. I told her my three sources. Streeter. Greg. And lovely little Shannon. 'I haven't any idea how to approach Shannon,' I confessed. 'She's like a butterfly. I'm afraid if I come too close I'll cripple her.'

'Let me do that,' Grace suggested. 'She's less likely to fly to pieces if some woman talks to her, particularly someone not a lot older than she is. Besides, I've got a legitimate reason. The case is still open, so I can take some of my own time to go back and look at Melody's murder again.'

'Shannon's taking some classes,' I suggested. 'You'd probably do better if you find her somewhere away from the family. Sometimes she walks the shelties, though I think she stays away from the park.'

'Leave it to me,' she said with a yawn. 'Suddenly I'm so sleepy again.'

I took the hint. When I left, she was curled up on the bed with Critter across her feet, the two of them making a corporate noise somewhere between a snore and a purr.

Since I was leaving Shannon to Grace—who would get to it as soon as she could—I decided to try Streeter again. She'd given us her number when we had talked to her at the Pancake House, so I called her the following morning and asked if she'd mind having lunch with me. She was doubtful, a little hesitant, but I told her we'd come up with some questions maybe she could help us with. I'd jotted down some notes. There was the money, of course. Plus the manuscript Lycia had written. Plus Fred's relationship with Melody Steinwale. That's what I really wanted to talk about.

Despite her hesitation, Sally Streeter seemed slightly more relaxed than the last time we'd talked with her. 'I've decided to forgive and forget,' she said with a rueful smile. 'I was spending too much time hating him. So I just decided to put it down to experience and forget it.'

'Not quite yet,' I begged her. 'There are three things we really need to know more about.'

'Three?'

'Fred's sister found a lot of money, cash, that Fred had hidden. We haven't a clue as to where it came from . . .'

Her face stayed blank, but a wave of red washed over it. So. She knew something about that.

'Then there's that book you told us about, the one he said his wife was writing. And last there's his relationship with the young woman you saw him with, Melody Steinwale.'

She fiddled with her food, thinking. 'Honestly,' she said,

'I don't know anything about the book except what I told you.'

'Which means you do know something about the other two things,' I said softly. 'Come on, Sal.'

She fiddled a bit more, gave me a quick look out of the sides of her eyes, then told me, almost in a whisper, without looking at me.

'It was a little while before . . . before I got really involved with him and then moved. I was in his apartment. I used to take him things to eat, and sometimes he'd offer me some coffee or a drink and we'd talk. I'd talk about my husband, and he'd talk about himself. So this time I was there, having a drink, and the phone rang, and he answered it and said her name. "Melody?" Like that.'

'You overheard the conversation,' I suggested.

'I didn't eavesdrop!' she exclaimed. 'I didn't.'

'I didn't think you did. You were sitting in the living-room, and Fred was on the phone right around the corner in the hall, right? You couldn't help but hear.' I hadn't seen Fred's apartment, but I'd seen one in the same building and there was a phone alcove with a built-in seat and table in the hall. It was a pretty good bet all the apartments were very much alike.

'I couldn't help but hear,' she agreed.

'And what did he say?'

'He didn't say anything at first. Then he said, "Besides having influence in high places, my sweet, I have enough to make life interesting, as I've told you before." Then he didn't say anything, then he said, "I have it. What I do with it is my business."'

She took a mouthful, without seeming to taste it, washed it down with iced tea, then went back to playing with her food.

'Sally?'

'Then he said, "That's pure supposition on your part." And "You'd have a hard time proving that." And, finally, "You little witch, try it and you'll be sorry." Then he hung up.'

'Was that all?'

'That was all, except he was furious. I could tell from the way he spoke. Those might not be the exact words he used, but pretty close. As soon as he hung up, I went into the kitchen with my glass, pretending I hadn't heard him, because he was really angry, and when he got angry, he was mean. When he came in the kitchen, he had red patches up on his cheekbones and he was breathing funny. He told me I should leave because he had to go out, very harshly, just like that. Like "Get out, Sally, get out of my way."'

'When was this, Sally?'

'Oh, when was it? I don't know. It was three or four days before I took my gun back and waved it at him . . .'

'Took your gun *back*?'

'He . . . he took it that same day. That day he had the phone conversation.'

'Sally!'

She bridled. 'Well, he did! He told me he had to go, so I left. Then, about an hour after that, he showed up at my apartment and asked me if I still had the little gun my husband gave me, and when I said yes, he said he'd take it someplace for me and have it cleaned and oiled.'

'And you gave it to him.'

'I don't know about those things. Don't you have them cleaned and oiled, like a car? I thought he was being kind, because he was sorry he'd been so abrupt.'

Honestly! Some women! 'You gave him your gun.'

'Yes. And he brought it back to me a few days later, and that's when . . . when he stayed at my place.'

'And you ended up waving it at him . . .'

'Because it was right there, in the box he'd brought it back in, on the coffee table. Usually it would have been at the back of the closet shelf, and I couldn't have waved it at anybody, but it was right there that time. But he took it away from me.'

'And he never gave it back.'

'No. I don't know what happened to it.'

'Do you happen to know what kind of gun it was?'

'A little one,' she said doubtfully. 'It held six bullets. A twenty-two? Does that sound right?'

I cut and chewed and ruminated. After a time, I asked, 'Sally, what did you think Fred's conversation with Melody meant?'

She flushed brick red. 'I think he was talking about sex. About having enough of it to make life interesting even though he was a lot older than her.'

'How about the "influence in high places"?'

'Oh, he was always saying that. He meant people he'd met in Washington or on the peace walks. I tried to tell him once they didn't even remember his name. You think the Prime Minister of England remembered the name of this guy trailing along after these kids with these candles? She might have been smiling a nice political smile, but she was thinking about the kids probably spilling candle wax on her carpets, believe me. When I told him that, Fred got real angry. That's the time he hit me. After that, I never disagreed with him.'

'And the rest of the conversation with Melody?'

'I told you he wanted to go to bed with her. I just know he did. He'd probably been propositioning her. So she said something nasty to him, like the thing he said to me. About his not being up to her standard or something.' She heaved a breath that was like a dry sob, and I reached across the table to pat her hand.

'Come on, Sally. He was a bastard. So you think she said something snide, do you?'

'I think she did. Something about his being too old or something. Then he said she was assuming, she couldn't prove it, and she said something even worse, and he called her a witch. Or maybe it was a bitch, I don't know.'

'When you knew he was angry at her, and then when he took your gun, and then when you read in the papers about her being shot, did you connect it up?'

She turned away from me, tears starting in her eyes. 'Oh . . . oh, of course I did. I'm not stupid. Of course I did. But then I talked myself out of it. I told myself nobody would

shoot somebody else just because that person didn't want
to go to bed with them. That's not enough reason to kill
somebody!'

I didn't really think so either. I made a few notes in my
pocket notebook, and asked, 'What about the money, Sally?'

'I saw it once. A whole box of it. He didn't know I saw.
I went over with some pie, and knocked, and he didn't
answer, but the door was open, so I just went in. And he
was in the living-room, bent over the coffee table, stuffing
all this money in a box . . .'

'You didn't tell him you saw it?'

'I went back out, to my own place, and I never said a
word. I'll tell you the truth, Mr Lynx. It scared me, there
was so much of it. What went through my head was drugs.
The only time I've ever seen that much money was on TV,
when they were doing drug deals, you know? And then,
later, when I had a chance to think, I knew how silly that
was. Whatever Fred was doing, it wasn't drugs. But it was
his business, and he got nasty when people interfered with
his business, so I never said anything.'

'When did you see the money?' I asked.

She shook her head. 'I can't remember. Last summer, I
think. It could have been before. I was his neighbour for
almost two years.'

I thought about it. If Fred had been blackmailing Lycia,
it had to be after Melody had died. But Sally hadn't seen
the money after Melody had died, because she'd broken
with Fred right after that happened. Was the money Sally
had seen some other money? Had he made a career of
blackmailing people?

We finished our pie and our coffee and I took Sally back
to her apartment building lobby, where she was greeted
with squeals of delight by three equally plump ladies who
wanted a fourth for bridge. I left her in their generous hands,
hoping I wouldn't have to bother her again.

The conversation she had overheard did not fit in with
anything else I knew about the Steinwale-Foret puzzle. It
had to be connected somehow. I ran over the sequence in

my mind. Fred had met Melody at a birthday party given for his daughter Shannon, had built on the acquaintance with Melody, and had propositioned Melody. That much was understandable. But the rest of it? That business about 'You'd have a hard time proving that.' Somehow that didn't sound like a sexual challenge.

Suppose Melody had found out that Fred was blackmailing someone. Not Lycia, someone else. Somehow, Melody puts two and two together and says to Fred, 'You don't have enough money to interest me, Fred.'

And he says, 'Aside from friends in high places, I have enough to make life interesting.'

And she says, 'Better be careful how you spend it, Fred.'

And he says, 'I've got it. How I use it is my business.'

And she says, 'I know where you got the money, Fred. You got it illegally.'

And he says, 'You're assuming that.'

And she says, 'You got it by blackmail.'

And he says, 'You'd have a hard time proving that.'

And she says, 'I could give some information to the police.'

And he says, 'You try that and you'll regret it, you little witch.' Or words to that effect. At which point, Fred borrows the gun from his neighbour lady, kills Melody, then cleans and oils the gun, pretends he's had it at a gun shop when he returns it to his neighbour. Then he goes to bed with the neighbor lady . . . Why? To establish an alibi? With some vague idea of getting her on his side in case anyone ever got suspicious?

Though Sally had talked herself out of believing her gun killed Melody, I wasn't at all sure it hadn't. Fred hadn't returned it. With Sally mad at him, perhaps he had had second thoughts about the wisdom of giving her a gun that could link him to murder.

How could I prove that's what had happened?

It only made sense if Melody knew about the blackmail! If Lycia knew Fred blackmailed people, she could have told Ross and Shannon could have overheard. Or Lycia might have told Harriet and Melody might have overheard that conversation, or Greg might have overheard, in which case he might have told his wife. Unless Fred, full of braggadocio, had told her about it himself.

No good to ask Ross or Lycia. No good to ask Harriet. Greg was so centred on his art, he probably wouldn't remember. Shannon was probably our best bet.

Grace would have to find a way to ask her if she had ever heard Fred Foret's name associated with blackmail.

It was only then that I remembered Greg's remark at his birthday dinner about sticky fingers. Melody had told Greg that Fred had sticky fingers. Greg had mentioned it; then Ross had interjected a comment, and I'd never asked him what he meant. I made a note. When I talk to Greg, ask him again what he had meant by sticky fingers.

Grace picked up a pizza and brought it to my place that night. We raided the wine cellar for something Italian and she stuffed herself with over one-half of a very large double-cheese hold-nothing pizza while I had two small pieces and Bela got the last ones. I'm sure some animal-rights person probably would hold me culpable for feeding Bela pepperoni sausage, olives, and anchovies, but he'd have been crushed to have been left out.

Afterward, Grace allowed as how she felt like spending the night with me. I asked her if my lascivious comments or my playing kneesies with her during supper had influenced her in any way. She said she hadn't noticed. I inquired whether my breathing heavily at her all evening had caught her attention, and she disclaimed any knowledge of such breathing. She said she just felt friendly. As a matter of fact, she felt extremely friendly for some little time. When she had finished feeling friendly, I gasped for air, washed my face in cold water, and then came back to bed to accept her head on my shoulder and put my arms around her silky bare skin. After feeling friendly (as well as before, but, thank God, not during) Grace usually feels either hungry or talkative. We talked about what Sally Streeter had had to say.

'You think he killed Melody?' Grace wanted to know.

'Only if he had a reason. It could have been because she spurned him, though I find that a little remote. A sexual refusal, even one accompanied by some raillery, wouldn't have been enough reason, not even for Fred. He'd have hit her for that, not shot her.'

'But if she knew something incriminating and threatened to go to the police?'

'It's all assumption, Grace. In order to establish a motive, we have to prove that there was blackmail and that Melody knew about it.'

'I'll talk to Shannon tomorrow,' she sighed, turning over and pressing her warm bottom against me.

'Be careful.'

'It's all right, Jason. I've met trembly little girls before. Sometimes they're only that trembly when the family is around.'

CHAPTER 6

I called Trish the next morning, told her I was looking into Fred's death for Marge, and also told her there seemed to be some connection between Fred's death and Melody's. I didn't go into the actual connections, most of which were rather theoretical, but I did mention the way the two bodies had been similarly arranged and the fact that the two victims had known each other and had talked occasionally in the park.

'Do you think Greg would talk to me about Melody?' I asked her.

Long silence.

'Jason, he's just getting over . . .' Another long silence. A sigh. 'It might be therapeutic.'

'Is he still grieving over her?'

'No. It's not grieving. I don't know what it is.'

'You'd be welcome to sit in . . .'

'No. No. Maybe talking about it would be good for him. I'll make a lunch date for you, how's that?'

I told her that would be fine, anytime, even today. She called back in about ten minutes, saying today. I said I'd pick him up at the studio about one, then spent twenty minutes trying to remember a restaurant with enough privacy so that our conversation wouldn't be remarked upon. There was a little French place on East Colfax that was usually half empty by one-thirty, which was probably as early as we'd get around to conversation. I made a reservation.

I was at my desk by eight, in time to receive a call from Gladys Duchesne. She said the putative in-laws loved the guest rooms. So comfortable. So colourful. Such an original shower-curtain design. The Mifflins wanted to know where they could get one like it. Such a pity the Mifflin son and the Duchesne daughter had had a big fight over the weekend and there wouldn't be a wedding after all.

I told Mark and we both broke up laughing, though Eugenia didn't find it in the least funny.

'All that work!' she fumed. 'That impossible deadline with virtually no profit, and there isn't to be a wedding!'

Mark and I decided later she'd been hoping for an invitation. Myron called, returning my call. Yes, the deal looked like it was going through on the furniture. I sighed a deep sigh, realizing for the first time just how worried I'd actually been. It looked like Fred's mystery money was safe, and I wouldn't have to fight temptation.

When I picked Greg up, I noted that Trish had managed to get him into a clean shirt and tie and jacket, though his eyes seemed still focused on something in the studio. By the time we'd driven across town, he'd come to a little, and he approached the restaurant and the menu fully conscious. He ordered lamb. So did I, telling them to please cook it pink, not raw. Steak, as in tartare, I can take raw; fish, as in sashimi, I can take raw; but not lamb.

'You had some questions about Melody?' he asked as he buttered a roll and took a big bite out of it, spraying crumbs in all directions and surprising me considerably. I'd thought I'd have to sneak up on the subject.

'I need to know more about what she was like,' I said. 'You probably knew her better than anyone.'

He shook his head, as though disagreeing. 'I knew her,' he admitted. 'I think.'

'What was she like?'

He got a faraway look. 'She could be angelic,' he said. 'Like a sylph. Like a pet bird. She could be funny. She could make me laugh. She could do sweet things that made me feel loved and cared for. And then she could turn around and be someone else. Sometimes I wanted never to see her again. Sometimes I wanted to lock her up to keep her out of trouble. She was always getting into trouble . . .'

I waited. He was gone somewhere. I needed to bring him back. 'What kind of trouble?' I prompted.

'With men. She flirted. All the time. With everybody. She was seductive. She seemed . . . oh, I don't know. Edible. Like cotton candy. Sweet, and luscious, and . . . insubstantial. Inconsequential. As though you could have her and it wouldn't matter. It wouldn't lead to anything . . . And then she'd be hurt.'

I waited again. He sighed, accepted his soup, and began to eat it hungrily. I didn't prompt him again. After a time, he said, 'When she got hurt, she'd begin spending money. Or she'd start saying we had to have a house of our own. Or something. Whenever her feelings got hurt, she'd start accumulating things. Shoes. Jackets. Even putting deposits on furniture for the house we didn't have . . .'

'I understand your mother offered you a house.'

'Yes. A modest house. Mom was right. Wherever we lived should have been within our means to maintain. Melody didn't want that. She wanted . . . I don't know what she wanted. Whatever she had, it was never enough.'

'Did she ever mention Fred Foret?'

'He was one of her conquests, that's all. She always told me about them. As though to tell me that other men found her attractive. She knew I loved her, but I couldn't always give her the things she wanted, so then she'd tell me . . . about other men liking her. Or she'd wear something Rich had given her. It was almost as though she thought, if I loved her enough, if somebody loved her enough, some miracle would happen and she'd get whatever it was she wanted.'

'She equated not getting what she wanted with not being loved enough.'

He nodded slowly. 'That's right. But no amount was ever enough. I went to Mom time after time, for this, for that, always for Melody. Eventually Mom said no, no more. In the hospital, the doctor told me that Mom was right. No matter how much Melody was loved, it could never be enough, because she was trying to make up for not loving herself, and she didn't love herself because of the way she was raised. It made sense. I could accept it. Maybe if she'd lived, we'd have . . .'

He fell silent. Our meals came, and we ate them, with me feeling like the worst kind of rat for dragging him through this again. He had obviously suffered enough.

Still, one must persevere. 'Greg, you said Melody had said something to you about Fred Foret's having "sticky fingers". Can you remember what that was about?'

He put down his fork and stared over my shoulder, that abstracted, concentrated look back on his face. 'Not really. It's just something she said about him.' He focused on my face then, as though he really saw me. 'Jason, sometimes I tried not to listen. Can you understand that? It hurt too much to listen. I just smiled and kind of made noises in my throat and didn't listen to her. She was telling me this man, this Fred Foret, who's connected with people my mother knows and likes, has propositioned her and wants her to go to bed with him, and she's making quite a song and dance out of it . . . More than usual, I mean. As though it was more important than all the other times. And I didn't want to listen. I didn't want to.'

'I don't suppose anyone else would know what was going

on there,' I said, more saddened by his tone than by the lack of information.

'Rich might know,' he said.

I cleared my throat. 'I thought she'd left Rich long before she met Fred.'

He looked at me, a clear, limpid gaze with pain at the bottom of it. 'She never left Rich,' he said. 'She always went back to Rich, now and then. She always had some new present he'd given her. Especially when I couldn't afford to give her anything much. Last Christmas, we were broke, and we agreed not to give each other presents. At Christmas dinner, Mom complimented Melody on her dress and she said Rich had given it to her.' He grinned, a brief, humourless grin. 'Needless to say, Mom wasn't pleased.'

'Did she ever say anything to you about blackmail?'

'Blackmail? No. You mean someone blackmailing her?' He sounded agitated at this.

'No, no. Someone else being blackmailed.'

He shook his head at me, then went back to his meal. When he had finished, he put his utensils beside one another, lining them up with finicky care. 'It's a funny thing. When I was married to Melody, I thought she made the sun rise and set. Only, when she'd been gone for a while, I realized how tired she made me. I was always tired around Melody, and worried, and apprehensive. Sometimes she could make me feel ecstatic, you know, but she seldom made me feel good . . .

'Trish makes me feel good. She takes charge of details, lets me get on with my work. If I yell at her about something, she says, "You're hungry. You're probably tired. After you eat and sleep, we'll talk about it." She's strong. She's calm. She knows I care for her. She doesn't ask me to prove it twenty times a day . . .' He took a sip of water. 'I love her. And yet . . . yet sometimes . . . sometimes I miss Melody so much I could cry.'

There was such yearning in his voice, I could hardly bear it. There didn't seem to be a lot to say after that. I dropped him back at the studio, hoping, whatever else he might say

to Trish, he would not say to her what he had said to me.
Honesty has to stop somewhere.

Grace had called and left a message saying she had talked
to Shannon Foret. I called her back, and she answered in
her 'official policeperson' voice, saying she would get in
touch with me later. That meant someone was at her desk,
or, considering how long she'd been gone, several persons.

Lucinda Hooper called. John had sent pictures of his new
highboy to some dealer on the Coast, asking for an appraisal.
It had come back ten thousand higher than he'd paid for
it. She sounded awed.

I bit my lip and kept my voice calm. 'That's a New York
price, Mrs Hooper. He might not get that for it here.' And
if the bastard didn't trust me, to hell with him.

'I understand,' she bubbled, 'but he's very excited. Anyhow, his birthday is next week, and I want you to pick
something out.'

I asked her how much, and she said some little thing in
the ten-thousand range. I went downstairs to see what I
had in the fifteens. Screw them.

'You have a Chippendale fire screen,' said Eugenia. 'It
has an impeccable history and is in immaculate condition.'

She was right. The thing had been around so long I'd
almost forgotten it. It was in the basement, so I went down
to fetch it. Eighteenth-century fire screens shouldn't be
confused with modern metal fire screens. The purpose was
quite different. Antique fire screens were not meant to be
put near the fire; they were meant to stand well away from
the fire and throw shade upon a person. They often came
in Ma and Pa pairs, and they have, typically, a gracefully
carved tripod leg with some turned ornamentation to lend
weight, and then a tall, slender pole. Fastened to the pole
with a brass adjusting screw is a square vertical screen
covered with needlepoint or, sometimes, printed cotton. The
screen can be raised or lowered as needed to screen the face
or hands from too much heat. The one I had was mahogany
with the screen worked in an all-over needlepoint design of

formalized roses and leaves. It stood about five feet tall, and the screen measured a few inches less than two feet square. Because they look a little bit like folding tables, some of them have been converted into tables, or vice versa. Converted tables are worth far less. This one was and had always been a fire screen, and the needlework was original and in good condition.

Chippendale and Hepplewhite-style fire screens are rare and expensive. Good American ones are worth more than most English or European ones, because there are fewer of them. The one I had had been in the same family for two centuries, had moved from Connecticut to St Louis in the 1800s, and from there to Kansas City at the turn of the century, and then to Denver. It had only been sold when the last surviving family member had died. The needlepoint was quite faded, as it would be, and the stand showed wear on the feet and on the adjusting pole, as it should. Dealers call this wear 'patina', a combination of tiny scratches and abrasions resulting from use. One never, never 'refinishes' to get rid of patina, though a quick rub with furniture polish is acceptable. Eugenia gave it the cleanup while I vacuumed the needlepoint screen, and we set it aside to show Lucinda Hooper.

'Of course, you're going to ask twice what it's worth,' Eugenia said sarcastically.

'Tell her fifteen thousand,' I said. 'Which is what it would sell for on the Coast. And a letter from me establishing its provenance.' Provenance is important when antiques are regarded as investments. Later purchasers may want to know who originally owned it and where the dealer got it.

'It was tagged at ten,' she complained.

'It's now tagged at fifteen.' I smiled sweetly. 'That'll give you bargaining room.' Actually, I'd paid almost seven for it at auction. We also polished up an Empire pedestal-base card table and a little Queen Anne country tea table. Myron had paid eight thou for the one and six for the other, at a winter auction in the middle of a blizzard with nobody there but him and, as he put it, three other lazy dealers. The

Queen Anne had had a loose leg, but the pieces were all there and after I'd repaired it, the only thing newer than 1714 was the glue. Once the selection was complete and I'd tagged the tables at fourteen and thirteen thou, respectively, I went back upstairs and left Eugenia to deal with Mrs Hooper. Any of the items would be a reasonable buy and would hold their value very well, or there were other things in the showrooms that might appeal.

Grace called me back about suppertime. I invited her over, and she showed up breathless, with a tape recorder in one hand and a sheaf of papers in the other.

'I recorded her,' she said. 'I had it hidden in my purse.'

'Is that legal?'

'This was unofficial,' she explained. 'On my own time.'

'What's all the paper?'

'The file on the two killings. Nothing there of any help, Jason. I just thought you might want to see them.'

'Is that legal?'

She grinned at me and wrinkled her nose. It wasn't legal. Or, rather, it wasn't in accordance with regulations, put it that way. While she threw together a vast and eclectic salad in my kitchen, I skimmed the files. She was right. There was nothing there of any help and almost nothing I didn't already know except the time of death for Melody. From the stomach contents, coffee and a roll, consumed, according to Harriet Steinwale's cook, at six-thirty in the morning, Melody had died about seven. When we sat down to our salads, Grace put the recorder on the table and turned it on. After the usual hiss of running tape, I heard her voice.

GRACE: I'm Detective Willis, Miss Foret. I'm interviewing people who knew Melody Steinwale, just to see if we can learn a little more about her.

SHANNON (*hesitantly*): I didn't know her all that well.

GRACE: Your art instructor says the two of you were fairly close.

SHANNON: No. That was her. She was close. She fastened herself on to me. (*The voice was petulant, almost childish.*)

GRACE: Can you tell me about that?

SHANNON (*sighing*): Mother gave me a party for my twenty-first birthday. Harriet Steinwale came down to wish me happy birthday, because Harriet is Mom's close friend, and Harriet brought her son, Greg, and his wife. Even though she lived right upstairs, I'd never really met Harriet's daughter-in-law before.

GRACE: Who else was there?

Grace tapped the off switch and said, 'This kid was really uptight, so whenever she got too nervous, I asked her something easy, okay?'

I told her it was okay with me. She got up from the table, fetched a loaf of whole-grain bread and a cube of butter, buttered three large pieces to go with her salad, sat back down, and turned the recorder back on.

SHANNON: There was our family, and Ross, and Harriet and Greg and Melody. And my father. He just showed up. And some of my friends from school, about six of them. And Keith's date. Not Stephanie, the girl he knew before. Julie somebody.

GRACE: And that's the first time you'd ever met Melody.

SHANNON: Yes. I'd seen her before, like in the elevator, but not really met her.

GRACE: But she 'fastened on to you'?

SHANNON: She did. At the party she found out I was taking an art class that summer, and later she showed up at the same class. Everyplace I went, she'd show up. Always asking me to have coffee or go out for a beer. I don't even like beer. She wouldn't listen when I said no.

GRACE: The art instructor says she stuck to you fairly tightly.

SHANNON: I couldn't get rid of her. I told her to leave me alone, I didn't like it, but she wouldn't.

The recorded voice had risen in both pitch and tempo. Grace was getting some leftover ham out of the refrigerator.

GRACE: Did she ever talk about her husband?

SHANNON (*surprised*): No. Why would she? I didn't want to hear about her husband.

GRACE: Did she ever talk about any member of your family? (*Pause.*) How about your father?

Silence.

GRACE: She did talk about your father.

SHANNON: I didn't want to hear it. I didn't want to hear any of it. She was at me all the time about it. About how he wanted her to go to bed with him. I didn't care! She asked me if I thought old men like that ought to go after young girls not much older than their daughters. She was always asking me things like that. Always wanting to talk about sex. I just didn't care! It wasn't my business. I told her to stop, but she just laughed.

GRACE: So Melody told you that your father had attempted or was attempting to seduce her.

SHANNON (*angrily*): I don't think that's the word. Seduce. He just wanted to do it to her, that's all. There wasn't any seduce. Both of them, that's all they wanted to talk about. I don't want to discuss it. It doesn't have anything to do with anything!

Grace tapped off the recorder again, finished building her ham sandwich, and refilled her salad bowl. Beneath our feet, Bela sighed. We weren't eating anything he especially liked.

'Where did you conduct this interview?' I asked.

'In her apartment. After everyone else had gone off to work.'

'What do you make of it?'

'I don't know.' Grace chewed some lettuce, rabbitlike. 'She was very upset. There's only one more question on the recorder. I asked her if she'd heard anyone in her family mention the word "blackmail". She said no. The way she relaxed immediately when we got off the subject of Melody and Fred Foret makes me believe she was telling the truth. The word "blackmail" didn't bother her at all.'

I rubbed my head. 'Greg Steinwale suggested I talk to Rich Beacon,' I said. 'Evidently, Melody never really severed that relationship.'

'You think Melody might have told him something?'

'He's about the only source we've got left,' I complained.

Grace, now building a second ham sandwich, nodded in sympathy. 'Something weird here, isn't there, Jason? All the time I was talking to this girl, I had the feeling she knew something she wasn't telling me. Not the blackmail. Something else. If I'd just known the right question to ask . . .'

'I've got a question for you. How many sandwiches are you going to eat, on top of half a loaf of bread on top of three helpings of salad?' I wondered in amazement.

'I'm hungry,' she said, sighing. 'I'm always hungry.' There was mustard on her lips.

It was one of the things I found most endearing about her, once I got over the initial surprise. Grace weighed around a hundred eighteen or twenty, dripping wet, but she ate like two starving stevedores. It took very little to make her happy. Just lots and lots of food. I leaned across the table and kissed her in the middle of the mustard. She looked both surprised and gratified.

Rich Beacon was not the kind of person I could simply drop in on. I could not get past his secretary at his office. At his home, I could not get past either of two adamantly polite-voiced servants. I thought about it the next day, thinking up different approaches and discarding each of them as unworkable. Beacon played golf, but I didn't. I didn't belong to any of the clubs he belonged to. We were both symphony supporters, but he was out of my league. Finally, I decided to ask Neal Ambler if he would make an introduction. Ambler knew Rich, and he more or less knew me. More importantly, he had cared about Melody enough to want her murderer found.

Ambler was out of town for a few days, so that whole matter had to go on hold. I went to see Nellie, who announced proudly that Willamae had been to see her three times. I dropped in on Jacob, who was in a fretful mood. Grace had to work late three nights running. Mark had received a final Dear John letter and wedding invitation from his friend Rudy, so he was about as gloomy as anyone could be and still survive.

'The bride's someone he's known for years,' Mark said. 'A girl whose older brother he went to school with. Her parents know his parents.'

'Catholic girls' college?' I wanted to know.

Mark nodded. 'She's thirty. He sent me a picture. She has more hair on her upper lip than I do. I'll bet she's a virgin.'

'Rudy tell her about himself?'

Mark shook his head.

'Well, you could always go to the wedding, and when the priest asks if there is any reason these two should not be joined together . . .'

'I don't think they do that at Catholic weddings,' said Mark. 'I don't think I could do that even if they did.'

'Well, visualize it anyhow,' I suggested. 'As catharsis.' Everyone else was having one. Why not Mark?

Ambler got back in town the next day. I explained what I needed to talk to Rich Beacon about.

'You're kidding!' he said. 'You mean, she went on seeing old Rich after she was married?' There was something in his voice very like pain.

I said so her husband had told me.

He sneered. 'What's the matter with that kid? No guts?'

'I think he told himself he was being understanding, Neal. I gathered he tried to convince himself that Beacon was a father figure to her and she needed to keep his friendship.'

'Father figure, hell. Money figure, more likely. Or good stud. He was still giving her things?'

'According to Greg, yes.'

'I'll be damned.'

'Can you get me an introduction?'

'Tell you what. Rich and some of us play a little poker at the Petroleum Club every Friday. That's tomorrow night. I'll take you as my guest, and you can see if he'll talk about it.'

'I'd rather just . . .'

'Draw poker. Table stakes. We generally have about five hundred to a thousand in the pot. Bring money.' And he hung up on me. He had sounded rather hostile.

At this point I must digress once more to say something about the Home.

'Homes' for neglected or abandoned children, as a class of charitable endeavours, do not by and large have much money. Even when state-supported, they are likely to have budgets which vary only from modest to slim. The Home in which I was reared was no exception to this rule. This means that the employees of such places, by and large, are either extremely dedicated or virtually unemployable. Only these two classes of people will accept the starvation wages offered.

Some of the people I remembered at the Home had been of the former type. May their haloes always shine in heaven. Some of them had been of the latter type, including Mrs Opinsky and Mr Josiah Basil, the janitor. Mr Josiah Basil, when I knew him, was a man in his seventies. He had spent his better years gambling through the length and breadth of these United States and several Latin American countries. Though he professed to know all about roulette and black jack and what he called chemmy, mostly what he knew about was poker. He knew straight poker and he knew crooked poker, draw and stud and six other kinds, and he taught me and Jerry Riggles and Prense Brown and a couple of older guys all of them. Old Josiah used to deal hands face up around the table and then cover them up and make us list all the cards that were showing. Then he'd bet a couple of rounds and make us list all the cards that were probably being held if nobody was bluffing. Josiah had memorized the odds on every possible draw of the cards, and he taught them to us as though they had been multiplication tables. Then, just in case that hadn't sunk in, he taught us to cheat.

Thus, when Neal Ambler hung up on me after making his little offer, I was not panicked. Yes, I could play draw poker with the big boys and probably limit my losses to what I could . . . well, if not afford to lose, at least compensate for

losing. I hadn't had any practise lately, but it isn't the kind
of knowledge you forget, and there was always Fred's money
in the basement.

This is by way of explaining why I didn't call Ambler
back and tell him to forget it. Hubris, I guess. Or stupidity.

I was introduced to the group the following night. There
were five of them. I made the sixth. Ambler, Beacon—call
the others Charles, Davis, and Evans. All about the same
age, well fed, well massaged, sleek, hair newly trimmed,
eight-hundred-dollar suits and handmade shoes. Something
a little desperate about Davis maybe: a little overeager to see
his cards. Beacon himself was the epitome of well-greased
money. Big. Extremely well tailored, barbered, and manicured. Black hair just turning grey at the temples. A beefy,
handsome face with a wide, recurved Greek-statue mouth.
Michelangelo's David at fifty. Not unlike the others, really,
all of them relaxed and easy or damned good actors.

Beacon said, 'Neal here tells me you're looking into
Melody's murder.' This was while the other four were
getting drinks and generally getting settled.

'I am, yes,' I said.

'Anybody paying you to do that?'

'No,' I said, shaking my head. 'I'm not a professional at
that. I don't take money.'

'Some kind of interior decorator, are you?'

Well, well. The man had done some digging. 'No,' I said.
'Basically I'm a dealer in antiques. I do décor as a sideline
to that, but I prefer to do it only for clients who have
bought antiques and want an authentically period look. My
education is in art and history, not in design.'

'What do those things cost?' he asked. 'Antiques.'

I didn't believe for a moment he was as naïve as that
question indicated. 'Some antiques are priceless. Many of
those are in museums. Some are cheap. Many of those are
in junk shops. Some antiques range in value from a few
hundred to a hundred thousand dollars, and I have stock
across that range.'

I didn't tell him the bank had a mortgage on most of it.

He probably knew it without my telling him. He probably ate bank vice presidents for lunch.

'Is that right?' He gave me a patronizing smile, pointed out a seat for me to occupy, and we settled down to play cards.

They began chatting about oil in the manner of men who spend a lot of time together, light, joshing conversation which betrayed an intimate knowledge of one another's pasts. Charles joshed Ambler about an exploration deal that had fallen through. Ambler teased Beacon about some wells they'd drilled in the early sixties. 'Those Magdalena wells were so dry, every mornin' we had to start over 'cause they'd blown away durin' the night.' My only excuse for being so slow to catch on was that I was thinking about what questions I wanted to ask Beacon rather than concentrating on what was really happening. I had three pat hands in a row, either in the initial deal or after I'd taken cards. I'd taken one little pot and lost the next two. It wasn't until I got the fourth pat hand that I realized what was happening. The fellas were having fun with the new boy. The only way they could have set this up was for every dealer to have an identical used, carefully stacked deck. I hadn't seen anyone switching decks, but then I hadn't been looking. They'd done it so smoothly I knew the sweethearts had played this little game with novices before.

We anted up and the dealer asked for cards. I kept one pair from my full house and asked for three. There was a slight, a very slight pause in the flow of the game. If I got three cards, the deck would be out of synch, and none of their hands would work either. Then we could play some honest poker. That is, if there wasn't any fancy finger work going on.

I watched the dealer pointedly enough to be almost insulting. Evans. He fumbled with the cards, but he dealt them off the top. I thanked him in a pleasant voice, my companions went around asking for ones and twos, and we settled down. I ended up with a full house again, if you can believe it. What I had received in the draw were the three nines Charles had been expecting. He was to my left and had taken two and three cards, alternately, each hand. My full house took that pot, and I was even.

Next hand was a nice little straight. I took two cards off the top of it and asked for two. I got a pair of the threes my neighbour'd been expecting, which went nicely with the three of clubs I'd held on to. Pure chance. That was the way they'd stacked them. Three of a kind was enough for the next pot, too. After that, I didn't notice any more chicanery, though the smoke got pretty thick after a while. After an hour or so, when I was a few hundred ahead, we broke for drinks and refreshments, and Beacon took me over to a table by the window where we could look down on the city.

'What did you want to know?' He was amused, if anything.

'I want to know anything Melody said to you about Fred Foret.'

He stared into his glass. 'To tell you the truth, son, I didn't pay a hell of a lot of attention to anything Melody said. She talked a lot, that little gal did, and most of what she had to say was like chickens clucking.'

'Anything you can remember.'

'One little thing did catch my attention. She talked about turning him over to the FBI to get even with him. Seems like he was putting the moves on her pretty hard, and she kind of resented it.'

'I didn't know the FBI had jurisdiction over seductions.'

'Don't ask me, son. I'm tellin' you what the lady said.'

'You went on seeing her after she was married?'

'Put that the other way, son. She went on seeing me. She'd call me up every now and then, and we'd have a little supper together. I'd give her some little present I'd sent my secretary to pick out, and we'd have a few drinks and a little snuggle for old times' sake. You know.'

The man's complacency angered me. 'Her husband thought she regarded you as a father figure.'

He reddened, I thought at first with anger, but then he bellowed with laughter. 'Damn, if she thought I was her daddy, she sure oughtn't to've done what we done. And her looking like she enjoyed it, too.' He went on laughing, gradually mellowing. 'Oh, son, she was an all right little girl so far's little girls go. Had cute little ways. Real sweet in bed. It was nice havin' her around makin' Ambler's eyes bug out. He was always crazy about her. I played fair with her. Had her teeth straightened out. Sent her to the best place to have her hair done. Sent her to school. Gave her charge accounts at good stores. Bought her lots of clothes, lots of shoes. Got her funny foot fixed . . .'

Something clanged. 'Funny foot?' I asked.

'She had this little old web between her toes. I got a doctor to fix that for her so she could wear those barefoot shoes the girls wear. Little old Melody, she did all right.'

I didn't answer him. As soon as I could, I excused myself and left (still ahead by about fifty dollars, which wasn't enough to make anyone at that table mad), thinking all the time of what Nellie had said.

It had been right there in front of me and I hadn't seen it. When I got home, it was late, but I called Silas anyhow and got Marge's number. I woke her up and asked the question I should have asked her long ago.

'Marge, what was Fred's full name?'

She sighed, trying to wake up. 'Fred?' she asked vaguely, as though she'd never known him. 'Oh, Fred. Frederick Charles Maudlin Foret,' she said. 'Maudlin was my mother's family name.'

I thanked her and hung up.

Rick Maudlin. Nellie was right. It was a wise child that knew her own father.

I had a pan of homemade lasagna in the freezer. Along about ten in the morning I stuck it in the oven, and it was ready to eat by the time Grace showed up at half past noon. Mark joined us while I made my revelations and we 'reviewed the problem'. We agreed that it was a toss-up between Lycia and Fred as Melody's killer; if Lycia had done it, then probably Harriet killed Fred. If Fred killed

Melody, then who killed Fred? Sally? Marty O'Toole? Simmons, for some reason unknown? Ross?

'Fred didn't know she was his daughter,' Mark marvelled. 'How could he not have known?'

'Why would he have?' Grace asked in a practical voice, taking a third helping of lasagna. She had her napkin tied around her neck and it was well covered with cryptic messages written in stringy cheese, punctuated with tomato sauce. 'He'd probably forgotten about ever being married to that woman. What was he, nineteen? Twenty?'

'But wouldn't he be the least bit suspicious when Melody talked about hunting for her father?'

'She wouldn't have said a word about that to Fred,' Grace opined. 'Not a word. The first time she saw him at that party, she heard about the webbed toe or saw it, and right then she figured him for her father. He knew her as Greg Steinwale's wife. If she didn't tell him where she was from— or if she told him a fib about it—why would he suspect?'

'Jason says the art instructor told him Melody said she and Shannon looked alike,' Mark went on doubtfully.

'That was her little joke,' Grace said. 'They didn't look alike. If they had looked alike, Fred might have realized, but they didn't look alike, so Fred hadn't a clue. Also, I think Melody was punishing Shannon for being Fred's daughter.'

Mark looked puzzled.

'Fred simply abandoned Melody. He and Lycia were divorced, but he still presumably acted like a father towards Shannon. Melody probably resented that. So she played this nasty game . . .'

'A vengeance game,' I said. 'Rich Beacon says she mentioned the FBI in connection with Fred. That and getting even.' There was still something wrong in the FBI reference, but whatever it was eluded me. My notebook had a list of things I'd thought of, and I referred to it, deciding what to do next. 'I've got a few loose ends I can work on. Melody's dog, for one.'

'What about me?' Mark asked in his depressed voice.

'You can find out whether Ross and Lycia have borrowed money lately. Or, since they might have had a half million to give to Fred, find out whether they've cashed in any stocks or bonds or sold any real estate. I need to know the same thing about Harriet Steinwale . . .'

'There are some brokers I know . . .' His voice drifted off. I figured Mark knew people he could ask questions I couldn't get answers to.

'How about me?' asked Grace.

'You can find out if Marty O'Toole has ever been charged with violence of any kind. Has he ever assaulted anyone? Or threatened anyone with a gun?'

If something didn't break, I would fire some bullets from that gun in the basement and give them to Grace to check against the bullets they'd taken out of Fred, but I didn't want to pull O'Toole in that deeply just yet. Poor guy. He'd already had quite a lambasting.

I kept the business about the collie dog for myself. When Grace had left and Mark had gone back to work, Bela and I went out for a quick walk to stir our blood and our brains. When they were sufficiently stirred, we sat in the middle of the park and let the muck settle. There had been something useful in my visit to Lycia's apartment, if I could just remember what it was. It lingered in my head, just out of reach.

I shut my eyes and visualized arriving, the half-open door, Lycia in a robe welcoming Marge. The living-room. Sunlight, plants, a lot of colour. We went through into the kitchen. It was a small room. Crowded. The shelties were in their baskets under the window. The door was a swinging door. When Ross got up from the table, I moved back to give him room . . .

The dogs' leashes had been hanging on the back of the kitchen door just where I hang Bela's. Plus . . .

Plus half a dozen framed certificates from community organizations. The Lighthouse. There were several from the Lighthouse.

What else? One from a child abuse prevention group.

One from an animal rescue organization. Not a name I recognized.

'Come on, Bela dog.' I nudged him out of a happy dream of freely chasing squirrels, and we ran home, with me ignoring the aching leg almost the whole way. I thought I would recognize the name of the organization if I saw it.

As I did immediately on looking at the list in the phone book. Ani-pals.

The phone rang and rang before someone answered. 'Hi there,' I said to the breathless voice. 'I hope I didn't catch you at a busy time? I'm calling for Dr Lycia Foret, actually. She brought an old collie in there last October. It was a Thursday, I think the eighteenth. She'd like to know what happened to the dog. Do your records tell you that?'

There was a frantic burbling at the other end.

'No, no. She has no complaint at all. She's just curious, and she asked me to find out for her . . .'

The voice retreated. There were paper noises. Eventually the voice returned.

'Put down the following week,' I said. 'Yes, well, she really didn't expect it would have been adopted. Thank you very much.'

Damn. Damn, double damn. Dr Lycia Foret had delivered an old collie dog to Ani-pals on Thursday morning, the eighteenth of October. Melody Steinwale had died while walking her dog on Thursday morning, the eighteenth of October. The following week, since no one had adopted it, the dog was 'put to sleep'.

And the person I least wanted to prove anything against had become my foremost suspect.

After struggling with myself for most of two nights, I decided to talk to Lycia Foret. I called her, told her I was looking into Fred's death for Marge, and asked if I could come over.

She told me no. Shannon was home, and she didn't want Shannon upset. Some policewoman had recently upset Shannon, and Lycia didn't want that to happen again. She would come to me.

I made a fresh pot of coffee, got out the good china, put on a pot to boil, in case she preferred tea, and was hunting for Agatha's linen napkins when she arrived. My preparations had breathed much of romance and very little of interviewing a murder suspect. I felt silly and a little undignified.

She, however, was charm itself. She complimented me on the shop, on the various pieces in the hall as I escorted her upstairs, on the office itself. She spoke knowledgeably of the Rococo Revival side chair by my desk, a chair much like one her grandmother had had in her sewing room.

'Grandma's had lions' heads on the back,' she said. 'I like the grapes better. I never liked leaning back on those lions. I was always afraid they'd bite me.'

'Where was that?' I asked, smiling despite myself.

'In St Louis,' she replied, returning my smile. 'Where I grew up. Mostly. Until I came out here when I was twenty to go to school.'

'That's when you married Fred.'

She nodded, no longer smiling. 'It seems so ridiculous now, Jason. May I call you Jason? It seems ridiculous now that we attached so much importance to sex then. I don't know if you can conceive of how important it was to be a virgin when one married. One was brave, clean, reverent, and a virgin when married . . .'

I tried to look encouraging, wondering what the hell she was talking about. She saw my confusion.

'You wonder what I'm going on and on about, don't you? Ten years later it was all different. The sexual revolution had happened, and it was all different. You grew up in a different time. But for me, for young women in my group, virginity was important. So a lot of us married too early and quite unwisely. We couldn't maintain virginity over the long haul, so we got married, and then we found we couldn't handle marriage either. That's what I'm trying to tell you. I didn't know Fred at all when we were married. I didn't know any man, really. My father was long gone. My older sister, who'd raised me, was . . . Well, she wasn't there to give me any good advice. So I married this man and had two babies, and things were so busy I didn't notice that I really didn't like him very much. And we went to Washington, and I liked him even less. And when Shannon was seven, we left him and came home, Shannon and Keith and I. I didn't divorce him, I just left him. It was only when he came back here five years later that I divorced him.'

'Amiably?'

She belied her hectic words with her tranquil smile. 'Oh, in the end it was amiable, yes. I would have preferred that Fred stay in Washington, but he said he needed a change. I think he may have burned his bridges in Washington. Something he said implied that he left just in time. In time for what, I don't know. I know he enjoyed teaching at the university. Shannon told me he had many plans for his retirement. He always had these enthusiasms, est, UFOs, one thing or another. He was always looking for final answers. Lately he was working on world peace again, I understand. I haven't seen him half a dozen times in the— what is it?—nine or ten years since.'

'But he saw Shannon,' I said. 'That was the trouble, wasn't it?'

She looked down at her hands. They lay quietly in her lap, but she stared at them, as though they were snakes, writhing. Perhaps they wanted to writhe, but she kept them quiet. 'Yes,' she said, almost in a whisper. 'He did see Shannon.'

'At dinner the other night,' I commented, 'Ross had something to say about it.'

'Ross would.' She smiled. 'Oh, yes. Ross would.'

'And then there's this,' I said, laying the manuscript on the desk in front of her. 'Marge found it. Among Fred's things.'

Her eyes fastened on the manuscript. 'I rather thought she might find it somewhere. I even thought of looking for it after he died, but decided against it. I hoped he'd lost it, but then, Fred wouldn't have done that.'

She tore her eyes away and got up then, only her haste betraying any agitation at all. She strode to the window, looked out at the building next door, through the office window into the neighbouring offices where, I knew, several pale persons bustled about all day like gnomes, shifting paper.

'Lycia,' I said. 'I'm not an enemy. I'm not the police. I'm not . . . I'm not official.'

'What does that mean?'

'Just that. If you can explain it away, do. If you can't, tell me to go to hell. I'm not going to give this thing to anyone.'

'But Marge might.'

I gritted my teeth. 'I don't know.'

She sat down again, sighing. The sigh made me remember my manners. 'Lycia, would you like some coffee? Some tea?'

'Jason, I would like a drink. Scotch? I'd even settle for gin in a pinch.'

I think my mouth dropped open. Maybe not. Why did I think she wouldn't drink? I went to the kitchen, got her a scotch on the rocks, sat down behind the desk, and waited while she gulped half the drink without ever losing that tranquil look. She set the glass down, took the manuscript in her hands, and flipped through it.

'I wrote this to save my sanity,' she said. 'Well, Harriet and I both did. We shared drafts back and forth. We had coffee and cried together. Then we decided we weren't killer types—I guess I decided that—and we said hell, let's figure out something else. Of course, that was before Greg went in the hospital. Before Fred broke up Shannon's engagement . . .'

'Are you saying you intended to kill but changed your mind?'

'I'm saying we'd never actually intended to kill anyone. We just fantasized the idea. It was fun, kind of. Like wiping out our problems with a big eraser. But it wouldn't have worked, we knew that.'

'Can you give me any information as to who killed your ex-husband?' I asked.

She gave me a thoughtful look. 'I honestly can't,' she

said. 'Though I could name a dozen who, like me, probably were glad he died.'

'You don't think Harriet . . .'

She laughed. 'We decided, I told you. We said we weren't the type. I remember the conversation. We were having lunch at that restaurant on top of the bookstore after a board meeting for the Lighthouse. One of the other members had been his usual obstructive self, and I looked at Harriet and said, "Let's blow him away, bam!" And we broke up. And I said I couldn't, ever, and she said she knew that.'

'But you bought a gun.'

'I did. Yes. Some time ago. Before I realized who was going through the apartment. I got rid of it, though, long since. Buying it was one of those silly things one does when one is frightened.'

'But Ross has a gun.'

She was silent for a moment, thinking. 'He did have one when he moved in with me, but his was stolen. Things being stolen is why we changed the locks.'

'Fred made a remark to one of his acquaintances about your writing a book, and about your paying him not to tell anyone.'

She laughed. 'That sounds like Fred. Yes. He told me he'd "gained possession" of that paper you have there. "Gained possession" sounds better than "stole", which is what he did. He asked me what it was worth to me to get it back, and I told him nothing.'

'Nothing?'

'Nothing. I didn't want it back. I don't know why I kept it at all. Fred knew I hadn't killed Melody. He knew I couldn't kill anyone. He just thought I might feel the manuscript was incriminating enough that I'd pay him for it. I told Fred to do what he liked with it, that telling tales out of school often went both ways, and we left it at that.'

'Would he have tried to get money from Harriet Steinwale?'

She laughed in honest amusement. 'After Fred and I

talked it over, I don't think he'd have asked for money from anyone again.'

'You had something on him?'

'We're not discussing that, Jason. You wanted to know about a plot for a story that Harriet and I wrote and I've told you about that.'

So she had had something on him. I looked over her shoulder, avoiding her eyes. 'Can you tell me one thing?' I indicated the paper. 'Did Ross know about all this?'

She shook her head. 'Ross knew Fred had been sneaking around in our apartment, yes. As soon as I figured it out, I told him. He knew Fred took things, yes. Ross didn't know about the story Harriet and I had written, no. Ross didn't know Fred had taken it and tried to sell it back to me. Ross gets very angry, and I didn't want him any angrier at Fred than he already was.'

'I'm afraid there's something else,' I said.

'Having met you, I was sure there would be.' She smiled, a tightly controlled smile. 'What is it?'

'The collie. Melody's collie.'

Her expression didn't change, but her colour did. It drained away. The rueful smile remained, but in an ivory face. Then a faint flush came back. 'Oh,' she said. 'Well, you'll have to talk to my neighbour about that.'

'Your neighbour?'

'Mr Stevenson. From across the hall. He saw it all. He'll tell you about it, I'm sure.' She stood up, drank the last few drops, rattling the ice with her tongue. 'I haven't killed anyone, Jason. Ross hasn't killed anyone. We didn't. We don't. It's not our kind of thing. Even Fred, insensitive as he was, knew that.'

She turned, stooped as though dizzy, but it was only to stroke the carved grapes on the back of the chair, the acorns and leaves, the twining vines. In a moment she walked out and away. I sat there, looking after her, wondering why I felt so bereft. After a minute, Mark came in and I told him what she had said.

'Stevenson? Who's he?'

I explained about the inventor of sickening ice cubes, the jokester with the poodles.

'Are you going to go see him?'

I was, of course. I had to.

The following morning I was waiting outside the Louvre, trying to look inconspicuous. I saw Shannon come out with the shelties, but she turned to walk towards town. Stevenson had said he sometimes didn't hear her, but evidently this morning he had, for he and the poodles emerged about five minutes later. I trailed them to the park, no downtown walk for Willie, and sat myself beside him on his usual bench.

'Did you solve your minnow problem?' I asked.

He turned, took a minute to remember who I was, then nodded, the corners of his mouth turning up, ever so slightly. 'Oh, yes. Yes, indeed. The problem was, we were thinking of whole fish, don't you know? No shock value in that, is there? Heh, heh.' His laugh was like his mouth, tightly managed.

'So what did you do?'

'Half a fish,' he crowed triumphantly. 'All raggedy, as though it had been bitten in half. Like half a worm in an apple.'

I considered this for a moment. 'Perfect,' I pronounced. 'True genius.'

'That's what the sales manager said.' He nodded, agreeing with me. 'He said exactly the same thing.'

We enjoyed his triumph in silence for a moment or two.

'I wonder if you could help me with something,' I asked him. 'I'm investigating a case that took place here in the park, and Mrs Foret says you were probably a witness.'

'Me? Oh, no. I haven't witnessed anything at all. Not since that accident on the freeway three years ago . . .'

'This wasn't that kind of thing. Mrs Foret said you would know about the collie . . .'

'Collie? Dog?'

'Last October? Mrs Foret and the collie?'

'Oh! The lost dog!'

I nodded. 'Could you tell me about that?'

'Well, I was here, where I usually am, and the dogs were over there in the bushes. I was reading a letter from my sister, one I'd just got, and this strange dog ran up to me. Kind of a fat, old dog. I thought maybe I'd seen it before, you know, but I wasn't sure. And it barked. It barked at me, and it wouldn't stop. I didn't know what to do. So I looked down the sidewalk, and Mrs Foret was coming into the park. So I yelled to her, about this dog. And she came over and took it for me.'

'She was coming into the park.'

'From the apartment house. She came down into the lobby while I was getting my mail, and then she came along behind.'

Behind him? 'What time was this?'

'Early. Very early. Before eight. Not long after seven.'

'Then what happened?'

'Well, she took the dog, and she said for me to come along, we'd look for the owner. So I got Mother's dogs, and we went around the park. And she asked people if the dog belonged to them, people on benches, you know. People are so rude. One lady didn't even answer. She was probably drunk.'

I could guess which lady. 'Over on the far side of the park,' I suggested. 'Sitting on a bench, with a magazine.'

'Yes. Only she wasn't sitting. She was sort of slumped over, and the magazine was on the bench. Mrs Foret helped her sit up and gave her her magazine. Maybe the woman was deaf. Mother used to say we have to make allowances for people. Maybe she was deaf and didn't hear.'

'Did Mrs Foret shake her or anything?'

'No. Of course not. She just helped her sit up, and put the magazine on her lap, and then she told me we probably couldn't find the owner, so she'd take the dog to a shelter.'

So Lycia had found Melody already dead. According to the police report, dead for a very short time. Why had she straightened up the body and propped the magazine in its lap? I knew an answer to that. When she found Melody dead, she was immediately reminded of the manuscript

Fred had offered to sell her. So she had gone quietly away. I didn't blame her. Stevenson was looking at me curiously, wondering what this was all about. I changed the subject.

'You had the dogs last fall, then? Your mother's been ill a long time.'

He shook his head. 'Oh, you thought she was still in the hospital? No, she was ill a long time, but she died. That's why I have to keep them, you see. I promised. They're very young dogs. I imagine they'll live years and years yet.' He sounded hopeless about it.

The pups deserved better than that. 'You promised your mother you wouldn't put them in a kennel. Did you promise her you wouldn't find them a good home? Somewhere where they could run and play? With someone who likes dogs?'

He looked up, hope dawning on his face. 'How would I do that?'

'Let me see what I can do,' I suggested.

He beamed at me. 'That would be wonderful. I never thought of that. I wonder why I never thought of that. I should have, because I'm not an animal person. I'm really not. It always surprises me when people are, like Mrs Foret, just taking that strange dog by the leash and taking it away, and it just went with her, just like that. It didn't even whine, except when she was with that drunk woman.'

Yes, that had surprised me, too. I toyed briefly with the idea that Lycia might have been making her second trip of the morning when she took the collie, but I could think of no reason why, if she had already shot Melody, she should have returned.

'Will you call me? Will you let me know? Can I help you?' Willie Stevenson wanted to know.

I smiled and told him no, I'd get in touch with him, that I had a particular person in mind who might like to have the dogs. He went away with protestations of delight, leaving me to sit there on the bench, glad of what he'd told me, and yet more confused than ever.

I was back with Fred as first suspect in Melody's death, except that if Lycia had told me the truth about there being no blackmail, the only feasible motive was wiped out.

And as far as Fred's death went? If I believed Lycia, I hadn't a clue.

CHAPTER 7

Believing Lycia seemed to be the only thing to do. By noon that day, Mark reported back to me that he had found out who handled Lycia and Ross's financial affairs and, since he knew the man rather well, had 'dropped in on him'. Mark had invented a story about an extravagant investment venture in partnership with Lycia and Ross, and his broker friend had told him frankly that the couple didn't have the resources to do what Mark proposed.

'He didn't come right out and tell me, that wouldn't have been ethical, but he gave me enough to put two and two together. From what he said, I know they've been putting what extra cash they have into annuity programmes and some rather modest investment schemes. My friend commented that doctors make good money, but that living takes most of it. The one interesting thing he let slip was that Lycia has cut back her contribution to her annuity programme lately. The broker has no idea why, except that she told him she was strapped for cash, but there haven't been any stock sales or borrowing against annuities or anything like that. What she's diverted from her annuities can't amount to more than a few thousand. In any case, the important thing is that neither Lycia nor Ross could have come up with half a million. They just don't have it and never have had.'

'She's strapped for cash? How much is a few thousand? And when is lately?'

'I got the impression we're talking about maybe eighteen hundred or two thou a month, Jason, for the last six or eight months. Moreover, it hasn't changed since Fred died. She's still starving her annuity plan.'

An interesting little fact which took us nowhere. A few

thousand a month, only recently, did not add up to half a million dollars.

'How about Harriet Steinwale?'

Mark shook his head. 'Her affairs are out of my reach, Jason. She could come up with half a million easy, that much I do know.'

'I don't think it's likely that she did,' I said. 'Why would she pay? The thing wasn't in her handwriting. I don't think she'd have paid Fred to suppress it, particularly after Lycia told him to do what he wanted with it.'

'If Lycia's telling the truth.'

It came down to that, always. In my judgement, she'd been telling the truth. I typed a short letter to Marge Beebe, telling her there was a witness to the fact that Lycia had arrived in the park after Melody was dead. Since Lycia had not killed Melody, it was extremely unlikely that Harriet had killed Fred. I told Marge the manuscript had been merely a way of letting off steam, not a plan for murder. I said the money she had found had not come from Lycia or Ross, that though Fred had tried to hit Lycia up for money, she had refused to give him anything and my research indicated that Lycia was telling the truth about that. I didn't mention that the money might have come from Harriet Steinwale. Maybe Marge wouldn't think of that.

Marge would believe Lycia was innocent just as I did, because she wanted to. She had never really liked thinking her ex-sister-in-law was guilty of anything.

Being well and truly stalled, I got out a pad and pencil and made a list. Making lists is often unproductive, though sometimes seeing a name in writing jostles a brain cell into making a connection.

Who did I have for Fred's murder?

Marty O'Toole. All other avenues having failed, it was time to fire Marty's gun and give the bullets to Grace.

Sally Streeter. She said Fred took her gun away with him, but maybe he actually hadn't. Or maybe she'd bought a new one. Perhaps I could find out exactly what kind it had been. Talk to Sally again.

Lycia or Ross. Who both had reasons to hate Fred for what he was doing to Shannon, but who also had an ironclad alibi along with the rest of the family. Of course, Marge had told me that. I could check it out myself.

Some X person who had known Fred before, on one of his peace marches, in Washington, at the university. Ask Simmons if Fred had mentioned any enemies. Hell, ask everybody. Check into Simmons himself, just in case.

Then there was Ancel Ancini, Shannon's fiancé. He certainly had reasons to hate Fred, and we hadn't even considered him seriously.

And Harriet. Couldn't leave her out.

Who did we have for Melody's murder?

Fred himself. He was the most likely candidate. Except that there seemed to be no motive if the blackmail idea was merely a will-o'-the-wisp.

There was Neal Ambler. He'd been half in love with her. Maybe she'd driven him to murder, somehow. Maybe he'd bought her paintings from her, then had an appraisal of them and had been infuriated. No. The man I'd talked to still thought she was a great artist. The man I'd talked to was besotted.

Then there was Harriet again, because of what Melody had done to Greg. Except that Harriet was out of the country when Melody died.

And Greg. Except that he was in the hospital. Of course, I hadn't personally checked either Greg's alibi or his mother's. I made a note to ask Grace to bring the police reports back again. The police had undoubtedly checked, and they had the facilities to do it better than I did.

I wondered if I should add Nina Hough to the list. Melody had been ruining the gallery business, and maybe Nina had felt strongly about that. She didn't seem the type to shoot anyone, but then, who did in this crazy bunch?

Rich Beacon. He was the shooter type. I remembered his hands, wide, hard, hairy on the backs. Not someone to let anyone get the better of him. But what motive? Had Melody

known something about him and tried to use it as leverage?
I put his name down. The man was tough and mean and
well protected. If he'd killed her, I'd probably never find
out about it. If she'd known something about him, it would
have to have been something serious. Something his lawyers
couldn't quite take care of. Murder. Rape. I toyed with the
rape idea for a while, but it didn't seem to jell. Melody
seemingly had been quite willing to continue her relationship with Beacon, even though he was old enough to be
her . . .

Wait. Could I possibly be wrong about Fred?

What had Ambler said at that poker game? Something
about a well he and Rich Beacon had been partners on. The
Magdalena well. He'd drawled it out. Mag-dah-lay-nah.
And Beacon had told him he didn't even remember how to
pronounce it. Something.

I called him.

'Well, well, the big winner,' he said.

'Fifty-two dollars is not big,' I contradicted him.

'If you include me, and you, and Rich, you were the big
winner,' he said. 'Charles walked off with the table. What
do you want to know now?'

'The other night, you mentioned a well you and Rich
drilled in Texas. The Magdalena well?'

'That's right. Right near Magdalena Creek in south-
central Texas, which is why we named it that. Nice, juicy
girl's name. For all the good it did.'

'Dry hole, hmm?'

'Drier than a spinster's twat. Why?'

'Why was Rich saying you didn't know how to pronounce
it?'

Ambler laughed. 'Rich, when he was nineteen, twenty,
he went to school in England, where his daddy was something big with the US government. He went to Oxford,
to what I'd call Magdalen College, only over there they
pronounce it "Maudlin". He was always calling that dry
well the Maudlin well on Maudlin Creek and snootin'
around in boots and a white shirt talking the King's English.

He only did it to make us crazy, not that we weren't crazy enough.'

'Neal, did he ever talk about that well around Melody?'

'Shoot, Jason, he talked about anything that crossed his mind around Melody.'

I hung up and thought about that. Surely not. According to Ambler, Beacon had spent a few thousand dollars hunting for Melody's father. He knew the story. Surely he couldn't have actually been . . .

Or had he only pretended to look?

Damn. Rich from Maudlin could have called himself Rick Maudlin. But had he? And wouldn't the same idea have occurred to Melody? Had she threatened to expose him as an incestuous old man? Had he killed her? What would he have been when she was living with him? In his mid-forties?

It was extremely farfetched, indicating exactly how frustrated I was. No, I was not wrong about Fred and Rich had been out of town when Melody died. It had to be Fred. It was his name. It was his style.

I threw up my hands and went out to lunch with Nina Hough. She had invited me to an opening at the gallery that afternoon, and I had invited her to lunch first. I needed a break from the whole stupid business. I couldn't remember a puzzle which had been so annoying.

Why?

Because the more I found out about the two victims, the less I really wanted to catch whoever had done it. I had promised Marge I would look into the matter. I hadn't promised her I would do anything about it. In fact, I told myself that today might be a good day to give the whole thing up.

I had decided to do just that, but when I got back that afternoon I found Mark and Grace waiting for me all shiny-eyed and bushy-tailed.

'Mark had an idea!' bubbled Grace.

'About money,' crowed Mark. 'Fred's money. Did you look at the series numbers?'

'Did I look at what?'

'Honestly, Jason. The things you don't know. Every time they change the money, like every time we get a new Treasurer of the US or a new Secretary of the Treasury, they start a new series of money. It says so, right on the bills. Series 1969, or series 1974, or series 1981. If you look at Fred's money, you can maybe tell how old it is.'

I think I gaped. It had never occurred to me. Since there was nothing else to occupy our attention at the moment, they came downstairs with me while I opened the safe and put the cardboard box on the old pool table I haven't been able to get rid of. When I opened the box, Grace gasped. Mark, as one might suppose, did not seem impressed.

We each took a stack of money and started looking for the series dates. I found lots of sixties and lots of seventies. Then a few fifties. A lone bill from the forties. We shuffled and muttered our way through a good dozen bundles before I said, 'There aren't any eighties.'

'There's nothing after 1977,' Mark said. 'Carter's administration.'

I put the bundle I'd been fumbling with back into the box. 'Do we need to look at all of it?'

'Not if it's all like this,' Mark said. 'Though some bundles might have later dates.'

I groaned, and we looked at all of it. Nothing later than 1977. I think I groaned again. Even though I had believed Lycia Foret, even though Sally's observation had seemed to clinch it, I hadn't been certain. This made it certain. 'This isn't blackmail money at all,' I said. 'But it does explain why Melody threatened him with the FBI.'

Mark gave me a puzzled look.

'If this money was accumulated before 1977, it was done while Fred was in Washington! Fred was working for the Department of Defense, and he was in charge of research contracts. This money had to come from kickbacks! When he was with the DOD he must have taken cash bribes for grant awards. When I talked to Lycia, I couldn't help thinking she had something on him to make him so docile about the divorce. He'd probably started doing it years ago.

I wondered how he could afford to fly all over Europe on that world-peace stuff, and he's been doing it for years. That should have told me the money antedated recent events. He must have bragged to Melody about having money he'd made in Washington. He probably hinted and winked and told her how sly he'd been. She told Greg he had sticky fingers. That's what she meant. She assumed he'd gotten the money illegally, and she threatened him.'

'How do you know that?' Grace wondered.

'Because of the phone conversation Sally Streeter overheard. Sally thought Fred and Melody were talking about sex. I thought they were discussing blackmail money. They were actually referring to bribery money dating from Fred's years in Washington. Remember, Melody said something to him about not being rich enough to interest her. So he said, "In addition to having friends in high places, I have enough to make life interesting," meaning money. Then she twitted him about where he got it and what he did with it, and he said he had it and what he did with it was his business.

'She said he got it illegally. He said she was assuming that. She said he was a thief, and he said she'd have a hard time proving it. She said she wouldn't try to prove it, she'd tell the FBI and let them prove it. And he told her she'd better not try it or she'd be sorry.'

'Then he borrowed Sally's gun and shot her?'

'I think it very likely.'

'Then who killed Fred?'

I shook my head, mentally adding a couple of names to my list. Ambler, in revenge, because he knew Fred had killed Melody. Greg, also for revenge, because he'd found out Fred killed Melody. And how had either of them found out?

I had no idea.

'This just gets worse and worse,' Grace said. 'Why did you think these two killings were connected in the first place?'

'Both the bodies had been kind of "arranged",' I said.

'It made me think maybe the same person. But that turned out not to mean anything . . .' I hadn't told them about Lycia's finding the body, and I didn't intend to. Somehow, I couldn't bear anyone else knowing anything bad about Lycia.

'No, it obviously didn't,' she fretted. 'Jason, I'm tired of this one. We're not getting anywhere.'

I agreed with her, soberly, then told both of them we needed a vacation from it all. Grace said okay, she was going to catch up on her paperwork and paint her bathroom. She didn't look at me when she said it, so I knew she was going through another one of her 'Jason and I are just friends' arguments with herself. Mark said he was going to take the weekend to meet some new people. I crossed my fingers for both of them, and for me.

A few days went by. My leg was better, so Bela and I were taking longer walks. We stayed longer in the park, meeting more people, many of whom wanted to know what had happened to my pet tiger. Grace had promised me a kitten, next time her cousin in Cheyenne's female cat had one of Critter's litters. I was looking forward to that. Bela missed Critter. He'd enjoy a kitten. Pets need pets, too.

As do old ladies. I called Willamae Belling and told her a sad story about two poodles condemned to live the rest of their lives with a man who didn't like them. She almost cried.

So it was with purpose in mind that I went searching for Willie Stevenson. He was on his usual bench, concentrating deeply. I hated to interrupt him.

When he heard about Willamae's offer for the dogs, however, he almost grinned. Almost. 'When?' he asked. 'Oh, how soon?

I told him I'd pick up the dogs that afternoon and transport them, a sack of kibble, their dishes and impedimenta, to Willamae's house. That they would love her. That they would have a fenced yard. That they would think they were back with Willie's mother again. That she needed them because she was a lonely old lady. The man was almost delirious with joy.

'It'll be so nice to walk without them again,' he said. 'To just walk, you know, at my own speed. Stop when I want to. Go when I want to.'

I admitted that was always a nice feeling.

He must have thought he had sounded ungracious, for he was quick to explain himself. 'Even people who like animals feel that way,' he assured me. 'Even Mrs Foret. She sometimes walks without the dogs.'

I smiled and nodded and said yes, I sometimes walked without Bela, trying to think of the last time I'd done so. Rarely. Very rarely.

'That day she rescued the lost dog, she didn't have her dogs,' he bubbled at me. 'That was a lucky thing, wasn't it? She might not have been able to manage three of them.'

I smiled and nodded again and told him I would see him that afternoon around two.

I was half way home before I realized what he had told me.

I didn't tell either Mark or Grace that I was going to Harriet Steinwale's, any more than I had told them about Lycia finding Melody's body. After settling the poodles in at Willamae's, I called Mrs Steinwale and asked if I could drop in that evening. I told her I thought I knew who might have killed her daughter-in-law. I half expected her to tell me to go to the police with it, but she made no objection to my visit.

It was raining slightly when I arrived about eight thirty. She took my wet coat and offered me a drink. I accepted. We went into the huge living-room. There was one table lamp on, in the far corner. She made the drinks at a bar-closet in that corner, then we sat across from one another in the dim room, looking out over the lights of the city. It was barely dusk, but the lights were beginning to come on—lights of traffic, lights reflecting along the wet streets, lights in the buildings, a sequinned pattern, shifting and glittering as darkness came.

'When my husband was alive,' she said, 'we used to love to sit here in the evenings, watching the lights. In the country, we always looked at water. In the city, we looked at lights. Rainy lights are best.'

'Have you been widowed long?'

'Twenty years. Too long.'

'This is a big place,' I said, looking about me. It was big, but elegant, with a well-used charm. 'Did you live here with your husband?'

'When Max and I first lived here, we had three children, and Max's father was living with us. It didn't seem large then. I've been in this building almost forty years. We own part of it, of course. The rent is reasonable.' She smiled to herself. Private joke.

'I didn't know Greg had siblings.'

'He doesn't now. Our daughters died very young.'

No wonder she was so passionately devoted to Greg. He was all she had left.

She was watching me intently. 'You didn't come here to talk about my family, did you?'

'I came to ask about Melody, actually.'

'I didn't know her at all well. Even though she lived here we had very little contact.'

'I think I know who killed her, Mrs Steinwale. Would you tell me, please, whether she ever said anything to you about Fred Foret and Shannon.'

'You know about that?' Whatever she had expected me to say or ask, it had not been that. I had upset her badly.

Not knowing what 'that' was, I equivocated. 'I know something about it, yes. Ross mentioned . . .'

'Ross shouldn't. Not to strangers.' She looked down at her hands, square capable hands, neatly disposed in her lap. When she spoke it was so softly I had to strain to hear her. 'Yes. Melody had found out about that. She seemed to think it would shock me or hurt me to learn of it. It did hurt, of course, though not in the way she thought. I'd already heard about it long ago from Lycia.'

'What exactly did Melody say?'

'She told me about Fred Foret's attempted incest with Shannon when she was only seven years old. She didn't say "attempted", of course. I already knew from Lycia that it was more than a mere attempt, though Lycia always refers to it as "attempted" around Shannon.'

I took a swallow of scotch to wash out the bitter taste in my mouth. 'Shannon remembers this?'

'Of course she remembers. She was seven, almost eight years old. Lycia found out about it almost immediately, packed up the children, and left. It was Shannon's abuse that spurred her to go to medical school, to work for the Lighthouse, to prevent other girls from suffering the damage Fred had done to her daughter. I'm surprised that Ross talked about this.'

'He alluded to it,' I murmured. 'Not in any great detail.'

She sighed, unaware she had told me something I didn't know.

'Lycia divorced Fred because of this incident,' I said.

She nodded. 'When Fred came back to Denver, he actually expected to be with his family again. Lycia told him she would make the matter public if he made any attempt to fight her divorce or gain custody of the children. According to Lycia, he told his sister a pack of lies, but he was reasonably sensible about it. Then.'

'How did Melody find out about this?'

'From Shannon. After that party in June, a year ago, evidently Melody tried to strike up a friendship with Shannon. She actively pursued the child, harassed her. Shannon told Lycia about Melody's almost persecuting her, and Lycia told me. Evidently Shannon tried to fight her off, tried to make Melody leave her alone, but Melody persisted. Melody twitted her for being a virgin, and Shannon broke down and screamed out how her father had attacked her when she was a tiny child. Even that didn't stop Melody. She went on plaguing the child . . .'

Like a crow, picking at a bloody wound, I thought. Like a carrion crow.

Harriet murmured, 'Lycia came to me for help. I said I'd talk to Melody. Greg was in the hospital. Melody and I were here alone in the apartment for a while, before I left for Mexico. Sometimes she ate with me rather than eat alone. At the dinner table I challenged her with her behaviour towards Shannon. She laughed at me. She said there was no reason Shannon should be allowed to be happy. She repeated to me what Shannon had told her about her father, and seemed disappointed when I said I already knew. She said she didn't give a damn about Shannon. She dragged Fred's name into the conversation by saying that Shannon wasn't the only one Fred had tried to have sex with, that he'd tried with her as well, that he'd told her he knew "what little girls liked". Melody said Fred bragged to her that he had accumulated a small fortune when he worked for the Department of Defense. She believed he had taken bribes for awarding contracts. It poured out of her, all about Shannon, all about Fred, like acid, bubbling out of her, uncontrollably. She seemed to need to tell me, as though I cared. And she said she would harass both him and Shannon all she liked. I don't know why she hated them so.'

I knew. 'Melody came here to Denver looking for her father, Harriet. A father who had abandoned her when she was an infant. At Shannon's birthday party, Melody learned that Fred, Shannon's father, was also her father.'

The colour left her face as though dusk had entered the room. She went grey, suddenly haggard. 'He . . . he was what?'

'Fred was married when he was very young to a woman in Baltimore. She died shortly after her baby girl was born. Fred left the daughter in the care of an elderly aunt, gave her a false name, and never came back. Subsequently he married Lycia without ever telling her he had been married before. The child in Baltimore was Melody. She came here to Denver to find her father. His name was supposed to be Rick Maudlin. Fred Foret's full name was Frederick Charles

Maudlin Foret. He never used his full name. Lycia knew it, of course, but she never knew Melody was searching for a father by that name. Marge knew it, but she knew nothing about Melody. Even though Melody lived here in this apartment with you for years, Lycia and the others seemingly never really met her until the birthday party.'

Her voice was harsh as she answered. 'Melody was never interested in meeting my friends. She had friends of her own. The rooms she and Greg shared had their own entrance. They ate out a lot. Though they shared this apartment, we seldom encountered one another. That was as much my wish as theirs. I didn't like her. I tried, but I couldn't. I saw what she was doing to my son.' She wiped her eyes. 'Poor child. No wonder she was so pitiably destructive . . .'

I looked away, stared out the tall windows at the lights of the city. 'You must admit that it's odd, living here in the same building, that Shannon and Melody had never met.'

'They met for the first time at that party, and it was a fluke that Greg and Melody were there at all. We had some legal things to go over that afternoon, Greg and I, and the lawyer was late. Greg was fretting about being away from the studio. Melody was sulking because he wasn't paying attention to her. I said, "Let's drop in down at the pool and wish Shannon a happy birthday." It was an impulse. It's the only reason we were there at all . . .'

I nodded my understanding. 'It was at the party Melody discovered that Fred had a webbed toe. Melody had had one, too. Someone had told her such anomalies run in families. Shannon had had similar webs, and probably said so at the party. From that moment on, Melody knew Fred Foret was her father. She didn't tell him who she was. When he tried to seduce her, she refused him but she told Shannon all about it. She wanted to hurt his other family, don't you think? Hurt him, hurt his other daughter?'

Harriet rubbed her hands over her face, as though trying to rub something away. 'I suppose. Yes. That would have

been like her. She always wanted to hurt me, because I was
Greg's other family. She couldn't bear to share him.'

'You used the word "persecuting", and what Melody did
to Shannon was that. Melody followed Shannon, bothered
her, probed for areas of discomfort, then insisted on talking
about them. She pushed Shannon. She brought up the
incest, again and again, and insisted on dwelling on it. She
drove Shannon out of her mind.'

Harriet rubbed her face again, lifted her glasses back,
over her head, rubbed her eyes, then put the glasses back
on, adjusting the band that held them. She looked old and
tired.

'Who killed Melody, Mrs Steinwale?'

'Why, I suppose Fred did, Mr Lynx. No doubt Melody
threatened to expose him for what he was, and he killed
her.'

'I think he intended to, Mrs Steinwale. I don't think he
actually did.'

She stared at me through her huge-lensed glasses, like an
owl. 'If not he, then who, Mr Lynx? You think you know.
You obviously came here to tell me.'

I did know. In a way Lycia had told me, Lycia who had
told me nothing but the truth. 'It was Shannon, wasn't it?
For some reason, Lycia was worried and went after her.
What was it? Did Lycia find a gun missing?'

'I don't know what you mean,' Harriet whispered.

'Lycia went to the park looking for Shannon. When she
saw Melody's dog running loose, she knew something had
happened. She took the dog and went looking for Melody,
putting on a show for Willie Stevenson by asking other
people as well. Then, when she found Melody, already dead,
she propped the body up on the bench, took the dog, and left
the park. That's inexplicable, Harriet. Simply inexplicable,
unless she was protecting someone. She wouldn't have
protected Fred.'

'Children,' she murmured. 'Families. There's nothing so
important.'

I waited, but she said nothing more. After a moment, I

went on. 'I suppose, after a while, she found Shannon and took her home. Or Shannon simply came home. Later that day, Lycia took the collie to the shelter. I don't know which happened first, but I'm sure both things happened.'

'Why would she have done that?' She wasn't really curious. She knew the answer.

'Taken the collie to the shelter? To give the family time. So there would be no questions asked. Greg was in the hospital. You had your own part of the apartment. If the dog was gone, no one would ask about it. No one asked about it even after Melody was found.'

She said nothing. I found her passivity irritating.

'Don't you think Shannon needs help?'

The words burst from her. 'She's getting help. Good Lord, Mr Lynx, Lycia is paying out thousands every month for help for Shannon! Do you believe putting the child through a trial and locking her in a hospital would help her more? She's been under psychiatric care since the day Melody died, just as she was for years after her father did what he did. She would have been all right if Fred had let her alone, but once he came back here, once she was no longer a child, he started in on her again. Between her father and Melody, they were destroying her. Such an unkind, evil man, Fred. And Melody! Such an angry, hating girl!'

'Couldn't Lycia protect her from him?'

Harriet made an impatient movement. 'Psychiatrists! Her therapist wanted her to deal with her father. Learn to handle him, put him in his place. Her therapist kept telling her to be strong, set Fred aside, put him out of her life, but she seemingly wasn't able to do that. He was like an evil genie, sitting on her shoulder, warping her. She needed to grow up, to have friends, to have a lover or a husband. She needed Fred to go away and let her grow up, to stop trying to control her!'

She was glaring at me. I glared back, taking in the huge round spectacles she was wearing, the low sensible shoes, the shapeless dress in an elegant fabric. Not a young woman. And yet a woman capable of much.

She turned away from me, speaking firmly. 'You mustn't think such things, Mr Lynx. Your imagination is running riot. Fred killed Melody. I'm sure of it. Let me freshen your drink.' She took the glass from me and turned towards the bar, turning on another lamp as she passed it. In the glow of the bulb I saw the band of woven elastic that held her glasses.

'You're not wearing your contacts tonight,' I commented.

'An infection,' she said, putting ice in my glass. 'I get them every now and then and have to do without my contacts. I hate glasses. I have funny bumps behind my ears and glasses won't stay on unless I use an elastic. Then if I use the elastic, they make blisters, so I have to put something under them . . .'

'I found a shred of that elastic,' I told her. 'On the tree where Fred died. It took me some time to figure out what it was. There was a tuft of fibre from a sweatband, too.'

Silence. Rigidity. 'Do you think I shot him?'

'What am I supposed to think?'

A long silence. Finally, a sigh. 'Yes. I shot him.' It was only a whisper.

'Lycia said you weren't the type, either of you. Not the killing type.'

'She isn't. Perhaps I found that I was.'

'Where did you get the gun you shot him with?'

Silence. She was thinking. 'It was Ross's. Lycia didn't know he kept it, but he had it hidden in his bedside table. One day when I was down there, I took it.'

'What did you do with it?'

She turned and looked at me again, stirring the drink. Then she handed it to me, calmly. 'I disposed of it,' she said, running her fingers through her grey hair. 'It and the sweatband and the clothes I was wearing. Somewhere they won't ever be found.'

'Why did you arrange the body that way? How did you know how Fred usually looked?'

She shrugged. 'I'd seen him there. I walk in the park,

too, occasionally. I don't walk a dog, but I do walk, and whenever he saw me, he always wanted to talk.'

Yes. Fred had always wanted to talk. 'Did you get the idea from that fantasy you and Lycia had created?'

She stared at me, then smiled, a remote, almost fatalistic smile. 'Perhaps. Yes. Fred couldn't or wouldn't understand that he was destroying his own child. Lycia told him. Ross told him. He only smiled, and said they were wrong, that Shannon needed him, needed his "protection". He was opaque to understanding, don't you know? He was so completely egocentric, she was only a mannequin for him to manipulate for his own gratification. He could not see what he was doing. He was killing her. I couldn't let that happen.'

'Because you and Lycia had planned it?'

She thought for a moment, reasoning it out. 'No. Because I love Lycia. Because I couldn't watch her suffer. Because she's my friend. Because Shannon is still a child, and sometimes children need more protection than the law can give them.'

Silence. I didn't know what else to say.

Harriet mused. 'It's strange that one can know all the causative factors that go to make someone like Melody, or Fred. One can know and sympathize. And one can still hate them for what they are. Were. I can be desperately sorry for them and still be glad they are gone.'

They were gone. Melody and Fred both. No one really grieved for Fred, but I remembered Greg's voice as he yearned for Melody.

Harriet stood at the window, musing. 'With them gone, maybe Shannon can forget. I hope Greg can forget. Shannon will go on seeing her doctor, and gradually, she'll grow up and get well. Greg and Trish will have a healthy life together. When you get to be my age, you long for family to go on into the future. I had three children. Both my daughters died very young. I have only Greg now, and Trish, and little Frosty, and maybe, I pray, another baby or two to come. I'm not worried about Greg any more. Trish will take care of Greg.'

'And all's well that ends well?' I asked. 'Murder is to be allowed to go unpunished?' Even to my own ears, I sounded shocked.

She shook her head at me. 'You know nothing about punishment, Mr Lynx, if you think that. If you want to turn me in, go ahead. I warn you, I'll get a good lawyer. I won't admit a single thing. It will be your word against mine.'

I stood and walked over to the window beside her. I didn't want to turn her in, though not for the reasons she supposed. 'What do I tell Marge Beebe?' I asked. 'She wants to know why her brother died.'

'Tell her . . . tell her his sins came back to get him,' she said. 'Does it matter which sins?'

It didn't matter which sins. There were a dozen victims who could have killed Fred Foret. A dozen who probably wanted to. As long as Lycia hadn't done it, did Marge care who?

'That place you and Lycia work for,' I said. 'The Lighthouse. Does it need money?'

'Always.'

When I'd talked to Marge last, she'd said she didn't want Fred's money. I had to do something with it. There was no way to return it. Fred had stolen much that couldn't be returned. Innocence. Joy. Youth.

I made up my mind, finally. 'I don't think anyone else needs to know what I told you about Melody being Fred's daughter.' Marge didn't need to know. Nor Lycia.

She agreed, with a nod.

I said, 'Thank you for the drink. I don't imagine we'll be seeing each other again soon.'

She cocked her head, waiting.

'Will you tell Lycia and Ross . . . tell Lycia I enjoyed knowing her.'

'You won't be seeing them either?' Was it hope in her voice? Or something deeper and more sardonic than that?

'I think they would find that more comfortable.'

Harriet would tell them I knew . . . what I knew. My

knowing would make them wary and defensive. Harriet might tell them she didn't think I intended to do anything about it, but they would doubt that. Any effort at friendship on my part would be suspect. They needed to let memories die as well.

I got up, found my raincoat by the door, slipped it on. 'I hope Greg and Trish will be very happy.'

'Trish has a talent for happiness,' she said. 'She creates it where there is none.'

From the way she said it, I could tell she knew. She knew her son still longed for the woman who had almost driven him mad. Ah. Well. As they say.

Grace and Mark seemingly had no trouble accepting Fred as Melody's killer. I told them Harriet Steinwale had confirmed Melody's assumption that the money had been taken as kickbacks when Fred worked for the DOD. I had told Marge Beebe that Fred killed Melody, and why. My conscience didn't hurt me over this. Fred might have done it. He had intended to do so, even if he hadn't done it. And if he hadn't done it, the only reason was that she was already dead. If we could find two guns and identify them as having belonged to Lycia and Fred, we would know for sure. I didn't think they would ever be found.

Grace and Mark still wanted to know, of course, who had killed Fred.

'I don't think we'll ever be sure,' I said. 'I told Marge about Fred's having stolen the money while he was at the DOD and about Melody's attempt to blackmail him or turn him in or whatever she had in mind. I think Marge understands what must have happened. The name of the actual killer—someone out of his own past or someone avenging Melody . . . I don't think Marge feels she needs to know exactly who.'

'And the money?' Grace wanted to know.

'The money has been sent to a charity,' I said. 'Anonymously, by a bonded messenger who stayed while it was opened in front of witnesses.' Remembering a previous charity rip-off I'd been acquainted with, I'd had sense enough to assure all that cash couldn't be made away with. 'Marge said she didn't want any questions from the IRS.' The Lighthouse would benefit, which was the only really good thing about this whole matter.

'I wish I could close the police file,' said Grace wistfully. 'But I can't do that without dragging in a lot of people, and the lieutenant would want to know why. I'd need the Beacon guy. And he'd have some high-powered lawyer. I'd have to question Harriet Steinwale, and so would she.' She gave me a long, level look.

'Let it go,' I suggested. Grace served the law, but she didn't mind serving justice, occasionally. In this case, we'd already achieved as close to justice as we were going to get. She made a face, but she let it go. Mark gave me a look, much like one of Eugenia's looks. He thought I knew something I wouldn't tell them. Well, I did. And I wouldn't. After a few days of hints which I pretended not to notice, he forgot about it.

Grace was another matter. Her seeming acquiescence had been only temporary. A week or so later we were lying at opposite ends of my oversized bathtub, two glasses of chilled champagne sitting on the tile and a selection of carefully selected nibbles on a platter within reach. I'd rationed Grace to one every five minutes so I could have some. It had been an intermittently slothful Sunday, and we'd enjoyed every minute of it.

Out of the steamy blue she said, 'You didn't tell me everything, did you? About Fred and Melody.'

I thought about lying and discarded the notion. Even though Grace kept insisting we were only friends, I had no intention of giving her ammunition for her belief that Agatha and I had had a relationship which Grace and I could never have.

'No,' I admitted. 'I didn't tell you everything.'

'Is it because I'm a cop?' she wanted to know, sounding more than a little hurt.

I considered that for a while. It was and it wasn't. 'I

thought you might think you should do something,' I said.
'I didn't want to put you in that position.'

'Don't you think you ought to let me make up my own
mind?' she asked. 'This isn't some kind of aristocracy, is it?
Or some sexist relationship where the educated male gets
to make all the decisions?'

Being male or educated had had nothing to do with it,
but try to convince Grace of that. So I slumped down until
the warm water bathed all the sore tufty bits of hair growing
on my scars and told her everything I thought. When I was
finished, she ate a few more bits and pieces very slowly and
thoughtfully, and finally told me I couldn't prove any of it
and she couldn't prove any of it, and she didn't think she'd
do anything about it. Later we went back to bed and made
love. There was something new between us, or from her to
me. Something almost like trust.

A time came, some months later, when memory was jogged
forcibly and her decision and mine reared its guilty head. I
was sitting at my desk on another Sunday, this a lonely
late-fall one, staring at another one of those newspaper
cutout messages (the fifth), which had been delivered in its
plain brown envelope with the morning paper. My would-be
informant was getting impatient with my unwillingness
either to be informed or to pay for the privilege. 'Last offer,'
this one said. Mr Anonymous didn't know it, but it was
getting harder and harder to ignore the invitation. I was
getting to the point where I wanted to know. Jacob's sweet
words notwithstanding, I really wanted to know. Or perhaps
it would be better to say that I was reconciled to knowing.
There were so many things I thought I recognized, so
many people, like Lycia, I thought I knew. It would be
good to know for sure. Or not, for sure. And put it behind
me.

I thought I'd talk it over with Grace. If it was an attempt
at extortion, I wasn't going to let the perpetrator get away.
I put the thing in the bottom drawer with the others before
spreading out the Sunday paper. The section that fell out

on top was the one chronicling the things people get up to when they aren't attending to business: the so-called society pages. Two pictures filled the upper corners of the page, and I knew the people in both. From the left-hand picture Trish smiled out at me like a princess, Greg's bony features close beside, off on their honeymoon to New York, where there would be a prestigious gallery showing of Grale's new paintings. I crossed my fingers and said a non-sectarian prayer. She looked radiant. I couldn't tell how he felt.

The right-hand picture was of Shannon and the Ancini scion, she in bridal white, he in tails and looking as though he'd worn such garments from birth. Her flowerlike face bloomed up at me as she clung to her handsome husband's arm. The photographer had caught another face behind the couple: Lycia, a little out of focus but with her mouth unmistakably curved in that familiar, tranquil, untroubled smile. An Etruscan smile. A smile that covered some mystery, some secret I needed to know now as much as when I had first met her.

I pulled my eyes away from her image and concentrated on the bride, noting once again that Shannon isn't a tall woman. In the news photo, the top of her head came to her husband's jawline, and I recalled him as being about my height.

Harriet Steinwale, on the other hand, is a very tall woman, over six feet. If Harriet Steinwale had left that bit of fuzzy fabric on the tree, it would have been slightly above my head instead of where I found it—below my chin. By itself, not proof positive.

Add to that, when I had brought Marge to the Louvre apartments the morning that Fred had died, Stevenson was just coming down with the dogs. He hadn't heard anyone go out from the Foret apartment, so he was late. And yet, when I got to Lycia's apartment, the shelties were comfortably curled up in their baskets, not nervously running to and fro as dogs do who need to go out. They'd been out. If Lycia had taken them, Willie Stevenson would have heard her and gone earlier. He hadn't heard, so Shannon must have taken the dogs out that morning, very early. The key to the door had probably been left in the door, not in Lycia's jewel box, though Lycia would have ostentatiously taken it from the jewel box later, after waking Ross to witness that fact. Wednesday was his and Lycia's day off, Marge had told me. Ross knew he wasn't on call. He would have allowed himself to sleep soundly until he was awakened.

Had Fred asked Shannon to meet him in the park so he could tell her once again how much better off she was without Ancel Ancini? What an irony if he had. Infuriated by him, spurred on by her therapist's suggestions that she be forceful and independent, and remembering that a gun had solved a problem once before, Shannon had decided to rid herself of another incubus. She had used Lycia's gun to shoot Melody, but Ross, ignorant of that fact, had kept an additional weapon in the apartment. Had Lycia suggested to Ross that he get rid of his weapon? Had he promised he would but then changed his mind? When Harriet said he kept the gun in his dresser drawer, it might have been true. Wherever he had kept it, Shannon had found it.

After Shannon had killed Fred, she had gone home and told her mother what she'd done. Lycia had called Harriet. And while Keith and Lycia and Shannon—I didn't believe Ross knew anything about it or he would never have talked to me as he had—had agreed upon an alibi, Harriet had gone back to the park and removed whatever evidence there might have been. The gun, if it had been dropped. The footprints, if there had been any. Harriet had arranged the body to look natural, as Melody's body had been arranged and for the same reason: to give the family time—time to tell Shannon what to say, time to get Shannon calm. Almost calm enough to make a good show when first Marge and I and then the police showed up. Her hysterics then had been put down to grief, or shock.

Perhaps someone had come down the path while Harriet

was there, behind the tree. Perhaps she had merely felt faint. For whatever reason, Harriet had leaned back against the rough-trunked giant, the side away from the path, where Shannon must also have hidden. The tree was a grizzled patriarch. Harriet hadn't seen the tiny tuft of white fibre from Shannon's sweatband. She hadn't realized she had left a shred of elastic from her glasses higher up on the tree, over a head higher. Pure coincidence.

Why had Harriet confessed? To lead me away from her friend's child? Like a ground-nesting bird, fluttering its wings, risking its life to lead the fox . . . the Lynx away.

As he had been led away. Looking at the bride's pictured face, I did not see any evidence of madness. It must have been there at least twice. It might still be there, hiding just behind those sparkling eyes. Obviously her young husband did not see it either. Perhaps he would always be faithful and kind and Shannon would always be happy and it would never reappear again. If so, my conscience would remain clear, Harriet would not regret her part in the puzzle, and Lycia could continue to wear that tranquil Etruscan smile. She had never actually lied to me. She had said Ross's gun was stolen, and it was—by Shannon. She had said she had gotten rid of her own gun long ago, and she had, when Shannon returned it after killing Melody. She had looked me in the eye and told me neither she nor Ross had killed anyone, and it was true. She had said she couldn't honestly tell me anything, and from her point of view, she couldn't. Not honestly. Each thing she had told me was individually true. I had heard the truth and had not seen what the truth was hiding: this girl in her white dress, smiling up at her new husband.

Something dark and evil whispered insidiously that it would not turn out well and I would have much to regret. I pretended not to hear it. Weddings are for hope. Weddings are for families.

Families. I thought grimly of the five ugly letters in the bottom drawer of my desk which offered me . . . what? A family of my own? Harriet had said nothing was more important than families. Grace had told me the same thing. And Nellie and Mark and almost everyone else I knew, in one connection or another.

I had to take it on faith.

Death for Old Time's Sake

CHAPTER 1

My foster father, Jacob Buchnam, died quietly on a February night with snow falling outside and the world muffled and still. He was eighty-one. A series of little strokes over a period of years presaged a bad one in late November. Once that happened, we knew him well enough to know he wouldn't live long. He simply wouldn't want to. When I got the early morning call from Jacob's nurse and companion, Francis Fairweather, I was shaken but not surprised.

Grief had been waiting in the wings, so to speak. It came surging in, and I sat there immersed in it, using the pain to expiate all the opportunities lost, all the kindnesses unaccomplished. I suppose everyone does that. People die and we use our hurt to assuage the guilt of all the things we could have done for them but didn't. Jacob had been my family, my anchor, my mainstay since I was thirteen. No amount of effort would ever have repaid his kindness, and I couldn't imagine being without him.

So I sat there and hurt, not hearing as Francis spoke earnestly about what had to be done. Finally I realized he was repeating himself, and I made myself focus on what he was saying.

'Jason, remember what Jacob said. He wanted things handled quickly.' Francis's voice kept breaking as he reminded me of Jacob's wishes. 'The doctor's on his way, and I've already called the mortuary. If you want to see him, you'd better come now.'

The Jacob of past years was the one I wanted to remember, not the shell who had lain in his bed for the last three months. It took a couple of tries to get the words out, but I told Francis it was all right: let the mortuary Jacob had chosen take him. Jacob was Jewish, and though he hadn't been at all observant he'd approved of the Jewish tradition of being buried before sundown of the same day one died.

He'd chosen cremation, which is not at all consistent with tradition, of course. Consistent or not, traditional or not, I'd promised him I'd do anything he wanted.

Jacob's only blood kin was his niece, Charlotte Grosbek née Buchnam, a rancher who lived about fifty miles south of Denver. I called her to let her know what had been planned. Like Francis and me, she was up and down half a dozen times as we talked, alternately crying and praising Jacob.

'He was such a really nice man. After Daddy died, Uncle Jacob was always so thoughtful, making sure I never wanted for anything.' Then tears would force her to stop talking.

When I told her that Jacob had left her a considerable bequest, she cried even harder. As Jacob's executor, I was to see to the bequests, the ones he'd left to Charlotte and Francis and the smaller ones to a few local and national charities. The balance of his estate, mostly books and furnishings of no great value, came to me. Jacob had arranged, however, that his sizeable monthly income from his former business (now mine) would end when he died. His death made me sole owner of Jason Lynx Interiors, the three-storey building at 1465 Hyde Street and a valuable inventory. Instead of teetering along in intimate partnership with the loan department at the bank, I was almost well to do.

If anything, that made me feel worse. I'd have given it all up and more to have Jacob back. However, no amount of resolve or guilt or grief would do that, so I did what people do when they lose someone: blundered my way through the day, stopping now and then in the bathroom to wash my face in cold water and swallow the lump that kept coming up behind my breastbone, sorry for myself yet glad in a sense that it was over because he had wanted it to be over.

Mark McMillan, my assistant, and Eugenia Lowe, the showroom manager, kept finding excuses to consult me about things, patting me (figuratively speaking) at each encounter. Grace Willis, who still says she is not in love with me, except when she forgets, took time from what she calls the cop-shop to phone every few hours to ask if I was all right. By evening, they'd stroked and poked me into some kind of shape, enough so that I could call Francis and tell him I was coming over to pick up the box of personal papers Jacob had kept in his bedside table. Everything else I might need as executor was already in the old iron safe in the basement of my shop-cum-residence at 1465 Hyde.

Francis made no effort to hide his feelings, and we ended up conducting a two-man wake, getting through half a bottle of Scotch in the process. Jacob had been abstemious. He'd had no patience with addictions—whether to alcohol, drugs, tobacco, gambling or sex. I could still call to mind his lectures to the fourteen-year-old Jason about all *that!*— and it was probably the memory of his outspoken attitudes that made Francis and me cap the bottle when we did. Of all Jacob's friends and relations, Francis was going to have his life the most changed. He'd been with Jacob since the first stroke, years ago. Now he'd have to make a lot of changes: who he cared for, where he lived. He was open about saying he thought it unlikely he'd find another patient he'd care about as much as he had Jacob.

It was almost midnight before I got back to the shop. The showrooms on the lower floor were dark, but I'd left a light on in my apartment upstairs. Bela and Schnitz met me at the backdoor. Bela is my old friend, a hundred and twenty pounds of white Kuvasz dog. Schnitz is a new friend, a twelve-pound Maine Coon kitten, son of Grace's huge tomcat, Critter. Schnitz is an orange tabby with tufty feet, and he'll weigh in at eighteen or twenty pounds when he's fully grown. Not as big as his daddy—there are no other cats as big as Critter—but then who needs twenty-nine pounds of cat.

The three of us went upstairs together. I felt tired but not at all sleepy, so I dumped the papers out on the kitchen table, put some coffee beans through the grinder and made a pot, poured a mugful and then sat down to see what I had to take care of. First thing on the top of a pile was

Schnitz, who had followed his usual habit of lying down on top of whatever I am working on. He knows it's an unfailing way to get noticed, especially when he revs up his basso purr, blinks at me slowly, and puts out a fat paw to touch my hand. I gave him a scalp massage with one hand while I fished from under him a thick blue envelope, unsealed. Inside were a stack of cancelled cheques. Big cheques. All made out to someone named H.Fixe. All signed by Jacob. I'd never heard of any H.Fixe, which puzzled me a little. Still, I wasn't upset until I turned the envelope over and saw written on the outside the word *Extortion!* The word was in firm black felt-tip, in Jacob's curly hand. *Extortion!* Underlined. Exclamation point.

It wasn't right. The mood was wrong. I'd been sentimentalizing, floating in memories, and that one black word brought me down with a clang and a shocking flush of red-hot anger, as though someone had set off a bomb in my head. I'd turned the papers upside down when I'd dumped them from the box, so this envelope had been tucked away at the bottom. Despite its location at the bottom of the box, the last cheque in the series was dated the past November, dated, as a matter of fact, the same day as Jacob's last stroke. Since then, I'd been taking care of his bills and payments because Jacob hadn't been able to. Writing this cheque to H.Fixe was among the last things Jacob had done!

I knew Francis wouldn't be asleep yet, so I called him and asked if he knew anything about the cheques or H.Fixe.

'Jacob paid his own bills and addressed his own envelopes as long as he could, Jason. All I did was stamp the envelopes and put them in the mail for him. You've been doing it all since November.'

'Did you mail cheques for him the day he had his stroke?'

He heard the anger in my voice. 'I may have. Jason, what's wrong?'

'Just something I found here, Francis. Makes me think maybe this guy was bothering Jacob, and I got furious at the thought of it. I never signed a cheque to H.Fixe. Jacob never mentioned anybody by that name to me. Did he ever say anything to you?'

'Never a word. I always assumed Fixe was an insurance agent or a broker or something.'

I asked another question or two, but Francis really didn't know anything about it. I apologized for bothering him so late and hung up.

Fixe wasn't an insurance agent or a broker, because if Jacob had been paying off a large policy or making some investment, he'd have told me. In fact, if he'd been doing anything usual or ordinary with that amount of money, he'd have told me. Why hadn't he wanted me to know about this? I tried to figure it out, feeling inexplicably hurt by the little mystery. Hadn't he wanted to bother me? Didn't he want me involved? You don't write ten-thousand-dollar cheques two or three times a year for almost ten years without a reason! Not if you're Jacob, you don't. And I knew Jacob well enough to know that when he'd written the word 'Extortion', he'd meant it. He'd been rigorous about the use of language. Words meant what words meant, and that was that. Extortion was extortion.

There was no address in the envelope. There was no 'Fixe' in the phone book, either. Francis hadn't remembered where the cheques had been sent. It was too late in the day to do anything about it immediately. I put the papers back in their box, and went to bed, thinking I might trace Fixe through the banks that had cashed the cheques. If I had to. Tomorrow.

As I lay there in bed, staring at the ceiling and thinking how unlike Jacob it was for him to hide something from me, it occurred to me that it was very like him to hand me a distraction. He had often done that when I was a kid, when I was sad or angry or just hating everyone, including myself. He'd find something to interest me, some puzzle for me to figure out, then he'd hang around, asking questions, demanding answers, until I turned from whatever emotion was running wild and began to pay attention to life again. He'd been everything to me any family could have been.

When I had wondered who I was and why I had been mysteriously abandoned as a child, it was Jacob who had insisted the 'why' didn't matter. Who I was, Jacob said, depended only on what I wanted to make of myself. He told me I was lucky to start with a clean slate, not burdened by other people's desires and failures, not thinking I had either to identify with or rebel against someone else just because they were related.

After a while, I accepted that, though curiosity still reared its head from time to time. Sometimes I still half-remember faces or voices. More recent and more troubling than the foggy memories are the half-dozen anonymous letters I've received, all of them mailed over the past eighteen months, letters offering to provide information about Jason Lynx, for a price. I'd been tempted, but Grace and I had talked about it at length, in the end agreeing it was a con. Even if it wasn't—what the hell!—I had Jacob. I didn't need any more family than that.

I'd never mentioned the letters to Jacob, mostly because I hadn't wanted to upset him, but also because I knew what he'd say. Jacob had had a firm rule about traffic in trash, one he'd drummed into me over the years. He wouldn't expend emotion or value on something he called (in a whisper and only for my ears) *dreck*. It didn't matter what other dealers did, buying and selling stuff that was essentially worthless, Jacob wouldn't do it, and he carried the same rule over to his private life. As kids will, I'd sometimes wanted things because other kids had them. It would have been easier for Jacob just to give in to me, as most parents who can afford it no doubt do. He never would. We always had to sit down together and analyse the value of whatever I thought I wanted. As a kid, sometimes I'd been furious with him, but I couldn't remember his ever being wrong.

So, if the cheques to H.Fixe had really been extortion payments, I knew the pain and revulsion it must have cost Jacob to write them. I also knew he wouldn't have done it to protect himself. He would have done it only to protect someone else.

My last angry thought, before I fell asleep, was that I intended to find whoever had been responsible and extract a fair measure of retribution on Jacob's behalf.

Thursday morning I didn't have time for retribution because John and Lucinda Hooper were coming in to see a Federal square-back sofa Mark and I had acquired in bits and pieces at the auction of the Morrison estate. When patriarch Morrison had passed on at age ninety, his children and grandchildren off in Arizona or Florida or California had been more interested in cash than they were in fine old furniture. At the time I had more inventory than I needed, but I went to the auction anyway. If one deals in antiques one goes to auctions. It's obligatory. If your competitors don't see you there, before you know it they've decided you're bankrupt or alcoholic or dying of some incurable disease. Antique dealers are like any professional group, revelling in jargon and fuelled by rumour.

So, though the bidding wasn't due to begin until one in the afternoon, by nine that morning I was walking up and down the dusty aisles between piles of great stuff (sternly advising myself that I did not *need* any of it), when I heard this poor crippled thing moaning at me from behind a bunch of dilapidated appliances. It was the strangest feeling. I may have glimpsed it subliminally from the corner of the eye, just enough to make me think I heard this weary little sound, like a tired child crying in a distant room. When I saw what it was, I stood over it for a long time, feeling pity. Such a lovely, elegant thing it was, like a crippled greyhound, lying there among the cast-offs with one arm and three of its four tapered front legs missing and the carved frieze coming loose from the top rail. It was a hundred and eighty years old if it was a day, and it was dying.

I raised my eyebrow at Mark when he came browsing by, and we conferred in hasty whispers. Sometimes people save broken parts of old furniture, thinking they'll have them mended later. Sometimes they put the broken bits away and forget about them. Sometimes they put them away in other old furniture. We spent the next hour fossicking around among dusty stuff, like domestic archæologists trying to do a dig without appearing to be doing anything except aimless wandering.

The missing arm rail, panel, and carved handhold turned up stuffed into the bottom drawer of a 1920's oak dresser under some faded curtains. We redoubled our efforts, surreptitiously burrowing through everything included in the sale. Lo and behold, Mark found the three missing legs at the bottom of a box of brass cupboard hardware. We looked around to see if anyone was paying any attention to us. No one was. Evidently we'd been sufficiently casual about the whole thing that no one knew the pieces were there. The delicate turning and reeding on the legs would have been unmistakable if anyone had been looking. It probably helped that none of my more knowledgeable competitors were present at the time.

When the auction got under way, we bid listlessly for this and that, making sure we didn't get any of it. Then, when the box of hardware and the dresser came up, Mark became less listless (though undetectably so) and got them both for under fifty. When the wreckage on the sofa was sold as part of an aggregation of junk, he bought that, too, while I yawned in a display of complete indifference and made inane comments about the weather to a colleague or two.

One of whom, Harold Feddleman, commented, 'Pity so many parts are missing on that Federal sofa. Almost be worth restoring it. Nice piece.' Harold knew Mark worked for me, and he was examining me suspiciously.

'Very nice,' I replied in a bored voice while my heart thubbed away in fear of imminent discovery. 'Too bad it's a total wreck.'

The only parts of our purchase we brought back to the shop were the disconnected parts of the sofa and the box of assorted brass hardware—which is always useful if one needs to match old drawer pulls or hinges or knobs. There were only shreds of upholstery left on the sofa back, literally shreds, but what was there served to identify the type of fabric used originally as well as giving us a hint as to the original colour. There are fabric houses specializing in period fabrics. Once all the mahogany and birch parts were cleaned up and reunited (*all* original parts, mind you, except for one four-inch piece of birch dowel going down the inside of a leg!) and the back and arms reupholstered in silk brocade with an elegant new seat cushion, the sofa turned out to be absolutely gorgeous. Near museum quality. Every time I looked at it with its exposed mahogany top rail and its elaborately carved Sheraton frieze, I felt sanctified by having rescued it.

Since the Morrisons had come originally from New England, my guess was the sofa had been made by Samuel McIntire in Salem, Mass. That made it worth at least twenty thou, more likely twice that. Mark had already worked up a nice comparison chart out of auction catalogues and notations of sales prices on similar items, as well as some information on Samuel McIntire and Salem furniture production in the late 1700s and early 1800s.

At any rate, John and Lucinda Hooper were coming over to take a look. I figured we'd dicker back and forth for some time. Dickering was the greater part of the fun for the Hoopers. They would amuse themselves thinking up new ways to approach the buy, such as trading me back such and such a piece they'd bought last year, or getting me to throw in such and such a piece to sweeten the deal. Eugenia and I had already conferred on what we might use as sweeteners. We could always sacrifice a few small things to make the bigger sale.

The Hoopers played it just as we'd thought they would. Hum and haw, and this and that, and no decision that morning, though Lucinda cast a worried look over her shoulder when they left, as though she feared another buyer might ooze out of the woodwork the moment she was gone. We had no other prospects for the sofa. Seeing the expression on Lucinda's face, I was pretty sure we didn't need any.

By eleven I was back upstairs in my office staring at the wall, suddenly at a loss.

'You OK?' asked Mark, giving me a sympathetic look.

'Yeah,' I said. 'Sure.' For the moment, dealing with the Hoopers, I'd actually forgotten about Jacob.

'You're going to miss him.'

I nodded and swallowed. 'We all knew it was inevitable.'

'I know. Still.'

Right. Still. Since Mark had reminded me, I fetched the box of papers from the kitchen and turned it out on top of my desk, drawing Mark's attention to the envelope with 'Extortion' written on it.

'Pretty firm hand,' he said. 'I thought Jacob was very shaky.'

'That was written before he got sick,' I said. 'Before I even came back to Denver. The first cheque was written almost twelve years ago.'

Mark had the cheques spread out in front of him. 'Who's this H. Fixe?' he asked me.

I shrugged.

'You're not looking for a puzzle, are you?' he asked with a faintly worried expression. 'You're not trying to make something out of this.'

I leaned over and tapped the word on the envelope. 'I don't have to make anything out of it. It's already made. If Jacob wrote that, he meant it. Somebody was holding him up.'

'Usually, I'd say go to it,' Mark commented, 'but you may be sorry if you go digging into Jacob's life. If he didn't tell you, he had a reason; maybe there was something in his life he wanted to keep private.'

'If it was something about Jacob himself, he'd have written the word *Blackmail*. Jacob was as much a stickler for accuracy as he was for honesty. Extortion is a different thing.'

Mark sat staring at the envelope. I could follow his thoughts on his face. Though he can do a poker face when he has to, his mobile, handsome countenance usually shows every nuance, every thought, every feeling. He looks like a blond Christopher Reeves, though his lips are fuller and his nose is not quite so sharply classic. He'd have made a great actor.

'Extortion is getting money by threatening someone, isn't it?' He gave me a puzzled look.

I was as puzzled as he. 'Jacob wouldn't have given in to a threat against himself, Mark. If he paid to protect someone, it had to be someone else. So who?'

'Who else is there?' Mark asked. 'You, or his niece, right.'

'Right,' I agreed. 'Me or Charlotte. In either case, I certainly should know about it. He'd have wanted me to help Charlotte, if necessary, and he'd sure as hell have expected me to look out for myself.' Why hadn't he told me about this whatever it was? He should have told me! It hurt that he hadn't.

Since neither of us could come up with a solution to the problem, Mark went back to his catalogues and I went back to the box, sorting the contents into piles. Jacob's birth certificate. Jacob's military service records, World War II. A picture of me at age thirteen, looking like a hippie. Tough guy. A picture of Jacob in the Colfax Avenue shop with me, age fifteen, wearing shirt and tie and dark apron, my hair long enough to hide the burn scars on the back of my head (the partly healed burns had been there when I'd been abandoned at the Home). After Jacob had caught me trying to steal from his antique shop, he'd hired me and put me to work polishing, repairing, sweeping out and packing up. Later on, he'd sent me to college, where I'd majored in art and history with the idea of becoming a museum curator. My graduation picture was there, cap and gown and silly grin. A few Navy pictures were there, too. I'd been twenty-three or twenty-four by that time. A shot of me with the rest of the guys from scuba school had a Happy Birthday message to Jacob written across our wetsuited forms. Nothing like seeing me busy learning to blow stuff up underwater, Jacob had written, to make him feel his years.

Next were two snaps of me in front of the Smithsonian

—when I got out of the Navy, I'd worked at the Smithsonian for several years—then me and Agatha, then the
two of us with baby Jerry. Agatha was dead. Jerry was
dead. I had learned to accept that, but still I turned the
pictures face down.

The next thing in the box was a packet of older photos
in wrinkled tissue that had obviously been wrapped and
unwrapped many, many times. Most of these I couldn't
remember ever having seen before, though the first one set
off an immediate tingle of recognition. I had seen this portrait—or a copy of it—years ago, hanging on the wall near
Jacob's bed. It showed a lovely young woman in her twenties and was signed *Dearest Jacob, all my love always. Olivia.*
Her light hair was arranged close to her head in those
too-tight waves women wore back in the 'twenties and 'thirties. Her dress had feathers at the shoulders, like little
wings, and she wore an ornate crucifix on a chain. The face
resembled someone else I knew, but I couldn't think who.

In another photo, a group shot of three women and two
men, the same woman stood against a car, her silk dress
moulded to her slender body in a single fluid line, a man's
arm around her shoulders. After staring at it for some time,
I realized the man was Jacob, a very virile-looking Jacob,
with a full head of dark curly hair. Jacob had been eighty-
one when he died; he'd been born in 1911. This picture
must have been taken sometime in the 'thirties. Looking at
that lovely, laughing face beside him, I wondered why
Jacob had never married. Had something happened to his
Olivia? Had she married someone else? Had he gone on
loving her, all his life?

Mark came by and peered over my shoulder. 'Gorgeous,'
he said, tracing the line of her body with one forefinger.
'Like a Botticelli goddess. She looks like someone I've seen
before. Wrong hairdo, though.'

I said she looked familiar to me, too, but neither of us
could decide who she reminded us of.

'I wonder what happened to the two of them,' I said.

Mark cocked his head, thoughtfully. 'Didn't you tell me Jacob was Jewish?'

'Yes. Not a religious Jew, but he always identified himself as Jewish.'

'She's probably Catholic.' Mark pointed out the crucifix, which I had ignored. ''Twenties and 'thirties were very bigoted times, weren't they? Height of the KKK and all that? Her folks probably went through the roof if they thought she was in love with a Jew. Wasn't there a popular stage comedy, way back, about some Catholic girl marrying a Jewish boy and all the problems they had with in-laws? I seem to recall Mother making some allusion to it when the son of a friend of hers made a similar *mésalliance*. I'm quoting. At any rate, marrying out of one's class and/or religion wasn't the done thing. Not among good families.'

'You think she was from a good family?'

He fanned the pictures on the table. 'Look at their clothes,' he replied. 'I'd guess that's a designer dress in the portrait. Even though feathers were in then, the way these are handled isn't cheap. Look at the car they're leaning against. That's a college crowd in a time when most people didn't go to college. If these people weren't rich, they were well to do, at least.'

If anyone would know, Mark would know. His family was among the wealthier of my acquaintance, not that they made much of my acquaintance. Mark's father had not yet forgiven his son for being gay, working as a designer, or failing to produce an heir for the family fortune, not necessarily in that order. Since I was the person Mark worked for, I received a full share of the elder McMillan's disapprobation. On the few occasions I'd met him he'd been polite but frosty.

'It's possible it was a prejudice problem,' I admitted, feeling sorry for Jacob if that had been true.

I was down to the final two items, the things Jacob had had at the top. One was a list of the charities he had left money to, next to each was a brief paragraph on how he wanted the money used. He'd asked me to visit the local charities on his behalf: the local Planned Parenthood. The Lighthouse centre for battered women. Several others.

And finally a snapshot which had come out looking like a nineteenth-century landscape, full of green and misty distances. I remembered when Jacob had taken it, from the porch of Charlotte's house on a rainy, early summer day. It showed a grove of huge ponderosa pines atop a nearby hill, the land falling away behind in multiple shaded horizons. I remembered the occasion, a family picnic after graduation, just before I'd gone into the Navy. Jacob had been about sixty then. I'd been twenty-something, home for the summer.

And that was all. There really wasn't a lot for me to do. Jacob had been methodical. He hadn't left a lot of loose ends hanging. I put everything back in the box except the list of bequests, the photos, and the envelope of 'Extortion' cheques. Those went in the bottom right-hand drawer of my desk where I keep pending matters. There was no good reason for me to assume that the photos of Olivia and her friends belonged in 'pending'. Maybe I simply wanted to look at her face again because Jacob obviously had, many times.

When Charlotte called later in the morning, I asked her if she recognized either the name Fixe or the name Olivia. Fixe didn't ring a bell, but when I described Olivia's picture, she recalled hearing that Uncle Jacob had had a sweetheart whom he'd never gotten over.

'Daddy told me about it,' she said, referring to Harry Buchnam, Jacob's twin brother. 'One time I asked him why Uncle Jacob had never married, and he told me about this girl Jacob was in love with, but her family didn't approve of the Buchnams. So they sent her off to Europe where she married someone who got wounded in the war, and later died. It was all very tragic.'

'Do you remember her last name?' I asked.

'Olivia sounds sort of familiar,' she mused. 'But I don't think Dad ever mentioned a last name.'

The day passed, Mark and Eugenia closed up shop and went home, I went upstairs to put together an Italian dinner for Grace Willis and me. We had a standing midweek dinner date for any Tuesday, Wednesday or Thursday she wasn't working, plus whatever time we could spend together on the days she had off. Lately she'd had weekends, which had been nice for us both. Grace is a cop. She says cop. She dislikes 'policewoman'. She is tiny, blonde, eats like three stevedores, has enormous drive and ambition, is honest to a fault and hard-working enough to make me feel guilty. She is about eight years younger than I am, which makes her thirty-two. We are at an indeterminate stage of our relationship. I think she's quit worrying that I may be comparing her to Agatha. I have quit trying to find Agatha all over again. Grace reminds me from time to time that she is not in love with me, though I'm not sure whether she's trying to convince me or herself. We have not talked about marriage, at least not marriage to each other, though I have waltzed towards the subject time and again without much response from Grace.

Grace occasionally says that I am not quite lively enough for her, so she goes out with other men from time to time. However, she tells me she does not go to bed with anyone else. She finds me lively enough in that respect. She has kidded me on occasion about being safe sex. I'm not sure this is flattering, but I'd be a fool to question the status quo. I think at the heart of the issue is that I am not at all gregarious, while she gets a high from being part of a crowd. She likes going Christmas shopping and attending football games, things I consider only slightly less agonizing than being trampled by stampeding cows.

Despite that, we enjoy one another. Sometimes Grace finds me moodier than she likes, and I occasionally feel her unquenchability is wearing, but we can say so, and neither of us ever expresses any animosity over these feelings. When I think about it, I find that very lack of irritation a little troubling. It makes me wonder, sometimes, if we are truly tolerant and accepting of one another, or whether we simply don't care quite enough. I like to think it's the former. I'm honest enough not to be sure. In either case, we are very close and fond friends. About that much, I'm positive.

When Grace arrived, I told her what I'd been discovering about Jacob. She got sentimental over the idea of Jacob having an old sweetheart, but when I told her about the 'extortion' envelope, she forgot sentiment and blazed up just as I had. We traded theories on what and who and why. Mine tended to be esoteric, as befits a puzzle-lover, while hers were more pragmatic, as befits a cop. Grace often says that most crimes tend to be a matter of ABC rather than the mystery of X. Someone gets drunk, then gets angry, then bashes someone with the nearest heavy object. Or shoots, or stabs, or runs down with a car. Simple. Despite having made this point repeatedly, she couldn't come up with a simple explanation for the cheques to H.Fixe.

'I don't think I've ever had an extortion case,' she said over the table which had held our Chianti, our antipasto, our minestrone, our veal parmigiana, our linguini, our salad, our cheesecake. I say 'our', though three-quarters of it had been consumed by Grace. In the year and a half I've known her, I've learned to lay in edibles sufficient for four large men and expect her to eat for three and a fraction of them.

'I did have a guy who threatened to kill his wife if she didn't give him custody of their kid, which was extortion even though he finally got charged with something else. Felony menacing, I think,' she said, polishing off the last crumb of her third helping of cheesecake. 'You think Jacob really meant extortion?'

Grace had met Jacob, but she had never had the opportunity to know him. I explained what a stickler Jacob had been for the right word at the right time. If he wrote a word, he meant it. Extortion meant extortion.

'I'll see what I can find out about H.Fixe,' she said. 'See if anybody with that name has a record.'

Then, having temporarily placated her craving for food and crime, she turned her attention to me and we found

other things to think about for the remainder of the evening.
She fell asleep before I did, on her back, soundlessly as a
baby. I lay on my side, my arm across her satiny breasts,
my hand curled around her far shoulder, looking at the line
of her profile against the light from the hall, thinking about
having a family again, starting a family again.

In the Home, all the kids, including me, had constantly
talked about families. Though some of us pretended otherwise, each of us wanted to be adopted. We wanted someone
of our own. Most of us were unadoptable. We hadn't been
relinquished properly, or we were of mixed race, or we were
too old, or we had serious physical or character defects,
some of them no doubt inherent, but some we'd acquired
during our years of institutional life. In my case, the burns
on the back of my head and on one ear (looking, one helpful
physician said, not precisely accidental) had left scars on
more than my body.

From about age fourteen, I'd worn my hair long to cover
the burns. In the year just past, I'd had hair implants
and surgery to smooth out the warped ear. In the Home,
however, we'd all had short institutional haircuts and I'd
been miserably self-conscious about the scars. They had
helped convince me I was unwanted and unwantable,
which had led me to boasting and strutting and accepting
a dare to steal, which had put me in Jacob Buchnam's
Colfax Avenue antique shop, where Jacob had caught me
at my first attempt.

He could have turned in the brat who had tried to rip off
his silver candlestick. Instead, Jacob saw all my cock-a-
doodle as mere cover-up and called my bluff. He made me
his foster son. He reared me. He sent me to school, he
accepted my wife as his own daughter-in-law and my child
as his grandchild. When my wife disappeared and my son
lay in a lifelong coma, he stood by me. When one was found
murdered and the other died, he grieved with me. He had
been my family, first and last.

And now I had none. I looked at Grace's quiet face
against the glow from the window and thought about asking

her to marry me. I decided not to, because I was afraid she'd say no.

Friday morning I made the rounds of the local charities on Jacob's list. He had asked me to call on them personally to explain how he wanted his bequest used. If they couldn't accommodate his wishes, they didn't get it. He'd been very firm about that.

I ended my morning's visits at the local Planned Parenthood clinic, where Jacob had wanted his money used for security against the anti-abortion picketers. I recalled visiting Jacob a year or so ago and finding him brooding angrily over a newspaper account of an abortion clinic blockade by some outfit called Operation Rescue. When I confessed puzzlement as to why he felt so strongly about it, he'd been almost angry with me.

'You, of all people, should undertand, Jason! How many kids were there in that place where you grew up? Over a hundred? Most of them "unadoptable", which means nobody wanted them, right? How many are there now in homes and hospitals all over the country? Half a million, maybe? A million? Minority babies? Half-grown children? Children with AIDS? Retarded children? Children born with addictions? Children who've been abused, as you were? And where is Operation Rescue for them? How many of those children are being rescued from fates far worse than never having been born? Hah?'

'Probably not many, Jacob,' I'd said, trying to calm him down. On the rare occasions when he got angry, he trembled all over.

He wouldn't calm. 'Oh, it's no doubt rewarding to spend a Saturday morning hunkered down outside a clinic, singing hymns and feeling holy, getting your picture in the paper, taking up the time of already overworked police, abusing women who may be more genuinely religious than you are. It would be too difficult and demanding to actually do something for a child in need! So-called Christians! Pah!'

I certainly had been one of those unadoptable children, which meant I could sympathize with his frustration even though I couldn't identify personally with the abortion issue. It had simply never come up in my life. None the less, I understood Jacob's point of view well enough to quote him at some length to Cynthia Adamson, the manager of the clinic, actually getting a smile out of her a couple of times. She looked both too thin and too tired, a pale woman of about thirty-five, lines of determination graven around her mouth and eyes.

'We can use the money,' she said. 'The anti-abortion groups like to claim we make a lot of money doing abortions, but we don't. All the non-profit clinics I know of try to provide abortions at close to cost, because most of our patients are poor.'

If the people in the waiting-room were any indication, they were not only poor but very troubled. As we had come through, I had noticed a woman sobbing in the arms of a friend. When we had settled into Cynthia's private office with the door closed, she told me the woman already had two children, victims of a genetic disease.

'She can't handle any more. Just taking care of the two she has takes all the strength she has.' She nodded towards the waiting-room. 'The first time that woman came in here for counselling, one of the male picketers grabbed her and started screaming at her not to kill her baby. She almost collapsed. All the poor woman has been trying to do is cope with this damned disease, and she didn't need the compassionate help of the so-called pro-life people, I can tell you that.'

She made a spitting motion with her lips, rubbing her forehead as though it hurt. 'Sorry. I get so angry at the pain they cause. I wish there were some way to thank Mr Buchnam for his gift. We need it badly right now.'

'Now more than usually?' I asked.

'Yes. A couple of years ago the police and judges got pretty tired of the demonstrations and started assessing fines that were commensurate with what it cost the city to enforce the law. That stopped the worst of it for a time. It's all very well to shout abuse at poor women and then return to your nice middle-class home for lunch, but spending several weeks in jail among unsympathetic prisoners wasn't what these people had in mind.'

'When did it start up again?'

'Just recently. This new bunch is very abusive. Mostly men. The few women in the crowd are usually brought by men. I won't go into what kind of men. Have you seen them in action?'

I admitted I had only seen pictures on the evening news.

'Drive by in the morning,' she said. 'I'm told we're going to get hit by a full-scale invasion about seven-thirty.'

I nodded, more or less affirmatively. I'm not sure whether I was just agreeing that I should or saying that I would. In either case, I promptly forgot about the clinic and did not remember it until very early on Saturday morning when Grace, who'd arrived late the previous evening with a small overnight case, began moving purposefully in and out of the bedroom at about five a.m.

'What are you doing?' I asked her in disbelief. She was actually wearing a uniform. Grace had been plain clothes for some time. I couldn't recall ever seeing her in uniform.

'Got to go,' she said. 'Duty calls.'

I knew she had the day off. 'What do you mean,' I demanded, furious at her. She had no business going anywhere at all on *our* Saturday.

'It's my weekend at the abortion clinic,' she said. 'They're going to be blockaded this morning. Some of us women cops moonlight there on the weekends, just to make sure nobody gets hurt.'

Oh, great, I thought, still half asleep and completely unsympathetic. 'Carrying limp bodies? Arresting protesters?'

'No,' she said, kissing me on the forehead. 'The guys on regular duty will do that. Those of us moonlighting are inside, to arrest anyone who breaks in or does anything violent. Personally, I'd volunteer, but the department has rules about taking sides in public disputes, like political campaigns or labour union clashes or controversial stuff.

Cops are always cops, even out of uniform, even off duty, so I can't volunteer for either side. What I can do is work for pay, enforcing the law.'

'Like moonlighting policemen at a concert or football game?' I asked. 'Paid extra, but working as cops?'

'Right. I'm not there to take sides. I'm there to provide extra law enforcement. But I donate my pay back to the clinic, which is my right, and that's the best I can do.'

'I'll drive you down,' I said as I struggled from among the covers, resolving, not for the first time, to be understanding. 'It's one of Jacob's selected charities, and I told the clinic manager I wanted to see what goes on. I guess this is as good a time as any.'

It wasn't. It was a lousy time. I had only one cup of coffee before we left, because Grace wanted to be there when the clinic opened at six-thirty. I was offered coffee when we arrived, but since it was to be made in a plastic cup from lukewarm water and a spoonful of brown gravel, I decided to forgo a second cup.

Grace and a colleague went off somewhere to decide on their strategy for the day. Cynthia put a green band on my arm to identify me to the staff as friendly, and I sat down in the as yet empty waiting-room waiting for something to happen.

First the cops showed up outside. Then a few patients straggled in. Then a cavalcade of cars arrived at the kerb, out of which poured the zealots. I watched the whole thing in a kind of frozen disbelief. It was a little like a soccer game, only nastier. The blockaders, mostly male, seemed to be keyed up, rushing the goal. They scrambled for the double glass doors (there were locked steel grilles inside), milled around there for a minute, and then hunkered down to begin singing something that sounded neither rousing nor holy.

From inside, all I could see was their backs, shoved up against each other like sheep packed into a stock truck. Out in front of the blockaders roamed the shock troops, evidently assigned to slogan-carrying and harassment.

Inside, the staff and patients went about their business as though nothing were happening. Whenever a patient arrived, clinic volunteers outside the clinic bulldozed a clear path through to a small back door. Someone inside unlocked it to let each patient in while uniformed female cops (Grace and her friends) stood nearby to make sure no laws were broken. They weren't allowed to help. Only to warn the protesters to stand back—which they did constantly, because every harasser seemed determined to intimidate the patients with shouted abuse—and to move in and make an arrest if something illegal occurred. After a while the regular duty cops outside made an announcement through a bullhorn. I could hear the bleat but not the content and assumed the protesters were being warned to disperse. Outside the doors there was some squirming and linking of arms. The bullhorn sounded again. I stood up to look over the heads of the protesters as the uniformed men began taking the blockaders off, one by one. Unlike some newscasts I've seen, the Denver police didn't bother carrying them. They twisted their arms up behind their backs and used pain to get them moving into the police vans. The remaining blockaders screamed about police brutality, but the police handling didn't look nearly as brutal to me as what the harassers had been doing to the patients.

It took about forty-five minutes to clear the doors. I watched as they moved each person until they were down to the last three. A skinny man with wild eyes screamed obscenities at the police. A woman with white curly hair glared at me through the glass as they led her away. The single remaining figure was slumped against the doors in a bulky down-coat, shapeless as a walrus, head sagging. As two cops took hold of the coat and shook gently, I thought maybe he or she had gone to sleep, bored by the whole business. Then the heavy figure slid sideways and toppled over. The younger cop yelled something and went off at a run.

Now we had a whole new scene. A doctor, at least one, from inside the clinic. An ambulance. Paramedics. More police. Cynthia went out and talked to the cops. Grace went out and talked to the cops. Grace came in and talked to me.

'She's dead,' Grace half whispered, so the few patients left in the waiting-room couldn't hear her. 'The woman by the door.'

So it had been a woman. 'Was it a heart attack?'

'We don't know. There was a note in her jacket pocket.' She consulted her notebook. 'It says: *She interfered. She's dead.*'

I stared at her, not believing it. 'She was killed?'

'Possibly. We don't know. I told them you'd probably seen the whole thing. The lieutenant wants to talk to you.'

'Me?'

'You've been sitting right here, Jason. She was crammed right up against the doors, and you've been watching through the glass. Sure he wants to talk to you.'

So Grace introduced me to Lieutenant Linder from homicide, and I talked to him. I told him I had seen the protesters arrive, had seen them squench themselves up against the doors, had watched them sitting there for almost an hour, and had then seen the police remove them.

'Anybody approach this woman?' He had a pale, middle-aged face with a long upper lip, pale lashes and brows so high on his forehead they made him look like a surprised rabbit.

I explained that the protesters had been at least five rows deep, that nobody had moved once they were in position because they couldn't, they were jammed in too tightly. Nobody stood up. Nobody came or went.

'How about when we cleared 'em out?' asked the Lieutenant. 'Did you see that?'

I had. The row in front of the fat woman had been cleared. Then the people at each end of the back row. 'The man to her left was skinny with crazy eyes, and he kept yelling obscenities at the cops. The woman on the other side . . .' I tried to think what it had been about her. 'She wasn't dressed for the weather,' I said at last. 'She was wearing trousers, but she had on a light shirt, no jacket. An older woman, sort of full-bodied, with glasses and white curly hair. Maybe . . . oh, sixty.'

'And this Fixe woman never moved?' asked the Lieutenant.

'Who?' I said it louder than I meant to.

He gave me a quizzical look.

'I'm sorry,' I said, recovering from the surprise. 'What name did you say?'

'The dead woman,' he said. 'Simonetta Fixe.' He watched for my reaction. When he didn't get one, he continued, 'At least, that's what it says on her ID card.' He turned his clipboard around so I could see it. He'd clipped the ID card by one corner so he coud copy down the name and address, written below. Simonetta L.Fixe. An address in the north-west part of town, North Zuni Street. I memorized the number.

'No driver's licence,' he commented. 'Just this card, her social security card and a credit card. You know her?' He gave me the standard cop stare, but he didn't have the face for it. No menace. Grace does better than that.

'I ran across the name Fixe recently,' I admitted. 'But it wasn't anyone named Simonetta.'

One pale eyebrow edged towards his hairline, but he didn't pursue the matter. 'And you never saw her move?'

'Once they sat down, she never moved from that place,' I said, running over various murder methods in my mind. 'I didn't see anyone come up to her but the police. I didn't see anyone touch her except the people on either side of her. I didn't see anyone hand her anything. I didn't see her eat or drink anything, though she could have done that without my seeing it. If she'd had a candy bar in her pocket, for instance. I could only see her back, not what she might have been doing with her hands or mouth.'

He shook his head, wrote down my name and phone number, and let me go. Police cars were moving away. Grace and I went back inside the clinic. We found Cynthia

Adamson kneeling on the mat just inside the double glass doors, staring at them.

'Cynthia, what are you doing,' asked Grace.

'If she was killed, they're going to think it was one of us,' she replied. 'Aren't they?'

'So what are you doing?'

'Wondering if there was any way anyone could have done something to that woman from in here. Like, you know, shoot at her through the crack between the doors or something.'

Grace pulled her to her feet. 'Nobody said she was shot, Cynthia. Besides, no one from inside could have put that note on her. Jason was sitting here the whole time. He didn't see anyone do anything to the doors, or to the woman.'

I nodded wearily, wondering if Cynthia was right, if someone would suspect the clinic staff. On our way home, I said this to Grace.

She shook her head. 'There are fanatics on both sides of the issue, Jason, but they don't work at the clinic. The people there aren't zealots. That's one thing that kind of surprised me when I first started working down there. I was expecting to meet militant feminists who think abortion is more a duty than a right and try to sell it like crazy. But the people there aren't like that. They know how hard the choices are, and they don't push for one choice over the other. If you're looking for a pro-abortion fanatic, you'll have to look somewhere else.'

I had no intention of looking anywhere, not for Simonetta Fixe's murderer. Her death was not my concern. My only interest in her was that she might have a relative with the initial H. When we left, I talked Grace into coming with me to the Zuni Street address, just on the off-chance H.Fixe might live there.

The house was tiny, set in a large plot of unkempt lawn. There was nobody home. Next door we found Mrs Walter Huggenmier, Vera, who came to the door in a light housedress and then stood bare-legged on her front porch, hugging herself to keep from freezing. We told her Mrs Fixe was dead. She said that was a terrible shame, but the words were convention, not feeling, so I assumed she wouldn't mind being asked if Simonetta had a relative with the initial H. Simonetta's husband was named Herby, she said, but he'd been killed in an accident a couple of months ago.

She added, 'Of course, the way Herby drank, I always figured he'd end up killing himself.'

I, exulting at the discovery of an H.Fixe, even a dead one, asked her how he'd managed that.

During a blizzard in the middle of the night, she said, shortly before Christmas. He'd driven off Spear Boulevard into Cherry Creek, had landed upside down and drowned in about eight inches of water. Because of the snow, no one ever saw the car until the next day.

We shook our heads over the vagaries of fate. 'The Fixes aren't in the phone book,' I commented.

'They had one a those unlissed nummers,' Mrs Huggenmier confided between shivers. 'Simmy said there was people lookin' for Herby, from somethin' he was mixed up in, a long time ago. She liked to be all mysterious about that, all the time sayin' she could tell us stuff if she wanned to. Walt says it's a lot of crap. Walt says Herby was too old to be mixed up in anythin' much, and besides he was half drunk all the time.'

'Your husband, Walt, knew him well?'

'Well, you know. A long time ago they worked at the same place. You wanna come back tonight, you can ask him. Walt'll be home about seven.' Already frozen into inarticulation, she was convulsing from the cold and her lips were turning blue. I wondered what was inside that she'd rather freeze than invite us in to see.

We said we'd be back, told her to go in before she solidified, and went off to find something to eat. Grace's early breakfast had long since metabolized, as had the several doughnuts she'd consumed at the clinic, leaving her in danger of imminent collapse. She has a favourite Mexican place on Seventeenth Avenue, where she stuffed herself on *chiles rellenos* while enlightening me on the various types thereof. There were, she informed me, five basic types. First, the *relleno autentico*: a whole mild green pepper roasted and peeled, strips of cheese inserted, the whole dipped in beaten eggs (preferably with the whites whipped separately and folded in) and fried, then covered with green or red sauce. In the authentic relleno, the seeds aren't removed, the cheese is a white, farmer type, and the chile itself is barely coated with egg, just enough to seal it.

Second, says Grace, we have the tourist relleno, in which the stem and seeds are removed before cooking. Third is the bulk manufactured restaurant relleno, which is made in a factory, and is covered with thick batter. The bulk relleno is very solid-looking, and is usually stuffed with bright orange 'cheese food' which neither looks nor tastes like cheese; it is shipped frozen and microwaved to order. Fourth, the yuppie relleno, in which cheddar and Monterey Jack cheese are shredded, mixed with chopped green chiles and sautéed onions and (depending upon the ethnic background of the cook) rolled into (a) a blintz, or (b) a crêpe, or (c) an eggroll wrapper, or (d) a tortilla, and then fried. Fifthly and finally, the *relleno exotico*, in which the stuffing may be most anything, including meat with raisins. My favourite place in Santa Fe serves them that way.

Grace finds four out of five of these acceptable. The place on Seventeenth Avenue serves the yuppie type. Grace had two and a half orders of two each, plus beans, rice, half a dozen buttered flour tortillas, and a basket of sopaipillas with honey. I had two stuffed chiles and nothing much else. Grace weighs one-eighteen and does not vary by more than six ounces over a year. I weigh one-eighty and can put on ten pounds by sniffing deeply outside a bakery. I need more exercise. I'm still not as mobile as I was before my leg got gunshot a year or so ago.

When Grace was toppped up, we ordered coffee, then sat for a while, trying to figure out whether Jacob's interest in the clinic and Simonetta Fixe's death and H.Fixe showing up in Jacob's cheques was all a coincidence. We thought it unlikely, but neither of us really believes in coincidences.

'Jacob's last cheque to Fixe was written shortly before Fixe died,' I said. 'It was dated late November.'

'I wonder if Jacob knew Fixe was dead.'

'I'm not sure how much Jacob really took in during those last few weeks. If they said Fixe's name on the TV news, Jacob may have heard it. Francis usually turns on the news around supper-time, so Jacob could have known. Not that it makes any difference whether Jacob knew or not.'

'Sure it makes a difference, Jason!' she said, reaching over to pat my hand. 'You said yourself you were hurt because Jacob hadn't told you what this was about. Well, if he knew Fixe was dead, he wouldn't have bothered to tell you about it, would he? Not if it was something painful. Not if it was a threat that no longer existed. He probably never intended for you to see the cheques, but he'd had that last stroke, and he wasn't able to destroy them or even tell Francis to do it for him.'

Since that last stroke, he'd been almost unable to communicate, but otherwise she was right. If the cause of his anxiety had been dead, he wouldn't have struggled to tell me about it.

We spent the afternoon at Grace's. I'd promised to help her lay tiles in a new bathroom she was putting in, and we made good progress. That evening, we cleaned up and drove over to the Huggenmier house, dressed warmly in anticipation of another front porch conversation.

We didn't stand outside, however. Walt Huggenmier, a stocky, bow-legged bulldog of a man, invited us into a house so painfully clean and neat we hesitated to sit down. I decided we had not been invited in that morning because it had not been neat enough for guests. As I watched Mrs Huggenmier moving about, tidying this and flicking at invisible bits of that, I knew she was one of those women who would have to clean the whole house before she could bring herself to call the fire department to report the kitchen was burning.

Walt was a salt-of-the-earth type, talky and jolly and

interested in hearing all about his former neighbour. Vera Huggenmier, now that she wasn't freezing to death, was similarly interested. Grace and I had already decided we'd get further if the inquiry was official, so Grace identified herself as a cop and asked for anything they could tell her about the Fixes.

'Well, damn,' said Walt. 'I'd knowed old Herb for a long time. Since we was kids. I should be able to tell you all about him, but you know, I can't. Herb got up to all kinds of stuff when he was a kid, and he'd brag on it all the time, but whatever he was up to lately, he only kinda dropped a hint, you know.'

'Illegal stuff?' asked Grace.

'The way I knowed Herb, I'd hafta say yes.' He didn't seem saddened by the admission. 'He was in with that North Denver crowd.'

'Really? *The* North Denver crowd.'

'Yeah. They were into gamblin', mostly. Started out bootleggin', back in the 'twenties, then got into gamblin'. Herby never tole me exactly what he did for them.'

Vera said, 'I'll tell you one thing. He drove that fancy car of his, so he had to have car payments, and insurance, and bills, you know, like we all do. But he didn' have a job. I said to Walt, I said, that tells you somethin', doesn' it? He had to have money comin' from somewhere.'

Walt nodded in agreement. 'Right. That's what she said. And she's right, 'cause Herb sure wasn't like, what they say, innepennennly wealthy.' He crowed with amusement. 'Not old Herby.'

'What did you think he was up to?' I asked.

Walt shrugged. 'These days? I thought maybe dope. What else is there?'

'How about blackmail?' suggested Grace.

Walt thought about it. 'That'd be good for ole Herb,' he agreed. 'He could talk tough. I guess he could scare somebody. Make somebody think he had somethin' on 'em. He was sneaky.' He nodded to himself happily, thinking how sneaky Herby had been. 'He used to all the time leave things with me, you know, stuff to keep for him, letters to mail. Five, six years ago, he left me a letter to mail if he died. Said somebody might do him in, and the letter was his insurance policy.'

'Did you mail it?'

'When he died? Sure, I told him I would.'

'Couldn't remember where you put it!' his wife challenged him. 'Never would've gotten it mailed if I hadn't found it for you, and took you near a month as it was!'

'Yeah, well. It'd been a long time.'

'Who was it addressed to?' Grace asked.

'Postmaster. It was addressed to Postmaster. There was another envelope inside, though. I could feel it.'

'What about his wife? Did you know her?' I asked.

Vera didn't need to think about that one. 'She was mostly by herself. He come here to see Walt oftener than he come to see her. Now here lately she got in with this anti-abortion bunch from her church and turned kinda crazy. She ast me to go with her, and I tole her I didn't hole with interferin' with people that way. People have to do what they think is right. I tole her that, but she'd just shake her head at me and talk about sin. I tole her, I said, "Simmy, you're gonna wear yourself out! You're too ole and you're too fat for this runnin' around." She used to get real mad when I called her fat, but she was.'

'Had they been married long?' I asked.

'Not all that long. She said ten years, I think. 'Course that was a couple of years ago. We only moved in here about—what was it, Walt?'

He thought maybe 'eighty-five, 'eighty-six.

Vera went on, 'I don't know why she ever married him, at her age.'

'Did she ever talk about her childhood?' Grace asked. 'About what she did before she got married?'

'Oh, she worked for people, doin' housework. I know that. She worked for some big rich family for a long time. Some eye-talian name.' Vera punched her forehead, as though she had an input key that needed manual operation.

'Somethin' happened to 'em, so she went to some other people and did cook-housekeepin' for them. Even after her and Herby got married, she worked for somebody named Sinclaire. She was always talkin' about 'em, Mrs Sinclaire this and Mrs Sinclaire that.'

There were several wealthy Sinclaires in the Denver area; two of them had been clients of mine. I asked which family, but Vera didn't know.

I turned to Walt. 'Your wife said you'd known him since he was young.'

'Oh, sure. We both grew up on the north side. Lots of eye-talians on the north side. Well, Herby was always into somethin'. Gamblin' mostly. With the rest of the eye-talian families over there, you know.' He winked at Grace. 'You otta know. Herby's name wasn't Fixe, not to start with. It was Fitteli or Fissoli, somethin' like that. They called him Herby the Fixer, that's how he got the name, an' he worked for the Leones. I guess that's how he got hooked up with Simmy. She was a Leone.'

'That's right!' exclaimed Vera. 'That's who she worked for before the Sinclaires! It was her uncle or somebody. The Leones.'

The name meant nothing to me. It meant something to Grace. She made a face.

'How about Herby?' she asked. 'Did he have any relatives?'

They shook their heads. They didn't know. There was nothing more the Huggenmiers could tell us. We thanked them for the information, refused an offered beer, and left.

'Who are the Leones?' I asked Grace.

'There were three or four families named Leone. One of them used to be a crime family, starting in the 'twenties and up through the 'forties, I think maybe the 'fifties. It never amounted to much. Not like the east coast. Not like Chicago or Miami.'

'Crime? Drugs?'

'They were never into drugs much,' she said. 'Walt was right. They started in bootlegging. Then, mostly, they went into gambling and protection, maybe prostitution, old-fashioned stuff like that. And there was only one biggish fish: Canello Leone. The rest were mostly small-time crooks. Everybody knew everybody, though. If there were any jobs going, one Leone would toss it to another Leone.'

'But it wasn't a Godfather-type family, huh?'

'Not really that powerful. Just rather incestuous. Like a whole family of little fish, feeding on what the big ones left, swimming around under the big fish's protection. Kinfolk. A tribe. Quite a few of them, but except for Canello, they didn't have any connections with other places.'

'How do you know about them?'

'Lieutenant Hector Haymart gives us an organized crime briefing every now and then. Nice guy. He was telling us about crime history in Denver, and he mentioned Canello Leone. It was way back, though. Nothing recently. Hector says what few crime families we had are pretty well defunct. Lots of the old-time guys were racked up on tax charges. They never amounted to much in Denver and now they're like a footnote. Everything's drugs, now. Colombian. Peruvian.'

'I wonder if Herby Fixe really died accidentally.' It was only a thought. The talk of organized crime had brought the question to mind.

Grace was way ahead of me. 'According to the traffic report, yes. I called the station this afternoon and had them read it to me. According to the autopsy his blood alcohol was almost point two.'

'Skid marks and all?' I asked.

'No skid marks. He was so bombed he didn't even touch the brakes,' she said. 'He was flying long before he left the road.'

She seemed sure. Still, I wondered.

CHAPTER 2

Grace did not stay at my place Saturday night. She said her Sunday was full of things to do and places to go and she wanted an early start. Without the distractions of soft breathing and silky skin and a six a.m. demand for breakfast, I woke late, stretched largely, took an extra long shower, and went down with only Bela and Schnitz for company to get the Sunday paper from (I hoped) the front portico where the paper boy sometimes manages to put it. Even though I was well aware of Schnitz's proclivity for escape, I wasn't really alert yet, and as I picked up the paper and turned to close the door, he slipped between my legs on to the threshold. I practically fell over myself making a grab for him, and the report of the rifle and the crack of the bullet into the foyer panelling came almost at once. I must have fallen to the floor, and rolled inside by pure reflex, with no thought behind it at all. When I came back to awareness, it was of dry mouth, trip-hammer heart, sweaty hands and labouring lungs, and me crouched in the corner where whoever-it-was couldn't get another shot at me. Schnitz stood halfway up the hall stairs, his tail fluffed out like a plume of pampas grass, back arched, eyes wild, growling. Or maybe it was Bela growling. Or me.

Somebody had goddam tried to kill me. I could see the hole in the panelling, right where I would have been if I hadn't bent over to grab Schnitz. I heard myself making adjectives out of four letter words, over and over in a raving somebody-else-not-me voice, so I shut up, embarrassed at the sound of it. By lying flat, I managed to stretch a leg and pull the door shut with minimum exposure. As it latched I recalled hearing, as though on delayed replay, a car starting up and speeding away. Not from the street out front, somewhere farther than that. The alley of the block opposite, perhaps, where most of the old houses had been converted into offices. Certainly less than a minute had elapsed since the shot, but it felt like an hour or so.

When my knees quit shaking, I got up and looked at the bullethole. A pencil inserted in the hole confirmed the trajectory was slightly upward and slightly to the left as I stood with my back to the front door. Whoever had shot at me had done so from ground level. Through a clear glass segment of the fancy window beside the front door I could see the driveway between the two conversions across the street. I knew it went through to the alley where the car had no doubt been. The rifleman could have shot from the corner of the nearest building.

I called Grace. She called Linder. He got there in about thirty minutes, which was twelve and a half minutes after she did. He brought two other guys with him who did what I'd done with the bullethole, then dug out the bullet, put it in a sack, labelled it and went across the street to see if the rifleman was perchance waiting around to answer questions.

'You think this has any connection to that woman's murder?' Linder asked me.

I told him I didn't know. It had no connection to anything, so far as I could see. Two persons had tried to kill me about a year before, but one of them was dead and the other one was still incarcerated somewhere at the pleasure of the FBI or the CIA or both. So far as I knew, and I think I'd have been informed if anything had changed.

'You were looking for somebody named Fixe,' Linder reminded me, as though I might have forgotten.

'Herby Fixe,' I affirmed. 'He had had some dealings with my foster father, who died recently. I wanted to know the details. It turns out Herby was Simonetta's husband. And yes, Grace and I went over to their place yesterday and asked the neighbours some questions, but they didn't tell us anything that would warrant somebody taking a shot at me.'

He asked whys and wherefores, and I told him what I knew. No point in not. Whatever it had been about, it couldn't hurt Jacob. Jacob's H.Fixe had probably been the now-dead-and-no-longer-threatening Herby Fixe from Zuni Street. Even in the unlikely event that H.Fixe was not Herby but Harold or Horatio or even, God forbid, Hermione Fixe, Jacob was no longer around to be extorted from on my behalf, or Charlotte's. The previous night I'd decided not to worry about the matter any more unless somebody came at Charlotte or me with malign intent. The decision had been premature. Somebody taking a shot at me definitely qualified as more than a little malign.

Lieutenant Linder put his notebook away and went off to help his men look for tyre tracks or witnesses or whatever. Grace, after exhorting me to stay inside with the doors locked, took the bit in her teeth and went galloping off to talk to her friend, Lieutenant Hector Haymart of the organized crime unit. I didn't hear from her again until Monday noon.

When she called she sounded altogether too chipper and pleased with herself. 'I told Hector about Herby and the Leone connection and you getting shot at, Jason, so he got a warrant and went over to Zuni Street this morning. I went along. Hector hadn't found anything useful up to the time I left, but I got names and addresses of Simonetta's family. She's got a whole bunch of brothers and sisters— at least one sister and two brothers here in town. The brothers both have sheets on them, but the sister, Dorotea, evidently got out of the neighbourhood and away from the family. She's married to a lawyer, Andrew Chapman. They live out in Cherry Hills, and the only place her name shows up is in the social pages.'

'Well,' I said weakly. 'That gives us somewhere to start, doesn't it.'

Grace was way ahead of me. 'She says she'll talk to us this afternoon, if you've got time.'

I hadn't mentioned Sunday's events to either Mark or Eugenia. They'd come in the back and hadn't seen the bullethole and I hadn't quite decided whether I was a selected target or a random one. Now, when I called through the connecting door to ask Mark if he could get by without me for the afternoon, I halfway hoped he'd think of a reason my presence was essential so I could stay inside for a while, out of range, so to speak. Mark, however, did not read my mind. Instead, he gave me a vague look and an affirmative grunt. I took it as an omen and stopped fighting the inevitable. 'What time this afternoon? I asked Grace.

'Mrs Chapman said three. It'll take half-an-hour to get out there. I'll come by your place about two-twenty.'

Which gave me time to enlighten the crew. The difference in their personalities was displayed fully when Eugenia went off immediately to call the painter while Mark was still asking me breathless questions. She, by God, knew that business came first and customers shouldn't be confronted by bulletholes! Mark was still shaking his head over me when Grace arrived, and he warned me to be careful as we went down the stairs. We were careful. Both of us scanned the neighbourhood from the front windows before I went out to her car.

'Did Linder find anything?' I asked, looking nervously around myself.

She shook her head. 'No empty case, no tracks, no witnesses, no nothing. On Sundays, Hyde Street is a tomb.'

I knew the fourteen-hundred block of Hyde Street was dead on Sundays. The restaurant on the corner doesn't open until noon. The next two buildings, 1487 and 1473, are office conversions. Then comes 1465, and south of my place are two more conversions before you get to the house on the corner, which has three apartments in it with the owner living on the ground floor. There are two owner-occupied homes across the street, but they too are at the far end of the block.

'How about across the alley?' I asked.

She shook her head at me. 'Some people live there,' she admitted. 'But they were all sleeping off Saturday night or they'd already gone skiing.'

Sunday morning was one time the shooter could almost

have counted on not being seen. Denver's Capitol Hill, bracketed on the north by Colfax Avenue (fifteenth) and on the south at about sixth, on the west by Broadway and on the east by University, is the closest thing Denver has to a round-the-clock city. The rest of the town is dead by nine p.m., with the sidewalks rolled up, the streets empty as a panhandler's pockets, and ninety per cent of the families tidied away into the residential areas. Downtown Denver after nine looks like a model city somebody forgot to populate. Capitol Hill, however, still seethes at midnight, with hookers prowling Colfax and restaurants busy and the fast food stores spilling people and cars. By three a.m. even Colfax is quiet. On Sundays nothing opens much before noon and half the population heads for the mountains at dawn, those who hadn't already gone the day before. That's what too many people move here for: the skiing.

'No hope,' I said to Grace with some gloom. 'I wish we had a clue, something. Anything!'

'You made anybody mad at you lately?' she asked, giving me a worried look.

I couldn't think that I had. Except for some nut, maybe, who had seen me at the clinic and followed us when we left. I mentioned this.

'It's a thought,' she said. 'There are a couple of demonstrators who've made threats against the clinic personnel. Maybe one of them took a shot at you. We'll check, of course, as best we can.' She sighed and cast me a sidelong look. 'I wish we could provide protection, Jason, but you know as well as I do the police can't sit on your doorstep. We don't have the manpower. We don't have the budget.' She was pink, embarrassed for her profession.

I soothed her, telling her I didn't expect protection. I didn't. None the less, the idea that I might need protection was intensely upsetting. I like to do something about problems. Nothing frustrates me more than getting into situations where I'm impotent, where I can't do anything. I don't like dealing with nuts. Logic won't work. Reason won't work. And, worst of all, society conspires to prevent the average person from protecting himself against craziness. Crazy people can't be punished, because they're crazy. So they're sent to hospitals to be cured. Then they're let out because they're 'Fine when they take their medication.' Then they stop taking their medication, buy a gun, and kill a few innocent bystanders, but they can't be punished for it, because they're crazy.

Obviously, people who cannot control what they do are more dangerous than people who can. So, in a properly run world, craziness—along with drunkenness and drug-use—would be an aggravating factor when considering guilt or innocence, not the other way around. If we could forget our Puritan obsession with punishment and decide that the only reason for looking people up is the safety of the population at large, we'd do better at law enforcement.

I said this, at length.

'Yes, Jason,' said Grace. 'You want to find the weather on the radio?'

I took the hint and shut up. Grace had heard it all before.

Cherry Hills is at the high-priced south end of the urban agglomeration. Ostentation is the norm. I fully expected the Chapman house to be yet another of the cheek-by-jowl multi-winged, many-gabled monsters that were hulked along both sides of the road in money-country. I have never been able to understand why anyone with the resources to build a house that size would put it on a skimpy acre or less with another monster house practically adjacent. Unless people live there *vide homolucrum*: to stare at people who have as much money as they do. Or to drive past even larger houses *vide supralucrum*: to stare at people who have more money than they do. Or, to regard the homes of the *summa cum lucro*: as in the lifestyles of the rich and famous.

I amused myself with such inanities during the ride so I wouldn't start shouting again, which I tend to do when I'm scared. If the truth be told, I found the idea of some nut gunning for me intensely disturbing. Not that I'd admit that to Grace. Not manly. Or something.

The Chapman house was not one of the side-by-side

monsters. It was a French château with pure continuous lines, old brick walls with multi-paned windows, a copper roof patinaed the colour of spruce buds, a matching flare of ribbed copper spread lily-wise over the front door, the whole set in sufficient grounds to give it gracious dignity. Inside were panelled doors and walls, well-proportioned rooms beautifully furnished with French and English pieces, many of them genuine eighteenth-century. I ran my fingers along the hall table and felt at home, among friends. I relaxed, feeling my frightened anger drain away. Nothing evil could happen in such a place.

We were shown into the sitting-room by the uniformed maid who had answered the door. Grace had on her wary expression. She gets it in the presence of—what? Monied surroundings? Servants? It isn't awe and it isn't resentment. It is a kind of watchfulness that comes from not being sure whether she knows the acceptable thing to do—not that she'd necessarily do it, but she likes to know what the rule is when she breaks it.

Dorotea Chapman was waiting for us: lean, elegant, about fifty, grey-blonde hair drawn smoothly back in a french twist, understated make-up, wearing the almost inevitable tweed and cashmere country clothes the house called for. We introduced ourselves.

'We don't want to take much of your time,' I murmured in what Jacob had called the intimate-elect voice, one that says, I know how important you are, let's get this out of the way. It was the voice he had often used when asking a buyer, 'And how will you be paying for this?'

'We need to know anything you can tell us about Simonetta Fixe,' I said.

Dorotea Chapman turned her recently manicured right hand into the slanting light from a multi-paned window and examined the nails, which were quite perfect. The hand itself was smooth and ageless. 'You're investigating her death?' she asked, almost as if she did not care.

'I am, yes,' said Grace, surprising me. Simonetta's death hadn't been her case the last I'd heard, and I'd supposed we'd have to skate over that question. 'Lieutenant Linder has assigned me to certain aspects of the investigation.'

'The doctor I spoke with told me she was stabbed,' said Dorotea, closing her eyes briefly, as though to shut out some private vision. 'Someone stabbed her with an ice-pick. She bled to death internally, sitting there.' Her voice was calm, but one eyelid twitched, over and over, fluttering, like a fly in a web.

Grace shook her head, for a moment shocked at this news. 'I hadn't heard the results of the autopsy. I was told there was no wound on her body.'

'There was no blood,' Mrs Chapman said. 'The doctor I spoke with says there often isn't, in that kind of wound. Particularly if the person is . . . fleshy.' She sighed and looked at us with a pained expression, no subterfuge in it at all. 'Remembering Simonetta is painful. I don't like talking about the family, can you understand that?'

I looked around at the graceful, ageless room, a proper setting for the graceful, more or less ageless woman, and thought of that walrus-like form hunkered down at the clinic. Oh yes, I understood. Grace did too. We nodded.

Dorotea took a deep breath. 'I talked to my husband about this, and he said if I could bring myself to be frank, it would probably be all over more quickly. I'd like it to be over. Remembering Simonetta isn't . . . well, dealing with her was always a frustration. What do you need to know?'

'Anything about her might help,' I said. 'We won't know until you tell us.'

She marshalled her thoughts. 'You know she was my sister. She was ten years older than I. The thing we always tried to remember about Simonetta was that she wasn't intelligent. We could get very annoyed with her when we didn't remember that. She wasn't exactly retarded, she just wasn't very bright, and we all had to keep it in mind. Mother had eight children who lived to grow up. Some of us are quite intelligent—intelligent enough to have left the old neighbourhood and traditions and become . . . acculturated. Of course, some of us haven't done that.'

Grace gave me a significant look. 'And Simonetta?'

Dorotea rose and stood at the window, thrusting a fall of brocade aside with one hand, staring out over her winter-dun lawn with her back to us, as though it was easier to talk if she didn't have to see who was listening. 'Simmy wasn't in the family and she wasn't out of the family, if by "family" one means the kinds of thing some of my brothers got up to. Papa was always very law-abiding, but some of my uncles were not. They had an unfortunate influence on some of us children. So did the toleration of them and their . . . lifestyle. We were always taught that blood was more important than the law. You can get trapped that way . . .'

We nodded again, though she could have seen only our reflections in the glass.

'Two of my brothers and a sister and I decided—quite independently of one another—to get out of the trap. Three brothers liked things the way they were. One of them is dead now. Simmy wasn't on one side or the other. She was just always there, always around, the way a young child is, or an aged relative.' She put her hands behind her, stretching her shoulders back. There was ache in that stretch, old pain.

'What was she like?' Grace asked. 'Her personality?'

Dorotea made a ladylike snort. 'Sometimes I felt Simmy had only instincts, or maybe habits. It was hard for her to learn things, but once she learned anything, it was set in concrete. She was intensely stubborn and intensely religious. We all went to St Seraphia's school as children, but most of us were selective about what we believed, you know. Heaven but not hell. Baptism but not the ban on birth control. Simmy swallowed everything she was told, and everything was of equal importance. Once she'd learned to read a little, and enough arithmetic to count her change—practical things like that—the nuns took her over to their residence and taught her housekeeping. They were pragmatic about it. They knew she'd never be able to hold any other kind of job, and certainly none of us thought she'd ever marry. She worked for the nuns part time while she was in school. They taught her to cook. She couldn't follow a recipe if it was at all complicated, but she cooked plain food very nicely. Italian foods, of course—she learned that at home—and fried chicken and pot roasts and pies, things like that. She learned one way to do it, and she always did it that way. You could rely on each of Simmy's dishes tasting exactly the same, each time she made it.'

Her reminiscences had come haltingly, almost without expression, like a list of things she'd purposefully evoked, intentionally called up out of the past. A kind of inventory: Simonetta, who and what she was.

'She worked for families, did she?' I asked.

Dorotea turned to face us. 'When she was eighteen, the nuns couldn't keep her any longer. Papa was worried about her being able to take care of herself, but he didn't want her at home where Mama would go on treating her like a child. He got her a job with Canello Leone. The Leone families in Denver are all related, of course.'

Grace twitched, and Dorotea saw the movement. She shook her head resentfully. 'I know. The Leones have had their occasional bad apples, but so far as I know, only Nello Leone ever had a genuinely evil reputation. One of those who tar all their countrymen with their brush, more greed than good sense, always stirring up trouble. Papa knew that, but he felt Simonetta wouldn't get mixed up in anything, that she'd be safe working there . . .'

Her voice drifted off into silence. She took a moment to find her narrative again. 'Nello Leone had two sons. Gabrielli and Geronimo. Nimo was oldest, he had recently married, and his wife was pregnant. Let me remember . . . her name was . . . Angelina? Something like that. At any rate, Canello didn't hire Simonetta to work in *his* house. He sent her to work for his daughter-in-law. She and Simonetta would have been about the same age, I suppose. Maybe Nello thought they'd be company for one another, or maybe he didn't know what else to do with Simonetta, or perhaps he just counted on his daughter-in-law being a kind person.

I heard that about her, that she was a very warm, kind person.'

'What was the kinship between your family and Canello's, exactly?' Grace wanted to know.

'I don't know,' exactly,' she replied, a bit impatiently. 'We're some kind of cousins, I suppose.' The idea did not please her; that showed clearly on her face.

She drew a deep breath and went on, 'So Simonetta worked for Nimo's wife as a maid: she cleaned and did laundry and was a kind of nursemaid after the baby came. Everyone in our family was pleased because Simmy was pleased. She loved the baby, she liked the work, and she worked hard enough that she didn't get monstrously fat. Big, but not monstrous. Simmy always had the tendency to put on weight.' She paused, pressing the skin under her eyes with her fingertips, perhaps reassuring herself that she was not fleshy, not fat, not like her sister. Perhaps she was only pressing an ache away.

'How long did she work for Nimo's wife?' Grace asked gently.

'She was with them three or four years, until there was some kind of accident. The wife and child died. I'm not sure exactly what happened, though I do remember going to the funeral. Papa insisted we all go, to show respect.'

'What did Simonetta do then?' Grace asked.

'Well, by that time she had some experience. Nimo didn't keep her on, but he gave her references. She was really quite good at what she did—slow, but faithful. She moved about a bit after that, working for different families.'

'When did she marry Herby?' I asked.

Dorotea flushed, a deep and ugly red. She started to speak twice before she got the words out. 'My father insisted that she and Herby get married about ten or twelve years ago. Papa claimed he'd found out Herby had been sleeping with her, when she worked for Nello Leone. Herby worked for Nello at that same time. Frankly, Papa's insistence didn't make much sense then, and I still don't understand it. I don't know if Papa really found out something definite or someone just made an allegation. Mama and I both tried to find out from Simonetta when this affair had started, or if it was still going on, or . . .'

She made a gesture of frustration. 'Simonetta was never able to talk about anything that might have been taboo when we were children. Sex things and bathroom things were simply taboo! Whatever Mama or the nuns might have shushed her about when she was eight, she still couldn't speak of forty years later! She would turn bright red and clamp her mouth shut and turn away. Mama and I are still not sure that anything ever happened between her and Herby, but Papa gave Herby the choice of marrying her or—' she blinked, suddenly aware of what she was saying—'or leaving town,' she finished bleakly.

We waited. She obviously had more to say. It simply took her a while to say it.

'Simonetta was almost fifty then. Mama and I tried to talk some sense into Papa. She couldn't possibly have become pregnant, not at that age, and Herby wasn't the kind of man who would ever make a good husband. Marriage made no sense, but Papa was adamant. He said it was a matter of honour.' She made a little face and turned away, hiding from us again. 'Lots of things were matters of honour to Papa. To him, and to men of his generation. I remember a great deal of talk about honour when I was a girl. One had to be very sure not to do anything that would reflect on someone's honour.'

We waited. When nothing more was forthcoming, I asked, 'What did you mean when you said your sister was religious?'

Dorotea sighed. 'I mean she was observant. Scrupulous. After her marriage she became even more so, if that's possible.'

Grace gave her a puzzled look. 'Yes, but what does "being religious" mean when you say it?'

Dorotea thought about this, turning to and fro on one foot, a little swinging motion, as a child might do, comforting herself by rocking. 'I mean she had always worried about sin. Well, one can't go to parochial school without worrying about sin, though most of us took it with a grain of salt. Not Simonetta. She had to know exactly what a sin was and how bad it was and whether she'd done it or not. She had to know if she could commit a sin by mistake. She used to drive Mother crazy with questions like that. She wasn't bright enough to figure anything out, or make allowances for herself. We were always having to reassure her that she wouldn't go to hell. After she was married to Herby, she talked a lot about being a bad sinner. She thought she'd committed some mortal sin, and I blame Papa for that. She didn't understand Papa's insistence on that marriage any more than Mother and I did. She thought it was a punishment, but she didn't know what for. I'm sure Simonetta was a virgin until Herby got to her, if he got to her, and given Simonetta's prudery and religiosity, I still doubt he did. If he did, there was certainly no one else but him, and the sins of the flesh aren't all that damning. Try and tell that to Simmy! She was sure she was going straight to hell.'

'She was frightened?' asked Grace.

'Until about a year ago, when she got involved with these anti-abortionists. She got the idea from something the priest said that working with them would expiate whatever her sin was.' Her tone was unsympathetic. 'A lot of nonsense,' she muttered. 'Positively mediœval!'

'You believe in freedom of choice?' I asked curiously.

'Of course not,' she snapped. 'I was reared Catholic and remain so. But I don't believe in mobs harassing women who are not breaking the law, either. It doesn't demonstrate the compassion our religion teaches; it sets a bad example of public order; and it's in very bad taste!'

We gave her a moment to calm down. 'Do you have any ideas who might have stabbed your sister?' Grace asked.

She shook her head slowly. 'Considering the tone of the message that was left on her body, I assumed it was someone connected with the abortion movement. Perhaps someone at the clinic itself.'

'No,' I said firmly. 'I don't believe it was. Your sister was where I could see her from the moment she arrived until her body was discovered. No one from the clinic went anywhere near her. In fact, no one except the people she arrived with went anywhere near her.'

She didn't contradict me, she just looked me up and down as though to say, 'And who are you?' None the less, she replied calmly enough, 'If *that* is the case, then who else would have done it? Canello Leone comes immediately to mind, but he's been dead for years. If she had interfered with *him*, he might have murdered her, but he would have done it then, not later. They say one should always suspect the spouse, and I'm not such a fool as to think Herby incapable of murder, but Herby drove himself off a road and killed himself before Christmas. So who?'

I didn't know. 'Am I right that you have very little contact with your family?' I asked.

She shook her head at me, giving me a slight, very ladylike sneer. 'To the contrary, Mr Lynx. I see my mother every week. She's in a nursing home, but she looks forward to my visits and we enjoy the time together. When Papa was alive, I saw him at least once a week. I talk with two of my brothers frequently: one is in Los Angeles and the other in Chicago. I see my sister Veronica whenever I get the chance. I left the family environment, not the family itself. My conscience, in case you are wondering, is quite comfortable in that regard.'

I think I flushed. 'I meant, you don't see your brothers here in Denver. You didn't often see Simonetta?'

She shook her head, bleakness descending once more. 'No,' she said with the same little sneer, only this time I knew it was at herself. 'I have not seen either of my convict brothers in some time. And I rarely saw Simmy. Of all the family, only Mama kept in close touch with them, particularly with Simmy, and since Mama's been in the nursing home, she's been unable to do that.'

We thanked her and left.

'What's this about your investigating Simonetta's murder?' I asked Grace, once we were in her car, headed down the curving drive.

'I asked for the assignment this morning,' she said. 'I told Linder I had the inside track, with you being there at the clinic and me working there sometimes. Also, he thinks maybe Simonetta's murder has something to do with whoever took a shot at you or *vice versa*, whatever. So I'm on the case. I have to share everything with Lieutenant Haymart in organized crime, but that's OK. He's not even all that interested. Nello Leone died twenty years ago, and since he's been gone, the family hasn't been up to much.'

'What about his son, Nimo? And what did she say Nimo was short for?'

'Geronimo. Nimo'd be in his sixties now. You know, I don't think I've ever seen his name on an arrest report. Our last organized crime briefing didn't even mention him.'

'That branch of the family must be defunct.'

'I'd think so. Except for what happened to Simonetta. And even that may have nothing to do with the family.'

'You know,' I commented, returning to my earlier frame of mind, 'except for that shot at me yesterday, I'd be tempted to drop this. I was after somebody who had bothered Jacob. Since I'm ninety per cent sure that was Herby, and Herby's dead, should I really be much concerned with the rest of this?'

She gave me a look. 'You might not be concerned, but I would be,' she said in a firm, no-nonsense voice. 'Forget somebody shooting at you. Jacob cared about that clinic, and right now everyone who works there is under a cloud. They're all worried. Dorotea isn't the only one talking as though the clinic people did it.'

'I told the police it's unlikely anyone associated with the clinic could have done it!' I exclaimed in irritation.

'So who are you? Mother Teresa? The Archbishop of Canterbury? The Chief Rabbi of Jerusalem? Who appointed you the last word on truth? All you can say is you didn't see anybody do it. Until we know who did do it, the clinic people will be under suspicion. And believe me, the anti-abortionists will do everything they can to make them suffer. Making false accusations fits right in with their usual pattern.'

I humphed and snarled at her when she said it, but the Tuesday morning papers proved she was right. One inflammatory quote followed another, both from those who had been arrested and those who supported those who had been arrested. All the rhetoric gave more heat than light. The words of the police lieutenant to the effect that the clinic personnel were not under investigation at this time were buried in the second column of a long overview story, and most people wouldn't read that far. I searched all the coverage for anything about Simonetta I didn't already know, but there wasn't anything.

I sat and stewed about being shot at for a while. I get this thing, sometimes, this hubristic conviction that if I concentrate hard enough I can find the answer to anything. Since I only do this when I'm not finding the answer to anything, it is invariably self-limiting. After thirty minutes of fume and glower, I still had no idea who was trying to kill me. So I went around my apartment being sure the curtains were pulled so that nobody could get a clear sight on me, then tried to give it a rest.

The sight of the scattered newspapers reminded me of the clinic, and my conscience started bothering me. I'd been so wrapped up in my own problems, I'd forgotten Cynthia Adamson and her problems. I called the clinic and left a message. When Cynthia called me back, I suggested additional security, saying I'd make some money available now if she needed it.

'We've already hired guards,' she said. 'We've been through these storms before, nothing quite this bad, but the pattern's the same. Over the next few weeks, someone will probably try to burn us out, or the staff will be harassed and threatened, or all of the above. There are a few real nutcases who hang around on the fringe of this issue. Any public spectacle sets them off, and they're unpredictable. Quite frankly, they worry us a hell of a lot more than the organized opposition does. The organized groups help incite these nuts, but the organizations themselves usually stop just short of committing a serious crime.'

'Are the nuts someones in particular?' I asked.

'Two someones in particular,' she said. 'Both male, both with histories of mental illness. Both very much into machismo. The kind of guys who would consider it honourable to pick up a semi-automatic weapon and knock off a dozen female staff and patients before you could say "gun control". Like the guy who killed all those female students at the college in Canada a few years back.'

'I can't understand that,' I said helplessly.

She laughed angrily. 'Try real hard,' she said. 'They're the same kind of people who put on robes and murdered civil rights marchers in the 'sixties. The same people who threw rocks at kids who were bussed to their schools in the 'seventies. It's all about dominance. You know, you've got to keep those black folks and those women folks where they belong!'

'What about saving babies?'

'Saving babies, hell. Once the children are born, they don't care what happens to them. You think it's an accident that the US has one of the highest infant mortality rates in the developed world? Men who vote against abortions for poor women also routinely vote against the programmes which would allow poor women to have healthy, well-fed children. Anti-abortionists by and large aren't pro-baby, they're anti-female!'

I thought she was overstating the case and said so as gently as possible.

'I'm not making it up,' she said angrily. 'Look at what they do—or don't do—instead of what they say. They scream "Adoption, not abortion," but they don't adopt kids who need homes. They scream "Don't kill your baby," but they elect representatives who cut the food and shelter programmes that keep those same babies alive. The people who picket us aren't interested in healthy children, they're interested in dominance. Didn't you watch their faces when you were here?'

I had watched their faces. Remembering those faces, I stopped arguing with her, admitting to myself that I couldn't look at those faces on a weekly basis, as she did, and disbelieve what she was saying. 'I'm sorry you all have to go through this,' I said inadequately.

'Me too,' she said in a calmer voice. 'I get upset sometimes.'

I let her get back to dealing with her problems, wondering whether I could have stayed calm under the same pressures. She was stressed and fractious, but she was keeping it together. She knew what she was doing.

Which was more than I did, at the moment. I had no idea what was going on. Though some famous person had once remarked that being sentenced to die remarkably focuses one's mind, being shot at hadn't had that effect on me. I was not focused. I felt irritable and decidedly scattered. I didn't really want to attract the further attentions of the gunman, whoever it may have been, who'd taken a shot at me. This meant, in turn, that it might be smart to stay away from further involvement with the clinic. Which meant, stay uninvolved in the matter of Simonetta's murder.

Grace, however, was not going to let me get away with that. Besides which, she'd been right in saying Jacob would have cared, about the clinic at least. So, for their sakes if not my own, it was up to me to stay involved, like it or not. I sat staring at my desktop while I made the conscious switch from the former question of 'Who is H.Fixe?' to the newer ones, 'Who killed Simonetta? What has it to do with the clinic? Has it anything to do with me?'

Stating the problem was as far as I got just then. The rest of the day was eaten up with odds and ends, most of them boring and none of them profitable. I didn't even think about Simonetta until Grace dropped by late that afternoon, bringing with her a fat envelope bulging with the records and photographs of all the people who had been arrested on Saturday. 'I need you to look at these,' she said, shoving them in front of me. 'Simonetta must have talked to some of them on Saturday, and I need to know which ones.'

'You want me to help with them?'

'No, it's official police business. Besides, I don't think they'd talk to you. Your face was all over TV. I think they mentioned your name, too.'

I hadn't known that. 'When?' I asked.

'Saturday night,' she said. 'The anti's always call the TV stations before they stage a demonstration. They want publicity. You just didn't notice the cameras. Anyhow, if any of these people watched the news, they'll know you were on the other side, so to speak, so they won't talk to you.'

I was considering whether the person who had shot at me Sunday morning might have been someone who'd watched the Saturday news. Pleasant thought. It only included a million or so people in the metropolitan area, excluding very young kids, very sick people, and those in jail. I tried to bring my mind back to the issue at hand.

'You're going to interview all these people? Alone?'

'No, not all of them. I told you, Jason. I'm going to find out from you who was next to her or who talked to her.' She waved a finger at me. 'Pay attention. That's why I brought the arrest records. I have to take them back as soon as you've looked at them. I only brought them over to save time!'

'Too much to hope any of them are still in jail, I suppose,' I remarked as I turned the sheets over one by one.

'Oh, they were out that afternoon, most of them. On their own recognizance. Except a couple of people who weren't from around here. They had to post bail. Anyhow, tell me which ones were next to the victim.'

I'd already found the man with the crazy eyes. He had a diagonal scar above the left eyebrow, and seeing it made my hand go to my neck where my own scars had been. I could still feel them there, under the bristly bits of new hair.

The transplants would never grow like normal cranial hair, but they already covered the scars.

Grace saw my unconscious movement and asked, 'Does your hair hurt?'

I laughed. My hair had hurt a good deal when it was being planted. So had the ear when it was being rounded off and reconstructed. The pain was over. The man in the mirror looked normal, though he still came as a surprise each time I saw him. I always expected someone else.

Grace hugged me and directed my attention back to the arrest reports. 'Anybody else?'

A few other people had been in the row in front of Simonetta. They hadn't sat facing me, but there'd been a certain amount of squirming around and talking to one another over their shoulders. I sorted them out and went on looking for the woman who had sat on Simonetta's right. After going through the sheets twice, however, I still couldn't find her.

'She's not here,' I said.

'I have a report here on everyone who got arrested,' said Grace, being patient with me.

'The woman to Simonetta's right had glasses and curly white hair. There is no woman here with curly white hair.'

She shuffled through the pictures finding no woman with curly white hair.

'Look,' I said, indicating the man with the scarred face. 'Ask this guy. He was on Simonetta's left. He should know who was on her right. Don't these people all know one another?'

'More or less,' she admitted. 'However, I understand people come in from out of town to take part, sometimes. People sent from another church or another group. They'd be vouched for, but not necessarily known to one another.'

'They were all arrested,' I said stubbornly, 'and she had white, curly hair. It was cut short. And she didn't have a jacket.' I thought for a moment and then asked what I should have asked long ago. 'Where was the wound?'

'In front. Slanting in from the right.'

'You're saying . . .'

'The doctor says she might have been stabbed even before she sat down. Maybe she didn'd die right away. People were milling around. We've subpoenaed the un-edited TV tapes, just in case the camera saw anything.'

'Would that mean the murderer was left-handed?' I was holding an imaginary ice-pick, jabbing with each hand in turn, trying to decide which hand could more easily stab to the right.

She shook her head. 'The doctor says from the front, easier with the left hand. From the side, easier with the right hand. From the back, reaching around her, easier with the right hand.

'Hell,' I said. 'You couldn't reach around her.'

'Well, if you could. Anyhow, I think you're right, I should talk to the people nearest her. This guy with the scar isn't local, so it may take me a while to catch up to him. Tomorrow morning. Now I have to go. I got these records out by promising to file them when I brought them back.' She kissed me and trotted off, focused as a cat with mouse on her mind.

I sat there stubbornly reviewing my recollections. The woman to the right of Simonetta had had white, curly hair. I could see her in my mind. A stocky woman, past middle age. Fairly tall. Five seven, maybe. Dark trousers. A long-sleeved shirt. A considerable bosom. Glasses. And white, curly hair.

I realized I was stroking the new hair at the back of my head, and with the realization came the thought that hair was not always attached to the person. When I'd looked at the pictures, I'd been looking for hair, not clothes or shape. The hair could have been a wig, but the woman wouldn't have had time to change clothes. I should have looked at the clothes!

I made a mental note, thinking that we still hadn't come up with any motive for someone killing Simonetta. Assuming there had been a motive, and the murder hadn't been an arbitrary act by one of the nuts Cynthia Adamson had mentioned.

I needed more information about Simonetta. Who might have known her? Dorotea saw her seldom if at all. Her neighbours had told us what they could, but they obviously hadn't been intimates. Grace said her colleague hadn't found anything of interest at Simonetta's house, and Grace herself had been looking only for names of the family. My interest was perhaps more general than either of theirs had been. I sat in colloquy with my conscience for some little time, staring out of the north window of my office as the sky darkened. The neighbouring building was unlit. Above its roof a bare branch flexed its muscle against the glow from a streetlight over on Colfax. A good time of day for burgling. People busy with their suppers. Too dark to see clearly.

My conscience gave up. I put out some food for the animals, then went to change into jeans, a navy sweater and a dark down vest. My burglar clothes.

Jacob taught me to pick locks years ago. One sometimes buys pieces of furniture that turn out to be locked. One does not wish to smash them to get them open, so one learns to pick locks. I do it now and then, just to keep in practice. I did it that evening on the Fixe back porch, while people moved up and down the alley and dogs barked and a brazen voice down the block yelled for Roger, Roger, Roger to come in for dinner. I wondered briefly if Roger was boy or dog. Or maybe husband.

The lock wasn't much. Once inside, I closed all the curtains that would close and drew all the blinds that would draw. The place smelled of dust and closed rooms, small rooms with too much in them and too little space for air. I listened to the sounds of the house, deciding Herby hadn't been big on household maintenance. Doors rattled on their latches. Faucets dripped. A loose window-pane clattered in a sudden breeze. No people sounds. Only the sounds of a lonely house, suddenly untenanted, relaxing into continuing decay.

I switched on the flash, and began to make my way through the clutter of Simonetta's life, Herby's life, wall by wall, drawer by drawer, closet by closet.

A typed list of numbers was posted by the kitchen phone: family names (including Dorotea Chapman's), the doctor, the public service company, the police. The paper was ochre with age, so brittle the edges had split and curled like dried leaves. Someone had prepared the list for Simonetta. Someone had posted it here years ago. It had never been moved or replaced. It was undoubtedly the source of the names and addresses Grace had found.

Aside from that one discoloured list, there were no address books, no phone numbers written in the back of the phone book, no orderly setting down of known people or places. There were scraps of paper stuffed in corners and between cannisters and stuck to the side of the refrigerator with fruit-shaped magnets. There were piles of unsorted mail, catalogues and letters piled in tottery heaps. There were boxes of junk on top of drawers and in closets.

One bedroom was obviously hers, one his. His was almost totally empty. Nothing in the drawers to speak of, a few bills, a few sheets of paper, two sets of underwear and as many socks. One fairly good jacket hanging in an otherwise empty closet. Why had he left it? He hadn't lived here. Was the marriage ever anything but a fiction?

Her room was a different matter. Here were all the stockings Simonetta had ever owned, neatly rolled into beige tennis balls and stuffed tightly in dresser drawers. Ditto underwear. Ditto shirts and blouses, the sizes decreasing as one burrowed down. The ones on the top were 3X.

Everywhere were rubber bands and string; pieces of aluminium foil, folded and flattened and stored; those little plastic envelopes of soy sauce and ketchup and mustard they pass out at fast food places, several hundred of them filling one drawer, along with plastic stirrers and paper packets of sweetener.

Simonetta had been a keeper. I cursed all keepers, everywhere. As I went on digging, I caught on. The drawers and boxes had been filled years ago. When they would hold nothing more, they became a geological stratum upon which later strata were laid down. Recent stuff was nearest the top. Recent stuff included articles of clothing and shoes and mail and little gift boxes with the ribbons put back around them, and Christmas cards standing in an accordion-pleated row along the mantel, their envelopes stacked neatly to one side. Almost all of them had returns. No Christmas tree. What had Simonetta done at Christmas time? Who had she been with? With her husband dead, the fiction of a marriage couldn't be sustained. Or could it? Was it easier for her family to sustain the fiction than to remember Simonetta was alone.

I came back to the Christmas cards. Considering the contents of the house, I was unlikely to do better. All the cards would fit nicely in a paper sack, one of a stack of perhaps five hundred paper sacks I found on the back porch, neatly arranged by size, folded, stacked. I snapped off the flash, opened the curtains, raised the dusty blinds and went out the way I had come, feeling I'd been in those claustrophobic, airless rooms for hours while down the street a tireless voice still called Roger, Roger, Roger. Maybe it was taped on a continuous loop.

Back at home, sitting at the kitchen table drinking coffee and trying to forget the hopeless, lifeless smell of Simonetta's house, I matched up as many envelopes and cards as I could on the basis of colour or size or names. Most of the cards were religious. There were a lot of Madonna and Child ones, a lot of Three Wise Men ones, a lot of Stars Over Bethlehem ones, and only a few on which holly or robins or reindeer made a generic reference to the season. It made me hopeful that these were cards from people Simonetta had known when she was young, in school. Perhaps I could hope for a few from people she had once worked for. Perhaps, just perhaps, one or more of them had known her well enough to have kept in touch with her over the years.

When I had as many matched up as I could manage, I

made a list of names and addresses. Most of the cards were not personalized and many of them were the same size, which meant I was at a loss to connect 'Betty and Joe' who signed the card with 'The Williamses' or 'The Bentleys' named on little stickers on envelopes. Sometimes the envelopes gave only the return address with no name at all. Where there was no match, I listed them separately.

It was only when I was a quarter way through and encountered the same little sticker for 'The Williamses' for the third time that I realized this wasn't one year's harvest. Postmarks verified it, making me feel like a fool. I should have noticed the changes of postal stamps from year to year. Simonetta had never thrown out Christmas cards any more than she had disposed of anything else. There were at least five years represented here, maybe twice that. The same people might be represented every year, or by four or five different addresses. My great number of possibles shrank suddenly to an entirely manageable and perhaps inadequate number. How many different people had sent cards?

Ah, well. I knew who to put on this particular job. I finished up the list, including the year dates on the postmarks, and sacked the cards, ready for return to their dusty mantel. Were Betty and Joe the same persons as Elixzabeth and J.B.? Were the L. Smiths on Baker Street the same as the L. Smiths on Lilac Way? Myra Sharp would find out for me. I was sure of it.

Myra is one of those extremely competent and ambitious young women who will turn their hand to anything at all, so long as it pays reasonably well and doesn't keep them from proceeding towards their well-thought-out goals. Myra has been studying accounting, and her goal is to become a very high-priced tax attorney. Myra pays attention to detail. She gets things done.

Except when she isn't available.

Mark made the call for me on Tuesday morning and came back apologetically. 'Her mother says she'll be back

Thursday,' he said. 'She's on some kind of an educational tour, looking at law schools. Her mother also says that her final semester leaves her some free time, so she can probably fit us in.'

I grumped, not sure I liked being fitted in.

'It's a slow Tuesday. Is it something I could do?' Mark wanted to know.

Well, of course it was something either of us could do. Or Eugenia Lowe, for that matter. Or possibly some office help hired by the hour. It's just that I had my mind set on Myra Sharp.

'I'm trying to find someone who knew Simonetta,' I explained, showing Mark the Christmas Card list. 'I wanted Myra to find phone numbers for these people, getting the right last names with the right first names, you know. Then I thought she could call them and weed the list down to the few who might have had some contact with Simonetta . . .'

'If you're determined to wait for Myra, you could try the nuns in the meantime.'

I looked at Mark blankly.

'You said Dorotea Chapman mentioned they all went to parochial school.'

'Sure. St Seraphia's. Possibly thirty-five, forty years ago.'

'Well, St Seraphia's is still in business and they undoubtedly keep records,' he said patiently. 'Maybe there'll be some old nun still there, someone who not only remembers Simonetta but can tell you who her friends were. Of course, you may not find any old nuns at all. There's a shortage these days.' He was no doubt quoting his former friend, Rudy, who had been reared in an Italian Catholic family and had endlessly described the glories of the heritage while eschewing involvement in it. Mark had inevitably picked up a bit of the cultural esoterica.

In this case, I already knew something about the subject because the history of some art *is* the history of monasticism. Many forms of mediæval art originated in monasteries, where there was no shortage of nuns or monks because monastic life was often longer and healthier than life on the outside. In mediæval times, women died in childbirth and men died in wars, fates generally avoided by the religious. Daughters with no dowries and younger sons with no land often had no future worth mentioning outside the convents. There, they'd get at least two meals a day and a roof over their heads while they engaged in peaceful pursuits such as gardening, carving, making lace, embroidering vestments, or illuminating manuscripts. Of course, that was during a time when both birth rates and death rates were high. When families are smaller and starvation is rarer, monasticism is not so attractive. Creating, as Mark said, a shortage of nuns.

Shortage or not, I found one.

She was Sister John Lorraine. When I called, I asked for anyone who had been at the school forty-five years ago, and Sister John was the name I was given. She was at the school still, seventy-five years old, clear of eye and mind, and she remembered Simonetta.

'They keep me around as a relic,' she told me when I arrived post haste, eager to pick her brain. 'I'm too old to change my habit, so I'm a historical exhibit.' Sister John wore the wide white head-dress I remembered seeing in my youth, one that made her look as though she had wings. 'I'm used to it, so they let me wear it.' She touched her wimple with affection and pride, like a little girl with a new dress.

I had introduced myself only as someone involved in investigating Simonetta's death. Sister John hadn't asked for identification, and I hadn't offered any. We sat in her office, a cluttered little room at the end of a side corridor on the ground floor of a school that looked and smelled like all schools, no holier than the one I'd attended as a child, for all its parochiality. Sister John said she no longer taught. All the teachers were lay teachers now. She was an administrator, she said, kind of a superior type clerk, and she would go on doing that until she grew too old to do anything. She lived as she had for the past fifty years, at the Sisters' residence next door, just behind the church.

And she, too, spoke of a shortage of nuns. 'There are only three of us over there. Used to be a dozen or more. Sometimes I wonder what's going to happen next.'

I sympathized. We spoke of the difficulties with education in a secular age. We spoke of the weather. Then we got around to Simonetta.

'She was a trial,' said Sister John. 'I suppose that's why I remember her.' She nodded to herself, then to me. 'What do you want to know.'

'Everything you can tell me. Anything might help.'

'Well, she was a great lump of a girl,' said Sister John. 'In all the time I've been here, there've only been two or three the size of Simonetta. Sister Julian and I tried to keep her busy so she wouldn't eat all the time. Any time she could, you'd find her stuffing candy, or sweet rolls, or cookies. That was her mother's fault. Mrs Leone felt sorry for Simonetta, so she always sent a sack of food with the girl when she came to school. I tried talking to Mrs Leone myself, but I didn't get anywhere. All she could say was poor girl, poor girl, she has to keep her spirits up.' Sister John looked away then back at me with a sly grin. 'It was my idea to teach Simonetta about the sin of gluttony. That got her, I'll tell you.'

'Sin?' I asked, remembering what Dorotea had said about Simonetta's concern with sin.

'Oh, sin, yes indeed. More than three moderate meals a day is gluttony, I told her. I had a talk with Father Waring, and he backed me up. He was a dear man. We got her down to a hundred and fifty pounds, among the three of us, Father Waring, Sister Julian and me. Kept her there, too, right up until she left us.'

'I should think she'd have appreciated that. It must have made her a lot more attractive.'

'You couldn't make Simonetta attractive. Being thinner made her a little less lumpish, that's all. Sister Julian and I used to trade her off as penance. She was very difficult to love. It was like loving a great chunk of . . . oh, I don't know. Clay, I guess. No. Something harder than clay. She was just . . . like a chunk of wood.' Sister John smiled ruefully at a memory. 'Sister Julian and I both thought that Simonetta was living evidence of God's inscrutability. We could not find any purpose for someone like her. It was a sin, of course, and I don't know how many times we confessed feeling that way and listened to Father lecture us about the sin of arrogance. I remember I'd do my penance, and then the very next week I'd find myself sinning again. Sister Julian felt just the same. Poor Simmy. She wasn't helpless enough to move us to holy pity. She was just . . . lumpish!

'Sister Julian and I, we'd talk and talk and talk at her, and she'd look at us, and we'd be sure none of it was getting through. Then, later, she'd come back at us with something we'd said, but it would always be whatever we'd said that hadn't mattered.'

I know I looked puzzled. I didn't know what she was trying to tell me.

She tried to help me. 'If I said to you, "When we add numbers, two and two always make four", what would I be trying to tell you?'

'That two and two always make four.'

'Not to Simonetta. She would come back at me, oh, maybe weeks later, and say, "Sister, when is it we're supposed to add numbers?"'

I thought about that. 'You mean, she thought you were giving her rules for living?'

The sister nodded, her head-dress fanning the air, the breeze brushing my face. 'Exactly. *Everything* was a rule for life. And all rules were unbreakable.'

'She made rules out of things that didn't matter?'

'Exactly. That's exactly it. She was always at me with questions about things that didn't matter. She thought there had to be one right way to do everything!'

I had seen the inside of Simonetta's house. Now, I started to understand it. Someone had told her to roll stockings.

Someone had told her to stack paper bags. That was the rule for doing it. There was no rule for undoing it, no rule for throwing things away. 'Strange.' I shook my head in wonder. 'She had no sense of humour, then.'

'She was completely literal-minded. I'll never forget the time Father preached on the text if thine eye offend thee . . .'

That one I knew. 'If thine eye offend thee, pluck it out.'

'Simonetta thought he meant her. Her weight, you know. She went on and on about plucking it out! Sister Julian and I had to talk like parrots for over a week to get that idea out of her head. We were frightened to death she'd start carving pieces of herself off. With most children, you can joke a little or poke fun, or tease. Not with Simonetta. She didn't think anything was funny except things the rest of us didn't.'

'As for example?'

'When one of our occasional parishioners tripped on the front steps and broke his hip, Simonetta laughed until she cried. She thought God had done it to him because he was sinful and didn't often attend mass.'

'She thought it was funny when God brought people up short?'

'She thought the miraculous conception was hysterical.'

I must have looked blank.

'The virgin birth,' she said gently. 'Jesus. Simonetta thought it was very amusing that God had arranged it, no matter what Mary might have thought about it.'

'I've always felt it would have been nice if He had asked her rather than just announcing His intentions,' I said.

I had been trying to be amusing, but Sister John gave me a look. I was sure she had perfected that look on whole generations of young Catholics. I felt the heat of it all the way to my coccyx.

'Is this conversation about Simonetta leading somewhere?' she asked me sternly.

'I was hoping it would lead to her friends. Did she have

any? Did she talk to anyone? Would anyone she knew at school have stayed in touch with her?'

'Why?'

'We want to know who killed her,' I said. 'Innocent people are being suspected. We need to know more about Simonetta.'

When I said 'innocent people', her face shut down like a garage door.

'The news said there was a note on her body. The note said, "She interfered; she's dead." And you don't think it meant she interfered with that slaughterhouse?' She gave me a glare, daring me to contradict. 'You don't think it means they killed her? Why wouldn't they? They kill babies all the time!'

She was going to put us on opposite sides; she was going to make us both angry; and then I'd go stalking out, or she would, relieving herself of any further responsibility. I wouldn't let her get away with it.

I smiled as I said, 'If you mean the clinic, no, I don't think that's what was meant at all. I was inside that morning, as an observer. I saw Simonetta sit down outside the doors. I was there the whole time. No one came near her except the people she arrived with. And the note doesn't say she interfered with the clinic. It may have been something else entirely. It's in the interest of justice that we find the truth. We need to talk with her friends.'

I could see her trying to decide her Christian duty. Part of her wanted to send me, an obvious heretic, packing. Part wanted to help. Neither side emerged winner.

'I'll think about it,' she said. 'If I think of anyone, I'll let you know.'

I had to be satisfied with that. Once more, I wished for Myra Sharp.

CHAPTER 3

Immediately after Jacob's death, Charlotte had offered to have his ashes scattered at her ranch near the little town of Elizabeth. Since the ranch stretches over the better part of two square miles, she didn't think the neighbours would object—not that she had any intention of asking them.

'Daddy's and Mother's ashes are here, too,' she said. 'They felt pretty much the way Uncle Jacob did about things like this.'

Grace and I drove out late on Wednesday, getting there just before dark. The weather was clear and cold. Though there'd been no snow for several weeks, we both wore heavy jackets and boots, more to keep warm than dry. I took with me the photo Jacob had shot years before, the one of the pine grove on the rounded hill. We could see that same hill from the front windows of Charlotte's house, a gentle slope in the middle distance, tree-fringed against the pale sky.

Charlotte exclaimed over the snapshot, then stumped off to get the jeep. She bumped us across the frozen pastures with experienced nonchalance, getting us half way up the hill before we were stopped by the terrain. We climbed from there. Jacob's ashes melted invisibly into the winter grasses among wind-curved eyebrows of lingering snow. Anemones would bloom there in April, so Charlotte said. I remembered them as pale and ethereal, like the spirits of flowers. Pasque flowers, they're called. Jacob told me once that though 'Pasque' means 'Easter', it comes from a root which means, 'To pass', so the pasque flower is also a Passover flower. Both holidays celebrate life triumphant, so it's suitable, one might say.

As we walked down the hill towards the car, the dusk gathered around us, sending the daytime landscape into another country. This world was shadowed and mysterious. I stopped to look back at the darkening grove, the tree-tops still sunlit, the wind sighing through the branches, moving them like waving hands. One ought to say goodbye, I thought. How does one say goodbye?

Charlotte asked us to stay to supper, and when we demurred for politeness' sake, she demanded we stay because she felt all alone and abandoned and sad, and besides, she had already cooked for us.

'Where's Richard?' I wanted to know. Charlotte's husband is usually more uxurious than otherwise. I'd been a little surprised at his absence.

'Richard is in Alamosa buying hay,' she said. 'It was so dry last year the pasture gave out, and we started feeding hay six weeks earlier than we usually do. We don't have nearly enough to last through March, much less April, or even May. God knows, the way things are going, we'll probably have no snow for months, then a freezing blizzard in late May, and drought all summer again. Anyhow, Richard went down to the San Luis Valley to see what kind of a deal he can make on forty tons or so. I told him just to call down there and see who has any, because we've pretty well got to take whatever they've got, but you know Richard. He won't buy anything without looking at it.'

'Besides,' Charlotte went on, as though she'd been reading my mind, 'you were asking about Jacob. You wanted to know about him when he was young? Well, I've found some stuff. Last time you called, when you asked about Jacob's girlfriend, it made me remember there was still an old trunk of Dad's in the cellar.'

We got back into the jeep, and Charlotte drove us to the ranch house, explaining as we went.

'The trunk was full of pictures and papers. I kept it because I thought my kids might want it someday. These days everyone seems to be into finding their roots. Jennifer and Jeremy haven't shown much interest in who Richard and I are, much less who *our* parents were, but I thought someday they might.'

From what I had seen of Charlotte's offspring, I doubted

it. They were far too poised and secure to need ancestrification.

She went on, 'I'd forgotten all about the trunk until you began talking about Jacob, and then I remembered they were twins, Jacob and Daddy, so anything Dad had kept from his school days would probably have been about Jacob, too.'

I didn't often remember that Jacob had been a twin. He had never made much of the fact. He and Harry had looked nothing alike, and of course Harry had been gone for over fifteen years.

'Anyhow,' Charlotte continued, 'I dragged out the trunk and sorted through the newspapers and letters and yearbooks from when they were young, before Dad got married to Mother.'

When we had divested ourselves of coats and boots, Charlotte took us into the kitchen where we found the table ready with three place settings, a large bowl of salad, and a pile of yellowing documents and newspapers. When we were seated, Charlotte thrust the salad bowl towards Grace and the papers towards me, then turned to the oven to bring out a casserole of chicken, a mixed vegetable dish, and a pan of au gratin potatoes. Charlotte had met Grace before. There was enough food for ten.

We looked through the papers as we ate. Under the newspapers was an envelope containing a duplicate of the photo I'd found among Jacob's things, the one of the young people and the fancy car. On the back of this one, however, someone had written, 'Left to right: Jake, Livvy Cerraverdes, me, Peggy Penrose, Vangie Curtis, Vangie's car. May, 1931.'

The 'me' had been Charlotte's father. 'Livvy' was the same girl as the one in the studio portrait among Jacob's things. Olivia. Her face shone from the dim old photograph like a moon reflected in murky water. 'Beautiful,' I murmured, echoing Mark.

Charlotte took the car picture and traced her father's features. 'Daddy looks so young. Half my age. I've seen pictures of him as a baby, but I don't think I'd seen one of him this age before. So young.'

They all looked young to me. Mere kids in love. The expression on Jacob's face as he looked at Livvy Cerraverdes left no doubt of that, though Harry's slight leer at Peggy Penrose was perhaps more lecherous than amatory.

'This is Olivia,' I said, pointing with my fork.

'Livvy. Not a pretty nickname,' Charlotte commented. 'Sounds like a bruise.'

'Mark says her family probably broke up the love-affair because of religion,' I commented.

'Oh, Daddy knew that was the reason!' Charlotte shuffled through the papers to pounce on an envelope with a foreign stamp. 'Read this!' She pulled out the folded letter and handed it to me.

Blue ink, in a round, childlike hand.

Dear Harry, I couldn't bear to write to Jacob but I couldn't bear his not knowing, either, so I'm writing to you. Please tell him for me. Tell him I don't take back anything I ever said to him. Not one word. Tell him I'm getting married because Mother and Daddy want me to. He's very nice. He isn't Jacob, but no one will ever be Jacob. His name is Octavio Desquintas y Alvares. He's a little older than I am. He's related to Daddy's family here, and he's a Don, and he speaks English, which is a good thing because I'm hopeless with Spanish. Most important, I guess, he's the right religion, and Jacob knows what I mean about that.

We're going to live here in Spain. Mother wants me to have maids and jewels and all the things Octavio can give me. They don't matter to me. Jacob knows that. Mother wants me to be married in the Church. That matters. Jacob knows.

Tell Jacob goodbye for me. Tell him I'll never forget him as long as I live. Tell him I will love him always.

It was signed, Olivia. Dated October 14th, 1932. Saragossa, Spain.

'Oh, that is sad,' said Grace, tears in her eyes. 'Poor Jacob.'

'She didn't get to stay there, though,' Charlotte said. 'Don Octavio got run out.' She sorted through the newspapers to find pages from the *Denver Post*, dated August, 1935. The social page reported the arrival from Spain of Don Octavio and Señora Olivia Desquintas y Alvares, together with their infant daugther. Because the Desquintas estates in Spain had recently been overrun by the forces of General Franco, the 'titled refugees', so gushed the reporter, would make their home temporarily with Señora Desquintas's parents, Mr and Mrs R. J. Cerraverde, of Cerraverde Imports.

'She didn't get her maids and her jewels, after all,' breathed Grace. 'Or at least, not for long.'

'So she came back to Denver,' said Charlotte. 'Right here where Jacob was. I wonder if they saw one another.'

I had picked up another newspaper, one from 1942, folded to display a story on page five: LOCAL MEN JOIN ARMED FORCES. Paragraphs of names followed under the headings of Army, Navy, Marines, Air Force. I searched for Buchnam on the alphabetized list, finding it almost at once under the 'army' heading. Harry and Jacob Buchnam. As I was putting the paper back on the pile, a name two lines below caught my eye. Octavio Desquintas. One name only. He had probably found Americans unsympathetic to his double-barrelled patronymic, so he had truncated it.

I found the article a little puzzling. 'They weren't drafting fathers that early in the war, were they? As a matter of fact, if he wasn't a citizen, would they have drafted him at all?'

'He could have volunteered,' Grace offered. 'Even if he wasn't a citizen. The Cerraverdes were probably taking care of Olivia and the little girl. Maybe Octavio had nothing else to do. He might have been eager to join up and get back at the Fascists, since they're the ones who ran him out of Spain.'

Both their names appearing on the same list was a bit of irony. Buchnam and Desquintas. I wondered if anyone else had noted that contiguity. Olivia's parents, perhaps? Olivia herself? Perhaps no one had remarked upon it until now.

'Coincidence,' said Grace disbelievingly.

'Coincidences have to happen sometimes,' I said. 'The laws of probability strongly favour that point.' Not that I believed what I was saying. When two related things show up together, it's because they're related, right? Common sense tells us that, and the hell with the laws of probability.

We found no more new information, though there were interesting pictures of the young Jacob, Olivia, Harry and Peggy playing tennis; of Jacob and Harry on a fishing trip; of Jacob and Olivia at a bridge tournament, smiling over a silver cup. I asked Charlotte's permission to take the papers back to my place so I could make copies, and on the way back to town I ruminated on what we'd found.

History has always fascinated me, but this was unlike the attraction of ancient history. Ancient history is mysterious, strange, like science fiction, a world in which we have no part, among people who were not personally connected to any of us. This was different, close, a time when people I knew were alive. I could see the faces and read the words and think, *I was almost there, like a character standing in the wings, waiting for my cue.* It almost seemed I should be able to remember that backstage existence. My real parents were alive then. Jacob had been born and gone to school then. He had fallen in love and seen his love taken away from him then, and I'd been almost there.

Jacob's remaining a bachelor all his life had been a mystery to me, but perhaps he'd never wanted anyone but Olivia. I wondered what had happened to her, and to Octavio. Women live longer than men, on average, so she might still be alive. And according to the newspaper account, she'd had at least one child: a daughter.

I had told Mark that Jacob would have paid extortion to

protect only me or Charlotte, because he'd had no one else. But perhaps there was someone else. If Olivia was alive, perhaps he had been trying to protect her, or her child.

The possibility was intriguing enough to keep me entertained during the drive home while Grace slept beside me, her breath making a little warm spot on my shoulder. I decided to add Olivia's name to the list I would give Myra. How many Desquintas y Alvareses—or even just Desquintas—could there be?

Myra came over Thursday afternoon, full of bubbling comments about the universities she'd visited and which ones she might attend. She had not changed at all since I'd first met her, three or four years before. She was still skinny and eager, with a little boy's freckled face, snub nose and haircut. She still sat in any chair balanced on her coccyx and the back of her head. She still talked to herself—I'd heard her chatting all the way up the stairs on the way in.

She still brought enormous enthusiasm and keen attention to every task she took on, as she did when I gave her the list I'd prepared, the picture of Olivia and the other young people, and photocopies of the two newspaper articles.

'We've got two separate things going here,' I told her. 'One of them pertains to the murder of Simonetta Leone. We want to find anyone who may have stayed in touch with her over the years, anyone who may have seen or talked with her recently. This other thing is personal. I want to find Jacob's old girlfriend. We know nothing about her except what's here, in these papers, and there's no Desquintas y Alvares in the current phone book.' I'd looked the night before, just on the off-chance.

'Myra Sharp,' she intoned in a dignified voice, 'Tracer of Lost Persons!' She giggled. 'Mom says there used to be a radio show about a tracer of lost persons. She'll flip.' She simmered over the photo, memorizing it.

'Olivia may not be lost at all,' I told her. 'The fact that

there's no Desquintas in the phone book doesn't mean much.'

'City directories.' Myra gave me a crafty look. 'Old city directories. Old phone books.'

'More power to you. I'm hardly in any hurry at all. How about tomorrow?'

'Monday,' she said firmly. 'Don't count on anything until Monday at the soonest, and you pay all expenses, right?'

Right. We shook hands on it and Myra left, reading the list aloud to herself as she went down the stairs and out the front door.

'Jason,' Mark said from the door.

'Ummm.'

'Do you think you might bring yourself to do a little business today or tomorrow? You've got a stack of messages on your desk you haven't answered, and one of them is from Lucinda Hooper.'

I bowed contritely towards the god of making-a-living and called Lucinda Hooper. Last year the Hoopers had bought a Chippendale oxbow-front chest of drawers from me for fourteen thou. Lucinda wanted to know if I'd take it back as a credit (full value) on the Federal sofa. We talked about that at exhaustive length. I finally told her I'd ship it to New York for her, sell it there, and she could give me the money towards the sofa, but I would not take it back in trade for the retail price.

'I can sell that sofa tomorrow for the asking price in cash, Lucinda. When you're in business, you buy at dealer prices and sell at retail, that's how you stay in business. If I take that chest back from you at fourteen thousand, I can't make a dime on it here in Denver. I'll have to ship it to the east coast.'

'Well, maybe we'll keep it,' said she.

Which is what I wanted her to do anyhow.

The next phone slip had Sister John Lorraine's name on it. I called Sister and received from her the names of two women: Cecily Brent and Yaggie Costermyer.

'Yaggie?' I asked.

'Don't ask me what it stood for,' she said. 'People give their children very strange names these days. When I was a child, you couldn't go to parochial school unless you had a Christian name. Come to think of it, she probably did have a Christian name that I've forgotten. Yaggie is what she was called.'

'Yaggie,' I confirmed, writing it down.

'Neither of those girls may be around any more,' she said. 'They knew Simonetta when she was in school, mostly because their families were neighbours. They weren't friends, but they were reasonably kind. You know what I mean.'

I did know what she meant. I thanked her effusively, and she told me she was praying for my enlightenment. I thanked her for that as well. She had evidently decided my eternal fate was still undecided and a little enlightenment might help. I called Myra, who had just arrived home, and added Yaggie and Cecily to the list she was already working on.

'Yaggie?' she asked. 'My God!'

The third phone slip down was a decorator I'd dealt with before. She was what one might call a hobbyist. She 'did decor' when she wasn't flying off to Europe with her husband or flying down to Tucson for the winter or flying somewhere else for something else. I didn't bother to return that call.

I did call Charles Nutting, a client I'd done a house for the year before. His boss at the brokerage firm (about whom I'd heard much, none of it good) had bought a big house which he wanted to refurnish. Charles had given him my name (thanks awfully, Charles) but he wanted me to know I should get everything in writing because the old bastard would try to cheat me.

The last call was to Kansas City, to Orvie Spender, an old friend of Jacob's who wanted to offer condolences. I'd met Orvie a time or two, a colleague in the antique trade, a warm and friendly guy whom Jacob had much liked.

'How did you learn Jacob had died?' I asked when I reached him at last.

'I was through Denver last week. I called Jacob's place, and that man of his told me about it.'

Francis was staying on in Jacob's apartment until we could get everything packed and into storage, and until Francis himself decided where he was going next.

'Orvie went on, 'I was real eager to tell Jacob about the table, but I guess I was just too late with it.'

'What table?' I asked.

'The one Jacob wanted.'

'I'm sorry. You've lost me, Orvie. What table did Jacob want, and why?'

'Oh, well, I thought maybe you'd know. Last time I saw him, he asked me to keep an eye out for an antique card table, a really good one. He wanted to give it to someone for a birthday present. Eightieth birthday, he said.'

'When did you see him last?'

'Oh, October, I guess. About the middle. I was on my way back from San Francisco, and I stopped over.'

'When did you say this birthday was?'

'Didn't say. Just told me to keep my eye out. I found the table before Christmas, but I've been so busy . . .'

'It wouldn't have made any difference. Jacob had a final stroke in November, and he wasn't able to communicate with us much after that.'

He made sympathetic sounds. 'You wouldn't want it, would you? The table?'

'Is it good?'

'This is a very nice piece, Jason. Jacob said it had to be special, and this is. Chippendale, five-legged, pre-Revolutionary. New York manufacture, I'm pretty sure. Mahogany, maple, and some poplar. Fancy top, inlaid with felt, and the felt's not even worn. I doubt the table top has been opened out more than half a dozen times. I could have got it for ten, but I paid twenty-five because the family was struggling and even though they'd had this piece forever, they had no idea what it was. I figured I'd let Jacob have it for thirty. Or you, of course. I suppose you know who he wanted it for?'

I made a noncommittal noise and asked, 'Can you send pictures and provenance?'

He could. He would. Thank you and sorry about Jacob and talk to you soon again.

And I sat there with my mouth open. Jacob had wanted a present for an eightieth birthday!

Mark asked me, 'What's the matter with you. Your mouth's open.'

I shut it, then opened it again. 'Olivia's alive,' I said.

'Olivia? How do you know?'

'It has to be her. She.'

'Her, she, who?'

I explained, not too coherently. 'Who else would Jacob want to give an eightieth birthday present to?' All kinds of possibilities and incredibilities were opening up. There had been that picture of Jacob and Olivia with the bridge trophy. Jacob had been a bridge fanatic. I'd disappointed him by remaining vulgarly addicted to poker. Right up to the time of his first stroke, Jacob had played bridge. Perhaps he had played with Olivia. Perhaps they had been lovers. If they could have been, honourably . . .

Though what was honourable where love was concerned? When Olivia turned her back on Jacob's love to marry the Spanish Don, was that honourable? Her parents and priest no doubt believed so. Jacob was, after all, a Jew. The Holocaust had not yet happened. The Nazis had not yet made anti-semitism revoltingly unacceptable to any civilized person. So Olivia had gone off to Spain, and both of them had no doubt wept at the unfairness of it all.

But what about when she came back? There were seven years from the time she returned until Jacob went off to war. What happened then? And what happened after the war?

Was it any of my business?

I had the feeling—though it was only a feeling—that Jacob would have said not. If this were purely personal, I should perhaps back off, grant privacy where privacy was due, remember that Jacob had never introduced me to the lady and therefore he had probably wanted to keep her to himself. Or such of her as he had.

However, there was the possibility that Olivia could be connected to the H.Fixe puzzle. If the extortion business had nothing to do with me or Charlotte (and I didn't, quite frankly, see how it could) then perhaps it had something to do with Olivia. I had to keep reminding myself, as I had reminded Mark, that it was extortion Jacob had written on the envelope, not blackmail. Blackmail would have been easier to understand. From what I knew of the early decades of the century, there had been many rather common shortcomings which were thought too shameful for public acknowledgment. That two people had been lovers, for example. I could imagine blackmail over that. Extortion was something else. Extortion did not mean that Herby Fixe would reveal something. It meant that something bad would happen. A threat. Though it seemed unlikely that anyone would threaten an eighty-year-old woman, the fact remained that Jacob had not gone to the police about this matter. He'd paid.

Mark and I talked it over, inventing scenarios: this had happened, that had happened. I offered as a hypothesis that Jacob and Olivia had not, in fact, been in touch, because if Jacob had been, he would have introduced me to her.

Mark considered this presumptuous.

'Why would Jacob have introduced you to her?'

'Because he loved us both,' I said, astonished at the question. 'Of course.'

'Oh, of course,' he replied. 'I always introduce my family to people I love.'

Well, maybe not. Jacob had loved me like a father. 'I suppose fathers don't tell their sons everything.'

'You've got that right,' said Mark. 'And *vice versa*.'

Mark went home. I wandered around the place, checking windows, turning down thermostats. Bela padded behind me, wagging his tail and whining softly. He wanted some attention. He wanted to go for a run. Schnitz did not want to run. He hid under a couch and growled at me, like a tiger. All right, cat, stay home and sulk. I got Bela's leash and we started for the park, stopping across the alley for a moment to visit our friend Nellie Arpels. Nellie's daughter and son-in-law, the Fetterlings, had recently remodelled their attached garage into a ground-floor suite for Nellie. After twenty years confined to a wheelchair on the second floor, Nellie had spent the past several months revelling in unaccustomed accessibility. In the summer she would be able to wheel herself out into the garden. Still, she had confessed she missed being able to see all up and down the block.

Bela and I slipped in through the back gate and knocked on Nellie's outside door, three and two, which means Jason and friend. I could hear Nellie's chair as it rolled up to the door, then the lock snicked and it rolled away. I waited until she had time to get out of the way, then pushed open the door and stuck my head around it. Nellie's cat, Perky, retreated to the closet when she saw Bela, though the dog only sat beside me quietly as Nellie and I chatted. Since Nellie enjoyed what she called 'real soap opera', I told her about our recent discoveries.

'This old girlfriend might be alive,' she opined, nodding firmly at me, as though she had to convince me. 'If I'm alive, she could be alive. Do you suppose she knows Jacob is gone?'

I hadn't thought about that. 'There was an obituary in the paper.'

'If she reads obituaries.' Nellie wrinkled her lips and nose. 'I don't. Too depressing. She might not know.'

Bela whuffed to announce the arrival of Nellie's daughter, bringing her mother's supper. Nellie preferred to eat alone, at her own pace, which was slow, rather than attempting the family dinner table. She said hurrying her meals made her gassy. After promising to come back soon, Bela and I left by the alley, jogged across Fourteenth and Thirteenth to the park, and did a slow, lolloping circuit as the light faded. It was dark when we got back to the shop.

There's no logical explanation for what happened then. I was pleasantly tired, quite hungry, and not thinking of anything much except supper. As I came up the back stairs, I got a whiff of something, an unpleasant frisson, the merest hint of smell, or perhaps part scent, part recollection. I was suddenly possessed by old dust, by curtains left hanging, carpets left lying too long. I was lost in claustrophobic airlessness, as though packed away in some ancient trunk or box, sealed against life, saved . . .

Imprisoned.

1465 Hyde had never smelled that way. Not when Agatha was alive, not since. The cleaners came every week and bustled about in a flurry of dusters and a slosh of lemon-scented oil. What I smelled was something else. The smell of old attics, old basement storerooms. The quintessential fragrance of Simonetta's house. A stored away odour, the smell of old clothes in the bottom of old sorrowful trunks. Renunciation of life. Habit and custom and routine.

Some rather long time later I found myself sitting at the kitchen table, the animals busy with their supper and I with no memory of having fed them. I with no memory of anything except loss and the revelation it had brought with it.

I didn't have to stay here.

The thought wasn't welcome or unwelcome, though it was chillingly unfamiliar. I didn't have to stay here. This had been Jacob's house. This had been Jacob's business. He had asked me to come back and take it over when he was too ill to go on with it, but I didn't have to go on with it now. Agatha and Jerry and I had been happy here, but they were gone, and Jacob was gone, and I didn't have to stay.

I didn't have to spend my life dickering with an endless series of Lucinda Hoopers—not that I disliked Lucinda, I didn't—or going to auctions or scuffling for inventory. I did those things because Jacob had done them, but it didn't matter to him any more whether I stayed or not. As long as he had been alive, yes, I'd owed him that. Loyalty. Security. Affection. But now he was gone, and I'd made no such commitment to anyone else.

I thought of Grace. Well, what about Grace? We'd considered the question. Or perhaps we'd only danced around it, like a couple of courting cranes who weren't sure about the nesting season, going through the motions of an uncertain gavotte. She had a career and was intent on taking it further. She had made no promises. And, perhaps, she had simply told me the truth, unflattering as that was. Perhaps I was not quite what she envisioned as a husband, being too sedate, too set in my ways, too quiet, too moody, too sad . . .

And perhaps I was that way because I had not only stepped into Jacob's business but also into his emotional shoes, into his life, his mould, his style, his habits. Like him, alone. Like him, devoted to someone I couldn't have, or didn't have any longer.

Now . . . now what? I wasn't required to stay in the mould, the rut. How did the old question go? What is a rut but a grave open at the ends? And what is a grave but the end of a rut?

There was no compelling reason I couldn't do something else. Anything I liked. Inside myself I could feel shiftings and rearrangements. Hard internal chunks pushed past one another, making momentary discomforts as they rubbed corners. Perhaps this was what a religious experience is supposed to be, though there was nothing ecstatic or beatific in it. Spaces were opening around me. Veils were lifted. Somewhere in my psyche, stagehands were shifting the scenery. I could almost hear the grunting and heaving.

When they had finished, they left a vast and twilit moor with roads leading in all directions and the air so clear I could see almost to the horizon along all of them. Jacob's words were upon every signpost. *You can be whatever you want to be. You are whoever you choose to be.* Almost as though he had come back to paint them, to focus my attention once more.

Well, who, at this late date, did Jason Lynx choose to be? Forty years old, still in reasonably good shape, still (so I'm informed) attractive to women, some women; well educated—though only in fields of art and the history thereof. Not gregarious. Not a man for crowds, team sports, or locker-room bonhomie. Not a man for sexual sniggers. A romantic, perhaps. Not a true expert on anything, lacking the experience to be an expert, but full of snippets and bits of disparate knowledge and irrelevant skills, none the less. A lock-picker, target-shooter (out of practice at the moment), Navy-trained demolitions man, antique dealer, puzzle-solver.

Who would do what, given the opportunity to do anything at all? Who would live where? With whom? Who would earn his bread how?

The questions bubbled and fulminated, and then, as suddenly as they had come, they drained away, leaving behind a feeling of empty repose. No need to decide now, I told myself. No need to do anything at this moment, so long as I kept in mind that decisions needed to be made.

Bela pawed at my leg. He'd had his head on my knee, and I'd been ignoring him. Schnitz sat on the table before me, at eye level, staring into my face. I'd been out of it, and they knew it. Where are you, Jason? Come back, person. Come back and pay attention to us, your creatures.

I wondered if God ever became distracted. Perhaps that is the purpose of prayer. Come back, Lord. Pay attention to us, your creatures.

I came back to my own creatures, tussling Bela and rumpling Schnitz and giving them both treats while I fixed myself a sandwich of leftover meatloaf. The mind-moor was still inside my head, placid and empty, all roads waiting. Anytime, Jason. Anytime at all.

Clearly, whatever else I did, I would have to take time to solve the twin puzzles of Olivia and Simonetta. They were not unlike other puzzles I'd solved for other people. I would finish them up for Jacob, just as I would finish up the rest of Jacob's business. So there would be no untidiness behind to haunt me later if I chose to go away.

Grace was busy for the next three days. She called me once or twice, but she had no time for us to get together. On Friday the Hoopers decided to buy the Federal sofa. On Saturday I took Bela and Schnitz, by invitation, to visit my friends Marge and Silas Beebe on their farm outside Littleton, where they introduced me to Celia and Bill Boniface, who had recently moved into a 'turn-of-the-century farmhouse' nearby. Marge had decided they should meet me. When they left, they gave me directions and asked me to stop by on my way back to town.

They'd described it correctly. It was a farmhouse, a sizeable one, vaguely Queen Anne, with a wraparound porch and a semi-tower on the south-east corner. It had a homely charm, though no particular elegance. The worst feature was a poorly built, tacked-on one-storey extension at the back, and it could come off without problems. I told them a good landscape plan would offset some of the architectural deficiencies, mostly, in my opinion, the fact that the place looked slightly 'tilted', needing mass at the north corner to balance the apparent weight of the tower. I thought a terrace garden would do the job.

The rooms were of good size, not chopped up with multiple doors or odd windows, and the ceilings were high. The Bonifaces intended to insulate the house, and to re-do the wiring, plumbing and heating, which immediately told me they were amateurs. Anyone familiar with such major renovation would have waited to move in until it was done. I suggested they rent a place in town or park a trailer on the property temporarily.

'Don't try to live in it, while they're working on it,' I advised. 'You'll hate it. You may end up divorced.' It had happened to more than a few couples I knew. Living in constant mess and annoyance carries over into personal relationships.

I suggested replacing windows with double glazing to cut down the heat loss, and recommended a couple of architects and builders I knew to be reliable. The furniture in the house had come from the town home they'd moved from, slick contemporary stuff in the still popular south-west pastels. I agreed with Celia that it didn't do much for the house. She wanted to know what the original furniture might have looked like, but she shuddered when I told her that turn-of-the-century farmhouse furniture, bought new then, had probably been either mission style or arts and crafts, which I have always considered fairly crate-like and not terribly comfortable.

'You could do it country,' I suggested.

'With churns and things?' She wrinkled her nose.

'That's country-cute,' I said.

'What's the difference?' Bill asked.

'In country, you leave the farm implements in the barn, where they belong. In country, you make your parlour and dining-room a little formal, with nice window treatments and carpets, because that's where company is entertained and one wants to show off a little for company. In country-cute you go for lamps made out of butter churns and chandeliers made out of wagon wheels, both with ruffled gingham shades. In country-cute, you put ruffled curtains on every window, with ruffled tie-backs and valances, and you put down 'rag-rugs', made in Italy out of new fabrics at forty bucks a square foot, and you go in for fireplaces which won't heat your rooms. In country, you might use wood stoves or coal stoves, sitting right out in the room because they can heat a room, and you use functional, well-designed lamps. You get the idea.'

They laughed and said they got the idea. 'But I don't want it severe,' said Celia.

'It doesn't have to be severe. It can be serene and practical and a little utilitarian, the way well-kept farms were. And are.'

They made an appointment to come in during the week and look at some Shaker things I had in stock. On the way back to town it occurred to me I'd gone through this whole exercise out of habit, paying very little attention, as though the revelations of Thursday night had never happened. I hadn't once stopped to think that I might not be around to do a job for the Bonifaces.

Sunday I took Nellie some chocolates and spent an hour with her before going on to dinner with Trish and Greg Steinwale. Greg is a very well-known artist. I'd met them both about a year before, and we'd become friendly. Trish tells me Greg likes me because I don't drool and grovel over his paintings, and it's true that I've tried to act sensible around him. When he shows me something, I try to see what he's aiming for, then I comment as briefly and intelligently as I can, after which I shut up.

At any rate, Greg's invited me on several occasions to showings or family meals at the studio, like tonight. Trish's pre-school daughter, Frosty, was with us, and we all sat on the floor slurping spaghetti and drinking red wine—or fruit juice for Frosty and for Trish, who was eight months pregnant.

Later in the evening Frosty fell asleep on the couch, and we three adults were chatting pleasantly over coffee when we were interrupted by the arrival of Greg's mother, Harriet Steinwale, and her friend, Dr Lycia Foret. I wished immediately for a cloak of invisibility. I'd been avoiding them both for a year, ever since what Grace and I called 'the dogwalker matter'. It wasn't that I disliked either of them, I was fascinated by Lycia, and had been since I first laid eyes on her. It was just that I'd come out of that affair knowing things they'd rather no one had known. I'd chosen avoidance in order not to embarrass them or me, in spite of my inexplicable fascination with Lycia.

There was no avoidance possible in the circumstances. The studio is all one big room with only a tiny bath and kitchenette arrangement on the balcony. So I smiled and said how do you do, so nice to see you again, and then faded as gracefully as possible into the wall surfaces. As it turned out, Harriet and Lycia had stopped by to pick up a small painting Lycia had bought from Greg as a birthday gift for her mother. I admired the picture; it was marvellous. Greg wrapped it carefully in bubble-wrap, and the two women left.

'Quite a nice gift,' I commented, relieved they were gone.

'Lycia's mom's a great old gal,' said Greg. 'She's going to be eighty in a couple of weeks.'

Everyone seemed to be turning eighty. I launched into the story of Jacob and his planned gift for someone's eightieth birthday.

'Oh, what a pity,' cried Trish. 'And you don't know who.'

'There's the possibility it could be Jacob's childhood sweetheart,' I confessed. 'But we don't know for sure, and so far we haven't located Olivia.'

Trish laughed, then Greg. I hadn't said anything funny.

'That's old Mrs Meyer's name, Lycia's mom. Olivia.'

My heart pounded. 'Olivia was married to a man named Desquintas y Alvares. She had a daughter in about 1929 or 1930. Does Lycia Foret have an older sister?'

Trish said thoughtfully, 'I don't think Lycia's mom was ever married to anyone but Mr Meyer. Besides, Lycia's an only child. She was saying just the other day it's too bad there aren't brothers and sisters to help her arrange her mother's party. Sorry.'

I was sorry too. It would have been a wonderful coincidence to confound Grace with.

Celia Boniface jumped her appointment and came in Monday morning to look at the Shaker furniture. We also looked at pictures of farmhouses, English style, American style. We talked about reupholstering some of her pieces. We talked about using leather instead. I gave her photocopies of things she wanted to think about. I didn't push. If they wanted me to do the job for them, they'd let me know.

About the time Celia departed, Myra arrived, her mouth turned down in a discontented curve.

'No luck?' I asked, feeling hollow.

'Oh, some,' she muttered. 'Just not as much as I'd like.'

She sat on her tailbone, slid down in the chair until the top of her head was against the back, paged through her notes, and began:

'These people who sent Christmas cards. I called a great number of these people, some of them gave me the names of other people, and I have to say that none of them knew Simonetta worth diddly.'

'No result.'

'Not diddly,' she said with gloomy satisfaction. 'They were friends of her mother, and they sent cards to Simonetta because her mother had asked them to . . .

'However, I did get this Yaggie person. It turns out the Cecily person is in Brazil for the nonce . . .'

'For the nonce?'

'That's literary for a few weeks. You know, if you look like me, you've got to sound like you went to a liberal arts college even if you are majoring in accounting. It's kind of hard to bring Principles and Techniques of Inventory Management into general conversation. Anyhow, this Yaggie, she used to live on the same block as Simonetta'a family. She doesn't remember all that much about Simonetta except for one episode that happened when the woman she worked for died. Simonetta had a fit.'

Myra looked up at me to see if I cared, and when I nodded encouragingly, she shuffled her notes, settled more slantingly into the chair, and said, 'Hokay! Now, here's how that went:

'Yaggie Costermyer was home from college, her junior year. She thinks it was spring break. Simonetta's family lived on the same block, though not Simonetta herself. She lived with the family she worked for. On this particular morning a cab pulls up in front of Simonetta's family's house and Simonetta practically falls out. She pounds on the door, which is locked, because her mother is off shopping or something. Yaggie is outside getting the mail out of the mailbox, so she sees all this.

'So then Simonetta starts up and down the block, knocking on everybody's door, telling everybody the woman she worked for is dead, she committed suicide, she committed this terrible sin, and stuff about the baby, and this thing and that thing. So Yaggie corrals Simonetta and takes her over to Cecily's house, and everything settles down. Later, Yaggie reads in the paper the woman died of a gas-leak, accidentally. From what Yaggie says, Simonetta had a real crush on her, the woman who died.'

'What year would that have been?' I wondered.

Myra pursed her lips and fiddled with a strand of hair. 'Yaggie said something about ages. What was it? She said she felt sorry for the woman who died, because she was only three years older than Yaggie was. That doesn't help, does it.'

'Sure it does,' I said. 'Yaggie was a junior in college, so she was around twenty. The woman was three years older, so she was around twenty-three. Simonetta was the same age as the woman she worked for, so Dorotea Chapman said, and she was sixty-two when she died. So we're talking about nineteen fifty-three, give or take a year, right?'

Myra nodded, ticking off on her fingers.

'Have you got anything else?' I asked.

'Not yet. We need that other person, Cecily Brent. Yaggie says Cees—that's Cecily's nickname, Cees—knew Simonetta better than anyone. According to Yaggie, Cecily aspired to sainthood. She planned on being a nun, and she spent a lot of time trying to be holy. One of her holiness kicks was being very sweet to Simonetta, listening to her, talking with her, explaining things to her. Yaggie said this was a real pain, because it was no fun for Cecily to be a saint all by herself, she had to do total recall at anyone who'd listen.'

'And Cees is now a nun in Brazil?'

'Cees is now a housing expert, currently in Brazil. She gave up on the nun business when she moved to California with her folks. She finished college and became an architect, and now she lives in Santa Fe, New Mexico, married to another architect, and the two of them design what Yaggie calls "technologically appropriate dwellings" for developing countries because, Cees told Yaggie, it's a more practical way of doing good.'

'When did Cees move to California?'

'Not long after this thing with Simonetta. Yaggie was talking with her, commiserating, saying it was too bad Cees had to leave all her friends, and Cees said there were some things she wouldn't mind leaving, like Simonetta Leone, because you could get in over your head with people like that.'

'And that's all?'

'One more thing. When Cees moved, Simonetta had another hysterical fit. Showed up again and screamed the neighbourhood down.' Myra sighed. 'That's all I've got on her. It isn't much, but I haven't given up yet.'

I thought she had a lot. 'How'd you find Yaggie?'

'She still lives there. Her real name is Amy Agnes Costermyer. She's been married and widowed twice, but she took back her maiden name when she moved into the old family home when her folks died. She's a funny old dame. She cracked me up.'

'And she's still in touch with Cecily.'

'Still in touch. She and Cecily talk on the phone all the time. Cecily's name is Stephens now, and when she gets back to New Mexico, we can follow up with her.'

'OK. Now what about Olivia?'

Myra shuffled papers, putting the top on the bottom. 'Nothing, Jason. Zippo. The Cerraverde family is in the city directory up until 1954, and so is the Cerraverde Import Company. Olive oil, cork, wine, that kind of stuff. After 1954, they're not there any more. Instead, there's somebody named Ralph Burnam at that address, and he's listed there for eighteen years, then somebody tore the house down and built a parking garage. I can't find Burnam after that, and there's nothing listed at the former address of the Import Company . . .' Her voice trailed off as she searched her notes.

'No Desquintas y Alvares shows up in any directory. There are lots of Alvareses, but no Octavio or Olivia. I called all the Alvareses with initial O. Some of them I didn't get, so I'll keep trying. So far as the city and the phone company are concerned, there wasn't any Olivia.'

'Ahhh,' I said, realizing for the first time how much I'd really wanted to find Olivia. I'd wanted to follow through on Jacob's plan to buy the table and present it, from him, as a sign of undying love.

Which she might have found, of course, intensely embarrassing!

Myra was ploughing on. 'Since I wasn't getting anywhere, I decided to work on the neighbours of the Cerraverdes. I made a list of the names in the neighbourhood, up and down the blocks on either side, from the years after Olivia came back. Then I looked them up in this year's phone book, looking for anyone with the same names.' She preened a little, waiting for the question.

'And you found?'

'I found a man named Daniel Brockman. He was a teenager in the 'fifties, and he had a terrible crush on Olivia's daughter. Maybe he'll talk to you.'

'To me?'

'Not to me. He doesn't talk to women. He's now Brother Daniel.'

'A monk?' I told myself it wasn't surprising. The Cerraverdes had probably lived in a Catholic neighbourhood, near their parish church. 'Catholic?'

'Don't ask me. All I know is what his sister-in-law told me when she gave me his name and the phone number you call to get hold of him. I found her because her husband is Arthur P. Brockman Jr, and his father was Arthur P. Brockman who lived down the block from the Cerraverdes. His wife says A.P. never paid much attention to the Cerraverde family, but his little brother was so crazy about Olivia's daughter it became a family legend. Daniel became a monk because his heart was broken. She said it was Romeo and Juliet all over again.'

'Jesus, Myra. What is this? *Lost Loves* season? Incredible Romances? We've got Jacob and Olivia. Brother Daniel and the Desquintas girl. Simonetta and the woman she worked for.'

Myra smiled understandingly. 'I know it. I feel like I've been up to my neck in that TV show about the unsolved mysteries. You're going to scream when you get my phone bill. I did the best I could with weekend rates, but I'm not finished yet.'

I nodded absently. All these spiderwebs spinning off in various directions produced no pattern at all. I approve of pattern. The lack thereof makes me itchy!

So, all right. There seemed to be nothing more Myra could do to locate Olivia, not at the moment. I would talk to Brother Daniel and Myra could concentrate on Simonetta.

'When is Cecily returning from Brazil?' I asked.

'In the next few weeks sometime. Yaggie said she'd let me know.'

We left it at that. She went away down the stairs, talking earnestly to herself, leaving me to stare at Brother Daniel's phone number, considering what I might say to him, what questions I might ask.

Any decision on the matter was forestalled by Mark, who came in waving an envelope, grinning widely. 'We did get it,' he cried. 'The bid on the Stanley job.'

I couldn't think what he was going on about. Then it came to me. Six months before we'd bid on an office furnishing and decoration scheme for a law firm: Stanley, Seeley, Meyer, Huffnagle and Wirtz.

'Damn!' I exploded.

Mark stared at me as though I'd lost my mind.

'Wasn't the thing due months ago?' I asked him.

He read the letter, his smile fading, then went out to dig through his files. He came back flapping several documents. 'You're right. It was due for award in November. At the time, I assumed they'd given it to someone else and neglected to inform us.'

'So did I. So, in the meantime we've sold a lot of the specific items we'd included in the bid.'

Mark flipped through our bid copy again. 'Of course we have. You're right. Damn.'

'I suppose we could renegotiate. We could offer to meet the bid price on everything except the items we don't have any more. We could supply replacements at cost plus.'

'You don't sound eager,' he said.

I wasn't. But then, recently I hadn't been eager about much. 'Well, the fact they're three months late on the award doesn't augur well for the job, does it? You can call them and set up an appointment. It won't hurt to talk.'

It never hurts to talk. While Mark went off to make the appointment, I went downstairs to check inventory with Eugenia, leaving Brother Daniel's number on top of my desk where it was covered by the inventory sheets when I brought them up. I knew the number was there. I just didn't think about it for a while.

Our relationship with Stanley et al. had been entirely through Elbert Stanley, son of the original and late Mr Stanley. I'd been told that Seeley and Meyer were also dead, and I hadn't met either Huffnagle or Wirtz or, need-less to say, any of the other personnel except the receptionist and Elbert's secretary, whom he had not bothered to intro-duce. I have an aversion to businessmen who refer to com-petent staff members as 'the girl' or 'my girl', which Elbert habitually did.

The firm had obtained an extremely favourable long-term lease on space in one of the high-rise office buildings with which Denver is greatly over-supplied. (During the oil boom buildings sprouted like corn; since the oil bust they stand largely vacant.) According to Elbert, the money saved on the lease was to have gone into decor. During our meet-ing late on Tuesday, however, Elbert did not carry the matter forward. Instead, he chose to be purposefully obtuse about the consequences of his own dalliance.

'Surely you can obtain other pieces at the same price.'

I explained yet again there was no surely about it. The original pieces had been authentic period furnishings, and antiques do not come available on order.

'Well, if you don't want the job . . .' he whined.

'If you'd wanted the job done,' I said in a not particularly ingratiating tone, 'you'd have awarded the bid as per your original terms. Since you didn't bother to do that, you can hardly expect us to turn handsprings for you now. I've told you what we can do. You can accept that or not.'

Someone came in behind me while I was talking, but I didn't turn. I was too interested in watching Elbert's face turn purple.

'Elby, why are you being an idiot?' a voice asked.

Then I turned. She was formidable, dressed in a fuchsia suit, iron grey hair drawn back in a complicated knot, massive jaw thrust forward, coming into the room like the USS *Imdomitable*. I almost expected to hear her say, 'Damn the torpedoes!' Luckily, she wasn't aimed at me.

Mark, meantime, had risen to his feet with every evidence of delight. 'Amelia,' he cried. 'I didn't know you were the Wirtz in this firm! Jason, I'd like you to meet a very dear friend of my mother's. Amelia Wirtz, Jason Lynx.'

'How do you do,' she said, giving my hand a single hearty pump stroke before turning back to her luckless partner. 'Elby, why are you being obtuse?'

She didn't wait for an answer, but turned to me, saying, 'My colleagues out-voted me and gave the bid to someone else who was a lot cheaper, only to find the low bidder had more or less vanished along with his defunct business. Didn't Elby get in touch with you then?'

'We heard nothing from Mr Elbert until yesterday,' I said in my most dignified tone.

She trained her guns on Elbert, who attempted an exculpatory explanation to do with our not meeting the terms.

'Well, *you* didn't, dear; why should they? My god, Elbert, do you want this firm cleaned up or are you content to go on looking like the shabby butt end of World War I?' She shook her head at him, part pity, part contempt.

'Come into my office,' she bellowed. 'We'll settle this

once and for all.' She snatched the papers from Elbert's desk and sailed out under full steam.

Mark grinned at me behind her back, and we went after her.

'How's your mother?' she asked him. 'I haven't seen her in months. Business has been far too good. Lots of people mad at each other. Lovely for lawyers, having people mad at each other. Nothing like the frustrations of a rotten economy to increase litigation. Are you and your father still not speaking?'

'We speak on occasion,' said Mark, trying not to laugh. Or maybe, trying not to cry. It was hard to tell.

'So difficult, I've always thought, having a gay child. Though not nearly as difficult as having a criminal one, or a drug addict, or something like that. And no more difficult than having one's child married to someone impossible. I have a daughter-in-law you would not believe. Not one brain in her pretty little head, but my son will none the less be aghast when his children turn out to need remedial reading classes. I'd far rather he were gay than married to her. I told your father so. I told him to count his blessings. He told me to mind my own business, of course.'

She settled into her moorings and let her eyes skim the agreement she'd swiped from Elbert's desk. 'From what I overheard, I take it you can do everything on the original terms except provide a few things you no longer own, correct?'

I nodded. She seemed to need no more than that. She leafed through to the schedule of specific items, where I'd listed each piece together with its provenance. 'You can find us similar items at cost plus. Cost plus what?'

'Shop overhead, which is eighteen per cent, plus profit, which is twenty.'

'Ten,' she said.

'Fifteen,' I countered, carried away.

'Done,' she said, pressing a button on her desk. 'We'll stick in a not-to-exceed figure, just so you don't go hog wild.'

A person came in, was introduced, and went out again after receiving instructions. The same person returned in two minutes bearing a bucket of ice. Amelia opened the cabinet behind her and asked what we would have. Every liquid made by man appeared to be available.

'I understand you have a new companion,' she said to Mark as she handed him an ice-filled glass. 'Has Rudy really married?'

Mark nodded, sipping. 'Yes, Amelia, Rudy has married. He went back to California and wed himself to a nice, convent-educated Italian Catholic thirty-year-old virgin with a little moustache. Rudy no doubt approached his marriage bed with his eyes shut while concentrating upon his duty to the family.'

'Meow,' she commented. 'Don't be a little cat, dear. Who's your current friend?' She gave me a drink and sat back with every evidence of having limitless time to bedevil us.

'His name is Bryan Langton. He's a professor of mathematics at C.U. Denver. He's thirty-nine. He rides to hounds.'

The hunt clubs in Colorado chase coyotes, not foxes, but aside from never catching anything, the sport is much the same as it is elsewhere.

'To hounds? That displays a certain level of social grace, if not of good sense. I'll tell your mother. She's been worried he may be unworthy of you.'

'That isn't what Mother's worried about, Amelia. Tell her he checks out medically and I'm not into chance encounters. That's what's worrying her.'

'And what about you?' she demanded, swivelling her head in my direction.

'I'm forty, heterosexual, neither married nor engaged, not into chance encounters, and have no mother to worry about me.'

'Pity,' she said. 'Overcoming parents builds character. Like overcoming a stutter, or being left-handed.'

Mark choked on his ice. I sipped and kept a serene countenance, trading her stare for stare.

'I thought you might be related to someone I know,' she said. 'You have a familiar look about you.'

'I'm not related to anyone I know,' I said. 'I was a foundling.'

'Really! Tell me!' She folded her hands beneath her chin and gave me her complete attention.

I told her briefly about my life, and about Jacob.

'What a good man,' she said. 'I like hearing about good men. In my business, you sometimes believe they are extinct, like the dodo or the moa. A marvel, created by God, but unable to sustain itself in the face of human depravity and natural selection.'

The person tapped at the door and came in, bearing documents which we all signed. We shook hands. She looked at her watch.

'I have to run. The firm is giving a dinner for the widow of our late partner, in honour of her eightieth birthday in a few days.'

'Would that be Lycia Meyer's mother?' I asked. 'Olivia Meyer?'

'You know her?'

'I've met Lycia. She and I have a mutual friend in Greg Steinwale.'

She smiled widely. 'Harriet's son, of course. Harriet and I are old adversaries. We do battle here and there. Well, small world, and other such clichés . . .

'Here's your copy. You'll get a cheque for the advance within a few days. I, personally, would appreciate your doing this as quickly as possible, though I know we've no right to ask. I'm heartily tired of the rest rooms in this building, as well as the slow elevators and the drab Edwardian look we've settled into. All fust and worn leather.'

'As soon as possible,' I promised.

'And we'd better do it, too,' said Mark on the way down in the slow elevator. 'Or she'll eat us alive.'

CHAPTER 4

We spent the following few days in the kinds of activity any large job involves. One good thing about Law Firm Jobs (Eugenia calls them that— we've done several) is that only busy lawyers can afford us, and busy lawyers have no time to get involved in details. Aside from getting a list of colour preferences from the partners, we had a free hand to get on with the work. Amelia had stressed that they wanted a solidly traditional look with some sparkle to it, and that's what they were going to get, with authentic period furniture used wherever it made sense and was not too expensive.

Desks are always a problem in period offices. Most desks made before the 1900s are simply inadequate for today's use, they're too small, they have too little knee-room. Originally, desks were simply boxes in which paper and ink could be stored, often with a slanted lid, hinged at the top, which could be used for a writing surface. The occasional literate individual strapped up the box, lugged it about, and set it up on any convenient bench or table. Later on, carpenters began putting drawers in the boxes and building stands to hold them; still later the French began putting drawers in the stand, all the way to the floor, and covering the writing surface with a fabric called bure, thus 'bureau' for any chest of drawers. By this time, the hinge had been moved to the bottom of the slanted top, giving us the so called 'fall-front' desk where the lid hinges down to make a level writing surface.

Eventually, the drawers in the base were split to yield a little knee-room, and this was increased over the years until we had something looking very much like today's pedestal desk, with two sets of drawers and a large, flat top. Women workers with short skirts led to the invention of the so called 'modesty screen' between the pedestals, but otherwise the basic design remains unchanged since the nineteenth cen-

tury. We planned to use good, but large, period reproductions for Amelia's job.

Chairs always have to be idiosyncratic: people have to
choose their own chairs. No two rear ends are built alike,
and even if they were identical, people have varying ideas
of what constitutes comfort. The clerical workers would
have contemporary chairs with every adjustment of back,
hip, and thigh known to man, as well as very modern work-
stations for their word-processors, printers, and so forth,
but their work space wouldn't be visible to most people
visiting the offices.

We'd ordered conference tables built to order. Any genuine period table that size would cost a fortune. The genuine
pieces we were using would appear in the halls and recep-
tion areas and the partners' offices. Mark spent all day
Wednesday and Thursday plus Friday morning at the
fabric houses and the carpet wholesalers. Eugenia called
dealers, asking if they had anything we could use, while I
conferred with our currently-favoured general contractor.
One problem with doing period styles in modern space is
that the surfaces themselves are inappropriate. Glass areas
are too large for traditional window treatments; walls are
too flat and ceilings are boring. It's necessary to break up
windows and walls with columns or panels, then treat the
parts individually. The resultant surfaces, if well done, are
more interesting; they look warmer. The dropped ceilings
found in most offices—if there aren't heating or air con-
ditioning ducts in the way—can sometimes be raised wholly
or in part by eliminating fluorescent fixtures.

Of course, there are purists who believe all this is
heresy, that buildings and rooms should be structural and
unadorned. I preferred rooms and buildings that made
people feel good, no matter how they were built.

The contractor said he could start in ten days. Friday
afternoon I talked to Myron Burstein in New York, read
him my list of things we hadn't found locally, and asked
him to do his best. That concluded the preliminaries. We

estimated the job should take no more than three months.
Mark phoned Amelia and told her so.

By four o'clock we were ready for a TGIF party, so after
Mark reconnoitred, the three of us sneaked down the alley
to the Painted Cow. I left a message for Grace, telling her
where we'd be. Mark phoned his room-mate. Eugenia said
she could have one drink and then had to run because she
had theatre tickets.

We sat in the bar. Grace showed up. Eugenia left. Bryan
Langton, Mark's friend, showed up. The four of us became
convivial and went elsewhere to dinner. Grace took
repeated advantage of the salad bar, then ate all her dinner
and half of mine. Throughout the evening—drinks, food,
conversation, laughter—I was aware that the days just past
had not occasioned any great excitement or sense of accom-
plishment. A year ago they would have. Even six months
ago I'd have been patting myself on the back at how well
everything was fitting together and how clever we all were
to have thought of this or that or the other thing. This past
week I'd done more or less the right things without thinking
much about them. The job would turn out well. The
lawyers would be happy—at least, Amelia would be. And
I, when all was said and done, would be glad their money
was in my bank, but I wouldn't care much otherwise.

I was a little disconcerted by the feeling, but I thought
I'd hidden it from everyone else. Grace, as she often does,
surprised me. When we arrived back at 1465 Hyde, she
wasked me, 'Is something wrong, Jason? You're not happy
about the new job. You're preoccupied.'

I started to say something evasive, but then decided not
to. Grace has a way of zeroing in on evasions that's most
uncomfortable. I told her nothing was really wrong, but I'd
been sort of preoccupied with the thought that with Jacob
gone, I didn't need to go on with the business unless I
wanted to. I said it in a casual voice, not making much of
it. I was prepared for any reaction except the one I got.

'Well, of course you don't,' she said in an exasperated
tone. 'Hadn't that occurred to you before now?'

Considerably piqued, I confessed it had not.

'It should have,' she assured me. 'I mean, we both know you came back here to Denver because of Jacob. If he hadn't asked you, you'd still be at the Smithsonian or somewhere like it. Now, if Agatha were still alive and you had children, you'd probably stay, because Denver's a pretty good family town. But since there's just you, I can't see why you haven't thought about leaving before now.'

'Maybe I didn't want to,' I offered, stung at the implication. I didn't want to think about the implication.

'It would be easier just to go on doing the same old thing,' she agreed. 'Changing your life is really hard. I know. I've been trying to change just a few things about mine.'

'Like?'

'Like not running every time Ron gets himself in trouble.'

Ron was her brother. He lived in San Francisco, being part of a casually gay and feckless lifestyle that was virtually guaranteed to get him either jailed or prematurely dead. Not, Grace assured me, out of malice or wickedness, but simply because he was both lazy and sensuous. It was easier for him to go along with people than it was to do anything requiring will or determination. Easier to get drunk than stay sober. Easier to get involved with druggies than to stay away from them. Easier to just have sex when he or someone else felt like it than to plan ahead and protect himself.

'How're you doing?' I asked.

'He called three times this week, and I said no each time. No, I wouldn't come out. No, I wouldn't send money. No, I wouldn't pay his lawyer.'

'Tough.'

'Really. I feel guilty all the time. I wake up feeling guilty. I go to bed feeling guilty. I cry a lot.'

'What was it you told me? You either do it your whole life, or you don't do it?'

'That's right. Only, if he dies, if he ends up in jail, then what?'

'Only, if you die, what happens to him if he's never

learned to stand on his own two feet?' It was a question she had asked me. I suppose it is a question every parent asks about every child. What happens to this child if he hasn't grown up by the time I'm gone?

'Some people never do learn,' she said, shaking her head angrily. 'Why are we talking about me? We were talking about you! I'll tell you one thing, Jason. This business isn't enough for you. Otherwise you wouldn't get all involved in these puzzles of yours. Maybe you do that because you're kind of bored. Did you ever think about that?'

I shook my head at her warningly. 'I haven't thought about that, no. And I don't intend to think about it today. You may be right, but I'm not prepared to deal with the larger issues just yet. There's no hurry. That's one thing I know for sure. There's no hurry.'

'Just so you don't get in a rut,' she warned. 'If you do, you'll ossify.'

I shrugged again. 'If I do, it means I didn't want anything else badly enough to go after it. Or, maybe, that what was here was what I wanted.'

She gave me one of those deep looks she occasionally pulls off, as though she had X-ray eyes and could see into places I'm not even sure are there. 'Maybe,' she said at last. 'Maybe, Jason.'

We made love that night, and there was a kind of carefulness in it, as though one of us—or maybe both—was fragile. It was sweet but painful, a reluctant engagement, a tender touching, careful not to hurt. Careful not to bruise.

Afterwards we lay close with her head next to mine on the pillow, her mouth next to my ear. I said to the ceiling, 'I am not going away. Not anytime soon!'

'Hmm,' she murmured. 'I'm not either.'

'We have to figure out who killed Simonetta,' I argued. 'I can't do anything before that.'

'And where's Olivia,' she whispered.

'And where's Olivia,' I agreed. 'And who's trying to kill me.'

'That's right.'

'Well then,' I demanded. 'Well then! What's all this part-ing lovers' ambience. All this melancholy.'

'Well, we don't know,' she whispered, half asleep. 'That's it, Jason. We just don't know.'

Then she was asleep, all the soft length of her against me, warm. All of Grace was warm, even her feet. She had no cold, bony places. Everything about Grace was comfortable except her habit of seeing things I didn't see.

It was a long time before I got to sleep.

At the breakfast table, Saturday morning, we avoided any recap of the previous evening's discussion. Instead, Grace filled me in on her attempts to find witnesses to Simonetta's death.

'The picture you picked out, the man with the scar on his face, he's from Utah. He posted bail and went back to Salt Lake City. Linder got him on the phone. He says he didn't know any of the other people, so he didn't know who the woman on the other side of Simonetta was. I went through the pictures again, and I double-checked to be sure I had them all, and none of them has curly white hair.'

I told her about my wig idea, and she promised to bring the arrest photographs back, so I could look at them again.

'The Lieutenant says if it wasn't anybody at the clinic who killed Simonetta, it must be somebody from her past. So Hector's been digging into Nello Leone. Turns out he died in a mental hospital back in 'sixty. Heck no sooner found that out than somebody told him Nimo died the same way. Some kind of inherited disease, father and son, both.'

It rang a faint bell. 'Yaggie told Myra that back in 'fifty-three or thereabouts, the woman who Simonetta worked for was accidentally killed—a gas leak, the papers said. That'd have been Nimo's wife, right? The one Dorotea told us about.'

Grace looked up form her English muffins and ginger marmalade, two furrows between her eyes, remembering. 'Right. Nimo's wife and the baby. An accident, she said.'

'The thing is, Simonetta said suicide. The papers said an

accident, but Simonetta said suicide. Why would a young mother commit suicide?'

Grace snorted. 'Married to Nello Leone's son? I can think of a dozen reasons.'

'Yeah, but when you mentioned an inherited disease, it occurred to me she could have discovered her husband had this disease. Which could have meant maybe her child had it?' I thought about it. 'Though I can't see how Simonetta could have interfered in that.'

'Well, suppose the wife died by accident. But Simonetta thought it was suicide, so she went around saying so. That would have been interference, for a Catholic family.'

There was a more convincing explanation. 'Suppose the young wife *did* commit suicide,' I offered, 'but the family tried to hush it up. Tried to claim it was an accident. And then Simonetta went to her family and said it was suicide. That would upset the family some.'

'But the baby died too, so it wasn't . . .' She looked down at her plate. I knew what she was thinking.

'We don't know how the baby died,' I said. 'All we know is Dorotea said the mother and child died, but she didn't really remember.'

'It could have been murder-suicide,' Grace offered. 'The mother finds out the baby has this genetic disease, so she kills the baby and then herself.'

'Even if that happened and Simonetta knew about it, why would that get her killed almost forty years later? I could see somebody trying to shut her up then, but now?'

Grace wiped marmalade off her lips and made a rueful face. 'I think we're clutching at straws.'

I had to admit she was probably right. The idea of murder-suicide was an interesting, if rather repulsive, idea. Parents killing their children to protect them from life happened now and then, but it always came as a shock. If and when we spoke with the peripatetic Cecily, maybe we'd find out.

'If she did, I know how she felt,' said Grace.

'If who did what?'

'If the mother killed her baby, thinking it had a horrible disease. She couldn't face the pain. Not her pain, not the baby's pain. She thought it would be easier. I know how she felt.'

I put my arms around her and held her, her and the muffin and the marmalade. She was thinking of brother Ron again, of his constant hysterical demands on her, of his inevitable pain and of her own. He kept on doing stupid things, and hurting himself, and passing the pain to her by asking her to make everything all right. Let Gracie kiss it and make it well. Let Gracie come up with the bail money, the rent money, the whatever. She knew she couldn't go on doing it, but it hurt to say no. There wasn't anything I could do to make it better, so I just sat there and held her, and after a long time she took a deep breath and said she was all right, so we got dressed and went to the Natural History museum in City Park to see the Aztec exhibit, the way we'd planned.

Rather, not quite the way we planned.

I'd wanted to see the exhibit. Grace had agreed to go along if we could go to a movie after.

'Doesn't gold set your little pulse hammering?' I'd asked her.

'Not other people's,' she told me soberly. 'If I had some of my own, it might.'

So I was going for the art and she was going to keep me company, and after that, we'd go to the movie. That was what was planned. We got as far as the parking lot. It was packed with cars near the museum, so we went all the way to the extreme northern end of the lot. We locked the car, then walked through the intervening lanes of parked cars and driveways, stopping under some bare oaks on a strip of ice-coated grass to allow two or three cars to cross in front of us. A few hundred yards west of us was the giraffe enclosure at the zoo. Whenever I'm anywhere near the giraffe enclosure, I look for giraffes, so I was staring in that direction, paying no attention to the traffic. Suddenly Grace threw herself into me, and we both slipped on the ice and went down in a heap. The car that had been in front of us screeched its tyres, bumped over two or three concrete kerbs, slammed through a planted area, and shimmied northward, over the frozen grass towards the golf course.

Then I realized there'd been a bang. A gunshot. Somebody had shot at somebody, and from the sound of the words coming from Grace's mouth, the somebody had been one or both of us.

'Did you see what kind of car that was?' she demanded, dragging me to my feet.

I shook my head mutely. I hadn't really noticed it until it started cross-country. 'Dark blue,' I said. 'Four door. That's all.'

'Damn!' she said. 'Come on. I have to get to a phone.'

'What did you see?'

'I saw a *gun*, Jason. What do you think I saw? Lions and tigers and bears?'

She was headed back towards the car, yelling at me over her shoulder, and I was limping after her. The fall had done my damaged leg no good. On the other hand, remaining upright would probably have done it no good either since it was attached to the rest of me. 'Which one of us was he shooting at?'

'I didn't have time to ask,' she said. 'The key, Jason. The key.'

I came up with the key, we drove across Colorado Boulevard to a 7–Eleven where there was a public phone, and Grace phoned her colleagues at the station. We waited until a car showed up.

'He was fifty-five, sixty, pasty-faced, half bald, and he had on a beige down vest,' she told them when she'd explained what had happened.

'Been throwin' your weight around, Grace?' one of them asked her.

She glanced in my direction and said something baleful. The glance was enough. She hadn't said so, but she knew the gunman had been aiming at me. That was twice. Even after the shot outside my door that Sunday morning, I'd been only marginally careful because I hadn't really believed it was meant for me. I'd convinced myself it was random. Some kid, maybe, playing lethal games. Now I had to admit to myself that it was a real threat. There really was a gunman and he'd really been aiming at me, and he'd missed once because of Grace and once because of luck. If I hadn't been lucky, I'd have been dead.

Somehow I no longer cared about the Aztecs. Grace and I went back to Hyde Street, and I limped upstairs to find an Ace bandage for my leg while she chivvied me from behind, like a sheepdog.

'So why me?' I asked her as she strode jerkily to and fro, her forehead furrowed in thought.

'The same damn reasons we talked about last time. You were on TV,' she said. 'Maybe. In connection with the clinic. Remember what Cynthia said about those nuts. Maybe one of them has decided you're the Devil incarnate.'

'It's an idea,' I admitted. 'You ought to tell Linder.'

'I already did. On the other hand, it could be something else.'

'Like what?'

'Like your looking into who killed Simonetta.'

'Nobody knows I'm doing that!'

'Anybody who's watched you knows you're doing that! You went to Zuni Street and talked to her neighbours twice. You talked to her sister. You've had Myra calling all the old neighbours. And there's Yaggie. Myra talked to Yaggie, and from what you say, it sounds like Yaggie probably talks to the world at large.'

Grace was angry. When Grace gets angry, she gets very pale and pinched-looking.

'You went with me to Zuni Street,' I pointed out. 'Both of us went out to talk to Dorotea.'

'I'm just one cop. Kill me and the department gets mad, then somebody else asks the same questions, only more so. Killing a cop doesn't make sense. Kill you, though, maybe after a while the department gets distracted, loses interest in Simonetta, and nobody gets anywhere.'

'Then whoever is doing this must think I'm getting some-where, right?'

She shrugged. It was the weak point in her argument, because I wasn't getting anywhere. Not yet. Unless I was getting somewhere without knowing it.

'If they get me, promise me you'll talk to Cecily,' I said, trying to be funny.

'Oh, Jason, shut up. This is serious. That guy really meant to kill you.' She clenched her fists and squinched her eyes and threatened me.

'Maybe it was just a warning shot.'

'He was looking right at you.'

'Well, if it's a nut, there's nothing I can do about it. But if it's because of Simonetta, then we have to find out who killed her.'

'That would help, yes,' she cried, giving me an accusing look.

'I have been a bit busy with other things,' I yelled. 'Like earning a living.'

'I know.' She shrugged apologetically and hugged me with tears in her eyes. I melted.

'I could set my mind to it.'

'Do that. Do that while I make a snack of something.'

So I set my mind to it and came up with nothing much. Until Cecily returned from Brazil, we were at a dead end. Except for the death which had set Simonetta off . . . the death of the woman she'd worked for, in 1953.

'Library,' I said, when we'd had Grace's snack. 'Let's go to the library.'

The Denver Public Library has a file of Denver news-papers going back to the turn of the century, all on micro-film. We wanted the spring of 1953 or, failing that, 1952 or 1954. Grace took one machine and I another, and we scanned away, she working on April, and I on March. I found the reference in the third week of March.

GAS LEAK FATALITY. YOUNG MOTHER DIES. The story told how Mrs G.R. Leone, 21, was overcome by gas during the night. The leak had been traced to an old gas log in the fireplace, one which was thought to have been sealed off. Comments from the Public Service Company. Funeral Friday at St Mary's.

I read it. Grace read it. Grace said, 'There's nothing about a child. I thought the child died.'

I read it again. She was right. The only reference to a child was the implication made by the headline, where Mrs G.R. Leone was identified as a young mother.

'Dorotea Chapman was rather indefinite about it,' I mused. 'She said she didn't remember what had happened except that it had been a tragedy and she'd gone to the funeral. She was still a child herself at the time.'

'But according to Myra, Simonetta was yelling about a baby.'

'So Yaggie said. But if the woman had been pregnant again, perhaps it was another baby in utero who died. If Simonetta thought the woman had committed suicide, and if she'd been pregnant . . .' None of it seemed to mean much, quite frankly.

'Damn,' said Grace feelingly. 'We don't have diddly.' She continued to inventory what we didn't have all the way home and then stalked off up the stairs.

Before I followed her, I gathered the small pile of Saturday mail from the hall floor. Mark had filed all the stuff pertaining to the law firm job on Friday, so when I dumped the mail on my desk I found it empty except for Brother Daniel's phone number. Which had nothing at all to do with Simonetta. Still, Grace had vanished into the bathroom, and while she was in there, maybe I could make an appointment. I called and got hold of someone with a Brooklyn accent. I explained I was attempting to trace a friend of my foster father and had been told Brother Daniel might have useful information. The voice told me I could see Brother Daniel on Sunday afternoon and advised me in a singsong voice that women who were not family members were not allowed entry. I mentioned this to Grace when she returned from the bathroom, but she only shrugged.

'Silly,' she said. 'If I wanted entry, I'd get it.'

'You want to go to the movie?' I asked.

'Probably safe enough, if you slip across the alley and go through Fetterlings and I drive my car and pick you up out front of there and nobody follows us.'

'Shit.' The idea was intensely annoying. 'We went to the library?'

'He didn't have time to re-group before we went to the library,' she said. 'Maybe we could stay home and pull all the curtains and watch a movie on the VCR? We never watched *Little Dorrit* and you've had it for ages.'

'Ten hours' worth of Dickens?'

'Well, until we get tired or run out of food or find something better to do.'

We didn't get tired, and we didn't run out of food, but we only watched about an hour of *Little Dorrit* before we found something better to do.

My predicament was not susceptible to easy solution. If an unknown man is coming after you with a gun, and if he's patient, he'll get you sooner or later. Even a rotten shot like the guy who'd tried for me twice will get the job done if he's given enough time. The Secret Service knows this. All those guys who guard the President spend their lives sweating and praying it won't happen on their shift. The truth is, if somebody is reasonably careful and absolutely determined, he can get to anybody. Guns are easy to get, and high-powered automatics are lethal even in the hands of idiots who can't tell east from west. Just point one of those in the general direction of the victim and he'll end up dead along with half a dozen innocent bystanders.

Figuring this out took very little time after Grace left on Sunday morning. Maybe the guy out to kill me hated antique dealers and had picked me at random by sticking a pin through the yellow pages. Maybe he had mistaken me for somebody else. The whys didn't matter. There were only two ways I could see to get at him. I could figure out why he wanted to kill me and therefore who he probably was, or I could catch him and then figure out why he wanted to kill me. Grace and Lieutenant Linder had already kicked that idea around. She'd suggested having me followed in an attempt to catch the guy. The trouble was the same old thing: the department had a limited budget, nobody knew how long it might take, and if they caught the guy, it might be *after* he'd shot me rather than before.

If he was following me, I might be able to lead him into a trap. If he wasn't following me but just taking a stab at me every now and then when he thought of it, trapping him would be difficult. Though, come to think of it, both attempts had been on weekends. The first time early Sunday morning, then again the following Saturday.

Which meant what?

Coincidence. Or, maybe, somebody who only had time off to go gunning at the weekends. Or somebody who was only in town at the weekends. Somebody from out of town. Which made no damned sense at all! However, if true, it made today more dangerous than tomorrow.

Though as a boy I was as much a show-off as any of my peers, I am no longer into feckless nonchalance. I do not like horror stories where the heroine goes off in her chiffon nightgown to see what's making the strange noises in the middle of the night. I do not like adventure epics where the hero walks around in enemy territory ignoring the most elementary precautions for protecting himself—like keeping his back against a wall—and lets people come up behind him and whop him over the head, escaping later only because someone else is even stupider than he is. I am disturbed at the low level of intelligence displayed by these characters, also at the amount of alcohol they consume, the number of times they fall into bed with high-risk sex-partners (asking no questions), and the number of times they end up in the hospital. If they were flesh and blood, they would have died of liver disease, AIDS, and trauma-related problems long before they reached volume four of the series.

In my book, hero(ines) should be at least a tiny fraction smarter than the low-lifes they so consistently encounter!

Thus ruminating, I decided I'd been living in a fool's paradise, just like the characters I despised. It was my duty to stop blundering around and out-think whoever was after me. Whatever the reason, twice was sufficient warning. I was not about to walk into another bullet!

First I went down in the basement, opened Jacob's old iron safe, and got out my four target handguns that had been in there for years. I took them upstairs, got out the fifth one, the one I keep in my desk, then cleaned, checked, and loaded all five. One went in my bedside table, one back in the desk, one in the kitchen. The fourth one went downstairs, inside a Chinese vase in the main showroom. The fifth one went in the basement, in its holster, which I strapped to the leg of an old square piano with duct tape. Just in case, I told myself. If I'd had that gun down there a year before, I might not have been shot.

Then I sneaked across the alley to Nellie's place and begged the use of her phone. This took care of the remote possibility my phone was bugged, as it had been on one previous occasion. 'Man who stumbles over same rock twice deserves to break fool neck,' Jacob had often said, claiming to quote Confucius. I called Mark who, fortuitously, was home, and asked him to pick me up outside the Fetterling house at twelve-thirty. I ordered a cab for one o'clock at Mark's apartment house, because he has a drive-in basement garage with entrances on two separate streets. When the cab got there, I'd ask Mark to meet it, bring it into the garage, and I'd take it out the other way.

All of which worked pretty much the way I'd planned, up to and including the use of a few props I'd taken along.

'Laugh all you like,' I said, pulling down the brim of my slouch hat over a pair of Jacob's horn-rimmed glasses I'd knocked the lenses out of. I'd also found an old raincoat down in the basement, the kind nobody has worn for thirty years. 'I was the one who got shot at, not you.'

Mark sobered. 'What can we do to help, Jason? We've got nothing planned. I could pick up a wig and false beard for you. Maybe a pair of elevator shoes?'

'If you really want to help, meet me outside this abbey I'm going to,' I told him. 'Either or both of you. I should be finished there about three. If I haven't lost whoever's gunning for me by now, he's too smart and I might as well give up!'

When the cab arrived, Mark brought it into the basement, I scrunched down in the back, and the driver took us up and out. After half-a-dozen blocks he mumbled, 'If there's anybody following us, Buddy, he's invisible. There's nobody on the streets but us.'

So I got up, feeling only a little like a fool, and we talked about the Broncos all the way to the abbey. Or rather, he talked, and I said 'Right,' and 'You said it,' and 'You just never know, do you?'

When I tipped him, he winked and said, 'I never saw you, right?'

'Right,' I said.

'You runnin' away to become a monk?' he asked me. 'I thought of doin' that once. Kind of nice life. Quiet.'

I shook my head. 'I'm not patient enough,' I confided. 'Besides, I like women. And good coffee.'

'Me, it's beer,' he said. 'Beer and sports. What you gonna do, right?'

'Right.'

'Nothin' like beer.'

'You said it.'

'When you're a kid, you think everything's gonna be a big deal. You never think much about the little stuff. Like havin' a few guys over for a beer. And a little bet on the game, just to make things interestin'. Life's not such a big deal. It's just, you know, kinda nice.' He smiled and stretched, the perfect picture of contentment. I envied him.

'You just never know, do you,' I said.

'You have a nice day,' he said, looking around to see that we hadn't been observed before he drove away. I took off the raincoat, the Indiana Jones hat and the glasses before ringing the bell at the gate.

Until my phone call to the place, I hadn't known there

was an abbey in the grounds of the Catholic seminary, which sits on a hundred acres or so of prime residential land south-east of downtown. As we'd turned on to the approach street, I'd noticed for the first time that one corner of the property was set off behind its own wall, making it a separate enclosure. The separateness of it was much in evidence from inside, for I was led down a brick-paved cloister beside a walled garden. I was left in a small room containing a few straight chairs and another door across from the one I'd entered by.

The silent man who came through that door didn't offer to shake hands. He was sixty, perhaps, with a pale, quiet face. He looked serene, but not well, like a man with a chronic illness who's gotten used to it.

'Mr Lynx?' he asked, as he seated himself on a straight chair across from me. He wore a brown robe and stout shoes. I'd expected sandals, but Denver's winter would be a little severe for sandals. He looked like a monk. 'You are Jason Lynx?'

I nodded, realizing I'd been staring.

'How can I help you?'

I sat down and told him about Jacob. I said Jacob had ordered a birthday gift for someone's eightieth birthday, and we believed that someone to be Olivia Cerraverdes, or Olivia Desquintas y Alvares, but we couldn't locate her.

He nodded, letting a tiny smile move one corner of his mouth. 'That was a long time ago. How did you come to connect me with the Cerraverdes?'

I told him about Myra and her research.

'My brother,' he said, letting the smile broaden into something real. 'Yes, of course. We were neighbours of the Cerraverdes. 'I'm not sure I have any information that will help you. I've been here since I was eighteen.'

'Anything you can tell us about the family. Even if you don't know where Olivia may be, some other member of her family might help us find her.'

'You believe this is important?'

He asked it rather sadly, like a man who found very little

of importance. I supposed from his point of view, such worldly things were rather picayune. I'd said nothing about Jacob's lifelong love. I didn't want to. I simply said yes, I thought it was very important because Jacob had thought so and I felt morally responsible for carrying out his last wishes.

Moral responsibility seemed to set well with him. 'Well, then, let me tell you what I can remember, though I didn't know Mrs Alvares well. Only the way a schoolboy would know the parent of a schoolmate. It was her daughter I knew.'

He seemed unable to get past that point. 'Your sister-in-law mentioned you were childhood sweethearts,' I said carefully, hoping I wasn't venturing on forbidden ground.

He looked surprised, then almost relieved, as though I had given him permission to say or feel something he'd been wary of saying or feeling. 'Yes. We were . . . we were childhood sweethearts. We loved each other very much.' He dropped his eyes, examined the hands knotted quietly in his lap, as though he had never seen them before.

'But you decided to enter a religious order,' I said politely, when he didn't go on.

He looked up, eyes blazing. 'No!'

I waited, dismayed at having evoked that fiery negation.

'No,' he said more calmly. 'She and I had decided to be married. We were both eighteen. She had just turned eighteen. We were old enough. Her father . . . her father was a very . . . strange person. That is, strange to me. He was Spanish. He had been, I believe, very wealthy, very important in his own country. That was before the war. He was driven out, forced to accept the charity of his wife's parents. It was very hard for him. He was very proud.'

Brother Daniel used words carefully and individually, each one placed neatly, precisely, in the formal manner of a man perhaps unaccustomed to narrative. Certainly in the manner of a man avoiding emotion. Except for that blazing 'no', there was no warmth in his words.

'You knew him?' I prompted.

'She told me about him. My angel told me.' Suddenly there were tears in his eyes.

'I'm sorry,' I said, starting to get up. 'Perhaps I shouldn't have . . .'

He waved me down. 'No. It's all right. It's a relief to talk about it, actually. If you have the time, I'll tell you the whole story.'

He waited. I nodded.

'His name was Octavio Desquintas y Alvares. She used to say it that way. "My father is Don Octavio Desquintas y Alvares." When America entered the war, he volunteered to fight in Europe. He was not a citizen, but he volunteered to fight against those who had driven him from his home. He was badly wounded, and his life was saved by a fellow soldier. They became friends.' He stood up and turned, grimacing a little, as though in pain.

'Mr Lynx, even now it's hard for me to tell this because I've never been able to explain it, not even to myself. Even now, after all these years, I can only imagine these things. I have never been in a war, never been wounded, never made such a friend. Here . . . here we are warned against making close friends, you understand?'

'I've read something . . . a little.'

'Too close a human friendship distracts us from God. We swear our deepest friendship to God. But Don Octavio swore an oath of a different kind, an oath of friendship with this man who had saved his life. In his oath, I do not believe he even considered God. His oath was that their two families should be united. His daughter should marry this man's son.'

'Your . . . sweetheart? Olivia's daughter?'

'Yes. At the time he swore this oath, she was only a child. Ten. Eleven, perhaps. He didn't tell her then, not when he first returned from the war. He was an invalid. He didn't talk to her much, and he never mentioned this oath until she told him about me, about us. Only then did he tell her she couldn't marry me because he had promised her to someone else.'

'Told her she was to marry someone she didn't know?' It seemed barbaric to me, like something out of the Middle Ages.

'It was on her eighteenth birthday. He told her that day. Less than a month later they were married. The banns were waived. It was all in a great hurry. The day she married, I came here and asked to be admitted. They did not take me then, but soon they did. It was my way of being faithful to her . . . then. Later it became my way of being faithful to God.'

'I can't imagine a father doing that to his daughter!' I exclaimed. 'This is the twentieth century, the United States, not . . .'

'Not mediæval Spain?' he asked me gently, seating himself with a grimace of pain. 'No, this country is not mediæval Spain. But Octavio Desquintas y Alvares was not from this country. He was only its unwilling guest. And he was a mediæval man in many ways, a man who had been wounded in the war and never regained good health, who had been treated for years as we treat sick men, dutifully, gently. A very arrogant man who saw his honour as the only important issue. He lived only long enough to see her married. It was a matter of honour. Not only for him, for the boy's father as well. A matter of honour.'

'But she agreed!'

He looked past me, out of the window at the sky, his eyes empty. 'Her father was ill. She was dutiful. She took seriously the commandment about honouring her father. She had that much honour of her own.'

I shook my head, trying to get myself back on track, finding it hard to put aside my outrage for Olivia's daughter. 'If you came here when you were only eighteen or nineteen, then you probably don't know what happened to Olivia.'

'Oh, I wasn't cut off from the world. My parents visited me regularly. They told me when Don Octavio died.' He shook his head slowly. 'They told me the Cerraverdes had moved away, to St Louis, I think. They took their granddaughter, Olivia's younger daughter, with them. Olivia left the neighbourhood too. Later she married again. I can't remember her second husband's name, if they ever told me.'

'Meyer,' I said, suddenly sure of it. 'And the younger daughter's name was . . .'

'Alicia,' he said, surprised. 'They called her Lycia. She was ten years younger than my angel.'

Everything fell into place. Lycia Foret was Olivia's daughter! She had always seemed familiar to me. Now it was clear why. She resembled the picture of her mother, the picture Jacob had always kept by him, hanging above the walnut cabinet beside his bed, lost among a clutter of other photographs, of his parents, of his brother, of places he had travelled in his youth. I'd seen the photographs there every day of my growing up, but they had been like the pattern in the wallpaper. He had never called my attention to them, never told me they were important.

I looked at the quiet man in the brown robe almost absently, my mind aswirl with sudden plans. I would buy the table Jacob had meant for Olivia. I would tell Lycia Foret about her mother and my foster father. I would . . .

I would do nothing at the moment, I warned myself. Nothing. Not until I knew I could do it without hurting anyone. Jacob had known details I didn't know. I couldn't go trampling in, like some mad elephant . . .

'Is that all you wanted to know?' he asked me.

'Yes. Thank you. I'm very grateful.'

'Remember me in your prayers,' he said. He stood up and was gone, silently.

The same person who had let me in let me out. Mark and Bryan were waiting in Mark's car. I got into the back seat.

'You look like you've found the Holy Grail,' Mark said.

'I found Olivia,' I told him.

'Jason, that's wonderful!' He turned to Bryan and filled him in on Jacob's lost love, evidently a topic they had already discussed. They wanted all the details. Even after

I'd recited them exhaustively, Mark wasn't satisfied. 'What's the matter with you?' he demanded. 'I should think you'd be excited and you're all gloomy. Where is she? Olivia?'

'She must be here in town, somewhere. Her family are planning a birthday party for her sometime soon.'

'So why the gloom?'

'Well, for one thing, I'm not sure how Olivia may react to hearing from Jacob's foster son. I'd like to talk to her daughter Lycia first, but since that matter a year ago, I don't really feel comfortable doing that.' Mark didn't know the whole truth of that matter, but he knew enough to explain my discomfort to Bryan.

'Oh hell, go ahead,' said Bryant. 'If she's like my mother, she'll love anything that will make her mama happy or interested. Mother goes crazy trying to interest Gram in anything at all.'

There was a certain amount of sense to that. No matter how Lycia Foret felt about me, she wouldn't deprive her mother of pleasure—assuming it would be pleasure. Besides, it had just occurred to me I could ask Trish Steinwale to explore the situation for me. That way, nobody would be made uncomfortable, at least not face to face. If they'd rather not, they could tell Trish and Trish could tell me.

Mark and Bryan dropped me off at the Fetterlings' house and I went home via the alley. Once inside I called Trish, asking if I could see her sometime Monday. She and Greg had recently bought a pleasant old house in Park Hill, which they were renovating slightly before moving in. Trish said she'd be at the new house in the morning and could drop by my place on her way down to Greg's studio at noon. I thanked her profusely, got myself a beer out of the refrigerator, and sat down to watch TV and think about things—such as how Olivia Meyer might have somehow attracted the attention of an extortioner. Or how her daughter might have done so.

Though perhaps it had been the other daughter, Brother

Daniel's love, the one he called his angel. I realized suddenly that the information about Olivia had come as such a welcome surprise that I'd neglected to ask Brother Daniel what had happened to his childhood sweetheart, Olivia's older daughter. On further consideration I decided that even if I'd thought about it, I would not have asked. The subject was obviously painful for him.

Besides, he might not even know. Lycia had commented that she had no brothers or sisters to help throw the party for Olivia, which might mean her sister had died or that she lived far away. Her sister could have ended up in some remote place, some foreign country. The family into which the girl married could have been European, like Octavio himself, or perhaps Latin American. I hated to think what the girl's life must have been like, married to a man she'd never seen, taken to an unfamiliar place, perhaps to an unfamiliar culture, leaving her childhood sweetheart behind, knowing she'd probably never see him again. Doing all that to fulfil her father's sense of honour, only to see him die very shortly after the wedding.

Had she ever come home to visit her mother and sister? Had she ever driven to the walled enclosure I'd visited that afternoon to sit outside, wishing she could go in? Had she lived a long time with her stranger husband? Had she grown old with him?

In a way, it was Olivia's story all over again. She, too, had married to please her family. Perhaps, having done so, she had felt she could not interfere in what her husband had arranged for their daughter. More likely, she'd simply felt impotent in the face of her husband's Mediterranean ideas of honour.

Myra and I had been right when we'd said it was like an episode of *Lost Loves*. Pure melodrama, except for the reality of the people involved. If the same situation had presented itself now, the daughter would tell her father he was out of his mind, and then she'd run off with her boyfriend to California or New York, they'd spend a few years finding themselves before settling down to middle class obscurity and one point three children in a suburb somewhere. Daddy might die without his honour satisfied, but every year on the anniversary of his death, his daughter would go to his grave and tell him how well everything had worked out. I could see the final screen credits.

It was infinitely more gothic the way it had actually happened. I knew Grace would think so. When she called about eight, I told her everything, and she remarked that it read like a mini-series, but she'd missed the final episode. I said the final episode might be yet to come.

'Did you check your windows and doors, Jason?' she asked when we had finished with Jacob's tale.

I told her I had, and that the alarm was on. I had also checked the three upstairs handguns, but I didn't mention that.

'And Bela's feeling alert, right? How about the dog door?'

I had both latched the dog door and inserted the panel on the inside which made it burglar-proof. If Bela needed to go outside during the night, he'd just have to tell me so.

This met with her approval. 'Good night, Jason,' she said. 'Be careful in the morning.'

I was immediately careful, not waiting for morning. I did not walk in front of uncurtained windows with the lights on. I had a long soak in the big tub, and went to bed. Despite the fact that someone seemed to be trying to kill me, I slept soundly. If I dreamed of anything at all, I didn't remember it when I woke.

Amelia Wirtz dropped by on Monday morning. She wanted to look at the drapery fabrics Mark had chosen for her office. Because she was a family friend, he was going out of his way to be sure she was happy. Because she was Amelia Wirtz, I thought that was a damned good idea.

'What's new in your life?' she demanded, plunking herself down in the chair across from my desk, thus forcing Mark to bring the samples into my office though he'd had them nicely arranged in his own. 'Did you find out who your foster father ordered the table for?'

I didn't remember having told her about that. I glanced at Mark and saw him flush dark red. So he'd told her—a kind of addendum to what I had told her about Jacob.

'As a matter of fact, yes,' I said. 'However, for the time being at least, this must be a professional confidence. We've found that Jacob's old sweetheart was the wife of your former partner, Theo Meyer.'

'Olivia Meyer? I'll be damned. Come to think of it, Theo mentioned she was a widow when he married her.'

'Her affair with Jacob was before her first marriage,' I said. 'When they were in school together. As a matter of fact, knowing Jacob, he probably respected her too much to have allowed it to be anything more than a very chaste relationship. Girls were into virginity in those days, weren't they?'

I hadn't meant the question to sound personal.

'Honey, how the hell would I know?' she bellowed. 'That was my mother's generation, not mine.' Then she laughed. 'So what are you going to do? Are you going to give her the table?'

'I haven't bought the table yet. It would be a fairly expensive gift, and I don't want to present something that would embarrass her or that she wouldn't treasure as Jacob intended.'

'Why a card table?' she demanded of Mark, who only shrugged and left it to me to explain Jacob's fondness for bridge. In the end I dug out the pictures I'd brought home from Charlotte's, and we looked at them together, including the one of the young people with the tournament trophy, eternally youthful, smiling into the camera.

'So what're you going to do?' She was intensely, vitally interested, and she carried me along, getting me to tell things I hadn't necessarily planned to tell. No doubt an appropriate talent for a lawyer. No doubt an excellent technique for questioning witnesses in court.

'I shall be silent on the matter,' she said when she'd wrung the last detail from me, taking a moment to glare at

Mark. 'As your flunkey here, who has blabbed, should also be!'

'I only blabbed because I counted on your discretion,' said Mark weakly. 'Which is, of course, legendary.'

She laughed and trotted out to Mark's office, making him move the fabric samples a second time.

She'd not been gone long before Trish appeared, and I told the same story again, this time with the doors closed to give at least an appearance of discretion. She listened and commented and even cried a little, burrowing in her coat pocket for a tissue to blot her eyes. 'That's so sweet,' she said. 'Honestly. Sure, I'll tell Lycia and she can decide whether to tell her mom. Wouldn't it be great if you could give her Jacob's present during the party.'

I grimaced. 'Great if she knows Jacob is dead and won't be offended by receiving a gift from beyond the grave. Not so great if she (a) doesn't know he's dead and finds out then, or (b) either knows or doesn't know but doesn't care much either way.'

'I can't imagine Olivia not caring,' Trish objected. 'I've only met her a couple of times, but she's . . . she's sweet. She's got a kind of lovingness about her.'

'If she still cared about Jacob, why didn't she marry him when her first husband died, I wonder?'

She took time to think about this. 'Probably because her parents were still alive. They wouldn't have liked her marrying someone Jewish any better then than they did when she was twenty. Maybe she wanted to bring Lycia up in a religious household.'

It sounded dumb but likely. Trish promised me she'd let me know what Lycia said. The birthday party was the following week. I called Orvie in Kansas City and asked him where the heck the pictures and provenance were, and he said he'd fax them to me.

'Can you get the table here by next week?' I asked him.

'If I have to,' he said. 'Did you find out who it was for?'

'I think so,' I told him. The only thing that remained

was to find out whether Jacob's old love would enjoy being reminded of him.

When Trish left, about noon, Mark and I went out (carefully) and lunched over a couple of sale catalogues. There were some auctions coming up in New York that Mark wanted to attend. An old friend of his was getting married in Connecticut; Mark thought he could go to the wedding, then go down to New York City for the auctions and to see a few shows. Bryan, it turned out, had some time off, plus a sister on Long Island. So we went over the catalogues, deciding what we could use and how much we could afford to spend.

'Buying the table Jacob had in mind will leave us a little short of cash, won't it?' he asked.

I shrugged. 'It amounts to what I'd have paid Jacob in three months. So it'll take us another three months to be in the black. We won't be any shorter than usual, and if it was something he wanted . . .'

'Sure. Well, I doubt we'll pick up many of these items, anyway. The local bidders will go higher than we can.'

'You're going to be there, so go to the auctions! Take the trip off your income tax. Half, anyway. If you're lucky enough to get something we need at a reasonable price, great. You've got vacation coming, so use some of it. Also, while you're in New York, take the Bursteins to dinner.'

He subsided happily into the catalogues.

We got back to the shop about two. At two-thirty, to my enormous surprise, Lycia Foret came wandering in, very casually, as though she did it every day. Aside from that brief encounter at Greg's and Trish's, I hadn't seen her in a year. I hadn't expected to see her at all, but she greeted me like an old friend.

'Trish came by,' she said. 'I'm taking off this week, getting caught up on some domestic things and arranging Mama's birthday party. Trish says you're of a mind to give Mama a present.'

'Not me,' I smiled at her. 'Jacob.'

'Mama's mystery love,' she said. 'Do you know, I have

heard about Jacob since I was about two, though she has
never once mentioned his name. She still says things like,
"No matter who you marry, there'll always be someone you
think of, wondering what might have been."'

'You think she meant Jacob?'

'Well, she didn't mean my real father. There was no
"might have been" about him. He was very real, always in
a chair by the window with a blanket over his knees, always
throwing terrible tantrums to prove who was boss, always
yelling for Mama to come do this, do that. He'd been badly
wounded in the war, but it wasn't just his body that was
wrong. Mama never had time for anything else with Don
Octavio there. Including me. My sister almost raised me,
at least until I was about nine . . .' Her voice trailed away.
She flushed, aware she'd raised her voice. Don Octavio was
evidently an old pain that still hurt to touch.

'How'd you find Mama, anyhow?' she asked, changing
the subject.

I explained about Myra's finding the son of a former
neighbour. Something kept me from mentioning Brother
Daniel. Perhaps the feeling that I'd intruded on him painfully and should try to keep him out of it.

'The neighbour spoke of your older sister,' I said.

She paled. 'Jason, please, if you come to Mama's party,
don't mention her. Don Octavio rode roughshod over her,
just as he did Mama. She died tragically. Mama still can't
think of her without a good deal of pain. I don't want Mama
upset!'

Speaking of it obviously upset Lycia as well. 'I'm sorry,'
I said. 'I know nothing about it except the mere mention.'

'That's just as well. Just pretend I'm Mama's only child.
I was the only child for a long time, hers and Theo's. He
adopted me when he and Mama were married, even though
I spent a lot of my time with Grandma in St Louis.'

'Didn't they want you with them?' I asked, surprised.

'It wasn't them, it was me. Everything here reminded
me of things I needed to forget. I had nightmares all the
time. I was better in St Louis . . .'

Seeing her consternation, I resolved not to ask her anything more about it.

She pulled herself together and said in a brisk voice, 'So do you want to come to the party and bring this present Jacob got for her? She'd be pleased, I think.'

'Does she still play cards?'

'Does she! She still wins tournaments! Very little ones, of course.'

'Then she'll be pleased. Jacob's gift is an eighteenth-century card table, a very fine piece.' I reached into the bottom drawer and pulled out the envelope of photos and papers I'd shown to Amelia only that morning. 'I thought I might have this old photo of your mother and Jacob duplicated as a kind of gift card.' I showed her the tournament photo, then the portrait.

Lycia did what Mark had done, touching the young face gently and saying, 'Beautiful.' Then she went back to the other photo, smiling down at it and saying, 'So this was Jacob?'

I said yes, that was Jacob.

'He was a handsome man. You're his foster son. No blood relation?'

'Right.'

'He told you about Mama.'

'In a manner of speaking. There were . . . instructions left among his things.' The instructions were only implied. Charlotte and Grace and I had read the young Olivia's letter. Her daughter didn't need to see it.

'Ah,' she said. 'Well, if you make a copy of this one, with the two of them at the tournament, she'll understand.'

'Small problem.'

'What?'

'Does she know he's dead? I'd hate to bring her a gift from him and have her find out only then that he's gone.'

'I'm sure she knows, but just to make doubly sure, I'll tell her you're invited, and who you are, and how you came to know of her. If that makes any problem, I'll let you know.'

We left it at that. She told me the party would be h.. in Harriet Steinwale's penthouse apartment, Tuesday a week, at six-thirty. 'Mama has quite a small apartment,' she said. 'Mine isn't what you'd call huge, and Harriet offered. You know where it is.'

I said yes, I knew where Harriet's apartment was. Neither of us reminded the other how I knew or what had taken me there before. It seemed we were to ignore that. By mutual consent.

I had a final thing to tell her. 'When I first met you, Lycia, I thought you looked familiar. I never knew why until I found this picture of your mother. I recall that it hung beside Jacob's bed when I was a boy. You look very much like her.'

'Do you think so?' She seemed honestly surprised. 'I'm flattered.' She looked at the portrait again, searching for the resemblance. She smiled, gave me her hand, and took herself away with a final stroke of the back of the carved chair she'd been sitting in. She'd done that the last time she'd sat in that chair. I watched her go, feeling satisfied and pleased and almost familial towards her. It was a good feeling.

I phoned Orvie and told him to ship the blasted table ASAP as it had to be here the following Monday. With the party on Tuesday, that would give me a day to clean it up, if it needed cleaning up, and arrange delivery to—to where?

Mark came in when I howled.

'What is it?'

'Damn it,' I said. 'Where do I take the table? The party's at Harriet Steinwale's place. But that's not where Olivia lives. Lycia said she had quite a small apartment.'

'Shush,' he said. 'Don't make mountains out of molehills, Jason. You'll give the gift at Harriet's, of course, because that's where the party is. You'll include in the card a note saying you'll have it delivered wherever she wants it. If she wants to make room for it in her rather small apartment, she will. If not, she'll say so.'

Sensible Mark.

I gathered up the photos to tuck them away with the other pending matters. When I opened the bottom drawer I saw the large manila envelope which had been festering away in there for the past year and a half. With some half-formed idea of getting rid of the contents, I took it out and dumped the half-dozen letters it contained on to my desk. Mark's eyebrows went up at the sight of the cut-out words and letters. I passed them across the desk to him, and he sat down in the chair Lycia had recently vacated.

'My God,' he breathed when he'd been through them once. 'When did you get these?'

'Not recently. The first one was postmarked about eighteen months ago, I think. The last one came in October or November.'

'You didn't pay . . .'

'No. I didn't pay.'

He ran his fingers across the glued-on words. 'Somebody went to a lot of trouble to hide their handwriting.'

'I've thought that. I've wondered if it's someone I know, someone whose handwriting I might recognize.'

'But you're not going to pay?'

'I haven't had one for a while, maybe the offer's no longer available. Even if it were, I tell myself I don't care that much—a kind of homage to Jacob. He always said it didn't matter.'

'It doesn't matter,' he said soberly. 'I know exactly who my parents are, Jason, and I'm no better off than you are because of it. Often I wish I were like you, without all that familial baggage. It gets very heavy sometimes.'

He made a face at the letters, gave them back to me and returned to his work. I put them back in the envelope. If ignoring this temptation was really a homage to Jacob, next time I went down to the basement, I'd take this along and burn it in the vast old furnace. Burnt offering. And about time.

CHAPTER 5

I continued careful, and busy, during the following week. Grace had one final weekend off before her schedule changed. We chose recreation in lieu of valour and on Friday afternoon drove down to New Mexico for the weekend, taking Grace's car, and going through a few well-thought-out gyrations to be sure we weren't followed. The first part of the drive is always sheer boredom, getting out of Denver and then getting through the clutter and fume of Colorado Springs, which has twelve square miles of new and used cars along the highway. Once past the cars, we saw hilly lunar landscapes runnelled with spaghetti-like tangles of motorcycle trails, pastures dotted with dispirited horses, winter-dun fields stretching away to mud-dun hills, bristly with yucca, lined with drooping fences and speckled with bored-looking cows either in the last stages of parturition or being butted in the udders by hungry calves. A dull fur of bare cottonwood twigs marked every watercourse, every gully.

I pounded a fist upon the steering-wheel and confessed a hatred for March, and February, and perhaps even January when it didn't snow. Grace yawned and stretched but otherwise ignored me. She had heard this opinion before. Grace has, without doubt, heard most of my opinions before.

The mountains were blue and snowcapped, but I longed for grass. There was no grass. Instead, tan succeeded dun succeeded greige succeeded a vile ochreous tinge betraying some kind of weed infestation. Yucca was reinforced by chamisa and choya, each trying to out-bristle the other. The University of Southern Colorado appeared on the southern horizon, arranged along the treeless bluff to the east of the road like a set of children's blocks set in a row, sun glinting from the squat cylindrical water tanks. Smokeless blast furnace chimneys jabbed upward at the southern edge of

Pueblo, one of only two steel towns west of the Mississippi. Traffic increased for a few miles, the mills themselves came up on the right, were succeeded by miles of slag heaps, barren as Mars, heading into an infinity of dun prairie and long stone-edged, sky-seeking diagonals rimmed with juniper.

At Walsenburg we turned west, over La Veta Pass and down into the San Luis valley, miles on miles of flat as we drove south out of Fort Garland, mountains gathering in from either horizon. I started to yawn. Grace and I traded seats, and I fell asleep before she'd driven a mile. I didn't wake up until we were just north of Taos.

As we drove through Taos, we decried on this sign of growth and that. We both remembered it as a historic core with a small shopping area to the south and a long bare stretch between Taos proper and Ranchos de Taos, the first town south. Now the built-up area stretched along both sides of the highway, joining the two towns with a miles-long clutter offering goods and services.

Beyond Ranchos de Taos the road led more or less along the Rio Grande, past small orchards, up and down juniper-speckled hills, through Espanola—we stopped to pick up a few groceries—and on down to Nambe, where I turned on to the side road that led east towards my friends' place, Los Vientos. The Wilsons, who owned the place, were in Hawaii until April, but the caretaker had been told I was invited to occupy the guest house. I'd earned the privilege by helping Mike furnish the place. I'd saved him a lot of money, and he'd reciprocated.

The weekend went by in the scent of pinon smoke and long nights full of unimaginable stars. When you live in a city, you forget there are such things.

While there, I tried to call Cecily Stephens. None of the firms listed under 'contractors' had the name Stephens attached, though there was a residential number listed for a C. Stephens that yielded only an answering machine. I did not feel like explaining to a machine.

We drove back on Monday, arriving about two in the

afternoon. Grace dropped me off in the alley behind the
shop. The sight of the Fetterling back gate provoked an
attack of conscience at having neglected Nellie recently, so
I set my overnight bag in the garage and went to say hello
to her.

'Some man was watching your house,' she told me. 'I
saw him through the gate. He even stuck his face in here a
time or two, but my son-in-law ran him off.'

'When, Nellie?' The sinking feeling I'd subdued over the
weekend was suddenly back.

'Saturday and Sunday both. Jeannie was here Sunday
when he showed up.' She was speaking of Jeannie Rudolph,
a teenaged girl who came in a few times a week to sit with
Nellie and her cat so Janice, Nellie's daughter, could get
out. 'When the man went off down the alley, I told Jeannie
to walk along the sidewalk out front, kind of see if she could
see where he went. He went around in front, walked right
past her, got in a car and drove off. He never even noticed
her.'

'What kind of car, Nellie?'

'It was blue, that's all she could tell.'

I sighed. Too much to hope for that Jeannie had been
able to come up with anything really useful.

'Of course, she got the licence number,' said Nellie, digging into the bag that always hung on the arm of her wheelchair. 'If that'll help.' She handed me a scrap of brown
paper bag with the number scribbled in Jeannie's schoolgirl
hand. 'Colo,' it said, then three letters, three numbers.

'You and Jeannie,' I said admiringly, giving her a hug.
'You're some team.'

A little further conversation elicited a description which
wasn't unlike the one Grace had given the last time I'd
been shot at. Pasty face, sixtyish, half bald.

I gave Nellie another hug and a promise of a longer visit
soon, then hurried across the alley and up to the office.
Grace wouldn't be home yet, so I called Linder direct and
gave him the licence number.

'If you want to talk to Nellie Arpels, send Grace,' I told

him. 'Nellie knows Grace.' I gave him Jeannie's number, as well.

Mark was standing at my elbow. 'What's this about a licence?' he asked.

I told him about the man and the car.

'I thought there was someone hanging around!' he said. 'When Bryan and I came over Saturday morning to feed the animals and let Bela out, I saw him. After I put Bela's food out in the kitchen, I went into your bedroom to be sure the windows were locked, and when I pulled back the curtains, I saw somebody duck away down the alley. By the time Bryan and I got downstairs and out the back door, he was gone, but Bela was sniffing and growling all over the back yard, as though some stranger had been in there.'

My unknown enemy hadn't given up. He'd shown up at the weekend, just as before. After worrying at that fact for twenty minutes or so, I called Linder again and pointed out that the assailant, whoever he was, seemed to prefer Saturdays and Sundays.

'That licence number is from Trinidad,' he said. 'Maybe the guy can only get up here on weekends.'

The town of Trinidad lies almost on the Colorado–New Mexico border, a hundred and eighty-odd miles from Denver. It had been (perhaps still was for all I knew) a mining town that had recruited a number of Italian workers to add to the original Mexican inhabitants. The miners sent for their families, then their relatives, then their more distant kin, and the town became an interesting Mexican–Italian mix.

'Whose licence number is it?' I asked Linder.

'Some roofing company. Snowy Peaks Roofing ring a bell with you?'

It didn't so much as tinkle. I said so profanely and at length.

My frustration must have come across because Linder said, 'Relax. There'll only be so many people who drive that car. I've already asked the local police to get us the names, and just in case the car's still in the Denver area,

we've put out a pick-up on it. We've got the bullet we took
out of your front hall, and if the guy's in the car and the
gun's with the guy . . .'

'It's Monday,' I complained. 'He'll be back in Trinidad
by now. He fired a rifle at me the first time, a handgun the
second. The rifle bullet is the one we have, but he'll have
put the rifle away somewhere already, and when he knows
we're on to him, he'll drive some other car and dispose of
both firearms.' I was fairly hostile about it, but my anger
wasn't directed at Linder particularly, just at the frustration
of the circumstances.

'Calm down,' he said again. 'Don't worry, Jason. I won't
let him get away. If I did, Grace'd kill me! We've got an
idea who the guy is, and we've probable cause to search for
the gun.'

Probable cause! I had no idea as to probable cause. Some
person from a smallish town on the Colorado border, someone I didn't know, had never met, had no reason to like or
dislike, was trying to kill me for a totally unknown reason!
Probable cause!

I took several deep breaths, got myself some coffee, and
was summoned downstairs by Eugenia to admire Orvie
Spender's card table, soon to be Olivia's card table, which
had arrived Friday afternoon after I'd left. In a private van,
no less. Special delivery. It was, thank God, every bit as
good a piece as Orvie had said it was, and Eugenia had
already gone over it with cleaning oil and a soft brush
followed by buffing cloths. The delicate curved corners
shone like cabochon gems.

The rest of the day went by doing this and that, none of
it very rewarding. The long drive had made my leg ache,
so when everyone left, I gave it a long soak in the big tub
and stretched out early with *Foucalt's Pendulum*, which I'd
been trying to read for a year. Everyone I knew claimed to
have read it back when it was first published, but I kept
losing my place or falling asleep or trying to figure out why
the characters were bothering to do what they were doing.
Of course, Jacob brought me up to be a sceptic, which

made me not entirely sympathetic to their metaphysical obsession.

The phone rang in the middle of the night, or rather about two o'clock Tuesday morning. The heavy book was still on my chest, though I seemed to have turned out the light. I fumbled the switch and dropped the phone twice before I got it to my ear. Grace.

'The station just called,' she said. 'Linder wasn't available and it was sort of my case.'

'What?' I mumbled stupidly, trying to get myself focused.

'That licence number Nellie came up with. They located the car on a street out in Aurora. The patrol car tried to pull it over, and the car took off south on Gun Club Road. I guess the driver got it up around ninety. He hit a gravel curve south-east of Buckley Air Base somewhere, skidded off the road, went through somebody's fence and ended up out in the middle of a pasture. The car rolled and burned.'

'Who was driving?' I asked stupidly.

'Hell, Jason, wake up! I said the car burned. One guy was driving, but he'd baled out before it crashed. It's black as a coalminer's neck out there, and they haven't found him. Maybe tomorrow we'll find out who it was. I thought you'd like to know we've got a line on him, that's all.'

She too had been awakened in the middle of the night. She too was grumpy about it. She hung up. I lay back on the disarranged pillows, provoking a baffled half-growl from Schnitz, who had inserted himself beneath one of them. He clawed his way out and stalked, frowning, to the foot of the bed, his tail fluffed out in annoyance. Not many cats can actually frown, but Schnitz shares that ability with his father. Bela whuffed from his basket. Phones aren't supposed to ring this time of night. It made us all edgy, even though the news was, from my point of view, good. Given the car and the description, my mysterious assailant was, presumably, identifiable.

If that had been he, driving the car, and not someone else. Of course, the man in the car might not have been alone; he could have had an accomplice or been an accomplice. If the driver had gone south on Gun Club Road, he might have started somewhere near Motel Row on East Colfax, where the rooms rent by the hour as often as they do by the night. Along there, nobody really paid much attention to who came and who went. Some other, unidentifiable person could be in a motel, just waiting for morning to take another shot. Or in my backyard. Or my basement.

I decided I was being paranoid and tried to think of something else. The town of Trinidad. Possibly a largely Catholic town. I didn't know that for sure, but it seemed logical. Catholic, therefore probably anti-abortion, therefore, someone from there could have participated in the clinic blockade. Someone inclined to fanatical enmities or explosions of religious fervour. I told myself it could be true, but I didn't believe it. No one would drive almost four hundred miles every week, round trip, to shoot someone they'd only seen on television, out of mere fervour!

Schnitz growled again and blinked his amber eyes. I turned off the light. It made no sense in darkness either. I gave up and went back to sleep.

•

Tuesday. Party day. Mark called Harriet Steinwale and arranged to deliver the table. He'd put a huge red velvet bow on it and made an oversized card of the enlarged photo. Before he delivered it, I double-checked with Lycia to be sure her mother knew about Jacob.

'She knew, Jason. When I mentioned his name, she was surprised at first, then she cried a little and said how much she missed him. They used to talk on the phone every few days. Did you know that?'

I hadn't known that. It seemed I had been wrong in thinking Jacob would have introduced me to her. He had kept her a secret, even from me. I had thought I shared deeply in Jacob's life, and this secretive bit hurt a little. Why hadn't he told me?

Lycia went on, 'Mama was seventy when Theo died. She says she and Jacob talked about getting together then, but they decided what they really wanted from one another was the companionship they'd have had if they'd been together always. So they met once in a while but mostly just talked by phone.'

I heard her sniffling. 'A friend of mine remarked that this whole business was like a romance novel,' I commented lamely.

'Well, it is, in a way. Anyhow, Mama read his obituary when it came out. You know, there was a time there a few weeks ago when I knew something was bothering her. She was very quiet and seemed not to hear when I spoke. She didn't say at the time, but it must have been Jacob's death.'

I murmured in agreement.

'Mama's looking forward to meeting you. Jacob often mentioned you to her.'

Well, at least he'd shared me with her even if he hadn't shared her with me. That was helpful. I wouldn't have to explain.

While Mark was delivering the table, I took an hour to visit the one and only barber who knows how to cut the transplanted hair on the back of my head so it looks like hair and not Spanish moss. He also manages to cover my odd ear (though it's not nearly as odd as it used to be before surgery). When evening came, I put on my most elegant and conservative grey suit, one I'd had custom made and only worn three times. White on white shirt, charcoal tie with little red diamonds in it, black dress shoes so new the soles were still slick. Seeing as how Olivia had heard such nice things about me, I couldn't let Jacob down. Confronting myself in the mirror, noting the new touch of grey at the temples, I told myself I was thoroughly acceptable.

I took a cab, thinking of another plot cliché I dislike, the one in which the hero, after exerting due caution for sixty per cent of the book, gets stranded through his own stupidity and becomes prey. Driving my own car in Capitol Hill would lead me down that road very nicely, since the area's packed with apartment buildings and short on parking space. I had no intention of having to park a dozen blocks away and making a target of myself. The cab let me out twenty feet from the front door of Harriet's building, and I made it inside unscathed.

Harriet Steinwale owns all or part of the building, in addition to living there. As I passed through the foyer, I resolved to mention the furnishings to her. Just because the place was called 'The Louvre' didn't mean it had to be quite so fakey-French. Next time it was redone, maybe I could get her something a little more classy. That is, if the tenants didn't prefer the bad fakes.

Harriet's elegant and spacious penthouse was on the top floor. Nothing fakey about that, at least. The affair was being catered. A black-jacketed attendant took my coat, another one offered me a glass of champagne, a third directed me to the buffet. Lycia saw me come in. She took me by the arm and led me through the crowded living-room to the enclosed area where the gifts had been assembled.

I would have known her anywhere. She was ensconced in a high-backed chair with the lights of the city spread behind her. Despite the fluff of white hair and the fine patina of wrinkles, she looked like the girl in the portrait. It was there in the hairline, in the curve of the brows, in the sweet set of the lips and the delicately rounded chin. The fine bone structure was still there, the shape beneath the years.

'Olivia,' I said. 'I'm so very happy to meet you.'

'You're Jason,' she responded. 'Jacob showed me pictures of you, such a handsome boy. He spoke of you all the time. He was so proud of you.'

I may have blushed. Jacob had never told me I was handsome, and I'd stopped thinking of myself as a boy about fifteen years ago. I sat down beside her and we talked. She had already seen Jacob's gift and read the card. She wiped her eyes, crying and laughing at the same time as she recounted times when she and Jacob had had great triumphs at the bridge tables. She didn't get technical about it, for which I was grateful, since I'd never been able to work up any interest in the game. Poker was, perhaps lamentably, a sturdy relic of my misapplied childhood.

Other guests came in to offer best wishes, and I retreated to the buffet table, wishing for Grace. She'd have loved both the food and the fact there was so much of it. I filled a plate and circulated and acted the part of a social animal, chatting with Keith Foret, Lycia's son, and with Ross Whit-field, her companion, room-mate, lover, what have you. We talked mostly about local politics. Then I spoke with Harriet, mentioning in passing her lobby furniture.

She glared at me. 'Every article of furniture in that lobby is stolen on the average of once each six months.'

I gaped, uncomfortably aware I'd hit a nerve.

'We've fastened chairs with steel chains through holes in the floor. We've bolted the legs through the floor into the garage ceiling below. We've attached alarms. The last time someone cleaned us out, I said the hell with it and bought a dozen replacements for everything, the cheapest I could find, and put them in the store room with my name sprayed on the bottom. They get stolen, I replace them. If they don't get stolen, they fall apart in a year, but they're usually stolen before that. One of these days, we'll catch somebody taking them.'

I expressed astonishment, and she snorted at me.

'You're naïve, Jason. People who rent apartments have the idea they're being exploited by the landlord. Some of them come from the east where they have rent control, and since there's no rent control here, that makes stealing from the landlord seem somehow cute and acceptable. After all, here they are, paying this enormous rent, three or four hundred a month, or maybe even more, and all they can see is this greedy old person just raking it in. So they keep pets without paying the pet deposit; then their animals ruin the carpets, and they move out leaving a thousand dollar repair bill which all the other tenants end up paying.' She pointed a long, bony forefinger at me, stabbing me repeat-edly on the shoulder.

'If the heat's included in their rent, they leave their heat on and their windows open. If you put meters in their apartments, they turn their heat off and let the people on either side heat them through the walls. They never see the mortgage payments, or the fuel bills, or the electric bills, or the insurance bills, or the elevator repair bills, or the janitorial bills, *or* the taxes. Last year, I made less than four per cent on my investment in this building. I could do better tearing it down and building a parking garage!'

Someone across the room waved at her, and she strode off in high dudgeon, leaving me gasping but rather glad she'd found something to harangue me about. If she'd felt at all uncomfortable with my being invited to the party, her discomfort had been well sublimated.

Seeing that Olivia's well-wishers had dispersed somewhat, I went to say good-night.

'I saw Harriet pounding on you,' she whispered, her eyes laughing. 'Was she going on again about building a parking garage? It was sweet of you to listen so attentively.'

I flushed.

'Jason, dear, I want the table with me in my apartment,' she said, putting her soft old hand over mine. 'I want to know about it, about its *provenance*.' Her voice put quotes around the word. 'Jacob would have thought that very important. Will you bring it and tell me all about it?'

I told her I'd come, getting the words out around the lump in my throat. Even though I'd sternly reminded myself that all this melodrama should be taken with several pinches of salt, I'd ended up awash in sentimentality.

'Tomorrow,' she said. 'Tea-time, if you can. I want to talk about Jacob.'

Her apartment was on the fourth floor of a building south of Cherry Creek, where the new mall has recently opened. Mark brought the table over from Harriet's place, then departed. Olivia's companion brought in tea and cakes and then made herself scarce, obviously by prearrangement. The two of us were to have tea alone.

When we were settled with cups and plates, Olivia did as she had promised and talked about Jacob and their youth together. She said little about either of her marriages, except to mention her second husband once:

'After Theo died, Jacob used to call me every few days. I didn't hear from him at Christmastime, so I called him. The nice young man who answered the phone said he wasn't able to talk, but he said he'd give him a message. Somehow I knew then I'd probably never talk to him again.'

'You could have visited him,' I said.

'We'd agreed not to do that, he and I. It was a sentimental promise. When I thought of Jacob, I thought of him the way he was before I married 'Tavio. He liked that. He said he liked staying always young in my mind.'

Until recently, I had not thought of Jacob as an incurable romantic. 'So you left him a message at Christmastime?'

'I said Olivia called to wish Jacob a happy New Year. He always used to wish me a merry Christmas and I'd wish him happy New Year, though I knew it wasn't the Jewish New Year at all.'

'Jacob wasn't religious,' I commented.

She nodded slowly. 'I know. I was and he wasn't. I thought my religion meant a lot to me. I wished that Jacob's religion meant something to him, too, so he'd understand.'

I said I thought he'd understand.

She shook her head at me, very slowly, making a sad clown's mouth at me. 'No. He couldn't have. Because I didn't. Later on I realized what had mattered most was my parents. I thought giving up Jacob and getting married to someone they chose was a religious matter because they told me it was, but it really wasn't. It was really about other things, but I didn't know that then.'

I sipped and looked inquiringly at her.

She saw I hadn't understood. 'Nineteen-thirty was a different time. Oh, I know it was supposed to be the flapper age and all that, but even so, girls didn't know then all the things they know today. Not *nice* girls. We didn't have TV and movies educating us about sex. We were ignorant, and we were supposed to stay that way until we got married and pregnant. I remember whispering with a girlfriend about pregnancy and babies when we were about sixteen. She said her babies would come out of her belly-button! And I believed her! That was our destiny, to believe in belly-buttons and marry some nice Catholic boy and get pregnant with nice Catholic babies and never know anything until it actually happened to us. Our families and our church knew that if we were kept ignorant—though they called it "innocent"—nature would take over and we'd be caught.'

'I can understand that,' I said weakly, though I couldn't. Not at all.

'*Good* girls weren't assertive, weren't rebellious. We were taught to be passive. We got into the habit of it, and it isn't an easy habit to break. Even years later, after 'Tavio died, my parents were still saying I owed it to Lycia to give her a proper Catholic home, so I married Theo. Not that Theo wasn't a nice man, he was; but I didn't love him as I loved Jacob. Jacob would have married me then! I was barely forty! But, no, I married Theo because it was the right thing to do . . .

'Of course, my making a good Catholic home really didn't matter to Lycia. After what happened to Angela, she spent most of her time in St Louis with my mother.'

I found my voice somewhere. 'Angela?'

'My other daughter. Lycia's older sister. Angela.'

Lycia had warned me not to mention her sister on the grounds Olivia would be disturbed. She didn't seem particularly disturbed. Weepy, yes, but not distraught. I managed an interrogative sound, somewhere between a hum and a grunt, wondering if Brother Daniel had been saying not 'my angel', but 'my Angela'. I hadn't known her name was Angela.

Olivia stared out the window as she spoke. 'When she was seventeen, Angela fell in love with Daniel Brockman, a neighbour boy a year or two older than she. She didn't need to tell me. Anyone with eyes could have seen what was going on. She glowed whenever he was around. Whenever I saw her face, it was like looking at my face in a mirror when I'd been that age.

'On her eighteenth birthday, she came to us, to 'Tavio and me, to tell us about him. Once she was eighteen, she didn't need our permission, not really, but she loved us both and she wanted us to approve. She was a loving girl, and she loved 'Tavio, even though I didn't, never had, not really. Poor child. As soon as 'Tavio understood what she was saying, he told her she could not marry the boy she loved because he had promised her to someone else. I couldn't believe it. The light went out of her. Like blowing out a candle. It was like my parents, all over again, like a nightmare.'

I couldn't keep quiet. 'Olivia, it wasn't the seventeenth century! Couldn't you have done something about it?'

She made a pushing motion with her hands, signalling impotence. ''Tavio was *dying*. You don't know what it was like, Jason. I was angry at him. I hated him. But it was a *sin* to hate him. He was a wounded soldier who'd fought valiantly. He was her father. He was my husband! And I was a sinful, angry woman always trying to catch up on my penance for hating him! Of *course* I tried to talk with him, over and over, but it was no use. I asked my parents to help me, but they refused to get involved. They'd picked 'Tavio for me, and it hadn't worked out as they planned. They felt ... oh, I think they felt guilty, so guilty they wouldn't do anything to "interfere" ever again ...

'The only one who could do anything with 'Tavio was Father Olivera. He was Spanish, like 'Tavio, first generation, and he talked 'Tavio's language. I thought maybe he could fix things, but it worked the other way. He sat us down, Angela and me, and preached at us how 'Tavio had sworn on oath before God, that the oath was an honourable one designed to unite two families, that the other family was a proper Catholic family, and that we owed it to 'Tavio to let his oath be fulfilled before he died.'

This time I didn't say anything.

'Father Olivera hadn't been here long. He was wrong. I

fought, Jason. Honestly, I did. But I was all alone. Poor Angela, she was like a little bird, trapped and fluttering and unable to do anything. Oh, I wish that boy had taken her away, run away with her. I wish she'd had it in her to be rebellious, but between how I'd raised her and what the school had taught her, she was just . . . lost. It had all been trained out of her, just as it had all been trained out of me . . .'

I put my hand on hers. She was in pain, and it was too late to do anything about these ancient tragedies.

She whispered, 'Even today I try not to hate 'Tavio. I try to remember the unhappy life he had. He was never loved as people should be loved.'

'Umm,' I said, patting her hand, wondering how Jacob had reacted to these revelations.

'Angela didn't love her husband any more than I had mine. She saved all her love for the baby, for little Michael. He had a huge awful birthmark.' She peered at me, waiting for something. 'It was dreadful-looking. A port wine mark, I think it's called. They can cure them now, but there was nothing they could do back then.'

What does one say? What I was feeling was irritation, something just short of anger, at Octavio for what he'd done, at Olivia for letting him, at Jacob for not kidnapping her and running off with her, even at poor Angela for not eloping with her boyfriend. I found all this passivity and helplessness a little unbelievable and more than a little sickening. I didn't understand how Jacob could have stood it, he who had always insisted upon honesty. How could he have loved someone like this, who had let these things happen?

'I'm sorry to hear about the birthmark,' I said. It was all I could think of to say.

She glared at the floor. 'It wouldn't have happened if she hadn't married that man. His father didn't even come to the wedding. He was sick, they said. Sick! He'd been sick for years, but when Michael was born, Angela's husband said the baby was cursed, someone had put a curse on the family. Oh, Angela was fierce about that! *Then* she rebelled! She said if there was a curse on the family it was there before Michael was born. She kept Michael with her, away from his father, so the little boy wouldn't hear such talk. She told me she would save Michael, no matter what his father was like. And after all that care, all that love, it was like she was doomed . . .'

I drained the last few drops in my cup as I prepared polite reasons I had to leave.

'Huntington's disease, it's called,' she said. 'A genetic disease . . .'

I sat with my mouth partly open, cup in mid-air.

''Tavio had sworn an oath to a man who had Huntington's disease. Three years after Angela was married, she found out what it was her father-in-law had. His family had tried to hide it, but she found out. And Angela's husband had a fifty-fifty chance of having it; and if he had it, there was a fifty-fifty chance the baby would have it too.

'Jenny came to tell me about it. She was Angela's friend, Angela's best friend. She was there the night Angela found out. She got me out of bed to tell me. She said she'd put Angela to bed, with a sleeping pill, but that Lycia and I should go over first thing in the morning to be with her . . .'

Her voice trailed away and she fell silent, grieving, unable to take the story further.

I waited for some time, then prompted her. 'What happened?'

'She died,' Olivia whispered. 'When we got there in the morning, Angela was already at the hospital. They'd found her in her bed, unconscious. The room was full of gas. She was in a coma for a long while. Lycia and I stayed at the hospital the whole time, but she never regained consciousness. Never said goodbye. A mercy. They said if she'd lived, she'd have been a vegetable.'

She wiped her eyes. 'The stupid woman who worked for her said it was suicide. It was an accident. She wouldn't have committed suicide. Lycia had nightmares about it. Everything here reminded her. Mother said if I married

Theo, it would all be different and we could make a home for her, but even then she preferred to live in St Louis. In the end, I lost both my daughters.'

'But Lycia came back.'

'Oh yes. I shouldn't have said I lost her, because you're right. She did come back. At first she came back for visits, and the visits got longer and longer. Finally she came back to stay, but she was a grown woman then. In college.'

'The woman who worked for your daughter was Simonetta Leone. Angela was married to Nimo Leone.' The two halves of my puzzle had come seamlessly together.

She didn't seem surprised that I knew. Perhaps she thought Lycia had told me. 'I never say his name,' she said angrily, keeping her face turned away from me. 'I swore I would never say the name of any of that accursed family.'

This time I didn't forget to ask: 'What happened to little Michael?'

'I wanted him. Even if he had that dreadful disease, I wanted Angela's baby. Besides, he wasn't safe with that horrible nursemaid. When I asked to have him, Angela's husband said the baby was already gone. Gone away. Sent away to relatives of theirs in Italy. So *he* wouldn't be reminded. So *he* could forget.'

'He?'

'Angela's husband,' she said.

'You didn't protest about the baby?'

'Protest!' She turned on me. 'What good was *protest*, with that family or with mine? What good had *protest* been with Octavio Desquintas y Alvarez? Every day, Jason, every day of my life since then, morning and evening, I have prayed that Michael is well and happy somewhere, that the disease passed him by.'

'You've never tried to find him?'

'Theo offered to help me find him, but it was a bargain I made with God. If I didn't look for the baby, if I let him go, he'd be safe. The priest I go to now doesn't understand. He says God doesn't make bargains. Jacob understood. He knew I had to do something, make some sacrifice so that things would come right. I'd done so much to let them go wrong. God has forgiven me, so the priest says, but I'll never forgive myself for letting Angela marry that man. If God is love, how can we turn our back on love? No matter what religion says.'

Tears were dripping from her jaw, running into the corners of her mouth. I gave her my handkerchief, and she buried her face in the white linen.

When she looked at me again, she gave me an ironic glance, 'Worst of all, my parents didn't want me to marry Jacob because he was a Jew. 'Tavio, though . . . he was Catholic, he was a Don, an aristocrat. But when we had to leave Spain, 'Tavio wasn't a Don any more. He was only an arrogant Spaniard who thought he was too good to take a job with my father. The last four years of his life, my father never even spoke to him.'

I left shortly after that, as soon as I politely could. I felt almost as grieved and battered as she obviously did. She was not the only one who had been sacrificed on the ugly altar of her parents' pride, of 'Tavio's pride. Jacob had been sacrificed too.

And he'd told me so, though I hadn't known what he meant at the time. There were several little lectures he used to give me when I was young: the self-reliance lecture, the work-ethic lecture, the honesty lecture, the values lecture:

'Some things that people treasure have no value at all, Jason. Ideas, customs. Scrutinized in the light, they're only husks, old worn-out things, not worth a nickel.'

I was fifteen when he'd first told me that. Olivia had long been married to Theo, but Jacob had gone on loving her. To my dismay, I did not think she had been worthy of that love.

Thursday morning the police identified the owner of the burned car as one Antonio Gabrielli (Gabe) Leone: sixtyish, pale-faced, half bald and rather plump. He was the owner of Snowy Peaks Roofing in Trinidad, Colorado, to which city and place of business he had not yet returned. The police files identified him as the son of Canello Leone and a former associate of known felons. Both a rifle and a handgun had been found in the trunk of the car. Bullets fired from the rifle matched the one dug out of my front hall panelling. Without doubt, the brother of Olivia's son-in-law had taken a couple of shots at me. Probably he'd try it again, if he wasn't lying dead somewhere.

Grace was an intrigued and surprised by the tie between Simonetta and Olivia as I was. She became even more interested when I suggested she bring over the clinic arrest record which I'd asked her for days earlier, this time because I thought I'd made a connection with Gabe's description. Sure enough, there he was. When I'd looked at the pictures before, I'd looked right past that pale, pouchy, very ordinary face. It had been just another out of twenty or thirty, with nothing distinctive about him. This time I was looking at the long-sleeved pale plaid shirt and the light down vest he wore. I put my hand over his baldness and imagined him with a white, curly wig.

'I think he must have arrived at the clinic wearing glasses, the white wig, and this down vest stuffed in his shirt-front to give him a bosom,' I told Grace. 'Later, during the confusion of the arrests, he pulled the vest out from under his shirt, put it on, took off the glasses and the wig. As I recall, he's got a lard-butt and heavy thighs. That plus the bosom and the wig was enough to make me think I was seeing a woman.'

'He must have killed Simonetta—he had no other reason to be there—and he must have thought you'd seen him do it.'

'I remember him looking in through the glass door at me, but it didn't mean a thing at the time.'

Grace showed me the picture of Gabe that had been faxed up from Trinidad, and it matched the one on the arrest report, so there was no question as to identity. She was still puzzled, however.

'OK, we'll say he killed Simonetta, but *why* did he do it?'

I wished I knew, because the puzzle was suddenly *my*

puzzle, having something to do with Olivia's family. The person who'd tried to kill me was not some nut who had seen me on TV or picked me at random from a phone book. He was a murderer named Leone who had not wanted anyone connecting him to Simonetta.

'One good thing,' said Grace. 'He'll know we've traced the car. It's his car. I saw him in it, and I can identify him. The rifle that fired at you was in the car, that ties him to the attempt on you. His picture from Trinidad matches the one on the arrest report, so we can place him at the scene of the murder. We don't need you to place him there. All the reasons he had for getting rid of you no longer apply. He'd be crazy to try and bother you again.'

I hadn't thought of that, but she was right. Gabe Leone had no reason to come gunning for me any more.

I phoned the clinic to tell Cynthia Adamson about Gabe, for a wonder getting to her before Grace did.

'Oh,' she breathed, 'oh God, I'm so glad it was somebody else.' I knew what she meant. She meant somebody not associated with the clinic. 'Why did he do it?'

I had to confess we didn't know, except that it had nothing to do with the abortion controversy. 'The only reason that makes sense for him to have killed her in a crowd like that is that it gave him an opportunity to make it look like something else,' I told her. 'He had some reason for wanting it to look like something else, possibly because he didn't want the real reason she was killed to be known. No doubt he thought it would be blamed on some fanatic pro-abortionist, and that'd be it. And if he'd let *me* alone, that might well have happened.'

She sighed. 'I'd like to get the anti's off our necks. Can I tell the papers?'

'Better they get it from the police. After that, say what you will. Has it been rough?'

'You have no idea what we've been accused of, Jason. One of the nuts tried to bomb the clinic the other night. They caught him. They haven't caught the person who's been slashing our tyres, though. Or the ones who call up and breathe threats. These people have so many psychological problems it's unbelievable, particularly the men. They're very, very sick.'

I knew about the men. If 'Tavio Desquintas y Alvarez had been alive, he'd have been right out there among the picketers. No, that would have been too undignified. He'd have hired someone to picket for him.

I phoned Dorotea Chapman and asked if she'd see me again, that we thought we knew who had killed her sister. I knew the police would probably want to see her as well, but I wanted to get to her first. She said she was coming into town to do some shopping, so she'd drop in later.

Grace had let me photocopy the two pictures of Gabe Leone, and when I gave them to Dorotea that afternoon, she stared at them in disbelief while I told her what we thought we knew.

'None of this makes sense,' she said.

I was sympathetic, admitting it made little sense to us either.

'Why in heaven's name would Nello's son kill Simonetta? Now? After all these years?'

'Has anything changed recently?' I asked.

'What do you mean?'

'I mean, has something changed recently that had anything to do with Simonetta? Anything at all?'

'Her husband died,' she said blankly. 'Herby. But you knew that.'

'Right. Anything else?'

'My mother went into a nursing home. That was last summer, though.'

'Up until then she'd seen Simonetta regularly?'

'Yes. Up until then.'

'Could it have been . . . perhaps something Simonetta used to discuss with your mother that she began talking of to other people? Talked of to Herby, maybe. Something she knew?'

She shook her head at me impatiently. 'I told you,

Simonetta didn't *know* things. Not like that. She believed things. Half the time, what she said was completely crazy.'

I shrugged helplessly. 'Perhaps someone didn't know that. Perhaps someone thought she was capable of spilling a secret.'

'I don't understand.'

I tried an example. 'We've heard that when Simonetta was about twenty-three, she came back to your parents' house one day and found no one home. She had hysterics all up and down the block. She said that Nimo's wife had committed suicide.'

'I remember. I mean, I don't remember it happening— I was at school. But I remember everyone talking about it.'

'Now, the newspapers said the woman died accidentally. So Simonetta had it wrong. Or, maybe, she had it right and the newspaper story was wrong.'

'All I really remember is Simmy being hysterical. Her job with the Leones ended when the woman died, so for weeks after that she was in and out of the house, back and forth, throwing fits. I remember that vividly. Sometimes she cried, and sometimes she laughed like crazy. She said God had fixed it so the baby wouldn't die. The mother had died, but the baby wouldn't.'

'You told us the baby died.'

'Did I? You're right! Why did I say that? Come to think of it, I guess it *felt* like the child had died, the way Simmy acted. I mean, she'd been taking care of them both, the mother and the child, and then suddenly she wasn't doing it any more. I guess the child was just taken away. I knew it was gone, because Simonetta kept having hysterics over it.' Dorotea fell silent, concentrating. 'I remember! Simonetta said God was the baby's father. She said, "Just like Jesus." Then she laughed like a crazy woman. Heavens! I haven't thought of that in years!'

It didn't really connect to anything I knew. 'Could she have said something then, or at any time, that might have made people think she knew something she wasn't supposed to know?'

'What could she have known? You mean, something she overheard? From Herby? From the Leones? How on earth would I know? I haven't seen her half a dozen times in the last five years.'

I made an apologetic face, but persisted. 'Would your mother know?'

She glared at me. 'Mr Lynx, I'll ask her. She has her good days and her bad ones. If I catch her on a good day, I'll ask her. If only to get you off my back!'

I chose to ignore her tone. She was no more irritable than I. 'See if you can find out what was on Simonetta's mind in recent months,' I suggested. 'Ask her what Simonetta talked about. Ask your mother particularly if Simonetta talked about Herby and what he was up to.'

'You really think it had something to do with him?'

'You said yourself that one of the things that had changed was his death. I think it likely that his death and Simonetta's are connected in some way.'

'But his was accidental.'

'So I've been told.'

'You don't believe it?'

Frustrated, I threw up my hands. 'I don't disbelieve it. I don't know. I know the police had no reason to question it, not then. Maybe they will now.'

At least, Grace would. Grace, who was still tracing decades-old crimes that had never been solved.

'Same M.O.,' she chanted triumphantly, when she came over that evening.

'Cops really do say that,' I said.

'Say what?'

'M.O. Same M.O. Why don't they just say "method"? Same method. Why use a two-syllable shorthand for a six-syllable Latin phrase when you can use a solid two-syllable English word?'

'Jason, hush, you're spoiling my triumph! Listen to this: back in the middle 'fifties there were some ice-pick murders over on the north side. The victims were involved with illegal gambling, which at that time implied Nello Leone,

but no arrests were ever made. So now we know who probably did them, and I'm very pleased with myself because
it isn't every day that a cop comes up with a probable
solution for murders that happened before she was even
born!'

'You think it was Gabe Leone.'

'When I say same *method*, I mean *exactly* the same. The
autopsy on Simonetta could have been written for any of
the other victims. I got filthy down in those files, but the
autopsy reports were still there, by God. Same weapon,
same angle, same internal damage, same lack of external
bleeding, the whole business. Gabe would have been in his
early twenties back then. If he didn't kill those people, then
it was the guy who taught him how!'

'So we know who, and we know how, but we have *no* idea
why. I'd really like to know why.'

'You'll figure it out,' she said, kissing me on one side of
my chin. 'You always do.'

I was glad she had such confidence in me. All I seemed
to have was loose ends.

Thursday evening I made myself go to Olivia's, osten-
sibly just to say hello. Actually a question had occurred to
me, and I was hoping I could get the information without
making a big deal of it.

She opened the subject herself. 'I should apologize for
yesterday. I had no right to unburden myself that way. I
haven't talked about Angela for years except with Jacob,
but yesterday was Angela's birthday. I couldn't get her out
of my mind. I wanted you to know I'm grateful to you for
being so understanding of an old woman.' Tears were filling
her eyes.

'You're Jacob's dear friend,' I said helplessly, regretting
my anger. 'So you're mine, too. No thanks necessary.'

'It would be so sad for Angela to go completely unre-
membered. After you left, Jason, I got out the old pictures.
Angela's and her friends. Daniel from next door. Jenny
Bruns.' She opened a drawer and took the photos out, laying them before me like an offering. I knew Angela immedi-

ately. She was like the young Olivia, and much, much like Lycia.

I pointed out a jolly young face. 'Jenny Bruns? She was the one you mentioned before, Angela's friend?' That had been the question I'd wanted to ask. Who had been close to Angela?

'Jenny Mattingly now,' she said. 'Mrs Maynard Mattingly the second, or is it the third? I can never remember. She wasn't married when she knew Angela.'

'They were close friends.'

'Best friends. You know how girls are.' She caught herself and waved her hands at me, erasing what she'd said. 'No, how would you know how girls are! Silly of me. Well, sometimes girls have real best friends. Good friends. Not the kind who are friends today and off in a snit tomorrow. Jenny and Angela were really close. Even after Angela was married, they spent a lot of time together. She was there the evening before Angela died.'

'You still see her?'

'She drops in now and then. Takes me to lunch once in a while with her aunt and a few other old biddies. She's a great-grandmother, can you imagine!'

She showed me pictures, and I made the proper noises. As we sat there together, I toted up how many hours I'd spent in similar activities. I seem to collect old ladies. Mark has remarked upon it. I've thought it's because I have no family of my own that I collect left-over pieces of other people's families. Today I was the attentive young(er) man who sits patiently and looks at old snapshots. I did it for some little time, as penance for yesterday's annoyance.

When I left a good hour later, I promised to drop in from time to time, just to be sure she was behaving herself. She bridled like a girl, fluttering her lashes and laughing at me. For a moment I saw the Olivia Jacob must have known and loved, laughing eyes and delighted smile.

The phone book yielded no Maynard Mattingly the third, so I called Mattingly the second. No luck. The veddy haughty voice on the phone told me Mrs Mattingly was in

Mexico and was not expected to return for several weeks. Would I care to leave a message.

I left a message, mentioning that it urgently concerned Angela Desquintas y Alvares, taking a perverse pleasure out of the confusion the double-barrelled name caused the voice. I had to spell it twice.

Friday came and went, spent mostly inspecting the progress on the Law Firm Job: chaos incarnate. At an early stage all jobs are chaos. Everything is torn apart; nothing is put back together yet; nothing hints at the eventual outcome. It would all come out right, but just now it looked impossible.

Grace would be on duty over the weekend, and I didn't feel up to seeking other companionship. Schnitz threw up on the kitchen floor—putting a second curse on what promised to be a lousy weekend. I had forgotten to give him his weekly dose of hair-ball preventive, so it was my fault, not his. I wondered, as I cleaned up the mess, what long-haired cats did in the wild. Threw up, probably. That's probably why they eat grass, as a purgative. The day ended in a mood of housekeeper's irascibility.

Saturday I woke feeling no better, depressed and anxious, as though something inimical were lurking outside the door. This despite the fact there was no reason for Gabe Leone to come after me now. His name and face had appeared on the late news as a suspect sought in what the media were calling 'the abortion clinic murder'. Killing me would no longer help him a bit.

Why, then, did I vibrate with a kind of premonitory tension? I was as irritable as a bear being tracked, feeling the need to circle and come upon my enemies from behind.

Then the phone rang.

'Cecily's back,' Myra said. 'She won't talk to us.'

'She what?' I snapped. My irritability increased and I felt almost clairvoyant. Somebody was up to no damned good!

'Don't bite my head off, Jason. She won't talk to us. Her friend Yaggie called me and said Cees was back, so I called

her in Santa Fe, but when I told her we were looking for
people who had known Simonetta, she shut up like a clam.
She wouldn't talk. And she says don't call back.'

'This is the holy one, right? The one who wanted to be
a nun?'

'Right.'

She gave me the address and phone number. Cecily
Stephens. Two addresses in Santa Fe. One home—the one
I'd tried when I was there—one office. The firm was called
Habitacion. I recalled seeing it in the Santa Fe phone book
when I'd looked at the contractor listing. '*Casas por las
gentes*.' Houses for people. I was reminded of Harriet's per-
oration on the same subject. Houses for all; information for
none.

The fact that Cees wouldn't talk was actually more
intriguing than Yaggie's bubbling on and on about funny
old Simonetta. We'd talked to a lot of people, and none of
them had had any hesitation about talking back. Dorotea
had found the family history distasteful, but she'd told us
what we wanted to know. Now, here, for the first time, was
someone who didn't want to talk.

She had something to hide, my puzzle-solving self
chortled as it sniffed along the trail and whuffed at the scent
of villainy. She had something to hide, old Cees did, and I
was going to find out what it was. I refused to consider that
she might be simply busy, or tired, or unwilling to get
involved. No, she was the person I'd been looking for, the
one who knew!

How was I going to get it out of her?

I could write her a letter. Which would do no damned
good.

I could drive down and try to see her. A six-hour drive
from Denver. Twelve full hours, round trip.

Or I could fly to Albuquerque in an hour, rent a car and
drive up to Santa Fe in another hour, but the round trip
air fare was extortionate. Ever since airline deregulation,
fares for lightly travelled routes have become ridiculously

expensive. Persons can now fly reasonably only so long as they go where everyone else goes.

Grace and I had made the same drive the past week, and it hadn't been bad. The roads were good; the weather was supposed to be clear for almost a week. The following week, so said the weathermen, we were due for big snow. Also, Mark would be off to New York, so if I did it at all, it would have to be now. This weekend, so I'd be there Monday.

No point in waiting around, making myself and everyone else even edgier. I left a note explaining matters to Mark and Eugenia, packed an overnight bag plus all the impedimenta that goes with travelling with pets, loaded up the animals and headed south.

The first part of the drive was just as it had been the week before, boring. I zoomed along, thinking of nothing much, three hours vanishing along with the yellow stripe in the road, until the blue Spanish Peaks made twin indentations against the southern sky, tops lined with snow. When Grace and I had come down last, we had turned west, through Walsenburg, across La Veta Pass, and down through San Luis and Questa. The other route led through Trinidad and the Raton Pass. I decided to go through Trinidad this time. I wanted to see Gabe Leone's home ground.

Walsenburg went by on the right, endless lines of coal cars parked on a siding below the highway, small homes gathered along the bluff, every washline full of flapping laundry. Atuomatic dryers had not yet come to Walsenburg, might never come to Walsenburg, falling behind me among the grey hills. Abruptly, as I approached Trinidad, the vistas were no longer Great Plains but south-western, the skyline broken in crenellated buttes and sheer-edged mesas above the town.

I stopped for dog and cat exercise, a drink of water for them, coffee for me. Acceptable coffee. The man next to me at the counter wore a sheriff's star on a chest that sloped down to a vast comfortable belly. I asked him if he knew where the Snowy Peaks Roofing company was, and he gave me directions.

'Guy that ran it wrecked himself up in Denver last week,' he said. 'Now he's wanted for something or other. Musta been drunk. Never knew Gabe to drive crazy before.'

'You know him?' I asked, a little surprised.

'Hell,' he said, 'I know ever-body. All the natives. All the refugees . . .'

He laughed. 'That's the story. This here's the hidey-hole for the Cosa Nostra. This is where they send their guys who're in trouble. Didn't you never hear that?'

I shook my head, no, I hadn't heard that.

'Sure. This is the Mafioso Rest Camp. Also the Sex Change Capital of the US.'

'You're kidding.'

'Nah,' said the counter man, shifting his gum from one side of his mouth to the other. 'He's not kidding. This really is. We got a doctor here does more sex change operations than anybody else in the whole country.'

They were still chuckling about that when I left. I wasn't sure whether these were local fables, used to astonish the tourists, or the truth, though later a journalist friend advised me neither story was fictional.

The Snowy Peaks Roofing Company squatted at the edge of town, a flat-roofed, cinder-block building with a long shed out back and assorted tat-encrusted wheeled machines dotted on the gravelled, weed-infested lot. The shed was stacked with bundles of asphalt shingles and wood shakes and fat black rolls of roofing paper. I parked and stared. Antonio Gabrielli Leone's home base. I'd looked him up in the phone book, finding him among a number of other Leones. There were many Italian names in the book. Maybe that's where the Mafioso story had started. I tried to think up some good reason for going in and asking questions, but I couldn't come up with one. Besides, it was Saturday afternoon. They were probably closed.

South of Trinidad, pinons grew along the tumbling creek as we went up the canyon towards the pass, past beaver

dams with ice frilling the banks, among winter-dark ponderosa pines, over the top and down into New Mexico, into
Raton, marked on its northern edge by one of those dreadful
farms that always make me cringe: stained and rotted
sheds, churned and trodden ground, with truck and auto-
mobile tyres lying everywhere among derelict machinery
and nothing which was or would ever be green.

I'd forgotten to get gas in Trinidad, so we stopped to fill
the tank in Raton before driving the long flat stretch south
to Cimarron. Then the good part of the trip began, Cimarron Canyon, where the road slaloms upward through forests
and along the tumbling stream, coming out at last at the
totally unexpected lake at Eagle Nest, around it and past
it and up once more, along the rock-cut road past Angel
Fire, and then down, through spruce forests, past little
houses lining the Taos Creek, and on to the flat where giant
Rio Grande Cottonwoods reach over the road with long,
winter-grey arms and twiggy fingers. Suddenly there were
adobes everywhere along the road, bed-and-breakfasts, art
galleries, historic thises and thats.

Another hour brought me to Los Vientos once more,
where the caretaker told me the guest house was mine if I
wanted it. Monday morning, as soon as office hours started,
I'd find out whether Cecily Stephens was present at
Habitacion.

Meantime, in the rounded adobe fireplace I made a tiny
teepee-shaped fire, the way Mike had taught me, shared
the hamburger I'd bought in Espanola with Bela and
Schnitz, had a few bottles of Negra Modelo beer, and looked
at the stars.

Mike had pets of his own, and he'd built a dog and cat run
to use when he was away for brief times. After the three of
us had a long morning walk down a dry river-bottom, I left
Bela and Schnitz sleeping in the run and spent Sunday
afternoon visiting art galleries in Santa Fe and having a
late lunch at my favourite restaurant, Casa Sena. They
have a prime rib burrito that has to be tasted to be believed.

I got back to the animals well before dark. We had another long walk before their supper, then yet another night of stars and quiet so deep I found myself holding my breath, just to listen.

Monday morning, I took the used linens up to the laundry-room off the main house and got them washed and into the drier, then called the number for *Habitacion*. The receptionist said Cecily Stephens was in but unavailable. I did not leave a message. Instead, I put the animals into the run, got into the car, checked the location of *Habitacion* on the map of Santa Fe I'd picked up the day before, and drove directly there.

Everything in Santa Fe is either real adobe or fake adobe, so it was no surprise to find *Habitacion* located in a purpose-fully massed mud house surrounded by plantings of native, dry-land flora. Mike Wilson has lectured me on the sculptural qualities of real adobe, enough that I can appreciate the nuances. The building before me was gently curved and surfaced, made of honest mud with a weather-resistant coating. It was not the cheap imitation: square-edged cinder-block covered with stucco. Beside the main building, a row of smaller structures stood shoulder to shoulder, complete with explanatory signs. These were examples of mud houses as they were built in North Africa, in Iran, in Arabia. Mud might be used anywhere, I assumed, where the rainfall was low. One of the exhibits included a ram device for making hard rammed floor and roof tiles of sieved earth and cement.

I took it all in as I walked past, not dallying but not hurrying. I wanted some idea of what Cecily did, hoping it might give me some idea of how to approach her. The exhibits didn't give me a clue. All I could do was present myself, provoke her into saying something or other, and then be hard to discourage.

She was in a meeting. I said I'd wait. The person behind the desk announced with a fine air of self-importance that the meeting would go on all morning.

'That's all right,' I said. 'Twice in the past several weeks

I have narrowly missed being killed by a man with a gun. I am reliably informed that Cecily Stephens can help me identify who that man is. At least, waiting here, I'm relatively safe, so I'll wait if you don't mind.' I gave her my card.

She stared at it nervously for a few minutes, then got up and edged out of the room, trying to do it casually but missing sang-froid by a mile. She was so nervous her eyelids were twitching.

A considerable time passed. If I had been she, or Cecily, I would have called the number on the card to find out who this maniac in the waiting-room might be. I assumed they were doing that. Though maybe they were calling the police, which could cause complications.

Presumably they stopped short of the police. A short, stocky woman came striding into the area where I sat, thrust my card in my face, and said, 'Why are you threatening my secretary?'

'I beg your pardon?' I asked in my most offended tone. 'I have done no such thing!'

'She seems to think somebody's coming in here with a gun.'

I smiled ingratiatingly, which she seemed not to notice. 'I do hope not. He's shot at me twice recently, but each time I was more or less in the open. He hasn't followed me inside anywhere. Are you Cecily Stephens?'

'I am. And I'd like to know what this is all about.'

'Do you want to discuss it here?' I said it politely, indicating I had no objection to discussing it on Main Street at high noon if she liked.

She snorted and beckoned. I followed her jeans-clad form down a brick-paved hallway to a room much like the one I'd slept in last night. Exposed beams, cedar splits between them, softly textured walls decorated with Indian rugs and baskets. A slanted drawing table stood to one side with a half-finished rendering on it. The waste basket was heaped with crumpled white-paper balls tokening inadequacy or frustration or both.

'Sit,' she said, pointing.

I sat.

'All right, now what is this? And make it fast, I have people waiting.'

'May I go into the history a bit first? Just so you can see the relevance.'

She gestured again, impatiently. I told her about Simonetta's death at the clinic. I mentioned Herby Fixe. When I said his name, she didn't move but her skin colour changed. She didn't quiver, but she turned grey. I went on talking, trying not to stare. It was like watching a chameleon. She changed colour from grey to red to grey again as I talked. I told her about Herby dying. About the attempts on my life.

When I finished, she sat unmoving. After what seemed a very long time, she said, 'You misled me. You know who shot at you. This Leone person shot at you. Simonetta's dead. Herby Fixe is dead. This man who shot at you has no reason to do so again. Correct?'

I nodded, not liking the finality in her voice.

'No one is currently being suspected of a crime they did not commit, correct? The people at the clinic are in the clear?'

I nodded again.

'No one's life is in danger.'

'I'm not sure of that. I don't know that Gabe Leone has given up on me.'

'But, as you yourself say, he no longer has reason to threaten you. It would not be logical for him to do so. Since that's the case, there's no reason for me to tell you anything. I knew some things about Simonetta, yes, but they were personal things, some of them things I would just as soon not have known. I talked about those things once before. I did so out of misplaced compassion, and evidently it only caused trouble.'

I waited, but she didn't specify what trouble. Instead, she squared her shoulders and announced, 'I have no intention of talking any further about Simonetta.'

'Not if my life depended on it?'

'Only if you could convince me of that, and I'd be hard to convince. This Leone person was afraid you'd identify him. Well, he's been identified anyhow. Your girlfriend has seen him. Your neighbour has seen him. His car has been identified, and the weapon that was in it was the weapon he used against you. Now that everyone knows who he is, what motive would he have for killing you?'

Grace had said the same thing. I wished I felt as sure about it as they did. 'Do you know why Simonetta was killed?' I asked her.

'Oh, I could make a guess,' she said. 'I'd guess that she got between Canello Leone and something he decided to do. That's what the note in her pocket meant. She interfered; she's dead. That would have been Canello's way of telling the world to keep out of his way. And Gabe's way. Like father, like son.'

'Why didn't he kill her years ago? Decades ago?'

'Because he didn't know what she'd done until recently.'

'Nello died in the 'sixties,' I said. 'He couldn't have known recently.'

'His family,' she said, making an inclusive gesture to show that the exact "who" was irrelevant. 'I said, like father, like son. It wouldn't have mattered which of them found out. Geronimo or Canello or Gabrielli—any of them.'

'After thirty-five, forty years!' I didn't believe her.

'After generations.' She sighed. 'Mr Lynx, I spend a great deal of time in Latin American countries. In Brazil, for example. In that country, if a man kills his wife or his sister for some reason of family honour—because she has taken a lover, or because he thinks she has, or because someone merely has accused her of it—no court will convict him even if the woman was innocent. I vividly recall one case that received a lot of attention in the newspapers. A woman refused to marry a man and chose his rival instead. The man shot his rival. He wasn't convicted because he'd killed in the heat of passion; his honour had been bruised. The woman entered a convent. Twenty years later, she left the convent and he murdered her. He was tried and set free. He could only let her live in a state of perpetual chastity, you see. Otherwise, his honour was still offended. If he'd died in the meantime and his brother or son or nephew had killed her, no court would have convicted any of them. The law doesn't punish matters of family honour.'

'Leone was Italian, not Brazilian.'

'It's the attitude I'm talking about, Mr Lynx, not the nationality. It's an attitude that goes with tribalism. Every tribe has a more compelling history, has suffered greater wrongs, and has a purer honour than any other tribe. They rejoice in long memories. My God, the Irish are still fighting battles hundreds of years old and the Shiites still have enemies they made over a millennium ago! You think a few decades is enough to wash out a debt of honour?'

'The thing a great many untravelled Americans forget is that our country is not the paradigm of the world! We've exported a number of mercantile superficialities, enough to make us think that people who eat McDonald's hamburgers and drink Coke and watch our sit-coms must be like us. Most are not like us at all. What you tell me about Octavio's oath would be perfectly understandable and acceptable in many countries. Uniting two families by marriage would be considered much more important than the wishes of the woman involved.'

'You say Octavio's point of view isn't unusual. All right. He was first generation Spanish, maybe I can buy that. But what about Nello? Why would he agree to the marriage?'

'Who would a proud Catholic father have wanted as a bride for his son? He would have wanted a virgin Catholic girl from a good family. If she could be pretty and healthy, so much the better. The Leone family had a bad reputation. Getting a girl like that might not have been easy. And what was Angela? Someone who fitted that description exactly. A girl not only from a good family but from an aristocratic one. And pretty.'

'She wasn't Italian,' I objected.

'Well, Nello's father was actually Sicilian, I believe, a

people who are no less obsessed by the notion of honour than Latin Americans are. Nello's mother was Venezuelan. The Mediterranean-Indian mix makes fertile ground for notions of honour. Self-esteem is very vulnerable. Threats against it are serious matters.' She stood up, unmistakably telling me our interview was at an end.

'You'll tell me that much, but no more?'

'Oh, I can talk to you all day about cultural differences. That's my field, after all. But I won't talk about Simonetta. She isn't my secret to share.'

'You shared it once.'

'With someone I thought had a right to it. With someone I thought was trying to help her.'

I cast about for anything I could ask her, any scrap of information I could get. 'How do you know so much about the Leone family? I can't imagine Simonetta knowing all those details of who came from where.'

She shook her head at me. 'I took the trouble to find out. Years ago. I needed to make sense of things Simonetta had told me. In those days I thought if one only knew the facts, it was easy to do the right thing. As I grew older, I found the more one knows, the harder it gets.'

'You found these things out before you moved to California?'

She turned grey again. 'Yes. I asked questions. I looked things up. I was young and innocent-looking, people talked to me. I put together some information. A few facts I've found out only recently. Such as the significance of Nello Leone's mother having come from an area near Lake Maracaibo. The people in the surrounding villages have the highest incidence of Huntington's disease known anywhere in the world. I found that out quite by accident in a hotel room in Atlanta, watching television.'

'I know nothing about the disease,' I said. 'Except that it strikes in adulthood and is invariably fatal.'

'Some live a long time with it. Some not long. Those who die quickly are, I think, the lucky ones. Nello lived quite a long time, as did Nimo, but Nello's mother died when she was only thirty-two.'

I sighed. Cecily knew what I wanted to know. She wouldn't tell me. All the principal actors seemed to be dead —except for Olivia.

'Let me take one more minute to tell you about Olivia,' I said. I proceeded to do so, briefly but with some detail about her age and the tragedy of her life.

For the first time, Cecily seemed to be concerned. 'I . . . No, I won't. The woman's daughter is dead. Don't you understand? I will not tell you what Simonetta told me! It could cause trouble and nobody you've spoken of really needs to know! This Olivia is eighty years old, her daughter's been dead for years, she hasn't seen her grandson since he was an infant . . .'

'I didn't say anything about her grandson.'

She stopped. Started to say something. Stopped. Started again. 'Simonetta, of course, was very fond of the little boy, so I knew of his existence.'

'How did you know Olivia hadn't seen him in years?'

'No comment. That's it, Mr Lynx. Go back to Denver. I'm sure you've many important things to do there. If you come back here, I'll run you off.' She was angry, angrier at herself than at me. She had said something she hadn't meant to.

I left. I sat in the car for a long time, adding and subtracting what she had said from what she hadn't said, coming up with only two new threads to add to the fabric of what I knew.

First: Simonetta's killing had been a matter of honour. Simonetta had interfered with something Nello Leone had wanted to do. Call it The Act. Simonetta interfered with The Act, but Nello didn't know that at the time. Which means either he thought he had accomplished The Act or he knew he had not but did not know why.

Second: years later some member of Nello's family— probably his son Gabe who was unaffected by the heriditary disease—found out The Act had not been accomplished because Simonetta had interfered. No matter that his father was dead, no matter that decades had passed, the family honour was still at stake, so Gabe killed Simonetta for interfering. Then, thinking I'd seen him, he tried to kill me.

I wondered if The Act had ever been accomplished? Had the matter of honour been taken care of?

Possibly not, else why Cecily's insistence upon silence? Though, as I had to admit to myself, it might be only that the incidents in question had been embarrassing for her personally and she didn't want to disclose them.

What had the matter of honour been? Cecily had mentioned adultery. Had Angela committed adultery? Had someone simply accused her of it? Cecily had also mentioned that rejecting a man might become a matter of honour. Angela could have married Nimo, gotten pregnant, then rejected relations with him subsequent to the child's birth. What did Simonetta have to do with things like that?

Nothing worked. Even the idea that Simonetta had somehow interfered with the cover-up of Angela's dishonourable suicide had holes in it. Everyone knew at the time that Simonetta had talked about it. She'd gone up and down the street proclaiming suicide to all and sundry!

In a mood of continued frustration and annoyance, I started the car and drove back to the Los Vientos guest house to remake the beds and put the clean dishes away. My deal with Mike was I could stay anytime, provided I left the place clean enough for the next guest. The animals and I were back in Denver by eight o'clock Monday night, March 10th, windy but not cold. Bela wandered around the yard, reinforcing his territorial smells. Schnitz did a shred job on his climbing pole. There were a few messages on my desk. Nothing that wouldn't wait until morning except one call from Grace. When she sleepily answered the phone, I asked her if I could come cry on her shoulder, and she said I'd have to cry tomorrow; she had to be at work at six in the morning.

All in all, I did not feel terribly clever or efficient or even sensible. I was almost convinced this particular puzzle had run its course and I had unravelled all available threads.

CHAPTER 6

Over coffee the next morning I reminded myself that some secrets remain secrets forever. Dead men tell no tales is an old saw, no less true for being old. There's no key to unlock the feelings and beliefs of people who are gone. Unless a man keeps a detailed journal, outlining his day to day, minute-by-minute emotional responses, his life-scape vanishes when he does. Even if such a journal were kept, there might be no one to read it.

Simonetta's journal, if she had one at all, had been in her housekeeping, in the obsessive performance of little rituals, the routine observances, ingrained habits, learned duties, each accomplished day by day, adding up to nothing at all. Dorotea didn't want to think about her. Cecily didn't want to talk about her. Even Sister John Lorraine had confessed to doubt about the purpose of a life like Simonetta's. There seemed to be little reason for remembering her now.

I told myself the time had come to put her aside. Her end was like her life: beyond my understanding. All puzzles begin with fascination, progress through intrigue to resolution—or, go on to unrequited obsession, and at that point one is wise to stop. So I have told myself before and so I told myself now. Puzzle addiction is not unlike other addictions. One either quits chasing drink or drugs or gambling or women (or answers), or one sickens in the chase.

I told myself to forget the matter, though Grace continued resolute. By now she had every member of the Leone family pinned to her collection board and was busy calling my attention to this one and that one while burbling happily that Gabe was the last, really the last, of the Nello Leone line. There were distant cousins, but there were no dangerous Leones left, no one to take up the banner of whatever 'honourable' crusade it had been. When we caught Gabe, she believed the matter would be ended. I was still curious enough to hope he would tell us then what it had all been about.

Sister John Lorraine called me and asked if everything was all right. I told her yes, the matter had resolved itself, the innocent were no longer suspected, all was well. She sounded a little miffed.

'Did you ever figure out what it was Simonetta did that got her killed?'

Here was Simonetta again! I gritted my teeth and said, 'Sister, I think Simonetta upset people just by being herself.'

Sister said that was cool. 'That's what the kids here at school say when they understand something,' she explained. 'That's cool.' She didn't sound cool. She sounded baffled and frustrated, which was how I felt, but I let it pass. Simonetta had interfered, she was dead. Now, as at the beginning, that seemed to be all we were destined to know.

So why this hulking, suppliant shadow lurking at the edges of my mind? I heaved it aside, resolving once more to forget it.

A foul-up on delivery of carpeting for the Law Firm Job helped me think of something else almost equally irritating. The mistake involved the supplier, the shipper, and the local distributor who had placed the order. It took two days and considerable annoyance to get fixed, because everyone involved was interested in covering his ass rather than helping us fix it. Grace wasn't around to remind me of the case because she was working an odd shift which left her too sleepy to be social. 'I'm filling in for three weeks,' she said, yawning widely over the phone. 'Then I'm back days.' I marked the calendar and tried to live in anticipation.

Mark left for New York with Bryan. Without him to answer the phone, things seemed busier even though not much more actually happened. The Bonifaces came in to talk about their farmhouse, gave me some money on account and asked me to work out a plan for them. I tried to get excited about their project and failed. I kept thinking of Simonetta and getting angry at myself for doing so.

Late Friday afternoon I answered the phone with a barely civil 'Jason Lynx,' and heard Dorotea Chapman's studiedly cultivated tones asking whether I would be in the office for an hour or so. I said yes, I'd be there all evening in fact. She said she'd be over and hung up, leaving me wondering, reluctantly, what the hell she had come up with. Having set the matter aside with some effort, I really didn't want to get sucked back into it again.

She arrived about six, after we'd closed, and I escorted her up to my living-room where I'd been having a drink before supper. She surprised me by picking Schnitz up bodily, sitting down with him in her lap and reducing him to delighted rumbles by scratching his belly fur.

'I do love cats,' she said. 'I always had cats as a girl. I can't have them now because Andrew is allergic. And then, too, the house is rather formal for pets.' She made a *moue*. 'So Andrew says.'

I gave her the wine she'd asked for.

'I saw my mother today,' she said, after a sip. 'Mama had a very good day, so I asked her about Simonetta. Frankly, Mr Lynx, I thought you were being rather stupidly obsessive about Simonetta, but it seems you were right. The poor girl had done something silly. Mother never told anyone, not until now, but you see, it can't hurt Simmy now.'

'What was it?' I asked, not expecting, or perhaps just not wanting much in the way of revelations. I was tired, and I'd been trying hard not to think about it.

'Well, remember I told you about Simmy taking care of the Leone child. Did I mention about the child being born with a birthmark? I'm not sure I'd remembered that before. Evidently Nimo Leone told his associates and family there was a curse on the child because of that. It seems it was all common gossip. Mama remembered hearing about it at the time.'

I told her I'd heard all about that, yes.

'What Mama told me today was that after Nimo's wife died, Nimo threatened to kill the child, or Simmy thought he did, so she took him to protect him from his father.'

'Took him?'

'The child. Simonetta kidnapped him.'

'Kidnapped him?' Whatever I'd expected, it hadn't been that. 'How? When?'

'You'll have to forgive this being rather fuzzy, Jason—you don't mind if I call you Jason? If we're going to share all these family secrets, we might as well be on the first name basis . . . You have to remember that all this happened almost forty years ago, and Simmy was never what one would call a reliable witness, even for things that happened ten minutes ago. When Mama's memory is good, it's very good, but she can only remember what Simmy told her. Simmy always called the child "the baby", even though she'd been taking care of him for several years. At any rate, Simmy told Mama she took the baby—that's a quote—from its nursery the day the mother died. She hid "the baby", and some time later she panicked and told a friend of hers from school what she'd done. That friend took the child. Either Simmy talked her into it, or, more likely the friend offered, just to get it away from Simmy . . .'

'Then, out of a clear blue sky, the friend left town.'

'Cecily!' I cried.

Dorotea wrinkled her forehead, then tried the name on her lips, silently nodding. 'It may have been. I remember a Cecily, sort of vaguely. If she was Simmy's age, she'd have been a lot older than I. Mother didn't mention that name today. Maybe Simmy never told her who it was. However, both Mama and I remember two hysterical episodes, the first one when Nimo's wife died, and another one a few weeks later.'

'Cecily left town a few weeks later.'

'She did? Well, at the time, no one could figure out why Simmy was so upset. If this friend left town, however, maybe she took the child with her and Simmy didn't know where it was. The friend didn't tell her, probably for good reason.'

'Your mother wasn't told this at the time it happened?'

'Heavens, no. She only found out about it a few years ago. And she's never said a word about it to me until today.'

'Could Cecily have given the child back to its father? Nimo said his son had been sent to Italy, to relatives.'

'That's entirely possible, even probable, but Mama said nothing about that. The only reason Mama came to know about this at all is that Herby Fixe tried to blackmail Papa about it.'

She watched my face, letting this information sink in before she continued. 'Remember, I told you Herby used to work for Nello Leone. Well, about twelve or thirteen years ago he came to Papa and said he knew Simonetta had stolen this child, that there was no statute of limitations on kidnapping, that he'd get her arrested for kidnapping unless Papa paid him to keep quiet.' She set her wine glass down and half smiled. 'It was a stupid thing for him to do, but Herby wasn't really intelligent. Clever, sly, like a rat, but not intelligent.

'I'll quote what Mama said: "*Herby should have had better sense than to mess with your papa.*"'

'I take it Papa didn't pay?'

'He not only didn't pay, he made Herby marry Simonetta at once so he couldn't ever be forced to testify against her. He also mentioned that Simonetta's brothers would break every bone in his body if he ever spoke of it again.' She laughed shortly. 'Papa didn't mean my lawyer brother or my professor brother, needless to say. He meant my Denver brothers, who were fully capable of doing exactly that.'

'I thought your father said the marriage had to do with Herby seducing your sister?'

'That's what he told Mama and me at the time. That was like Papa. I think he didn't want Mama to know Simmy had done something illegal. Being seduced isn't illegal, it's just immoral. Mama could always handle immorality. She had the church to help her with that. She could trust in

God's forgiveness, but not the law's. Not long before Papa died, though, he told Mama the truth. He told her she needed to know, so she could protect Simmy. And once Mama knew about it, she asked Simmy about it.'

'So your mother has known about this for a while?'

'Since Papa died. Evidently, Mama talked to Simmy about it every now and then. Mama didn't turn a hair when I asked about it today, just came out and told me. She said Simmy was safe with God now, so it didn't matter if I knew.'

I tried to assemble the information in a form that made sense. 'Nimo thought the child was cursed, Simonetta interpreted that as a threat . . .'

'Or she may have heard Nimo actually threaten the child. Not that it necessarily meant anything.'

'Right. She heard an actual or implied threat. So she kidnapped the child and gave it to Cecily.' Despite what Cecily had said about other cultures, the whole thing still sounded unlikely. Children being threatened because of birthmarks! We were talking about the 1950s, after all. And why hadn't Cecily told me this? She'd told someone. Someone who had, so she said, a right to know.

'You never met Herby, did you?' asked Dorotea, interrupting my train of thought.

I shook my head.

'He was a nasty piece of work. Ingratiating in a terribly slick way that made you feel you'd crawled through something slimy. He flattered people, sucked up to them, all the time looking for something he could use. Looking at him, you wouldn't think he could be violent, but he was bad. He ran errands for Nello from the time he was a kid.'

'Errands?'

'You know. You've seen the movies. He threatened people and beat them up. Maybe he even murdered a few, I don't know. My brothers used to bring him around, and he always made me feel dirty.'

'I take it Herby never really lived with Simonetta. I saw

their house. One man's jacket in the closet, I think. Nothing else to show he ever lived there.'

'No, thank God. He didn't. Papa put Simmy on an allowance and bought her the house when she was married. Herby may have dropped by once in a while, to use the phone or pick up mail. When Simonetta died, the house went to Mama. As a matter of fact, after Simmy died, Mama asked me to have it cleaned out so one of my brothers can use it.'

'One of your . . . ?'

'One of my Denver brothers, yes. Even jailbirds get old eventually.' She sighed. 'It's my brother Carlos, another one of Nello Leone's former employees. I saw him the other day at the nursing home when he came to visit Mama. I remember him as a big, burly, threatening man, but now he's just a sad old person who doesn't see very well.'

'That surprised you?'

'Well, I thought he and my brother Joe were devils when I was a young woman struggling to get away from all that. Them and the uncles.' She gestured helplessly.

'You were afraid they were somehow going to drag you back, drag you down?'

'Exactly. You're very perceptive.'

It wasn't perception. It was what I'd gone through myself at age thirteen or fourteen with Jacob offering respectability and dignity and all that dull stuff while some of the kids I'd grown up with were offering inducements of quite another kind. Not only the kids. Some of them had by that time acquired older acquaintances, mentors, men who would have been only too glad to include me. I remembered juvenile nightmares in which I'd been caught with those men, caught doing something shameful—not necessarily something sexual, though there had been some of that going on, just something I didn't want people to know about. My childhood friend Jerry Riggles had succumbed to that kind of life. Last I'd heard, he was back in prison for the third or fourth time. Burglary or fencing. It had been Jerry who'd dared me to steal from Jacob in the first place.

I smiled grimly at Dorotea, and she gave me a similar smile. I realized the truth of what Jacob had said. Knowing who you had been wasn't always a help in becoming who you would be.

I told her I appreciated her telling me the story.

'It was the only thing I could do. After being so reluctant and annoyed the other day. One tries to put it all behind me, but . . .'

'I know,' I said.

'They're still family,' she said unwillingly. 'I tell myself if I could lop certain ones off from Mama and just keep her, I'd do it, but she'd never allow that. If I take Mama, I take them all, the whole family, willy-nilly.'

'I'm going to tell Grace Willis about this. Even though I don't think what you've told me is pertinent to anything she's doing, I can't guarantee she won't want to ask you some questions.' If I knew Grace, she would.

'It's all right. Mother said it for all of us. Simmy's beyond hurt. Nothing we can say will injure her now.'

While she was talking, I'd had an idea.

'Your brother's living at Simmy's old house?'

'Yes. The Salvation Army emptied it, all but the furniture, and I had a cleaning firm go through it. Carlos is there now. I refuse to ask Mama, but I'm pretty sure she's supporting him. Sending him a little cheque every week or so. You don't earn social security in jail.'

She finished her wine, gave Schnitz a last pummelling, and left me. She was right about the social security. I wondered if the cheques Mama sent Carlos stretched to beer.

On the theory the cheques didn't stretch that far, I picked up a sixpack on the way to Zuni Street, along with a couple of double hamburgers and some fries.

The place looked the same except that a few lights were on and the porch held some empty cartons. When Carlos opened the door, I smelled something burning. It wasn't an improvement over the previous smell. Dorotea had been right about him. He was an old man with squinty eyes, a contemporary of Nimo's and Herby's, a grey sexagenarian.

He peered at me near-sightedly.

'Carlos Leone?' I asked.

'Yeah.'

'I'm a friend of your sister's. She thought maybe you could help me with some information. I brought along some beer and burgers, just in case you hadn't had dinner yet.'

He stepped back uncertainly, motioning me inside.

'My sister?'

'Dorotea.'

'Oh, Dor'ty. I thought you meant Simmy. Yeah. I seen Dor'ty the other day.'

'She said she'd seen you. Visiting your mother.'

'Mama, yeah.'

We stood confronting one another in the living-room while he tried to see me. I lifted the beer in front of his face, so he couldn't miss it.

'Yeah,' he said again. 'Come on in.'

He led me through to the kitchen. The pan holding whatever had burned was now in the sink. A small fan whirred, trying to clear the air. He fell into a chair at the soiled kitchen table. The house might have been cleaned before he moved in, but Carlos was busily conforming it to his lifestyle. I passed him a hamburger and package of fries, opened a beer and added that to the array. Hungrily, he went for the fries first.

'Ya got'ny ketchup?'

I found the packets of ketchup in the bottom of the sack. There had been a drawer full of such packets when I'd been here last. The Salvation Army had probably taken it, along with the rolled stockings and the paper bags. Carlos wasn't going to invite me to sit down, so I sat without invitation.

'Whudja wanna know?' he asked, around a mouthful.

'You remember Nimo's wife?' I asked him. 'Angela Leone?'

'Sure. Ya don't forget stuff like that.' He made a lewdly descriptive gesture, but there was no lust behind it. It was a meaningless, habitual response to the mention of woman.

'She had a child,' I said.

'Right. Kid 'uz born 'uth this big red blotch on him. Nimo had a fit. Kid got to look better later on, but Nimo never liked him much. Not like a son, you know.'

'Do you remember when Angela died?'

'Remember when Herby Fixe did her? Yeah.'

I guess my mouth dropped open. He laughed between ill-fitting dentures which clacked and slipped as he chewed.

'Ya didn't know that? Hell, everbody knew that. Nimo told Herby to kill her an' the kid.'

'Why?' I gasped.

He chewed reflectively. 'I used ta think it was maybe 'cause of that blotch the kid had on him. But ya know, I think it was Nimo had that sickness. Went kind of crazy.'

'Not then, did he? I thought he didn't get the disease until later, a lot later.' Besides, did Huntington's disease cause that kind of madness?

Carlos was still thinking about it. 'I figure maybe he was already a little crazy. Didn' make sense to kill the kid over that mark on him. He was a good-lookin' kid 'ceptin' for that. Talk your ear off, too.'

'And why kill Angela?'

'Thass what I mean. Like, it was crazy, ya know. But Nimo said kill her, so thass what Herby did. Made it look real good, lika accident. He told me about it. How he fixed the old gaspipe so gas'd go through there again. How he turned it on when she was asleep up there.'

'What happened to the child.'

'Little boy? Herb said he killed him.'

'Killed him!'

'Said he did. Nimo paid him for doin' it. I always figured he did, but Simmy said he didn'. Simmy said she took the kid.'

I no longer had any appetite for food. I put the half-eaten burger down on the table and breathed deeply.

'When did Sammy tell you this?'

'I dunno. After Herby died, I guess. I usta come around, get somethin' to eat. Simmy, she'd talk yur ear off. She usta talk to Mama, but when Mama went in that home, Simmy, she didn' have nobody to talk to.'

'Did you tell anyone what she said?'

'Well, prob'ly. You know. Guys I usta know. Guys that worked for Nimo. Herby was dead, so it didn' matter. Lissen, when Nimo said do somethin', ya did it. If Herby didn' do what Nimo said, he'd've been in deep shit, I tell ya that.'

I stayed a little longer, but Carlos had nothing else to tell me. When I left, I was thinking of Dorotea Chapman growing up with brothers like these. When Carlos had told me about the murder, he hadn't even stopped chewing.

All along, ever since I'd talked to Sister John and to Dorotea that first time, I'd been thinking of Simonetta as a little crazy. Not it seemed, whatever she might have been, she had not been crazy. There really had been a threat to the child, and she really had stolen the child to protect him.

Like it or not, Cecily Stephens had to tell me what she knew! She was the key to this whole mess!

I called her home in Santa Fe. Nobody there but the damned machine. I did not discuss the matter with the machine. Saturday morning, I called again, both home and business. Business was closed, said its machine, until Monday. The Stephens were away, said their machine, until Monday. I roamed the house like a caged bear, up and down stairs. Bela whined at me. Schnitz fluffed his tail and raised his back, hissing. Both were saying the same thing. You're a stranger. Where's our two-legs? What have you done with our two-legs?

I gave up and went to a movie at an art cinema, some festival offering an Oriental film I couldn't remember ten minutes after it was over. Perhaps because I'd been too distracted to read the subtitles. Chinese histrionics don't soak in subliminally. Or had it been Thai?

At least one visual scene had penetrated my fog. A notable banquet depicted in loving detail midway through the film had started my stomach making demanding noises. I was on South Colorado Boulevard, only a dozen blocks from a good oriental restaurant where I ordered warm saki plus dumplings with spicy peanut sauce and something monosyllabic with lobster in it. When I came out into the parking lot with my leftovers in a little plastic box, it had started to snow. By the time I got home, I skidded into the garage on the coat-tails of a full-fledged spring blizzard. March is the snowiest month in Denver. It looked like we'd be under a couple of feet of the stuff by Sunday morning.

I let Bela out, and he jumped around in the snowfall for a few minutes just for the novelty of it, then came in shivering. I red him and Schnitz before turning on the gas log in the fireplace. Wood fires are largely *verboten* in Denver because of our pollution, so I lit a stick of pinon incense and tried to imagine I was back in New Mexico with Grace. I called Grace. She was out, said her machine.

The whole world was out except the machines. I decided to give up. The night was fit for nothing but sleeping anyhow. Bela and Schnitz seemed to agree. As soon as I turned off the light they both jumped up on the bed and curled against me, as though to make sure I did not sneak away in the darkness.

For a wonder, somebody had traded a day with Grace, and she had Sunday off. She called me at ten and arrived about noon. We raided both the refrigerator and the freezer, and I fixed an enormous brunch, with eggs and sausages and Canadian bacon and hollandaise. Grace ate her way through a pound of bratwurst while I told her about Dorotea and Carlos.

'It's now obvious how Gabe found out about Simonetta. Carlos told him, or told some third party who told him,' I said.

'OK, I can accept the Leones were maybe sort of super-stitious, but do you really think anyone would kill a child because of a birthmark?' she asked me around a mouthful of eggs Benedict. I am very proud of my eggs Benedict, and of my eggs Florentine, and of my cooking in general. I wish

Grace would occasionally pause in her ingestion of it to tell me it tastes good.

We talked about motivation. We agreed that the birth-mark theory was not believable, the suicide theory had serious holes in it, and the disease theory was only marginally acceptable.

'I figure Cecily knows the real reasons for all this,' I said.

'Are you going to go after her? You know, I could maybe make it a police matter, and that way you'd have some clout.'

'Police matter?'

'Well, knowing about the baby maybe goes to the actual motivation for Simonetta's murder.'

'With Gabe identified as the killer, does Lieutenant Linder need to know what the motivation was?'

She shrugged in her turn. 'I wouldn't say he really cares, no. Even the D.A. wouldn't care why provided he could prove Gabe did it. When we catch him . . .'

'If you catch him.'

'He'll turn up, sooner or later. You know, I could at least call Cecily and ask her if she minds answering some questions.'

'You couldn't force her to come here, could you?'

'Not unless we arrested her for something, then she'd have to be extradited. Of course, if this case goes on developing this way, the D.A. might want to depose her, or subpœna her, but that'll be a long time from now.' She chewed thoughtfully. 'We could always go down there again. But you said she travels a lot. If she flies in and out of Albuquerque, she probably connects either through Dallas or Denver. She might be coming through here some-time soon anyhow. Sometimes people will cooperate just because the police ask them to, if it isn't too much trouble.'

I'd met Cecily and I considered it unlikely. Still, nothing ventured, nothing gained. Grace promised she'd call *Habitacion* on Monday.

We spent the rest of the day in a clutter of Sunday papers and sequential snacks and several bottles of wine and tangled bedclothes, trying to forget there would be a Monday. Along towards evening, Grace put her head on my shoulder, stared at the ceiling, and asked what I'd decided about keeping the shop or giving it up. It took me a minute to recollect what she was talking about. I'd gotten so involved in Olivia's life, I'd forgotten that great decisions pended in my own.

'Don't put the decision off forever,' she said.

I promised her I wouldn't, wondering why she was pushing me. Maybe she wanted me gone. No. She'd have said so if that was it. Maybe she couldn't get on with her life until I got on with mine. That was more likely.

Mark was back Monday morning. A spring blizzard in New York the day of one of the auctions had kept people away in droves. Mark had bid, quite successfully, for several goodies we'd wanted, and he was full of himself over it. The things were being shipped, but by the time he was through describing, neither Eugenia nor I needed to see the actual pieces. We could have recognized them from half a mile away.

Grace called to say Cecily had been surprised by her call, infuriated at what Grace had told her about Dorotea's and Carlos's stories, and was now amenable to disclosure. 'I told her we'd been told Simonetta had taken the child, and that she, Cecily, was probably involved. And I told her part of what Carlos told you, about Herby probably killing the mother, and I said maybe she'd better straighten us out as to what had really transpired, because we had some unanswered questions regarding Simonetta's death.'

'And she said she'd tell us? I am astonished.'

'Well, technically at least, she's probably guilty of something—aiding and abetting, maybe conspiracy to commit. I think she figures she'd better straighten it out. Anyhow, there's some kind of international conference she's attending in England, and she can connect flights here in Denver, probably on Thursday. She'll let me know when.'

The following day, I dropped in to see Olivia. She looked

a little tired and said she hadn't been sleeping well, that
she'd been dreaming about Angela.

'I wish I really believed in heaven,' she said. 'I don't,
you know. I used to, as a girl. I believed we'd all meet
there, those of us who'd lived good, religious lives and been
scrupulous about the sacraments and worried about our
sins. But the longer I've lived, the more I've thought how
tiring heaven would be. Father Garson tells me I'm just
worn out and going through a little spell of anomie. You
know that word?'

I said I did.

'I don't think it's anomie. I think it's reality. Man has to
be made for something more important than merely getting
to heaven, Jason. Something more worthy than that. I
mean, if we were made only for that, only to spend our
lifetimes picking and prying at our consciences, it hardly
seems worth it, does it?'

I saw her working away at the puzzle of that thought and
wondered if this was why Jacob had loved her. She was so
intent on life, so frequently disappointed and yet so intent.

'What do you think?' She looked to me for help.

The best I could do was to get her off the subject. I talked
to her about getting up a dinner-party at a restaurant with
a couple of friends of mine. (I was thinking of Nellie and
her old friend, Willamae Belling.) I made up an outrageous
tale of love and piracy to do with the cardtable. I set myself
out to be amusing, and when she laughed, I considered it
a job well done. She might be right about the ultimate
purpose of human life, but today wasn't the time to go
fretting over it. It was too close to home.

All of which led me to wonder how much of what we did
in our day to day lives was simply to distract us from certain
thoughts that were uncomfortably close. Age and death,
pain and betrayal, love and all the consequences thereof.
Maybe football, fishing, grand opera and all the fruits of
the worlds' detective story authors are just buoys to keep
us from drowning in our ancient fears.

Cecily intended to stay in Denver Thursday night. Grace

and I were to meet her at the Brown Palace Hotel, in her suite, no less, at six o'clock.

We were there, on time. She'd thoughtfully laid in a tray of drinkables and a bowl of nuts.

I introduced Grace. We got through the small talk and the obligatory chat while drinks were fixed and we all sat down in comfortable chairs at a table by the window.

'I took a suite because I wanted a private place to tell you this,' she said. 'And I don't like talking in hotel bedrooms. Conversations in hotel bedrooms always seem illicit to me. Less than truthful.'

'You have something true and licit to tell us,' I said, trying to jolly her along. Cecily had the air of a woman who doesn't want to say anything, but has decided she must.

She sighed and gritted her teeth, really ground them together, making a gravelly noise. 'First thing I have to tell you is that Herby Fixe got this same information out of me some years ago. I don't remember exactly what year. It was maybe 'seventy-nine or 'eighty.'

'Why did you tell Herby?' I asked her.

'He came to me and told me he was Simonetta's husband. I'd never heard of him before, but he was plausible. He said Simonetta had told him she'd taken this child. He convinced me he had to know what had happened to the child, because she was having a mental breakdown and her doctors needed to know the facts in order to treat her effectively. Anyone who had ever known Simonetta would probably have believed that. She was constantly on the verge of breakdown!'

'And you knew what had really happened?'

'Hell, yes, I knew.'

'So you told Herby.'

'I thought he had a reason to know,' she said angrily.

Grace intervened. 'Well, he did. But it wasn't the reason you thought, Ms Stephens. Suppose you tell us what you told Herby Fixe.'

Cecily stirred the ice in her drink with her finger. I could see the muscle in her jaw jumping.

'I should probably have a lawyer here.'

'You certainly can have a lawyer if you wish,' said Grace, starting to stand up.

'Oh no, no,' Cecily waved her down. 'No. If I'm guilty, I'm guilty, damn it. I've carried this around long enough!' She sighed. 'Let me tell it my way, though, all right? I'd like you to understand what . . . what I was like when this happened.'

I remembered Myra's report on what she'd been like—determined upon holiness. I kept my mouth shut.

'I was young,' she said defensively. 'I thought most of the world's problems were caused by people who refused to do good. I thought doing good was simply a matter of following the rules or following your conscience. I hadn't a clue how unreliable either one of those can be.' She stopped and chewed on a fragment of ice for a while before she could go on.

'I was home from college on spring break. This was in 'fifty-three. Yaggie Costermyer, she was one of the neighbours, had been in parochial school with me, and both of us knew Simmy. I won't say she was in school with us because she wasn't, but we knew who she was and what her problems were. I was very much into being . . . good at the time. Part of that included being *understanding* where Simmy was concerned.'

She went silent again. I squeezed my fists and tried to be patient. Grace gave me a warning look, so I stared out of the window and counted cars passing the traffic light down the street.

'All right, so on this particular afternoon, I was home. Simmy came home in a cab, then went up and down the street having hysterics because her mom was away and their house was locked. When she got to Yaggie, Yaggie suggested she come over and see me. Yaggie was being . . . well, you'd have to know her. She doesn't take anyone very seriously and she was needling me, putting me on the spot.

'So, anyhow, here came Yaggie, leading Simonetta by the hand, with Simonetta blubbering and yelling. I invited

Simmy in, told her she could stay with me until her mom came home. Then, when she calmed down a bit, she told me she'd taken this baby.'

'She had him with her?' I asked, confused.

'No. No. She didn't. She said she had him hidden. Only he was hurt, and she'd given him pills to make him sleep, and she couldn't wake him up. I thought she'd killed some kid, I really honest to God did.'

'What did you do?'

'I told her I'd drive her to wherever the baby was and we'd get him, and if he needed a doctor, we'd take him to the doctor. She practically screamed the house down, yelling that we couldn't take him anyplace, yelling that his father would find out and then he'd kill the baby, yelling that he'd already tried to kill the baby.'

'Did you belive that?' Grace asked.

Cecily got up, moved about restlessly, sat down again. 'You've got to . . . you've got to understand this was almost forty years ago and I was only twenty. I didn't know much. However, I *did* know who she was talking about. She worked for Nello Leone's son. Nello Leone was in the papers all the time. He was a crime boss. He was into gambling and beating up on people. Everyone knew he had people killed, only nobody could prove anything. To a kid like me, brought up the way I was, he was the Devil incarnate. So, yes, I sort of believed it. A kid like me . . . I could believe anything evil about him or his family. I think anybody could have.'

'Why was the baby in danger?' I asked.

'I couldn't really get anything sensible out of Simmy. She said the baby was like Jesus. She said something about how he wouldn't get sick. She said his father hated the birthmark. She said she'd fixed the birthmark, but she was still afraid Nimo would kill him.'

'So what happened?' asked Grace.

'So we got in the car and went over to the Leone place, where Simmy had lived, in through the alley, to the garage. She'd been yelling about a *baby*, and I was expecting a *baby*, but she went into some kind of tool-room in the garage and brought out this little kid! God . . . !'

'He was asleep?'

'Thank God, yes. She'd fixed his birthmark OK. She'd burned it off. Pushed his head down on a stove and burned it off him! The whole back of his head. God!'

I wasn't ready for this. I hadn't had a clue. The world shivered and stood still. A kind of crystalline structure formed itself around the universe, shattering light, making sound reverberate in strange ways. It was as though I had taken a drug and become suspended, outside the earth.

I said something. I must have said something, because she answered.

'She said the birthmark had been on the back of his head, but all I could see was this horrible burn. He wasn't a baby at all, he was at least two and a half, three years old . . .'

Grace looked at me, her eyes very wide. She put her hand over mine, willing me to be still. She needn't have bothered. I couldn't have moved.

'What did you do?' she asked Cecily.

'I took the kid. Of course I took the kid. So far as I was concerned, I was the Good Samaritan! I took him to my place. Nobody was home. My folks were down in Arizona with my Gram, she was in the hospital. I bandaged the little guy's head.'

'You didn't call a doctor,' I said from somewhere distant.

'I couldn't call a doctor! No doctor was going to take this kid without wanting to know who his parents were, how this had happened to him. If I told them, they'd give him back to his father and he'd be killed. I *believed* Simmy when she told me that. I kept him. I got some sulpha ointment the doctor had prescribed when my dad burned his arm, and I put that on it. I used my mother's sleeping pills, quarters of ones, to keep him from screaming. I fed him. I went to the library and found a book on treating burns. I did what it said. All the time with Simmy running in and out of my house day and night, pulling at me, getting hysterical.

'Every day my folks called, wanting to know why I hadn't gone back to school, and I said I'd been sick, nothing serious, just felt too lousy to study. And then one day my mother called and said she and Dad were going to have to move to California right away because Dad had this new job, rush, rush. They said they were coming home just long enough to pack, and I'd probably want to stay at CU to finish the spring semester . . .' Her voice trailed off. She put her head in her hands and left it there.

'What?' prompted Grace.

'My mom was worried I'd take it badly, having to switch universities. Once they moved out of state, they'd be non-residents, and they couldn't afford the non-resident fees. She was really worried about that. I remember I almost got hysterical when she said how worried she was about that. Here she was thanking me for being understanding when all I wanted to do was escape from the mess I was in! I told her I'd already missed too much of the spring semester, and I'd go with them when they went.'

She raised her head. 'This . . . it all comes back. I was in such a panic the whole time. Well . . .

'There was this boy I'd known forever, we were good friends. He was living on his own for a year while his folks were in Canada, so when my folks came back, I got him to keep the little boy for me. Four or five times a day, even while my folks and I were packing and getting ready, I'd go over there to feed the little guy and take care of him. And then the night before we were supposed to leave, I picked him up and took him to the foundling home. I had it all planned. I'd looked it up. I'd even called around to be sure it was a nice place, not like in *Oliver Twist* or anything. I didn't tell Simmy where I was going. I didn't tell Simmy where I left him. I couldn't trust her . . .'

She went off into a gale of weeping, a forty-year-old tragedy being relived.

From somewhere, I heard my own voice. 'Evidently Simmy believed you'd taken the child with you.'

'That's what I wanted her to think. I didn't want her to

know where I'd left him, but, God, I couldn't take him. My family wouldn't have stood still for that, not for a minute . . .'

Things whirled. Grace said, 'Jason, would you like to wait outside? In the car?'

I said yes, but I didn't wait in the car. I went home. Later, Grace arrived, so I guess she figured out where I'd gone.

'Jason,' she said. 'Jason.'

'I'm here,' I said.

'I know it's a shock,' she said. 'But you've wanted to know for ages . . .'

'Yeah,' I said in a blank, careless voice. 'Sure. Not exactly the background one might have hoped, but who cares.'

'Oh, come on, Jason. Jacob always told you that things like this didn't matter. So your dad and grandad were little mafiosi. That's not so bad . . .'

'Not so bad,' I agreed calmly from some distant part of myself, thinking I really meant it because long ago I'd come to terms with the possibility that Ma or Pa might have been a murderer or a traitor or a pimp or drug-dealer or whatever. Jacob had said it didn't matter, so it didn't matter. The thing that *mattered* was the one thing he'd never thought of, and while Grace sat there staring at me, her eyes wide and a little scared, I started to laugh about that little oversight and couldn't stop.

It was a while before I could tell her why I was laughing. Nello had had Huntington's disease. So had Nimo. Which meant there was an even chance I had it too.

Friday, I left a note for Mark telling him I wasn't feeling well and shut myself into my apartment. There's a seldom-used door across the hall outside Mark's office, one Agatha got me to put in when we first moved in, to separate home from shop and give her some privacy. It had been standing open for years. I closed and locked it and the one between my living-room and my office. I took my private phone off the hook. Not many people knew that number, but I didn't want to hear from any of them. I wasn't thinking. It was impossible to think. I wasn't being panicky or scared or fearing death or any of that, I was just in a void, a vacuum, where nothing connected. I lay on the bed, staring at the ceiling, thinking nothing.

I'd been very ill once in my life that I remembered—not counting injuries now and then—and this was like being ill again. My body was disconnected from my mind, occupied by some other force. My mind was on standby power only, the little red light flickered dimly and I didn't care. Bela whined, and I put him out of my bedroom and shut the door. I wanted silence to wrap around me like a cocoon, shutting me away from life and all living things.

Some time later Grace found the doors locked, went around back and came up the elevator, came into my room and hit me in the face with a cold, wet towel. 'Up,' she demanded. She got me into the kitchen, put a mug of coffee in my hand, insisted I drink it, kept poking me and jabbing me and not letting me be still.

'There's a test,' she said. 'I called around and found some information about this thing. There's a test. You can find out if you have it.'

'I don't want to know,' I said.

'Don't be a goddam coward.' Her nose was inches from my own. 'Anything is better than this.'

Anything else meant I'd have to do something. I didn't want to do anything.

Grace wouldn't leave me alone. She fetched Mark, sat him down beside me and told him all about it, so he'd start chivvying me too. 'How many people do we need to get on this?' she asked me. 'You want me to call Olivia? She's your grandma, Jason, you want me to call her? You want me to call Lycia? Angela's sister? She's your aunt. You've got cousins now, Jason. You want me to call them?'

As I recall, I started to cry and couldn't stop. It was Sunday before I remember being part of the world again. Sunday. She must have been working on me for two days.

I was sitting at the kitchen table with Grace, resting a stubbly chin in one hand.

'There's a test?' I asked her.

She patted me and said yes, there was a man at the medical school who knew all about it, and so on and so forth.

'You didn't tell anybody, did you?' I asked.

'Like who?'

'Olivia. Lycia Foret. You didn't . . .'

'No. No, Jason. Jacob didn't tell them, and he probably had reasons. Even though he had to have known.'

'How do you figure that?' I asked dully.

'Come on!' she demanded. 'Wake up!'

I tried to focus.

'Herby tried to blackmail Simmy's papa and got nowhere. He knew it had to be Simmy who'd taken the little boy after Angela was killed, but at the time he kept quiet about it because he didn't want Nimo to know he hadn't done what he said. Like that huntsman in *Snow White*. Yeah, he said, I killed the kid. Sure I killed the kid, here's the kid's heart. Right? He didn't dare make anything of it so long as Nimo was around.

'But, after Nimo was in the hospital, Herby got Simmy to confess. He was sly, she wasn't too bright, so he got it out of her. But, he didn't know where the child was—*where you were*—any more than she did. Simmy told him Cecily took the child, so he traced Cecily. That's how he found out Simmy had burned off the birthmark and Cecily had left you at the Home, right? Now, if he knew that much, how hard would it have been to find out where you went from there? Hmm? Herby could've bribed some employee at the Home. He could've burglarized the records. Whatever he did, he found out. So then Herby puts the bite on Jacob. He says to Jacob, "Either you pay me or I'll tell the Leones that Jason Lynx is really Michael Leone, and when I do, they'll kill him."'

'Jacob knew I was Olivia's grandson?'

'I doubt he knew when he took you in. How would he

have? Olivia didn't know, how could he know? No, that was pure coincidence. But he knew once Herby told him.'

'Jacob didn't tell Olivia.'

'Of course he didn't, for two reasons. One, it would have terrified Olivia; and two, he couldn't take the chance with your life.'

'That was about the time Agatha and I were married,' I mused, awed at everything that had gone on below the surface of the lives around me.

'Whatever,' she said impatiently. 'Jacob believed there was still a threat to your life, and maybe that was true.'

I shook my head. 'Grace, look, we've tried and tried to find a motive here. It's no good. Neither of us really believes that Nimo Leone wanted to kill his son—me—because I had a birthmark! We're arguing backwards. Because he wanted to kill me, we say there must have been a reason. But what was it?'

She nodded agreement. 'Maybe it was about the disease, Jason. Maybe he didn't want you to grow up and have to face this thing. Or, Nimo's superstitious, right? So he has this kid with the birthmark, and then *after that* he finds out his daddy has this disease. So, maybe he decides you've brought a hex on the family. I can imagine his wanting to stop it. Listen, there was a hot book back then about this kid that was born evil. *The Bad Seed*. They made it into a movie later. I've seen it on TV. I mean, it's a superstition some people have, that evil can be born in somebody. Look at that movie, *Omen*, and all those Damien thises and thats.'

I shook my head stubbornly. We were creating motives, making up stories. There was no basis for any of it.

'Never mind,' she said, shaking me by the shoulders. 'It doesn't matter why! Just concentrate on finding out if you've got the damned disease. If you don't, then all this misery's for nothing. If you do, then you can decide what to do about it.'

'Herby should have killed me when I was three,' I said, irrationally.

'Shut up,' she said. 'He didn't. And you have Simmy to thank for that.'

She pushed me into the bathroom and put the electric razor in my hand. She asked me if I'd brushed my teeth. She got clothes out for me and helped me put them on. I felt like a toddler. Or an old, old man who'd been ill a long time.

Over the weekend, she talked on the phone, to Mark mostly, and to her cop-shop. She'd taken time off, she said. Personal time. Emergency time.

It came to me that I was as bad as Ron, her brother. Doing whatever came easiest. Collapsing under the burden of life. Letting her do it all.

'I'm OK, Grace,' I told her, making the effort. 'Really.'

'You sure?' she asked, staring at me through slitted eyes. 'You sure, Jason?'

'I'm sure,' I said, tugging at the edges of my life. It was like hauling in a wet sail, bringing heavy, unwieldy pieces of myself into reach. 'You think it was Herby who sent those letters to me? Offering to sell me information about who I was?'

'Of course it was. He found out Jacob was sick, you were here running things, he figured maybe he could play both ends.'

'He'd have had Jacob paying not to tell who I was, and me paying to know who I was.' I laughed, without amusement. 'Dorotea said he was slimy.'

'How do you feel about finding out who your folks were?' she challenged me. 'Really, Jason. You've got to tell me.'

I shrugged.

'That's not good enough,' she said stubbornly. 'I mean, there's Nimo. A real slime ball, probably.'

'Raised to be one,' I said, quoting Jacob. 'He might have been all right, raised by someone else. And his dad, likewise. How do we know? Look at Dorotea Chapman. She's got the same parents Carlos has. So, one brother's a jailbird and one's a lawyer.'

Grace made a joke about there being less difference than

one might suppose, and I actually managed to smile. Nimo being a criminal didn't bother me that much. Anybody could be taught to break the law. Rectitude, so Jacob had always said, was inculcated, not inherited. All babies are born lawless.

Despite my assurances, Grace didn't leave until Monday morning, when Mark arrived. By that time I was seated at my desk with the phone number of the man at the medical school in front of me. I dialled it at eight-thirty. His secretary told me the doctor usually arrived at nine. At nine-o-two I called again. An appointment had just cancelled, he could see me that morning. Maybe that was true. Maybe he heard the panic in my voice and made room for me.

I found the department of genetic diseases. I found the doctor's office at the end of a long corridor, an institutional space littered with computer terminals and piles of books and stacks of paper with holes down the edges. The doctor himself was insignificant-looking except for his eyes. They knew things. I told him I was adopted, that I'd recently found out my biological father had Huntington's disease.

'Ah,' he said, frowning. 'Do you know any members of your father's family? Do you have siblings? Does he? How about grandparents?'

I shook my head. 'My father is dead. His father is dead, of this disease. If my father had any uncles or aunts, they are now dead. My father had a brother, but he is dead.'

He frowned again. 'Mr Lynx, let me explain something to you. You obviously know this is a genetic disease or you wouldn't be here.'

Since this was the department of genetic disease, it was a fair guess.

'We've made a lot of progress in recent years, not in curing the disease, we can't do that, but in finding out if people are carrying the gene.'

'That's what I want to know,' I said patiently.

'Let me explain, please. We don't know exactly what the gene looks like. When we test for it, we don't even look for the gene itself.'

He saw my incomprehension.

'The gene for Huntington's disease is located down at the tip of chromosome number four. We know it's there, but we're not sure what it looks like. What we do know is that elsewhere on the chromosome, family members with the disease have a different DNA sequence from family members who do not have the disease. We call this other sequence a marker.'

I still wasn't with him.

He said, 'Let me try an analogy. There's a buried prehistoric village along a certain stretch of coast. You don't know where it is, but you do know that ninety-nine times out of a hundred, prehistoric villages of this kind were accompanied by shell middens on the shore, places where the village people threw away their clam and oyster shells. You with me so far?'

I said I was, impatiently, wondering what the hell he was getting at.

'Villages are buried, but shell midden aren't. So you look for the midden.'

'And that's a marker.'

'That's a marker. If we have access to your relatives we make DNA sequence maps of a long section at the end of chromosome four. We do maps of your kinfolk who have the disease, and maps of your kinfolk who don't. We run these maps through computers that are programmed to look for identical sequences in the people who have the disease and, we hope, a different sequence in people who do not. We find the sequence that's the marker in your family, and then we see if you're carrying that marker. If you don't carry the marker, you're probably not carrying the disease.' He looked pleased with this explanation.

I said, 'But you can do this only if there are enough relatives to test.'

His face fell. 'Yes. Only if there are enough relatives with and without the disease for us to find the marker that works in your family.'

We stared at one another for a long time.

'It's only a matter of time until we'll be able to identify the gene itself,' he said, rather weakly. 'A couple of years, maybe.'

'A long time to live in doubt,' I said.

'Some people prefer not to know,' he remarked, holding the idea towards me, like a toy for a kid, a distraction.

'Some people do not live well with uncertainty.' What I was actually thinking about was my son, Jerry. He had never lived to grow up. Perhaps there had been good reason for that. I was ashamed of the banality of the thought. I remembered Jacob telling me that any God who could create this universe wouldn't stoop to being purposefully sadistic with man. 'Omniscience,' he'd said, 'is incompatible with horseshit of that kind.'

No, I told myself sternly. Jerry had not died young to prevent his dying later. This disease was not why he had died. This was not *why* anything. It was not *because* of anything. It simply *was*, and it was up to me to handle it. One way or another. But thank God I had no family to worry over.

'You've shown no signs of the disease, right?'

'Not that I know of,' I said.

'You'd know. You're, what? Thirty-six, thirty-seven?'

'Forty,' I said. 'Almost forty-one.' Then I laughed. I didn't know that! I assumed that. 'I'm not sure, doctor. I've only recently found out about my biological parents. Now that I know, I can get a copy of my birth certificate. Then I'll know exactly how old I am.'

He asked a few questions about my childhood, which I answered absently.

'You might be older than forty, but surely you can't be younger. The people at the Home thought you were three when you were abandoned, right? It's fairly easy to tell the difference between a two-year-old and a three-year-old. You might have regressed a little, because of the trauma, but the reverse wouldn't have been true. You might have acted younger, but not older. If you've shown no symptoms by now, I'd consider that an extremely good sign. Onset of the disease varies, but it often happens in the twenties and thirties.'

'Or waits until the forties and fifties,' I said. 'I think it did with my father and grandfather.'

As a hopeful sign, being healthy now wasn't hopeful enough.

I promised to stay in touch, to keep *au courant* with all the wonderful progress they were making. He gave me some photostats of articles about the disease. I didn't go home. There were people at home who knew all about this and I didn't want to be with them.

Instead I went to the library where I could sit at a table and read and no one would bother me. The articles I'd been given were mostly about current research, technical and dry and full of what I thought of as cumbersome evasions about the possible side-effects of counselling or treatment. Sometimes I think the human body is only a battlefield to doctors. They fight disease across it, paying no attention to the person inside. I left the articles lying on th table when I went to ask the librarian if there was a list of associations or societies set up to deal with various diseases. She had a whole book full of associations and groups, charities and educational institutions. I found a National Huntington's Disease Society of America in New York City. I called them from a pay phone down the block, and they said they'd send me materials written for the layman. The man I spoke with also came up with the phone number of a 'support group' in Denver for patients and families of patients. He said absolutely nothing about people—who had no idea whether they would ever be patients or not.

I thought of going out to the department of vital statistics to get a birth certificate, but it was too late in the day. Mark and Eugenia would have gone home by now, and Bela and Schnitz would be hungry, wondering where I was.

Bela and Schnitz didn't know anything about genetic diseases. Whatever I did, they would not look at me with pity in their eyes. I went home to them.

CHAPTER 7

During the night, I came to a decision. I would sell Jason Lynx Interiors to Mark. He had plenty of money to buy it. He was as qualified as I to run it, more qualified, really, since decor is what he really wanted to do. I would set up the sale the way Jacob had, payments every month, enough to support me, to let me travel a little, see the world—at least those parts of it one could see without meeting a bullet or bomb in the process. Maybe I'd go to some places formerly behind the Iron Curtain, places people couldn't visit easily until the last few years. I could go to museums, add to my art education. Then, if I was permitted the time to live normally, I'd be more qualified for the kind of job I'd once hoped for.

There was no longer any question of marriage, not to anyone. The sooner I went away and let Grace find someone else, the better. If I didn't develop the disease, I'd hate myself for having left her, but if I did, I'd never forgive myself for having stayed. The next few years were the years in which she should have children, if she was going to, and I wouldn't father a child who might inherit this tragedy.

I told myself it was my decision to make. I could imagine Grace doing something fine and sacrificial, and that couldn't be allowed to happen. Olivia had sacrificed herself for her parents' sake. Jacob for Olivia's sake. Angela had done it for her father. Daniel for Angela. Even Cecily had made sacrifices for poor Simonetta, and carried the guilt for years. I wouldn't let Grace repeat the pattern.

Though, I reminded myself with a certain wry honesty, she said she wasn't in love with me and might not be inclined to do any such thing. Continuing the attempt at honesty, I admitted I didn't want to know if that was true. The doctor had said some people preferred not to know. About Grace's feelings in this matter, I agreed. I preferred not to know. I was going to say goodbye to her, but not just yet. I had to work my way into it. Little by little.

When I saw her next—it was Wednesday evening—I told her there was no test they could do for me. She looked shaken.

'Nothing they can do?' she whispered.

'Nothing,' I said in the calm tone I'd been practising all day. 'I'm not sure I'd have had the test done even if they could have done it.'

'Why not?'

'The doctor was very frank. Some people get along better not knowing for sure. If they know in advance, they kind of give up on life.'

She dropped her eyes, and I knew she'd been thinking about something else. Children, maybe. She needed to know for her own sake if I had the damn thing, and there was no way I could tell her.

'Grace, hey,' I said. 'What I'd really like is for us both just to relax for a few weeks. Let time go by. Let me get used to the idea. Then we'll talk.'

She hugged me and left me alone to consider a small dilemma I'd come up with. Did I tell my grandmother anything? Olivia, my grandmother: did I, for example, make up a story about Angela's son being alive and well in Sorrento or someplace. I could explain that he didn't know who he was, and therefore she could not write to him, or see him, but the knowledge he was safe and well would be a relief to her. I had no moral compunctions about telling her a new lie to replace the old one. My lie would at least be more comforting than Nimo's lie had been.

I did not consider telling her the truth.

I did decide to get a birth certificate. If I was going to travel, I'd need a passport, so why not get one with my own birth certificate? The legalities didn't even occur to me: the problem that would arise with a change of name from the one I'd been using, the different dates of birth. I just trotted over to the Department of Health, Bureau of Vital Statistics, paid my money, gave the names of my

parents and the year of birth—'Nineteen-fifty, I think.
There's been some confusion in the family, and it could
have been the year before or after . . .'

It was nineteen-fifty. December 1st. I went back home
and sat down at my desk to look at this document. Mother's
name, Angela Leone, née Desquintas y Alvares. Father's
name, Geronimo R. Leone. Mother's birthdate, March 5th,
1932. Place of birth. Attending physician. Date of marriage,
March 25th, 1950. She had been just eighteen years old.

I found myself counting weeks. Angela had gotten pregnant on her honeymoon, and I felt a wave of pity. She'd
certainly been given no time to adjust to anything. Not to
her husband, not to being a mother, not to anything. My
poor mother. I tried the word on, *mother*, to see how it
sounded, but it didn't work for me. Angela was, and forever
would be, only a girl, less than half the age I was now. If
I remembered her—and perhaps I did remember her, for
she looked a lot like Lycia, and I'd always thought Lycia
looked familiar—it was as a girl. Forever young. Never to
be white-haired. Never to be the baker of cookies, the helper
with homework. Only the girl in love who died tragically
soon.

I put off making any decisions about Olivia. I was desperately resolved on keeping everything very loose and very
calm. I went on automatic pilot. Bela and I went back to
our pleasant routine of running twice every day. Schnitz
got his fur rumpled regularly. I paid scrupulous attention
to what Mark and Eugenia were doing in order not to think
about what I was doing. Of course, I woke up a lot in the
middle of the night with my heart pounding, terrified. It
usually took an hour or two to get back to sleep. I drank
more than usual. I tried not to think, not to feel. I kept
going. March went out, the days warmed, crocuses stuck
their heads up beside the portico out front. Blue crocuses
and some little yellow cup-shaped flower with a green fringe
around it.

It was a Wednesday I first saw the old guy. A derelict,
really, a typical skid row type in layers of clothes. He was

considerably the worse for the contents of the paper bag he kept tipping to his mouth. He was at the corner when Bela loped by with me staggering in pursuit. A stagger was the best I could manage because I hadn't totally recovered from the fall I'd taken the day Grace had saved my lfie. I'd twisted an already injured leg, and it was still stiff and painful. So, as I staggered by I saw the old guy and he saw me, stared at me in fact.

The same man was there when we returned.

He was there again Thursday afternoon. And Friday evening, about supper-time, when Bela and I returned from our run. This time he stepped out on the sidewalk, blocking my way.

'You're Jason Lynx,' he said.

I stepped back from the miasma he was exhaling and admitted I was.

'I have some letters which refer to you by name,' he said with owl-eyed, professorial dignity.

All I could think of was that he'd been pilfering mail, reaching through mail slots, maybe.

He must have read my mind. 'I found them,' he said. 'In the course of my du . . . duties. With the Salva . . . Salva . . . shun Army.' His careful diction was starting to slip.

It still didn't connect.

'Inna pocket of this coat,' he cried desperately. 'We took all the stuff outa this house on Zuni Street, an' they was inna pocket!'

The quarter dropped. Simonetta's house. Dorotea had had the house cleaned out for her brother. 'Letters with my name in them?' I asked. 'Did you want to give them to me?'

'Mushisit worth to ya?' he asked, giving up all pretence at enunciation.

I shrugged. 'I don't know. What do they say?'

He shook his head drunkenly. 'Not 'less you pay me.'

'OK. Who're they to? Who're they from?'

'One's to you,' he said. 'Thas who.'

I fished out a ten. He reached, then craftily said it wasn't enough. We settled for twenty. He shambled away with his money, and I walked along the sidewalk examining the first of the two wrinkled documents he'd handed me. It was completely familiar in appearance. I'd seen several almost exactly like it: cut-out letters, glued on a sheet of typing paper.

Jason Lynx. You need to know who you are because somebody wants to kill you. Ten thousand buys it. Put an ad in the personals, say J.L. wants to know.

Found in Herby's jacket, where I'd have found it myself if I'd looked. Where Herby had left it last winter, intending to mail it, but not getting around to it before he died.

Bela whuffed at me. I looked up from the paper I was holding, totally at a loss.

Before he died?

Why would anyone have wanted to kill me *before* Herby died? Gabe had wanted to kill me only since Simonetta was killed, only because I was a witness, but he hadn't wanted to kill me last November. Had he?

The idea was fairly chilling. Since Gabe's car had crashed, I hadn't worried about taking precautions. Everyone said he had no reason to come after me now; *I* thought he had no reason to come after me now. If he did, Bela and I had been inviting assassination each day during our slow circuits of the park. Preoccupied with this thought, I stuffed the papers in my pocket and went around to the back of the house in a considerably chastened mood. I approached the back door. Bela hung back. He whuffed at me, sniffing along the fence, then growled at the back door. I reached for my key with one hand and the knob with the other. The knob gave. Unlocked.

Bela went on growling.

The light over the back door was sufficient only to throw a dim glow on the steps. It was not designed to illuminate the lock, a fact which had annoyed me in the past. I leaned down and peered at it from four inches away. Maybe there were scratches. Of course, I could have made them myself, fumbling with my key in the inadequate light. On the other hand . . . I hadn't left the door open.

If someone was in there, where would he be?'

I slipped through the door, into the laundry-room which opens at the left into the old kitchen, used for showing country-style furniture, mostly Shaker stuff. To my right was the small storeroom, the back staircase, and the slow, cumbersome elevator Jacob had installed. Bela slid in behind me and faced the kitchen, rumbling very softly. Both stairs and elevator go from the basement all the way to the attic. I went down the basement stairs in the dark, Bela beside me, nose down. He was silent. He didn't smell anyone on the stairs.

The square piano was in the storeroom next to the furnace with the holster still taped to the inside of the leg where I'd left my Smith and Wesson .38 automatic, model 52, a target gun, one no longer made. I'd left it with one round in the chamber and six in the clip. When I released the safety and cocked the pistol, the soft double click seemed as loud as a gunshot. I held my breath, waiting. Bela remained quiet.

Though there'd been a time when I'd known the .38 very well indeed, I had not fired it in years. Relying on reflexes from ten years before was probably not a good idea. I told myself not to take any stupid chances. I did not tell myself the sensible thing: to call the police. Later I wondered why. At the time it seemed self-evident. Somebody was after me. It was up to me to stop them.

A flashlight from the furnace room enabled me to find my way to the front stairs without tripping over anything, including Bela. A lighted EXIT glowed over each door, as required by the fire code, but they give very little light. The front stairs lead to a service corridor at the rear of the ground-floor hallway. From that service corridor, doors open in every direction: west into the old pantry by the kitchen, north into what was the dining-room, south into the main showroom at the front of the house.

I stood on the top step, my forehead against the door, silently counting the possible hiding-places on the ground floor, including the north front parlour and the south back parlour and the two toilets I'd put in, one for staff, one for customers, plus a number of nooks and crannies and several capacious closets. Normally we keep the closets locked, but an intruder who could pick locks might be almost anywhere.

With the flash off, I opened the stairway door very slowly. The exit sign threw a dim greenish glow on a shadow crouched before the pantry door. The shadow turned two glowing circles on me. Schnitz, his eyes reflecting the dim light like two moons. He turned back to the door, crouched once more.

Besides me Bela trembled. I laid my hand on his shoulder and felt the silent growl.

My intruder was somewhere behind that door, in the pantry, or the dining-room to the right of the pantry, or back in the kitchen. Maybe he'd been waiting for me to come past him from the back of the house. Probably.

There were a number of ways I could get into the pantry and dining-room. I could come at him from almost any side. If I knew exactly where he was. Which I didn't. Besides, he could be somewhere else by the time I got there and would be if he'd heard me come in.

I said 'heel' to Bela in my fiercest whisper, stepped forward, scooped Schnitz off the floor, and went to my left, into the main showroom, continuing the circle around into the front hall and up the curving front stairs, quickly and quietly. Bela came beside, still rumbling softly. I was counting on his letting me know if there was anyone ahead of us, but he didn't bark.

We went through the door between my office and my living-room. I locked it and bolted it. Out in the hall, I closed the seldom-used door across the hall and bolted that as well. The intruder might pick a lock, but he could not pick the bolts. I put Schnitz in the bathroom, shut the door on him and went to the top of the back stairs. Until then, I'd been as quiet as possible. Now I talked loudly to Bela. 'You'll be a good dog and go out if you need to go, won't

you, Bela boy. Yes, he's a good dog. He'll go downstairs if
he needs to go, won't he. Sure he will.'

At the top of the stairs, quite loudly, I told Bela to lie
down and stay. I wanted the intruder to hear me moving
around, but I didn't want him sneaking up on me. Bela
would make sure of that. We'd been gone almost an hour
on our run to the park. Whoever was in the house, assuming
he had watched us leave, had had plenty of time to get the
layout of the place. Whoever was in the house had no doubt
watched us for several days before he came in. He would
know all the ways there were to get at me.

Schnitz yowled in complaint, and I took him a bowl of
food. He could drink from the toilet bowl and usually did.
I left him shut in. After a while he shut up.

Meantime, I moved around, rattling pans, shifting this
and that, making a pot of coffee—the person hiding downstairs would smell that—taking up time. It had been almost
seven when we'd come home. It was now almost eight. A
little early for bedtime. Still, I'd been under stress lately.
Early bedtime might be believable. Believable or not, I
couldn't continue the charade for much longer. My stomach
was doing backflips.

When as much time had elapsed as I had patience for, I
took Bela down the hall to the front bedroom, the one
Agatha and I used to share, and put him inside. 'Lie down,'
I whispered sternly, then, 'Stay!'

He looked at me reproachfully, but he lay down and did
not move when I closed the door on him. That would keep
him safe, as well as Schnitz. One final thing. I took both
phones, business and private, off the hook. Nothing like an
unexpected phone call to distract people's attention from
the work at hand!

The door to the back stairs is across the hall from my
bedroom. I pushed it almost closed. Another of the
ubiquitous exit signs glowed greenly above the door, and
I unscrewed the bulb, leaving only the dim light coming
from the tall, narrow window at the end of the hall. I

went into my bedroom and pulled all the curtains tightly shut.

My bed is on the same wall as the door, which means it can't be seen very well from the hall. My favourite leather wing chair and its hassock are near the north window, across from the door. Once my eyes adapted to the dim light, I could barely make out the stairway door in the streetlight filtering through the hall window. If someone pushed open the door and came into the upstairs hall, I could see him, but he could not see me. So I believed.

I've never liked ceiling fixtures in bedrooms. Lamplight is warm and intimate. Ceiling fixtures are cold and remote. So my bedside lamp and the floorlamp beside the chair are on a three-way circuit, one wall switch beside the door, one switch on the bedside table, one beside my chair. I unplugged the floor lamp before I sat down in the chair and took off my shoes, dropping them one by one. Then I waited. Every ten minutes, the furnace cleared its throat. People went by on the street, and in the alley. The luminous dial of my watch said nine-thirty. I stayed where I was.

The first sound came a quarter of an hour later, from the door across the hall, the second one I'd bolted. Not much of a sound, really. A creaking. As though someone had leaned on it, hard. Then the same thing from the door between the living-room and my office. That took care of his coming at me from the front of the house.

Would the fact the doors were bolted scare him off? Probably not. So far as he knew, I bolted them every night. But he'd heard me telling Bela to go downstairs if he needed to go, which implied a way left open back here. I'd have been more frightened of the dog, myself. Though he could have made plans to deal with the dog. A silenced gun, perhaps. The idea infuriated me.

I put my left hand on the light switch beside the chair, shifting slightly and breathing slowly, deeply. Anyone coming up the back stairs would expect to hear someone breathing slowly, deeply. As though asleep.

On the back stairs the fourth step from the top creaks. I heard it sooner than I'd thought I would. The barest whisper.

The door opened. I saw the shadow emerge. It paused there. I went on breathing. The shadow came to the door. From my position in the chair, I waited until it was inside, beside the bed, before I pressed the switch and said, 'Drop it.'

He didn't drop it. He swung it towards me, wide-eyed, panicky in the sudden light. I saw the gun come around towards me, saw his black torso silhouetted against the bedside light, and my hand took over. I didn't even think about it. He was a target, that was all. The old reflexes I hadn't wanted to count on did it for me. I shot him. He fired at me then, a whisper, but the bullet came nowhere near me.

'Why?' I cried at him, as I crouched over him, trying to stop the bleeding. 'Why!'

He only looked at me stupidly. I thought he tried to speak, so I leaned forward, but he was trying to spit, instead. His mouth was full of blood. 'You bastard,' he said. By the time I got back from the phone, he was dead.

One does not need a licence to own a gun. One needs to be licensed to carry a handgun, but I had not been carrying one. I had merely kept one in my house. I had heard an intruder. The intruder had entered my house and come into my bedroom with the intent of doing grave bodily harm. No one, least of all me, doubted that, especially since he was quickly identified as Gabe Leone. A rather battered, bruised and bandaged Gabe Leone, probably injured when he jumped from his car before it crashed, and only recently recovered enough to come hunting me. So the police theorized while I was being questioned briefly. They took my good old S&W for evidence, then both the body and the police were gone.

There was blood on the bedroom floor, less of it than one might expect, most of it on the braided rug beside the bed. I took the rug down to the laundry-room and put it to soak in the tub. I got most of the rest of it up with wet paper towels. I let Schnitz out of the bathroom, then opened the door to the front bedroom and joined Bela on the bed.

I didn't start shaking until later, until I was stretched out in the bed, warm under the blankets, with the tension slowly draining away. Then I thought how simple it would have been if I'd just let him tell me. All my troubles would have been over. All these terrified night-time panics I'd been having. All these attacks of horror at the thought of what might happen in the future. All over. And I hadn't even considered it. Instinct had taken over. Preserve thyself, said all the little cells. Well, I had.

I prodded my conscience, seeing if I felt guilty over killing my uncle Gabe. Not much. I'd warned him; I'd given him a chance to drop the gun; I'd intended to turn him over to the police. He'd been the one who'd tried to kill me, and though I would have given anything to know why, I didn't figure it was my responsibility to grieve over him. The Leones had not behaved in what I'd call a familial manner towards me.

Morning found me hollow-eyed, not precisely sleepless but not rested, either. I got up early, made coffee, cleaned up the bathroom where Schnitz had demonstrated his irritation the night before by tearing a whole roll of paper into confetti, fed him and Bela, gradually worked myself up to going through the motions in a kind of weary haze, where nothing quite connected.

Still, I was shaved and dressed when I went down for the morning paper. It was about a quarter to eight. I arrived at the front door, coincident with a shiny older car driving up in front. It slowed, backed up, and parked at the kerb as I searched the portico for the paper-boy's newest hiding place. A chauffeur got out and called to me, 'Mr Lynx?'

I stopped where I was. 'Yes?'

He came around the car and opened the near door. First

out were two canes, the kind with braces that go around the arms. Next out was a little woman who took the canes and began a slow progress towards my front door. Her driver walked beside her, up the short flight of stairs to the portico. She moved slowly, carefully, obviously in pain. When she was beside me, she fixed me with a birdlike stare. 'Jason Lynx?'

'Yes, ma'am,' I said. 'What may I do for you?'

'I rather thought you wanted me to do something for you, young man. You left a message at my home. I'm Jenny Mattingly. Angela's friend.'

My mouth dropped open. I didn't plan what came out, it just emerged. 'Jenny,' I said. 'I'm Angela's son.'

She made a little cry and sagged on the canes. The driver caught her and supported her weight while I unlocked the front door. I didn't try to take her upstairs, not even in the slow old elevator at the back. We went into the showroom, where the chauffeur seated her on the nearest sofa, hovered around until she waved him away, then went back to the hall. I could feel him out there, within earshot.

'Ma'am, may I offer you some coffee? It's fresh.'

She thought that would be nice. I took the stairs three at a time, my leg screaming protest, though I came down more sedately, bearing a tray. I'd brought a cup for the driver, too, and he nodded his conditional thanks at me.

I put the tray on the table before her and poured us each a cup. 'I'd forgotten I'd called you,' I said. 'Olivia showed me your picture. I should have recognized you.'

'I've been away. I go to this clinic in Mexico sometimes, for my arthritis. I'm so sorry I was away when you called. I got back yesterday, late yesterday. I got your message, but it was so late, and I was tired. Then I heard your name on the news this morning. That man, trying to kill you. I said to Bentley, I have to go see Jason Lynx. I know about the Leone family. I have to go see him right now. Bentley thought I was being hysterical, I'm afraid. And then, when you told me! I thought you were dead. I thought Angela's son was dead.'

I shook my head at her. 'Not yet, no. I think there was some confusion about that. I get the distinct impression I was supposed to be dead.'

'You were,' she said. 'Oh yes, you were. I heard it all. I knew all about it.'

'Why don't you tell *me* about it?' I asked her.

She reached out to take my hand, as though she couldn't believe I was there. 'Angela was my dearest friend,' she said.

'I know. Angela's mother told me.'

'I mean, really my friend. I've never had another like her, not in all the years since. Did you know about her marriage?'

'Her mother told me.'

'It was so foolish and tragic. I told her not to do it. I told her she and Daniel should run away, anything would be better than marrying that man. But that priest talked to her and talked to her—about her duty, about her religion. Any other priest in Denver would have told her not to do it, but that man! He was like that Russian, that Rasputin! He hypnotized her. We all knew what he was like! Machismo, isn't that it? Proud as the devil . . .

'Poor Angela. She was as white as her dress the day she was married. I stood up with her because she said she couldn't go through with it otherwise. There were only a dozen people there. Her parents. His mother. Angela didn't even *know* him. It didn't get any better after she got to know him. I used to go over there every chance I got. She'd phone me and beg me to come. He didn't like for her to go out. If she went out, one of his goons went with her. That's what she called them, goons. I don't know what you'd call them now.'

She meant Herby, or Carlos, or men like them. 'I'd still call them goons,' I said.

'Angela got pregnant right away. Really, that was good, because she told him he had to leave her alone then. And he didn't care if I was there with her. He had this retarded maid who watched her all the time, a great, huge woman.'

'Simonetta,' I said.

'I guess. Simmy. That's right. Well, Angela had the baby, and he was beautiful, except for that blotch, but when his hair grew in, it hardly showed. The way Nimo took on, you'd have thought he was deformed. He kept howling about the evil eye, and how bad luck was settling on the family . . . Listen to me. I keep saying *he* and *him*. Not *you*. It was *you*, when you were a baby . . .'

She sat back, shaking her head and saying it over and over. 'You. You as a baby.'

I patted her hand and refilled her coffee cup, and after a while she calmed down.

'I was afraid she'd get pregnant again, right away, but she didn't. I think she was using something.' Jenny Mattingly blushed. 'She wouldn't have told me if she was doing that. Either that or she wouldn't let him . . .'

I nodded, to show I understood. Jenny blushed again.

'The baby . . . you, you grew up, such a handsome child. You would have been, oh, about three when the terrible quarrel happened.'

'The quarrel?'

'I was there. I'd had supper with Angela. Nimo had been out somewhere, but he came home about eight. Then his mother came from the hospital to talk to him. They were right in the next room when she began to cry and tell Nimo about the disease his father had. His father had been in a hospital for a long time, but no one had ever said what exactly was the matter with him.

'Angela and I heard every word she said. And we heard him, too, when his mother told him he might have the same disease. He was screaming like a crazy man. They were right there, in the next room, where we could hear everything!

'When his mother said it wasn't only him, but his children too, I reached for Angela, thinking she'd be horrified, but she was shaking her head at me and smiling this tiny little smile . . .

'I couldn't believe it. She was smiling. And she said,

"Don't be afraid, Jenny. Michael's all right. Nimo isn't Michael's father." Just like that. "Nimo isn't Michael's father."'

I had no sense that the woman sitting beside me was talking about me. She was talking about a stranger, not me. Michael, not Jason.

'And?' I choked out.

'That maid heard her say it. And she came at Angela, gabbling, waving her hands, demanding to know who the baby's father was, whether Angela had committed a sin. And Angela smiled at her—oh, so sweetly, and she said, "Simmy, God is Michael's father, just like God is Jesus's father."

'The maid began to laugh, this loud, hooting laughter she had, and Angela gave me a look. And that's when I knew she'd been pregnant, before the wedding.'

I couldn't believe it. I'm sure I stared at her stupidly. It had never occurred to me. Even though I'd noticed the dates on the birth certificate, it had never occurred to me!

Jenny took my hand again. 'But that crazy woman went straight to Nimo, I heard her. The nursemaid. She walked out of the room where we were and went to him, laughing like a crazy woman, and told him not to be so upset. The baby wouldn't get sick because he, Nimo, wasn't the baby's father! I couldn't believe she'd do such a stupid thing. What she was saying was all garbled up, but he heard part of it. He came raging into the room where we were. He said he'd always had his suspicions, she'd always been cold towards him, now he knew he wasn't the father, she'd taken his honour from him, she'd have to die, her and her bastard baby both! Oh, he used language . . . language people never used in front of women.

'Angela was frightened, really frightened. She tried to reason with him. She said she'd told Simmy that God was the baby's father, so Simmy wouldn't be upset about the disease, but he didn't listen. He just went on screaming, and then he left. Angela was shaking all over. I got her to bed. I gave her a sleeping pill. I wanted her to take the baby—you—and leave with me, go over to her mother's house, but she wouldn't. She said her husband would calm down the next day and she'd talk to him then. But the next day she was dead. They said an accident. I always thought she did it herself, just to escape.'

I remembered the last letter I'd had from Herby. I remembered what Carlos had said. I remembered the look on Gabe Leone's face as he died. 'She didn't do it herself,' I said. 'It could have been an accident, but more likely it was murder. Nimo meant what he said. He killed her. He tried to kill . . . me. If it hadn't been for Simmy, he would have. She saved me. Maybe only because I was Angela's son.'

'But not Nimo's,' she said. 'Angela knew you weren't. That's what she was telling me. I'm sure you're not. You even look like him. Or like he did.'

I'm sure I looked at her stupidly once again. 'Like him?'

'Daniel,' she said. 'Daniel had hair the same colour as yours. Nimo was dark, but Daniel had that same auburn hair. He was the only one who could have been your father. The only one.'

And of course she was right. He was the only one who could have been.

We sat there for a time, each lost in our own thoughts. 'You never told Olivia about Nimo threatening Angela and . . . me?' I asked at last.

'No, no,' Jenny said. 'Poor Olivia. I told her about the disease, I had to tell her about that, so she'd know the reason. I didn't tell her the rest. She felt badly enough as it was. Why add to her pain? I thought you were dead, but Nimo told her you were in Italy. I let her believe that.'

After a time, she asked me to call her driver, then got herself levered up on to her canes and left. I know my face was wet, maybe with relief, maybe with sorrow. I remember going upstairs and falling into bed again. All those nights of waking up in terror had taken their toll. My body and mind had some catching up to do. When I got up later that day, Mark was there. He'd heard the news about the shooting and had come over in case I needed him. He greeted me with a good deal of concern, but when I told him about Jenny Mattingly, he yelled so loudly it brought Grace running in. The two of them had been keeping watch over me. She said we had to have a celebration. It occurred to me while all this was going on that it was the only time I had ever heard of a celebration in honour of someone's finding out he's a bastard. I hoped I was a bastard. Gabe had thought so. He'd accused me of it with his last breath. Even so, a tiny, lingering doubt remained.

Monday morning, on the strength of what I remembered reading about all the children who had disappeared in the Argentine and how blood tests were used to determine what parents or grandparents were related to what children, I went back to the physician at the genetic diseases department and told him my problem. Nimo had died in a hospital within the last twenty years, I said. There should be records. Angela had died years before, but there had probably been a post-mortem, and there might be records. If they had not been kept all these years, Olivia might not mind giving a blood sample for this particular purpose.

'Can you get a sample from the man you think is your father?' he asked me, eagerly setting down the names and dates and facts I had.

I shook my head. 'Who my father is is unimportant,' I said, really, honestly meaning it. 'All I'm interested in knowing is who he's not.'

He said he could understand that, in the circumstances. He took a sample of my blood and promised to do what he could. He could find out where Nimo had died by getting his death certificate. He would call me if he needed a sample of Olivia's blood.

Grace was free that evening, and though we'd already celebrated for two days, we went to Charkeys for dinner, a new place that specialized in mesquite-broiled everything. I showed her the last letter from Herby and told her about

Jenny once more. She cried, and wiped her nose on the napkin and then cried again.

'So she didn't just go along,' she said at last with great satisfaction. 'Good for her!'

'Who?'

'Your mother. They may have talked her into making that stupid, stupid marriage, but she didn't just go along. She loved Daniel, she wanted his child, and she made sure she had it. I like that!'

'I'm still not entirely sure . . .' I said.

'I'm sure,' she said stoutly. 'It just feels right. I never could believe you were related to the Leones. Not even to the nicer ones, like Dorotea. You just don't look anything like that family!' She turned her attention back to her second helping of onion soup, warming up her stomach for the very large steak which was coming next. 'How did Gabe find out you weren't dead, after all those years?'

'I believe that once Simonetta's mama was in a nursing home, poor Simonetta had to talk to someone else about her sins. So she told her brother about the child she'd stolen when she worked for Nimo, and Carlos talked about it to someone. The word somehow got to Gabe. That's why he killed Simonetta.'

'But how did Gabe know who you were? Simonetta didn't know.'

I got out my wallet and took from it the much-creased letter the old man had given me the night I'd found Gabe in my house. Not the one with the cut-out words; the other one. I'd forgotten it was in the pocket until after Gabe was dead. I handed it to her.

'It looks like a draft,' she said. 'You can hardly read his handwriting. Or his spelling.'

'Right. It's dated a few years back. I figure he wrote a clear copy to leave with Walt Huggenmier, and he stuck this one in his pocket, and forgot about it.

Dear Gabe [it said],

I'm leaving this with somebody to mail in case something happens to me. That kid of Nimo's, he isn't dead. He grew up. His name is Jason Lynx now. He has a place here in town on Hyde Street. I never did him like I told Nimo. Since you made that promise to Nimo, I figured you should know.

Herb Fixe.

She laid it down on the table and stared at it. 'Herby left this for Gabe?'

'Don't you remember Walt Huggenmier saying Herby left a letter for him to mail?'

She looked stricken. 'I'd forgotten. And this was it?'

'I think this was it, Herby's protection. The proverbial letter-left-to-be-mailed if the bad guy gets killed. Good old Gabe found out about Simonetta from Carlos, but he found out about me from Herby. He'd made his brother a promise, and he tried to keep it.'

'Sick,' she said, with an expression of distaste.

'Sick,' I agreed.

'I simply can't imagine anyone doing such a stupid thing, after all those years. It's ridiculous. Angela hadn't done a damned thing to make the Leone family behave that way.'

'She'd broken their code of honour. She'd been represented to them as a virgin whom Nimo had to marry to keep a promise made by his father. You know, the one thing we've never considered in all this is that Nimo may not have wanted to marry Angela any more than she wanted to marry him. Their fathers had sworn an oath, however, and that was it. So he married the girl who was certainly not loving and undoubtedly sexually frigid towards him. She was pregnant immediately and asked him to leave her alone, which he may have been only too willing to do. Then the child was born with what Nimo saw as a deformity. That would have been a blow to masculine pride, so it had to be her fault. Then, later on he found out this thing about Huntington's disease, which was definitely his family, not hers, but it would be human nature to try and deflect the blame on to her or the baby. And then, hard on the heels of that discovery, here came Simonetta saying the baby wasn't his anyhow.'

'So he blew.'

'He obviously did more than merely blow. He swore to avenge his honour, and Gabe was his surrogate. Angela was dead, her child was supposed to be dead, but Gabe was prepared to act if the real father of the child ever showed up . . .'

'I guess Brother Daniel wasn't available as a victim,' said Grace.

'Myra located Brother Daniel purely by chance. I doubt Gabe ever had a hint as to who he was.'

She ate in silence for a time, then asked, 'Have you thought any more about what you're going to do?'

I almost told her what I had decided before Jenny's revelations. I caught myself in time. 'God, Grace,' I said soberly. 'Up until today, I thought I was doomed. This changes everything. I need to take a while just to be relieved!'

My relief was confirmed when the doctor phoned to say Nimo Leone's records were complete as to blood type. He had been type O and I was type AB. No matter what Angela's blood type had been, a type O father cannot produce a type AB child. It was one of those results which didn't require equivocation. There were no maybes. Nimo Leone had not been my daddy.

Which meant everything was solved except a few final and minor puzzles.

What should I do about Olivia? What should I do about Brother Daniel. What about Grace? And what about me?

A week or so went by.

Grace and I were playing kneesies at my kitchen table when she asked me when I was going to tell Olivia about me.

'I'm not,' I said, without even thinking about it.

She gave me a long look.

'No reason to,' I said defensively. 'She's accustomed to the idea that Angela's son is in Italy. No point in rearranging her world.'

'I thought you always wanted a family,' she said.

'Well. Yes. But I can be familial towards her without telling her anything. Being Jacob's son allows me to do that. I'm taking her to lunch with Nellie and Willamae next week, as a matter of fact.'

'So she's just another of your old ladies,' she said. 'What about Lycia?'

'Lycia's fine. She has plenty to keep her occupied, she's not grieving over her long-lost nephew.'

'And you? What about you?'

I shrugged. I hadn't figured that out yet.

Grace was very silent the rest of the meal. I'd planned on her staying over, but she excused herself, saying she had some things to take care of at home. The whole episode left me irritated, first at her, but then at myself. By morning, I'd decided it was time I quit fooling around and did something about Grace. Put up or shut up, as they say. Did I want to marry her or not?

I did. However I looked at it, yes, I did. If that meant staying here in Jacob's house, in Jacob's business, well, so be it. If that meant buying a house in the suburbs and raising two point one children, so be that, as well. I loved Grace, and it was time I made that clear to her. Enough fiddling about!

I'd bought tickets, months ago, for the roadshow of a recent runaway Broadway hit. The tickets were for the following Friday night, a long-agreed-upon date. We enjoyed the show, which was mindless fun, and went on to supper at a little place off Third Avenue which would have picked up a lot of after-theatre business by merely remaining open after ten, but also happens to have an interesting menu. The food's always tasty, the wines are exemplary, and the place stays crowded into the wee hours.

So we scrunched together at a tiny corner table, enjoying our meal, and when I figured Grace had had enough food to be able to concentrate on something else, I asked her to marry me. I said, 'Grace, will you marry me?'

She put down her fork. Her face turned pale. She got that pinched look she gets sometimes, when she's upset.

'Hey,' I said, suddenly very worried.

'I don't think so, Jason,' she said. 'I don't think you'd be happy with me.'

I'd been prepared for a yes. I'd been prepared for a 'No, there's someone else.' I'd been prepared for, 'I don't love you, Jason.' I was not prepared for her thinking I'd not be happy with her.

'Why would you think such a thing?' I demanded a little angrily.

'Because I'm not perfect,' she said, staring at my chin, avoiding my eyes. 'You only want a family that's perfect. I knew that when you said you weren't going to tell Olivia you're her grandson. She's not perfect. You told me that. You said she wasn't worthy of Jacob. You had Jacob and you believe he was absolutely perfect. You had Agatha, and she was perfect—'

'That's not true,' I cried in an outraged whisper. 'You know that's not—'

'Oh, I know she wasn't, but you *think* of her as perfect. You don't think about the dumb things she did. She's dead, and all her failings are sort of washed away. You didn't live together long enough to grind on each other.'

I held on to my temper. 'That's true, Grace. We didn't live together very long. But Agatha and I knew we weren't perfect, for God's sake—'

Grace interrupted, 'And I'll tell you something else. Jacob wasn't perfect either. Jacob decided he'd rather play the part of the faithful lover than be a real live person. All his life he was faithful to Olivia, but he never once *did* anything about her! You told me Olivia wasn't worthy of him because she didn't save your mother, but you might just as well blame Jacob for not doing anything about Olivia!'

'There was nothing he could do!' I cried, stung.

'Shit,' she said. 'He could have tried. If not when she married Octavio, then before she married what's-his-name Meyer. He could have offered his home as a sanctuary for Angela. He could have talked to her, tried to undo what that priest had done. Fact was, he never did anything. And he didn't get on with his life, either. His whole life he spent mooning over her. No wife, no children, just mooning. Kind of a sentimental warm bath. You may call that perfect, but I don't.'

'He was wonderful to me!'

'To you, yes. Well, he was over fifty when he took you in. He was doing well financially. It wasn't much strain for him, was it? No diapers. No up all night with the colic. You were easy, weren't you? You didn't give him a hard time. That's one thing about you, Jason, you're basically really a *nice* person. But he never adopted you. That way, you didn't have any real claim on him. So it worked out, and he felt good about it. Especially after he found out you were Olivia's grandson. That must've made it really romantic. Paying out all that money, year after year, never once doing anything sensible like trying to put the extortioner in jail and put an end to the threat.'

'He thought it would endanger me!'

'Yeah, well. Maybe. As it turned out, it endangered you a hell of a lot more not to tell you about it!'

'Grace, I don't know where you've come up with all this, all of a sudden . . .'

'It isn't all of a sudden. It's been months. I've watched you, and I've talked to you, and I've made love to you, and I've thought about you all the time. And I've wondered if maybe we could make it together, but we can't. We can't, because you've got this dream of some perfect family to match up to Jacob and Agatha, and I'm not perfect. I'm just not, but I'd try to be for your sake, and I'd end up destroying us both by trying.'

She got up, spilling her wine in her haste, and went out. I thought she'd gone to the rest-room to cry and then fix her face, so I waited, angrily marshalling my arguments.

Only when she'd been gone about twenty minutes did I realize she wasn't coming back.

What she'd said was unfair. It was unfair to Jacob, unfair to Agatha. I was sure of that. As the night wore on, however, with me sleeplessly replaying what she'd said, I wasn't at all sure it had been unfair to me.

She didn't call. After ten days, it became obvious she wasn't going to call. When I called her, I got a machine.

I talked to Mark. We had quite a long, involved conference during which I yelled some and sulked some and listened to someone else's opinion about my character. Always enlightening, that. Salutary, I suppose. After which, he went to see Grace on my behalf. His message was simple. If she and I were going to split, we owed it to one another to split as friends, to leave things peaceful between us. Would she please have dinner with me.

He had to go back twice, but he got her to agree. Yes, Saturday. Yes, I could pick her up.

I did, dressed in my conservative best.

'Where are we going?' she asked in a subdued voice.

'A place we haven't been before,' I said. 'I hope the food will be good.'

When we drove up in front, she said, 'I didn't know there was a restaurant in this building.' It was the first thing she'd said since we left her house.

When we got out of the elevator and walked down the hall, she gave me a curious look, maybe a little hostile. 'I have to pick up something,' I said lamely . . . and truthfully.

She didn't know the woman who opened the door. She did know the people assembled in the living-room.

'Grace,' I said, 'I'd like you to meet my grandmother, Olivia Meyer. This is my Aunt Lycia and her friend Ross. Grandmother, Aunt, this is Grace Willis. I'm trying to talk Grace into marrying me.'

She was too dumbfounded to say anything at that point,

and by the time she thought of something (I could see it in her eyes), it was too late. Dinner was served.

Not that I got an answer. I didn't. She seemed to enjoy herself, however, as did everyone else, even though I'd forgotten to warn Aunty and Granny about Grace's appetite and we had to stop at a fast food place on the way home.

From the time we left Olivia's to the time I dropped her at her house, Grace didn't mention my proposal. I didn't really expect her to, not this soon. I didn't bring it up either. Maybe she won't marry me, but she'll damned well have to refuse me for some other reason than the one she gave me. She's got to know I'm ready to accept a family, perfect or not. She's got to know I want her to be part of it.

A few loose ends.

Cecily: I wrote her a letter, thanking her for her intervention on my behalf. I told her who I was and that she had saved my life. I thanked her for that. I told her not to blame herself for telling Herby where she'd left me as a child. In the end, it had all worked out all right.

Brother Daniel: My father. I called the monastery and spoke with the same voice I'd spoken with some weeks before. Brother Daniel, said the voice, had died several weeks before. He'd had cancer for some time. It had been only a matter of weeks even at the time I'd seen him.

I counted up the days and realized he'd died before I'd known he was my father. There had been nothing I could have told him at that time. Perhaps there had been nothing I should have told him, even if he had lived. 'Remember me in your prayers,' he'd said. I was not much for prayers. But I would remember him.

Simonetta: The day after our family dinner, I went to see Sister John Lorraine to remind her of what she'd said about Simonetta being proof of God's inscrutability. I told her the whole story, starting with Olivia and Jacob and including Brother Daniel. If I wasn't one for prayers, I supposed Sister John was.

'If you're looking for purpose in Simonetta's life,' I concluded, 'consider this, Sister John: she saved my life. All her craziness saved my life. I'll be remembering Simonetta.'

'Kindly,' she said in a hushed, wondering voice, tears in her eyes. 'Remembering her kindly.'

I agreed. Despite the burns and the craziness and the long years spent in the Home, I'd be remembering Simonetta—and Cecily and Brother Daniel—kindly. And Jacob. Who, despite Grace's calumny, had been a fine and wonderful man. Though not perfect.

None of us is perfect. Thank God. What would we do for puzzles if we were?